INDECENT DEMANDS

A Dark College Romance

MARLEE WRAY

AVERY

The sun sets, and shadows give way to darkness as I trek to a frat party at Beta House. Other students bustle around me, bumping off each other like twigs floating in a stream, seemingly unworried. I analyze every sound and scent. Bonfire smoke, bubbling laughter, leaves crunching underfoot. Staying vigilant is crucial, because somewhere in the night, there's a predator called Casanova.

The last abduction was four weeks ago, and many people have already let their guard down. They say Casanova has probably moved on now that there are more campus police patrols, more lights along the walking paths, and more girls traveling in groups.

I'm not reassured. Four weeks isn't that long. A lot of serial offenders go weeks or months in between the times they strike. A frown tugs at the corners of my mouth. Too many details about criminal behavior have seeped into my consciousness over the past three years. That's a hazard of listening to stories from my stepfather's law practice.

The last missing Granthorpe girl is a sophomore who's in my

Macroeconomics class. We look so alike it's eerie. Her seat still sits empty.

Apparently, there are no leads. The girls, ones exactly like me, are just gone in the night. I look around, my breath not quite fogging the air. It's fall and the weather's mild, warmer than this time of year usually allows in the Northeast.

For a couple of weeks, I've felt like someone's eyes are on me, watching, waiting. Maybe it's just paranoia from streaming too many true crime shows, but these days, I get tense every time I'm out after sundown.

At the stately white Victorian mansion, I have to push my way inside because there are already too many people. Beta House's common room is a blur as my eyes adjust to the bright light.

My breath catches as my vision sharpens because it's filled with *him*. My stepbrother Shane. Who despises me.

Turn around and walk back out, a small voice inside me advises. My heartbeat counts off the seconds with a stuttering thump, thump, thump. Do I flee? Or stay?

Shane's hair is the color of champagne on the surface and Angostura bitters beneath. It's a mirror of his personality, which is golden at first glance but harbors a dark anger lurking below. Today, he has a few days growth of a beard that matches his carelessly wild hair. It's not long, but it's longer than he ever wore it while we lived in the same house.

The party rages around me, but I can see him and his friends clearly because they're standing on the platform with a few of the fraternity's leaders. There's nothing unusual about finding Shane at the top of the food chain at GU. When has he ever been anything else? He and his best friend Declan Heyworth were high school royalty when I met them.

Tonight, Declan wears a cobalt shirt, which offsets the black of his hair and his vibrant blue eyes. He has the kind of beauty that stuns people, so profound it creates an ache of lust or envy, depending on the person who witnesses it. Worse is that there is no vulnerability to make him seem human. In addition to his good looks, he's a stellar athlete from an obscenely rich family.

It's strange that, in my eyes, Declan doesn't outshine Shane. Maybe because they're two sides of the same gold coin. Each a few inches over six feet, each muscular, each sharp-witted. They're evenly matched in the friendship, with neither as a sidekick. Two alphas who, instead of tearing each other apart, rule synergistically.

Next to the legendary duo of Shane and Declan, there's the new addition. Erik Sorensen, aka the Berserker, looks like a Viking and dominates like one on the football field. Shane and Declan are tall, but Erik's a monster. He's six-foot-eight-inches tall, and his golden hair has lightning streaks of white-blond running through it. By contrast, his beard is copper-colored, like a new penny. The team's on a winning streak, so as a tribute to the football gods he hasn't shaved. Declan is the quarterback, but apparently ritualistic hair-growing is not among his superstitions, because he's clean-shaven.

The crush of the crowd is oppressive. I wish I could stand on the platform above the teeming sea of bodies just to get some air, but that position's reserved for the chosen ones.

Near me, drunk girls stare and gush, "Oh, my God. Erik Sorensen can pillage my village any day!"

"Look at Shane Moran! That lawless vibe makes me want to drop to my knees at his feet til he begs me for a ride."

"That guy doesn't beg for anything. He's the one who makes people beg."

"Declan's a god. Willing sacrifice here!"

Among my female peers, apparently all three men are coveted with equal fervor. I admire the trio's looks because it's impossible not to. But since I arrived on campus four months ago, I've done everything I can to avoid entering Shane's orbit. It's not been difficult since he doesn't want me in it.

I'm keeping a low profile for my own reasons, too. Tonight, against the backdrop of short skirts, plunging necklines and kitten eyeliner, I'm wearing faded jeans, a navy cable knit sweater and almost no makeup under my black-rimmed glasses. Everything about my outfit says I should be walking a dog in the park right now, rather than partying in one of the most powerful Greek houses on campus.

I don't want to be here tonight, but I was coming undone from cabin fever while in my dorm. I've been holed up every night, carefully locked inside after making sure the main doors were closed tight. Tonight, a starter party in the residence hall meant all the doors were propped open. It's like the other women aren't even reading the headlines.

Since my dorm-mates are still going to parties, I walked here with them. Safety in numbers, I thought. I didn't want to be the lone girl left in the building. Unfortunately, I've lost track of the other women from my hall.

If I'm left with no one to walk back with, I may call campus security for an escort. They announced that young women are encouraged to call for one if out alone after ten at night. I wouldn't have thought it necessary with the extra campus police patrols, but somehow no one's managed to get a glimpse of Casanova. Caution seems appropriate.

Declan passes me on the way to the bar. He does a double take but doesn't smile or acknowledge me before continuing on his way. As per usual, I'm a ghost where he and Shane are concerned. I wonder how much he knows about why Shane hates me. Probably all of it. A burning blush consumes my face. It's not as if Shane could avoid spilling the details of our family drama to Declan when Shane moved in with him for their high school senior year.

That move caused all sorts of fallout, but Shane does what he wants. Still, I don't deserve their scorn. I never did. It was just a misunderstanding that escalated farther than it should have.

I glance Shane's way, and he's leaning forward as a gaggle of girls speak to him. I roll my eyes an instant before his moss green ones lock onto me. My entire body stiffens so hard you could stretch me out between two sawhorses like a board.

I don't smile. I don't wave. Neither of course does he. His gaze is so hard that eventually I look away. As always. Just once, I'd like to win a stare-down with him. I also wish his scowl made him ugly. Instead, the intensity makes him more attractive. Unfair on an epic scale. The handsome face and broad shoulders on the tall, muscular frame...everything about him says, "I'm not trying; I was born looking this way." I can testify to that. I met him when he was seventeen; he's gorgeous when he rolls out of bed.

"Hey," a male voice says.

I turn my head and find Declan standing over me, his electric blue eyes boring into me.

"Who are you with?" There's no emotion in his voice. It's not hostile, the way it was during his last year of high school when he painted me as a betrayer of his friend—which I never was.

Not trusting my voice, I don't speak. Instead I shrug, trying not to notice the delicious way he smells. It's probably Rebel's Creed cologne. Our All-American quarterback is their brand ambassador.

His brows crowd together. "Why are you always alone? You've got a clean slate here. Use it."

A clean slate. That's exactly what I want.

His critical tone makes me reluctant to speak because I'd like to flip him off for his arrogance, and I don't want that to come across. For almost a year, I tried to defend myself against rumors and sneers, tried to recover my status in school. Nothing worked. Declan and Shane made sure it didn't. I'm angry and frustrated with the pair of them, but I know better than to say so. It would be social suicide, and I've had a big enough taste of that.

Declan shoves a hand through his black hair, showing off bulging biceps. I almost scowl at his physical perfection, which has been bred into his billionaire bloodline through a succession of stunning trophy spouses. Not that I'm one to talk. My mom's a trophy wife too, or so she likes to joke with a twinkle in her eye.

"You know about the disappearances, right?" His tone is impatient.

My scowl deepens, but I manage to hold back the tide of sarcasm that wants to spill out. Does he think I'm clueless? How could anyone avoid seeing the Casanova news?

"Yes, I know."

"So if you didn't come with a group of friends, why don't you go back to your room before it gets too late?"

This little show of concern, even with its less-than-friendly tone, creates a warmth inside me. Which annoys me. It's ridiculous to be buoyed by such a minuscule show of humanity, but after such a long time of being out of favor, any crumb of positive attention feels like a victory.

"If something happens to you, I'm not going to have it said you were at a party with Shane and me, and we let you walk home alone. That narrative will never be spread."

Oh, right. He's not concerned about my safety. He's concerned about *how things will look. For them.*

"I don't think anyone even knows my connection to Shane."

I wait for him to contradict me, to say that he or Shane has mentioned me to their circle. Nothing comes. At least, they no longer seem interested in making me a pariah.

I glance around for an opening amongst the bodies that I can walk through to escape talking to him.

"Our families know," he says. "No one wants to see your mother unravel again over nothing."

My head turns back, so I can study Declan. Would my vanishing at the hands of some freak be nothing? Because there's no misunderstanding that something sinister is happening at Granthorpe. Women have been disappearing without a trace. Their purses and phones found dropped on sidewalks or in bushes along with a lavender rose. The flower makes it all the more creepy, since we all know he's taking them for some dark purpose. Rape? Torture? Murder? Maybe all of the above. And the not knowing is excruciating and scarier.

My glare doesn't faze him. By Declan's expression, all he seems to want is for me to disappear again. They were probably furious when my stepdad said I was coming to Granthorpe. Even with great grades and SAT scores, I wouldn't have gotten in without Ethan to cinch the deal. Shane's father Ethan and his paternal grandfather and great grandfather all went to undergrad here. Even though I'm just Ethan's stepdaughter, I guess I still count as a legacy child.

I doubt that matters to Shane or Declan, who are *real* legacy students. As demigods, they take privilege as their due. It probably doesn't register how important graduating from Granthorpe could be for someone like me, someone whose family legacy is more McDonald's Big Mac than filet mignon.

Declan glances at a text. He responds and slides his phone into his pocket. "You ready to go? I'll walk you back."

The shock of this casual offer from him overtakes me, and for a moment, I'm speechless.

I'm also torn between wanting to take a physically imposing man up on his offer to make sure I make it home safely and not wanting to give Declan Heyworth a reason to complain it's a pain in the ass to have Shane's stepsister on campus.

"I appreciate the offer, but it's not that late. There should be enough people around."

I glance at my phone. Enough time has passed for the doors to have been closed and locked. Most people migrated to the next party at the same time I did.

"Let's go," he says impatiently, putting a hand at the small of my back and nudging me forward. The fact that he ignores my declining his offer of help is telling. He's already made up his mind. And what he decides is what goes. In that way, he and Shane are very much the same.

Deciding not to argue, I step forward.

For him, people part like the Red Sea.

Looking back over my shoulder, I lock eyes once more with Shane. Does he care that Declan and I are talking? And walking out together? In high school, he would've seen it as a mark of disloyalty. None of his friends were allowed to socialize with me.

Shane's expression now is dark, but that's typical when he looks at me. I want to feel nothing, but the raw intensity of his gaze affects me. As he looks me over slowly, a rush of heat pours through me, making my nipples pucker. Thank God for my thick sweater, but what the hell is up with my physical reaction to him?

I lick my lips, studying his face across the room's expanse. The distance is meaningless. With his eyes on me, I'm flushed and completely aware of him, remembering the way his hard six-pack was revealed beneath a t-shirt when he stretched to get something on a high kitchen shelf. During the year we lived under the same roof, I had plenty of time to memorize all the things that make women fall at his feet.

I turn away as the DJ returns from his break. Music blares from the sound system, and people dance wildly. Suddenly dodging flailing limbs becomes part of our trek toward the door. We hustle through the horde.

Getting outside is a relief, and the path to my residential hall is quiet and familiar. With Declan accompanying me, I don't examine every shadow. But I hate that I need a guy around to feel safe. When I first arrived on campus, I walked alone all the time and never worried.

"If you wanted to finish the semester from home, I'm sure Ethan's pull could arrange it. I know a couple of girls who are finishing online."

Is my safety the reason Declan suggests this? Or does he just want me gone?

"I can't do that. It would mean forfeiting my chance at a summer internship I plan to apply for."

"An internship the summer after freshman year? Why?"

Do I want to confess my academic hopes and dreams the first time I'm talking to him in two years? No, I definitely don't. "Someone I admire works for the company. It would be really great to get a chance to learn from them."

For a moment I think he might ask who, and I tense. It feels dangerous to say too much. Declan's ties to power are endless. If he or Shane bad-mouthed me, it might sabotage my chances.

I'm the only female and the only freshman in an upper-level business course. I really need to shine, and I don't want anything to come up that would make my professor have concerns about my character or professionalism.

We walk on in silence for a moment. I feel the pressure to fill it. "When you and Shane were in high school you were the dynamic duo on the football field. How come he's not playing here?"

"He's busy with other things."

Excessively vague. "Like what?"

Declan frowns, as if he regrets having said anything. "If you want to know something about Shane, ask him."

We both know Shane wouldn't tell me anything. By now, that should be fine with me. But somehow it still isn't. Shane is like a wooden splinter buried deep in my heel. I tell myself to forget it, but with every step it's there, creating an uncomfortable sensation.

"Someone said Erik Sorensen is Shane's cousin. I've never met him. Is he from Shane's mom's side of the family?"

Declan stares straight ahead, his expression shuttered.

"Sorensen doesn't sound like an Irish name," I add.

"It's Danish."

"Is he from Denmark?"

"No."

Small talk has never been so small. Thankfully, we've reached my building.

"This is me. Good night."

I don't wait for a response. Instead, I trot up the steps and let myself in.

When the main door closes behind me, I exhale in relief. Tonight was the first time I've come face to face with Shane and Declan, and it went better than expected. As Declan said, this is a good time to make a fresh start. The trouble from two years ago is ancient history.

There's a faint smell of rum punch near my room door as I unlock it. A lot of drinks sloshed on the floor during the party.

Inside, I turn the light on and check the closet to be sure it's empty. It's become a ritual. Two of the women who were taken were outside at the time, but it's less clear how Casanova got the third. The rose and her phone were found in her dorm room.

As an extra precaution, I check under my bed, which is of course empty.

Get a grip, Ave.

I shut and lock the door, and then change into yoga pants and an oversized t-shirt. I never sleep in a tank and my underwear the way I did when I first got here. It makes me feel too vulnerable.

When I'm ready, I pull back the blanket, and what I see makes me freeze. Lying in the bed is a long-stemmed lavender rose.

The whole world feels as if it's closing in on me, stealing the breath from my lungs, suffocating me.

Casanova has been in my room.

❧ 2 ❧

SHANE

Seeing Avery last night ruined my good time.

I thought about bringing someone home to distract myself but didn't. My place has too many secrets for it to be a good place for casual hook-ups to sleep over. I also wasn't convinced it would take my mind off my trespassing little stepsister.

So, I did a shot of Jameson's and slept hard on some fancy Egyptian cotton sheets that feel like butter's been churned into them. I'm addicted to all kinds of luxury items from the year I spent crashing at Declan's because of her.

How would Avery look lying naked against these sheets? All I have to do is ask myself the question, and an old image is conjured. My cock gets hard as the memory of her naked body hits me. The girl, minus the glasses, minus the attitude and minus the clothes, sound asleep on the basement couch. Squarely in my domain. At sixteen, she was all creamy skin, smooth legs, and perfect tits with rosy pink nipples.

And just like that my cock's a steel pipe.

I press my lips together, scowling. I want her gone from my head. I exorcised her from it for almost two years before my dad sent her here.

I try to replace her in my mind with other coeds. Unsuccessful. I move on to actresses, models, and even random porn stars. Nothing works.

Fuck her for coming to the Beta party. I close my fist around my cock and stroke impatiently.

Remembering the sight of her naked makes me groan. Her glossy dark hair spilling over her shoulder, the part of her soft lips, even the smudged eye makeup that looked like soot. Flesh-and-blood forbidden fruit.

Letting the memories come does the same for my cock. I get myself off in record time.

Fuck. I need her gone from Granthorpe.

On the nightstand, my phone rings. I glance over to see the profile picture. Dear old Dad. I don't answer or even pick up the phone. To hell with him. He's the one who sent the little phantom here to haunt me.

Instead, I head to the shower. I'm fifty-fifty on whether I'll listen to his voicemail after or delete it unopened. We'd mended our relationship about halfway when he pulled this shit about sending Avery here. I told him she should go *anywhere else*, but he ignored me. So now, I'm back to ignoring him when he reaches out.

When I get out of the shower, the doorbell rings. I've got no shipments scheduled for today, and it's not even nine am, so I don't know who that could be. It won't be Dec or Sorensen. We didn't leave the party until four, and those guys have practice today. When they crash, they crash hard. No way either of them is awake yet.

My Spidey sense isn't tingling, but it could be dampened by my being a little hungover. Taking my time, I towel off and get dressed. Whoever's out there will either wait or give up and leave. Either is fine with me. As a precaution, I grab the pistol from the nightstand. I don't expect trouble on my doorstep at Granthorpe, but being prepared isn't just a motto for the Boy Scouts.

When I get downstairs, I conceal the gun by resting my right hand against my back. No need to wave it around and scare some random Jehovah's Witness.

I use my left hand to open the door, and—*Are you fucking kidding me?*

Avery Kershaw, baby beauty queen turned coed, is hiding her big blue eyes behind black-framed glasses. She's hiding her body under worn jeans and a sweater. What I wish is that she was hiding her entire person back on campus where she belongs.

"Hey, Shane."

What the fuck did Dec say to her last night to make her think she should come here? Avery and I have barely spoken in the past two years. I broke her of the habit of trying within three weeks of what her bitch mother calls "the unfortunate misunderstanding."

Avery's five-five, female, and unarmed, but I still consider her dangerous. Not in the way that made men are dangerous. Or the way guys with big mouths are dangerous. No, she's more insidious, like meningitis sliding in to infect a brain.

"Can I come in to talk to you?"

"No."

Her exhalation comes out as a sigh, which pisses me off. She's going to act as though she's the long-suffering victim of my neglect? Be fucking serious is what I want to say, my blood starting to simmer.

It has not escaped my attention that, at eighteen, she's an adult and could have chosen to attend any college in the country that I didn't happen to be going to at the time. Her presence here is as much her fault as my dad's.

"I need to talk to you. It's important."

Her emphasis on the word important doesn't impress me, and I let that show on my face.

"Let me come inside, okay, Shane?"

My gaze finally notices a blue duffel bag on the porch next to her booted foot.

"Going somewhere?"

"Yes, into your place as soon as you step back."

I give her a hard look that would make anyone else turn tail and flee. She doesn't.

"Why would I invite you in?"

She licks her lips and swallows. "Shane, come on." Her voice is soft and sweet, just the way I remember. A siren song. Which should make me toss her off my porch and slam the door, but instead it makes me want to toss her onto my couch to fuck her. This is why I prefer to keep my distance; I have made her off-limits for myself, and, therefore, it's a bad idea to be around her.

"No," I say, then I step back and shut the door.

I think about the call from my dad. Did he want to give me the heads-up that the princess was on her way? He'd better not have told her it was all right to come by. And voicemails complaining that I didn't let her in will only piss me off more because they should know better.

But he's a lawyer who never loses a case. Relentless arguing is what pays his bills and keeps him in seven-thousand-dollar bespoke suits. He has never given up on the idea of "getting the family back together."

I jog up the stairs and into my bedroom. My phone's blinking.

Text messages and the voicemail.

"Do not start this shit, Ethan," I whisper into the empty room. When I check, only the voicemail is from him. The texts are from random Granthorpe people.

I tap the screen, and his voicemail plays.

"Shane, it's Dad. Second message. I'd appreciate a call back today. We haven't been able to reach Avery this morning. If I haven't heard from her by this afternoon, I'll need you to drive to her dorm to check on things. You don't need to talk to her. Just be sure she's all right."

The princess is dodging calls from the king and queen? That's new.

I send my father a text.

> Shane: Saw Avery. She's fine.

> Dad: Where did you see her? Are you sure it was her? Because Sheri's calls and mine are going to voicemail.

> Shane: Yeah, I'm sure. Saw her across room at party last night. Spotted her alive n well today too.

I'm curious about why she's not answering their calls, but I don't take the bait. There's a plan. I never falter from it. Keep my distance. Pretend she doesn't exist.

The doorbell rings.

Seriously?

Then there's knocking hard enough to carry up the stairs and into my room. Goddammit. If she thinks she can manipulate me the way her mom manipulates Ethan, she's very much mistaken.

The seconds tick by into minutes. The knocking stops, then starts again. Anger brews inside me. Who the hell does she think she is?

Avery has never been this pushy with me. But she's gotten away with plenty in the past, so maybe habit has her thinking she can do this even with me.

The thought of bending her over the couch and spanking her ass before I fuck it hits me full force. My cock stiffens. *Jesus Christ.*

My hard-on gets harder at the thought of an Avery hate-fuck.

I take the stairs slowly, my palm tingling to smack her ass. It's been a long time since I've played dirty games with a beautiful girl. Lately, I've been too busy for anything more than a quick fuck with a parade of pretty coeds.

The gun goes into a living room console table. Opening the door carries in a cool wind and a view of the girl who destroyed my home life.

"Hear me out," she says quickly. "I promise I won't take more than five minutes to explain why I'm here."

My gaze rakes over her. Perversely, I like the female Clark Kent persona she's adopted the past year. It followed on the heels of the insane boyish short haircut after the "unfortunate incident." Under the placid surface, she's a lunatic of course. And that's inherited, of course. But I'm not interested in listening to her bang on my door all day. Especially not when I might do something more interesting with her.

"What's in it for me?" I ask, applying the same bored tone I always use with her when simply ignoring her is not an option.

"Does something really have to be in it for you to have a conversation with a member of your family?"

"You're not family. And yeah, in this case, there does need to be something in it for me."

"You need to let it go. Nothing even happened to you. Not really."

My blood, which was simmering slowly, starts to truly boil. "That's not the approach to take if you want to get into my place. Try again."

Her expression goes back to looking cautious. "I don't know what you want from me. Money? I don't have any to spare. I'm not taking an allowance from them because I want to be independent like you are."

Is that supposed to move me? Any money she and her gold-digging mother have comes from my dad, including the money that pays for Avery's tuition, her clothes, and her meal plan. She's not exactly destitute. Last I knew, all Avery has to do to get money from my dad is ask.

When I don't answer, she waves a hand to push that aside. "Please let me in."

"Why should I?"

"Are you really this heartless?" she asks softly, and her eyes take on a sheen. She is so much her mother's daughter right now, turning on the tears to get what she wants. My dad caves every time. I don't, which she should know.

"What do you want in exchange for hearing me out?"

"You can scrub my bathrooms and do my laundry." It's not what I really want, but it should be enough to run her off.

Avery blinks and then looks surprised. After a moment, her head bobs in a nod. "Yeah, I can do that."

She earns points for not whining or acting outraged. In my dad's house, the maid comes every day. No one touches laundry except her.

I have a cleaning lady here too, but I only have her in the house once a week. I don't want her around when I'm expecting shipments that I don't want seen.

I draw in a breath and exhale, then I step aside. Avery comes in, sets her duffel next to the console table, and looks at me. Pointing at the couch, I get hit with my second flash of the day of her lying on it naked.

Avery sits without hesitation. Either she doesn't recognize the couch or doesn't place any significance on the role it played in our demise.

"You know about Casanova?" she asks.

"Of course."

Everyone knows about the disappearing girls and the mysterious asshole who's been taking them. The word is that a light purple rose was found in a copy of Casanova's memoir left at the scene of the first abduction.

I assume he's a rapist. Gotta be. What else would a man want with pretty young women? One thing's for sure, his acts have wreaked devastation far and wide. Missing girls, distraught families, and a campus that's on edge. We've all felt the fallout.

"Last night, there was a lavender rose in my dorm room. No other girls got one. Just me."

My brows rise. Did the fucking degenerate actually target my stepsister?

"No one's ever said anything about him leaving a rose as a threat." Raking my eyes over her, I decide she's fine. "I thought he leaves the rose when he takes them?"

She shrugs, hunching forward. "I talked to the police. They said the same thing. But it was there. I gave it to them as evidence." She looks up, her blue eyes searching my face. "I don't know what they think, but they don't seem to think it's him."

I'm sure the cops don't know what to think. The situation's murky. There was a girl who claimed she'd been raped by Casanova in her dorm room. Everyone thought the perp was escalating by assaulting her with other women only a few feet away who might hear her scream. A few days later the truth came out. She'd made it all up and had planted a rose in her own room. It was a ploy to get her boyfriend's attention back after he'd blown her off.

Of course, there have still been three legit abductions. I'm not trying to actively keep track of the case, but not noticing is not an option when the headlines are constantly screaming about him. It's not clear why the cops can't seem to get a line on him. They've had time. Someone must have seen something, even if they don't know it.

"I want to stay here until the end of the semester."

"Where? At Granthorpe?" I'm sure her mother and my dad have urged her to come home to finish out the last couple of weeks online.

"Yes, at Granthorpe. But also here." She looks around my house meaningfully.

I barely manage to keep myself from barking out a surprised laugh. "No way. I don't know what Declan told you, but my sending him to walk you home should *not* have been considered an invitation to come over. Or even to talk to me."

"You sent Declan?"

My eyes narrow. Did Avery think Dec came over on his own because he was interested in protecting her himself? What bullshit.

"It was a nice thing to do, Shane. I appreciate it."

I don't answer. Looking out for Avery is not something I'm going to do on the regular. I stopped that a long time ago. Sending Declan to her last night was a moment of weakness, probably because I was buzzed.

"Just a one-off. Your safety is your own problem. If being on campus worries you, leave."

"How will it make you look if your little sister gets taken from right under your nose? When you're supposed to be such a tough guy?"

"Is that my reputation?" I ask with mock curiosity, ignoring that she's trying to saddle me with the label of older brother. What interests me more is her saying I'm supposed to be a tough guy. That's not something she should know. My father always claims he never tells anyone about my mom's family. Has that changed?

"Even us lowly freshmen hear things. Like that there's an underground fight club. Like that you keep the peace at those events by carrying a gun."

Ah. The fight club. I did have to pull my gun once to keep spectators from getting in on the action when a frat boy was getting the shit kicked out of him by a townie.

"Those old rumors will not die," I say casually.

"But you do have a gun, right?" She tucks strands of shiny hair behind her ear.

I remember how silky that hair is, and my fingers want to reach out and touch it.

"You had a gun in Ethan and my mom's house. My mom said so."

"And we know she's a reliable source of information," I say sarcastically.

Her eyes rise to meet mine. "I saw it."

"How could you have?" I counter, my tone even. "The basement was off-limits to you, just as the second floor was off-limits to me. No way to see each other's stuff, right?" I always suspected she snooped around my bedroom when I was out.

"I broke the rules one night. Which you already know."

"You didn't see a gun that night. You were on the couch in the lounge area. A gun was not."

"I saw it," she says firmly, refusing to even look embarrassed. No apology. No remorse. Like mother, like daughter.

"Hmm."

She smells like spicy vanilla-scented body wash. It makes me want to lick every inch of her. No matter how much time passes, no matter how many times I remind myself that she betrayed me, there's a part of me that does not care. The physical chemistry between us is fucking relentless. Being near her is a mistake.

"So can I stay? In exchange, I'll do your housework for you. And cook. Breakfast every morning. And dinner, maybe three nights a week?"

"I've got a maid. And I don't need a cook, especially one who can barely fry an egg."

The color rises in her cheeks. It's the first physical sign of emotion I've seen today. Even when she talked about the rose, she didn't seem agitated. I usually like it when people are cool under pressure, but in her case it's suspect.

"Oh, so you remember that day when I tried to make everyone breakfast?" she says, trying for friendliness. "You were great actually."

My muscles tighten. There's no way we're strolling down memory lane to the time before everything went to hell.

"You've had your chance to talk, Avery. The cleaning supplies are under the sink in both bathrooms. The laundry room's in the basement. When you finish, let me know, so I can lock the door when you leave."

Avery shoots to her feet. "I don't feel safe in the dorm. Someone's always leaving the main door propped open for a boyfriend, even though it's insane to do that right now with Casanova on the prowl."

"Not my problem."

"You really don't care if I'm abducted and victimized?"

I school my face to give nothing away. "I don't," I lie.

Avery's blue eyes go wide behind her glasses. "What a prick you've turned out to be."

I almost tell her to be careful, but I don't. Let her stomp out in outrage. I don't even really want her in the house long enough to clean. It was a mistake letting her in. I wanted to play with her, but it's fucking with my own head too.

She surprises me by not using what I said as an excuse to stalk out without doing the cleaning.

"If I thought you didn't care that girls are getting hurt, I wouldn't have come." Her tone is accusatory. Like she expects me to cave in and admit I lied, which I won't. That would open the door on a conversation I do not want to have with her.

"But," she continues, "you kept your word to hear me out, so I'll get to work."

Good enough. Her in some other part of the house will be better.

I jog upstairs ahead of her to be sure the middle room's door is locked and then I head back down to the main floor to stay as far away from her as possible as she works.

After about an hour, she's finished, and she comes into the kitchen to wash her hands. Then she walks over to the kitchen table where I'm sitting.

"I'm done, but I want to ask you one last time to let me stay here. There must be something you need, Shane. A personal assistant to run errands? Everyone says you burn the candle at both ends. Taking classes, side hustles, aggressive partying. When was the last time you slept in? You look as if you don't even have time to shave these days."

She has me there. I've blown off classes and even some appointments. A haircut's long overdue. And I need one before I go to the next family meeting. But if I was going to hire someone to help me, it definitely wouldn't be the precious little princess who swung a wrecking ball through my life.

"The only thing someone like you could do for me is drop to your knees and suck my cock on command."

She stares at me, and her lack of reaction is one for the books. After a pause that seems to last forever, she asks, "Are you serious?"

"Yeah, I'm serious."

She presses her pouty pink lips together, maybe to keep them from parting to let a string of curses spew. "You're such a jerk."

I shrug.

After a moment, she says softly, "Not on command. But once a week I think I could manage."

My body goes still. What the fuck? Is she playing right now?

I keep my voice even. "Once a week is nothing."

That's a complete lie. Having her on her knees with my cock in her mouth even once would be satisfying as hell. I'm silent a moment, reveling in the dawning surprise that she'd consider trading the use of her mouth for a place to live. How scared must she be to even contemplate something like this?

I try to put myself in her place, try to imagine how a woman must have to worry when there's a monster lurking nearby who likes to carry girls just like her off to unknown places to violate them. No matter how I try to relate, I can't. I've been in situations where I had to fight for my life. When it was over, it was just over.

"Not any time all day long. I can't be in sexual boot camp with you telling me to drop and give you..."

"Head?" I offer, pleased by the flush on her face. For once, she's actually flustered when the situation warrants it.

"Yeah, that. I have work to do. I need to be able to concentrate." Her eyes dart to my face, then away. "Three times a week?"

"Once a day. Final offer."

She glances back at me and is silent. The seconds tick by, and then she finally says, "All right."

It's a complete mind-fuck.

My innocent little stepsister's just signed on to be my sex toy.

AVERY

A single hour of sleep, filled with nightmares, is probably not a good foundation for sound decision-making. By the time I got to Shane's, my mind was running on adrenaline and espresso, and I had one thought in my head. Destiny is testing me, and for once, I am going to win the stare-down.

I'm staying at school until the end of the semester because I want an internship that would allow me to work for Roxie Keller, a twenty-seven-year-old badass whose career I started following after I heard her on a podcast about entrepreneurship.

Her background is similar to mine in that she was raised by a single mom who wanted her to fit a certain mold that she didn't. There were so many things Roxie said on that podcast that made me feel like she was talking directly to me. She spoke of her obsession with finance and technology and how she practically dropped out of society for a couple of years to pursue her passion. Software that uses computer modeling to choose high-return investments was born of her single-minded focus. Six years after starting it, she sold her company for nine figures.

When I learned she was consulting at Ralston Enterprises and there was an internship available to work with her, I felt like it was meant for me. That maybe this opportunity was the whole cosmic reason I ended up at Granthorpe, where I didn't want to come because of Shane. The Ralston founder is a GU alum who has ties to its faculty. Even after the third Casanova abduction, I told myself I would not leave.

And then the rose appeared in my bed. After the police were no help, I almost called Ethan in a panic to ask him to pick me up. Instead, I white-knuckled it out in my dorm room until dawn and then came to Shane's. It's the one place at GU that I know I'll be safe from Casanova.

The semester is almost over, but I knew convincing Shane to let me move in would be almost impossible. I told myself to keep going until I found something he needed.

Bartering with sex never entered my mind. But as soon as he suggested it, I knew it was the only winning card I had. So I played it.

If I let myself think for too long about our new filthy arrangement, my mind reels. So I'm trying not to think. Instead, I'm riding the adrenaline-and-coffee express to the end.

I spend a couple hours heading back and forth between my dorm room and Shane's house by bus, bringing clothes and books to his place. Every time I glance at my bed where the rose laid in wait I feel a new surge of determination. I am not going to let a smug woman-hater force me to leave my school.

Casanova's hunting ground is the campus. My stepbrother's house is safely off campus. Also, Shane is prepared for trouble. When we both lived at Ethan's, I discovered a gun in Shane's nightstand. He never mentioned it, or even hinted that he had it. But I knew that if anyone ever broke into the house, they would get a nasty surprise.

Once in high school, before Shane and I had our falling out, a creepy guy tried to put his arm around me, and I pulled away. The guy joked, "Careful. I'm the guy who gets mad enough to show up with an AK to shoot up the school." Everyone laughed nervously, except Shane. With ice in his voice, Shane said, "And I'm the guy who ends your run before you clear the first hall." Then it was the guy's turn to laugh nervously and quickly say he was joking. Shane nodded but didn't laugh. I could tell he was serious, especially when he added, "Don't ever try to touch her again."

There is a sharp serrated edge to Shane that I've caught glimpses of when someone acts threatening. There's no doubt in my mind that if Casanova tries to force his way into the house, Shane will stop him.

Sure, the price of feeling safe is higher than I ever imagined, but I'm willing to pay it so I can sleep at night. I settle into the plum and light gray guest room. A gorgeous purple and glowing orange photograph of Boston at night hangs over the bed. Except for that picture, the room feels very generic.

There are two other rooms on the second floor that interest me. One door is locked. The other is open a crack to reveal a king-sized bed with massive wood and aluminum head and foot boards. It dominates Shane's room and draws more than my eyes. I resist the temptation to walk in and look around.

I head downstairs to the front room where Shane sits on the familiar black couch...the dreaded one. I thought Ethan threw it away or donated it to charity. No. It's here. A dark reminder of the past.

Shane leans back, his feet resting on the coffee table as he looks at his phone.

I glance at a large black-and-white framed photograph on the wall. In it, Shane's shirtless and in sharp focus with a cigarette hanging from his lips. There's a white bandage on his shoulder that's partially obscured by the smoke. In the blurry background, there's a bikini-clad girl lying on a wooden deck next to a hot tub. Steam and mountains rise behind them. I presume the picture was taken at Declan's family's house in Aspen, probably by Declan. I wonder about the cigarette and the bandage. I've never seen Shane smoke, and I've never seen him wounded. The image reminds me that I don't really know him anymore. Maybe I never did.

"There's a room upstairs that stays locked," he says, drawing my attention. "It's off-limits."

I walk away from the picture to join him. "Who's up there? Your sex slave?"

"No. My sex slave's standing in front of me." The statement is deadpan, and I think he's joking. At least I hope he is. The line still makes my stomach flip and my face flame.

I give him a blistering look, and for the briefest second, the corner of his mouth twitches like he'll smirk, but he doesn't. His formidable resistance to engaging in any friendly moments with me is not new. It's been in place since that terrible morning when our parents turned on him because of me.

I sigh, trying not to think about it. We've all thought about it way too much since it effectively broke up the family.

Walking away, I turn my attention to next steps. First, I grab my last small bag and head back upstairs. I approach the secret room, glancing at the door handle. Pausing to examine the lock, my fingers explore the smooth curves of the brass.

"If I catch you trying to get in there, you'll be sorry."

I jerk, surprised by his voice. I didn't realize he'd followed me upstairs.

"Yeah, got it. No need to bark at me."

"Did I raise my voice?" His gaze travels over my face, lingering on my mouth, possibly admiring his new property.

I start to walk away, and he catches my arm to stop me. His grip isn't rough, but it's firm. His bicep bulges, straining his t-shirt. His arms, as always, can't go unnoticed. The air between us crackles with electricity, and where our skin touches there's more than body heat.

"Hey." His green eyes narrow, but his voice is low. "Just so we're clear, this is my house. I bought it and pay the mortgage." He lets that sink in. "I make the rules."

I don't acknowledge out loud that I'm impressed he's been able to afford a nice house in this affluent neighborhood where real estate must be very expensive. Instead, I counter with, "You must like that. I know you hate following other people's rules."

"That's not what I hated." He leans closer, so I can smell the mint flavor of his toothpaste. "So we understand each other? You're the help, with one important difference." His gaze drops to my lips. "If someone who works for me doesn't meet expectations, I fire them. But you, I'll punish."

Punish? What does that mean? And why does the threat seem so sexual? It draws me in, like a planet to the sun. But I shouldn't forget that to get too close would be dangerous. When Shane shut us out of his life, it broke my heart. I don't intend to get caught up in him ever again.

"I'm not planning to break the rules."

"You never do." He gives me a little shove away from him as he releases me. "Now don't tempt me to make you get on your knees. I'm saving that for later."

My body stiffens. "No, you're not. Today, I cleaned. The other... service can start tomorrow. I have to work on a project all evening since I lost the day to moving in and doing chores."

"Not my problem."

"Shane—"

"Not. My. Problem."

He walks away, leaving me to watch him warily. I'm attracted to his body and the thought of touching it makes my mouth water, but I'm not naive enough to assume it'll change things between us.

Shane is uncompromising. His resolve itself can be punishing, and that's what is in store for me. Why else would he let me be here? Plenty of women would give him blow jobs on command, and they wouldn't have to be given a place to live in exchange. He doesn't really need me. This is his way of getting revenge.

With anyone else, I would never have made this kind of deal. A frown tugs at the corners of my mouth. Was my subconscious operating with more in mind than Casanova and the internship? Maybe.

I really want to settle things with Shane, but he's never made that a possibility until now. If we're forced to live together—to do intimate things—his walls will finally have to come down.

I want closure. I'm so desperate for it, it tastes like a snow cone on a hundred-degree day. Imperative, almost.

Because every time I see him or hear about him, the ongoing cold war slices me like a knife. Living with him will shake us out of the status quo. It has to.

And we'll either get past our bitter past, or we'll reach a new level of toxicity that makes me not care if we ever do.

✤ 4 ✤

AVERY

Shane has his dinner delivered. The Thai food smells amazing and makes my mouth water. I feel like an idiot for not thinking about what to do about dinner. I have the school's meal plan, but while living with him, I'm off campus. I don't have time to take the bus back before dark tonight, and I don't have room on my credit card to get food delivered.

"Hey, I don't have any of my own groceries here," I say. "I guess I could text one of the guys I know to bring me food." I wait, hoping he'll offer to share.

He doesn't look over. "No visitors in my house. If you wanna see someone, see him somewhere else."

"Can I have some of that? I'll buy groceries for me tomorrow."

"There's plenty of stuff in the fridge. Eat whatever you want. No need to buy groceries."

"Thanks." It's generous and even, shockingly, a little kind. "What are you eating?"

His gaze slides to me. "You want some of this, huh? I'll tell you what. You can have it, and as payment, I'll bend you over the couch and fuck you hard from behind."

My jaw drops, and my hands come up in silent protest. Then my shock wears off, and I glare at him. Before today, he was never this crude and abrasive. I can't help but wonder whether his sexual harassment is intended to drive me back and keep his walls fortified lest I slip through a crack.

He digs into the food and takes a bite, his eyes never leaving my face, which I'm sure is as red as the chilies in his dinner. He chews and then holds out the carton to me. "Take it. I dare you."

My heart slams against my ribs, and things low in my body come alive. "No thanks. Just lost my appetite."

"If you say so." His voice is sexy and rough, which makes my nipples tighten. I've never heard him sound like this before. No wonder women all chase him like catnip.

I glance at the clock, relieved I'll have a distraction soon. My video call with the annoying men I'm doing a project with is in ten minutes. I'm the only woman in the upper level entrepreneurial e-commerce class, and all the guys are super arrogant and aggressive. Two asked me out. One I actually kind of dated. But now, because I've made it clear that hooking up is off the table, they're all surly or dismissive.

I've had the top score on two exams and a paper, but I'm not sure anyone knows. Sometimes, when none of them will let me get a word in during discussions, I want to wave my paper in the air like a banner. See what Professor Smith-Hall wrote? *Best in class. Top score.*

But if I did tell any of them the truth, it would only make them hate my presence in the course even more. And it would make me feel like an insufferable show-off. I want my hard work to speak for itself, so I keep calm and carry on. British Empire, all the way.

Still, I know the pressure is on. I need to show Smith-Hall more than my ability to memorize and to craft a clever paper. The internship will include doing pitches and presentations. The application outright says those without leadership potential need not apply. If I want a shot at an interview, I need a strong letter of support from Professor Smith-Hall.

I set up my laptop on the screened-in porch. It's cold, but at least it's quiet. I forgot to bring my heavy winter coat to Shane's. I'll get it after class tomorrow, but for now, I'm huddling in my jacket as I log into the meeting.

My two classmates, Todd and Daniel, are already onscreen and engaged in conversation about our project. Am I late? I glance at the clock. No, I'm on time.

"Hey," I say.

Daniel offers a quick greeting before launching back into conversation.

Daniel and I went on a few dates. He's tall and wiry, with a beanie and short beard, and I liked his hipster style, which he counterbalances with a dry, self-deprecating wit. Too bad my first impression of him wasn't his true self.

After a decent first date, we met a couple of days later to study over coffee, and he was rude to our overwhelmed waitress. His voice carried when he said scholarship students should stick to cafeteria work, not drag down businesses where efficiency is key.

I told him to ease off, feeling the sting personally since before Mom married Ethan, we lived paycheck-to-paycheck a lot. Instead of being nicer, he doubled down with digs like "so many women are too sensitive to run a business. You guys don't have the killer instinct." When I countered with, "Companies with women on the boards are more profitable," and coolly spewed examples, he turned surly.

When we left, as if to hammer home his disdain for the weak, he was nasty to an elderly homeless person who was panhandling for change. That left me momentarily breathless. Completely mortified, I gave the man my last five dollars and apologized while Daniel fumed, rolled his eyes, and muttered.

I told him to lose my number.

Crazily, he texted on and off for several days after, saying we'd just had an off day and should go out again. I resorted to ghosting.

So it was *super* awkward to be assigned to a group project with him. Though, to give him a small amount of credit, he did apologize for acting so arrogant that day and has tried to be nice since. Unfortunately, when he's with Todd Bardoratch, I see shades of the pretentious asshole he was on that coffee date.

The screen door creaks, and I look up to see Shane step out. I don't have time to ask what he's doing. I need to understand why they're talking about accounting and the spreadsheets I created. I was supposed to go over that in the second part of this meeting.

"Hey, hang on a sec, guys. I thought we were going to review the mock-up of the website first?"

"Did that. And the product choices. We went with the graphic t-shirts," Daniel says.

"Wait, you made a product decision without me? And which t-shirts? Not the Trekkie ones? The margin on them isn't great, and there's so much competition that I—"

They talk over me, going on with a discussion of the spreadsheets and my automated workflows. I wonder if Todd's over-the-top dismissiveness is a show of solidarity with Daniel or if Todd's just always a fellow asshole.

"I like the workflows," Todd says. He's got floppy hair that he's always tossing like a wanna-be model. Tragically, he's our team's de facto leader because he hails from a long line of investment bankers and dabbles in investing with money he acts like he earned but didn't.

"They'll work fine," Todd continues. "And the recurring reports feature is really good. Great work, Daniel."

"That's *my* code," I say, my voice rising. "I wrote it. I created the workflows and reports."

"What?" Todd demands impatiently.

I lower the pitch of my voice, careful to not give them an excuse to call me hysterical or some other sexist adjective. "It's obvious you guys met up without me. When? And why?"

"Hey. Chill. We were already together at Todd's townhouse for some beers, and we got to talking. Your name will still be on the project. No big deal that you haven't done as much work."

I feel the blood drain from my face. "I've done a ton of work. All the spreadsheets, all the code—"

They aren't listening. In fact, they raise their voices to drown me out again as they decide to revisit the profit margins on the t-shirts.

"Didn't someone do the research on cost? Where's that sheet?" Todd asks.

"I did the analysis," I say, rigid with frustration.

"Good girl. Upload that, so we can take a look."

A shadow looms above me. My gaze jerks upward.

"Tell them to fuck off." Shane speaks so low that for a moment I'm not sure I've heard him correctly.

I ignore him, sticking with calm, and try again to make myself heard. "I'm not really comfortable with being cut out of meetings. We all have to do that peer review at the end. How are you guys planning to rate me on my presentation skills when I haven't had a chance to explain the work I've done?"

"We're not. You're a freshman. You shouldn't even be in this class," Todd says with a scowl.

"I did the pre-reqs as AP classes back in—"

"Just upload the product research," he says, cutting me off.

I shake my head, my heart pounding. "I want to present it, as an equal member of the team."

"Yeah, that's not happening," Todd sneers. "Now just upload everything you've got right now, or we will sink you in the review and tell Smith-Hall you didn't contribute to the project at all."

My stomach twists into knots. Impotent rage makes me feel like I may vomit. This can't be happening. When I lift my fingers to the keys, they shake from the adrenaline rush.

Shane's big hand plucks the laptop off the table and turns it around so the camera's on him. "Are you for real? Did you just gang up on a teenage girl and threaten to tell the teacher on her for not helping you? What kind of fucking pussies are you?"

A shocked silence follows.

After a beat, Shane reads their names out loud from the screen. His voice is so menacing and deep he could be a wolf growling. "You boys have heard of the pit, right? Where douchebags are turned into ground beef? Expect to find yourselves there soon if you act on the threats you just made."

His stony expression and everything about the way he looks and speaks has cowed them into speechlessness, something I've never seen from these guys.

Shane flips the screen down with a snap and sets it back on the table. Then he whips out his phone and starts texting.

For several seconds I'm frozen, then I grab his arm. "Hey, um—"

He looks at my hand and then at my face. "Hey yourself. If you want to put a hand somewhere on my body, go lower."

I withdraw it like I've been burned. He may have defended me, but it's apparently not an invitation to be friends.

"What's the pit? Did you make that up?"

Inside, I'm horrified but also fascinated. Is there really a place where men who step out of line are brought down by some form of dark vigilante justice? I know it's wrong, but a little part of me enjoys the idea.

Shane exhales a chuckle. "If I were lying, do you think they'd call my bluff?"

Yes, they might, I think nervously as he continues to lean over his phone.

When he looks up, his expression is serious. "Get into the project folder or wherever you uploaded your files to and delete them all before those assholes get a chance to download them."

"I—why? I have to participate."

"It's your leverage. Do it now," he says, yanking the screen up.

His voice is so firm that I don't stop to think. Instead, I enter the communal workspace and delete the documents.

"Done." I check the log. "No one has downloaded anything." I lean back and then grimace. "But doing this won't help. They'll exclude me from the project and destroy me in the peer evals."

"No, they won't." His tone suggests that my worry is laughable, but he doesn't know my two pampered and misogynist group members like I do.

"I know you're very popular, but these guys won't care about that. They've got huge egos, and they're not used to being humiliated. Threatening violence will probably just get you reported to campus police or Granthorpe administration."

"You think so?" His tone is mild as his brow quirks like he can't imagine it.

"I do. Guys like that—they'll never let this go. Remember the way you and Declan destroyed me socially in high school? The way no upperclassmen would speak to me or look at me?" My voice falters and trails off. The corner of my mouth tugs down and, inwardly, I cringe. I do not want to revisit that topic.

He watches me. His face is impassive as if he's unmoved, but his shoulders square.

"When guys with power get angry, it never ends well," I say.

Shane's brows rise again. "In high school, you got what you deserved."

"I did *not*. My mom made a mistake. That she regretted by the way. But you were furious, and you ruined my life at that school because of it."

"Your mom was the only one who made a mistake?" His eyes cut into me. "No." His tone is measured, but a deep frown appears. "And for the record, I never said anything to anyone."

"Well, Declan certainly did then," I say softly. "People didn't stop speaking to me overnight for no reason."

"You should have told the truth. Right when your mother accused me."

I wince. "I didn't know the truth. I blacked out and woke up naked. I didn't know what happened to me."

"You sure as hell knew I hadn't had sex with you. You were a goddamned virgin back then. You'd have known if a guy shoved his dick in you. Even if you couldn't remember the details, you'd have been able to tell."

"I felt sore all over that morning."

"From a hangover. Sore muscles from dancing on tables and around the basement. Not sore between your legs."

"It was my first hangover. I was innocent and dumb! And I never accused you of anything."

"No, you didn't. You stayed silent while she accused me. You let it go on. She called the fucking police."

His fury and frustration rams into me like fists, until I can't breathe.

"I *told* her I didn't think you had."

"When?"

"When she and I were alone in the bathroom. I tried to tell her to hold on until we could figure things out."

"So you say now."

"I'm not lying."

"What I know is that you disappeared to the second floor, the princess's tower, and left me to twist. After the cops talked to you, they seemed more convinced than ever that I was guilty."

"Shane, no—"

"I was proven innocent by video footage. Which existed because your bitch of a mother made my own fucking father distrust me so much he had cameras stashed all over the basement." He grinds his teeth, and then adds, "Security cameras, my ass. He was watching me. Even after I let them run me out of my own goddamned room, so you could have it and we wouldn't be on same floor. I lived in the basement for a year, but it wasn't enough."

My throat is tight as I swallow. I can't believe I'm finally getting to have this conversation with him. He usually immediately shuts down any discussion of the past.

"She's really overprotective, Shane. She was scared and irrational that morning from the shock of finding me that way."

He rolls his eyes, taking a step back. Toward the door.

I have to stop my hand from reaching out. I want to settle this with him.

"Shane—"

"It wasn't just that morning," he says, cutting me off, a flash of anger in his eyes. "And she wasn't the only one to jump to conclusions that morning. You went along with her when you had to know it wasn't true."

"Is that what you thought? That I actually knew the truth and didn't speak up?" My God. He believes I lied? My stomach plummets.

"How can you claim you didn't? When you moved in, I made sure I was nice to you. More than nice. When did I ever say no when you asked for my help with anything? *Never.*"

I open my mouth to speak, but he doesn't give me a chance. He's more animated now, the anger spilling out like oil from a tanker that's been ripped open.

He steps forward and leans into my personal space. I can feel the rage wafting off him like heat from the pavement.

"By then, you'd lived with me a year, Avery. So don't pretend you didn't know you could trust me. You *knew!*" He jerks back, his lip curled. "How could you act like I'd rape you while you were unconscious? The way my dad looked at me..." He swallows, his eyes distant, as if recalling the moment in horrible, vivid detail. "That was a knife you buried in my fucking heart."

The pieces, which I now realize I've had all along, shift into place. His lingering anger finally makes sense. He's in pain. The bone-deep kind.

Shane and his dad were incredibly close...right up until the moment I was found naked with Shane standing over me, dressed only in a pair of boxer briefs that failed to hide his obvious erection.

My mom lost it. Though I couldn't remember anything, she was adamant that her worst nightmare had come true, that Shane had exploited my incapacitating drunkenness to take what she said teenage boys want most. Mom accused him of coming back for more when she caught him.

Once awake, I'd been shaking and tearful, my brain in a hung-over fog. Shane glowered at us in a way he never had before. For the first time since we moved in, he'd seemed menacing to me.

Then Ethan came downstairs and saw his wife distraught and me dazed and confused, clumsily trying to cover my naked body. It was a horrible mess. And once the police are called, they investigate. It didn't matter that I told her to call them back to tell them not to come.

When the police talked to me in my room, I told them I didn't think Shane raped me, or that he would rape anyone. But maybe I wasn't forceful enough about it. I couldn't get animated because I was so sick to my stomach. Any sudden movement caused me to throw up.

Thank God Ethan remembered he had security cameras and thought to check them. It proved Shane was already in his room asleep when I came downstairs, wildly drunk and completely out of my head. I'd shed my own clothes, like I was changing for bed, but then I didn't put anything else on. I'd been blackout drunk and pretty much comatose all night.

I was mortified at having the police and my stepdad watch my indecent drunken behavior, but it was hard to focus when I still felt wretched physically.

My mom and Ethan were relieved. They cast the blame for my drunkenness on the older kids who'd given me liquor and told Shane they were sorry for suspecting him of an assault.

All three of us had just wanted to pretend that night and its aftermath never happened. But Shane's white hot rage at us burned out of control. Our apologies fell on deaf ears, and he packed a bag the next day and left, refusing to speak to us. It took almost three months before he even took a call from Ethan. He was shockingly distant. It was as if we'd all died.

"It was a terrible mistake," I say, hoping he hears the truth in my voice. "She's sorry. We all are. I should've defended you more strongly, but I was just so stunned and sick. So disoriented." When he's silent, I try to explain more. "It all happened so fast. Can you—"

"Whatever." His expression shutters, his rage disappearing behind the cool, unfeeling mask I've seen him wear the past two years. "The real mistake was my not moving to Dec's sooner. I should've left the minute they said they didn't want me on the second floor, like I was a fucking dog that couldn't stop himself from humping someone's leg."

My mouth drops open. Why had I never realized this was how he felt? Ethan had made it sound like living in the basement was what Shane wanted. That having his own in-house apartment was a good move for Shane.

"They must have been trying to protect me—"

"Fuck all the excuses and rationalizations," he says through clenched teeth as he shakes his head. "You know what? Enough of this. Let's go in the house. It's time for you to pay the rent."

5

SHANE

My cock's rock hard and raging to get out because even fighting with Avery makes me want to fuck her. As soon as we're back in the house and facing off in the living room, I jerk the zipper of my jeans down and free my erection.

Avery stands a few feet away, watching me with wide eyes.

I crook a finger at her. When she doesn't move, my eyes narrow.

"The deal means I don't need to coax you."

The slight tremor that goes through her makes me clench my teeth. For an instant I think she's going to balk. Given the mood in the room, if I were in her place, I would tell me to fuck off. But we're nothing alike. I bow to no one, but I'm also loyal till the bloody end, and I never need anyone to convince me of things I should already know. I also don't defend actions that are indefensible.

"This is really how you want to handle things?" she says, her voice low and furious.

As opposed to rattling on about the past? Of course, I want a blow job instead. I'd rather have a root canal than revisit that morning. "Yeah, it is."

Avery surprises me by grabbing a cushion from the couch. She lifts her chin and, with thunder in her expression, walks to me.

Anger on both sides works just fine.

"No teeth."

She drops the cushion at my feet without acknowledging what I've said. Maybe that warrants more conversation, but talk is the last thing I want. What I need is her mouth too full to speak. What I need is to wipe away the toxic cocktail of emotions that being near her always stirs. I was good to her once, and it came back to bite me. Avery Kershaw is a bomb in disguise, the kind that can detonate and take out everything around it.

She lowers herself to her knees, and I like seeing her there. Avery's hand flutters over the base of my cock. Her fingers are cool against my feverish skin, but the touch is too light.

I draw in a harsh breath. The wait is killing me. Brushing her hand away, I fist my cock in my hand, then I rub the head over her pouty lips, leaving a salty glaze on them.

She licks her lips, as if it's a taste test. It's maddening but so fucking hot it almost brings me to my knees. Then her tongue leaves her mouth and strokes the head, and my mind explodes.

My lids fall, and I groan when she takes me in her mouth. My hands drop to my sides, and I draw in a ragged breath.

Her mouth's so soft and wet and perfect that I let her tease me by just sucking the tip. Until I can't. My hand reaches for her head, and I find her ponytail. It usually annoys me to see it. Too much like the way she wore it in high school. But right now, it's the perfect handle.

I pull her forward, and she shudders. She grips my thighs to brace herself, and her mouth goes slack. Not what I need at the moment.

When I speak, my tone's a warning. "Avery."

Her lips close around me, and she sucks hard. Pleasure rips through me.

"Fuck, yes."

Her movements are stilted, like she's trying to work out what to do. A fleeting thought that maybe she's got limited experience passes over my mind. The more limited the better as far as I'm concerned, even if it means she needs direction.

MARLEE WRAY

She doesn't resist my hand controlling her head. I drag her forward onto my cock until it's halfway down her throat, which feels so fucking good.

I groan as her throat convulses. Then I pull back, but keep a tight grip on the ponytail, making sure her mouth stays where I want it.

"Wrap your fingers around the base. Tight fist." My voice is gravelly and rough with need.

She follows instructions.

"Yeah, like that." I move a hand over hers, showing her how to stroke me into her mouth. I set the rhythm.

After a few minutes, I'm fucking her mouth roughly, and she's taking it. More than taking it. She plays my cock like an instrument.

I savor every second. It's not smooth. It's raw and deep, which is better than smooth.

My balls tighten, and fire shoots from me. My head tips back, my hips jerk, and I come like it's been a year since the last time I did.

It wipes my mind blank, which also feels good. My heartbeat echoes in my ears, along with the sound of my breath as I catch it. Standing still, calm washes over me in ways it never has.

When my thoughts unscramble, I step back and look down at her. Her lips and cheeks are blushing a dark pink. She licks the corner of her mouth and swallows. If I hadn't just come, that would give me an instant hard-on. But for the moment, I'm beyond sated.

For so long I've avoided being near Avery, which I now realize wasn't a solution to our problem. Deep down, the unresolved fury—and more—was still simmering. Right now, the anger's gone, like I made her swallow it.

I put my cock away, staring at her.

She rises, looking embarrassed and something more that I can't name.

"You haven't given a lot of blow jobs, have you?"

Her arched brows draw together for a moment, then she frowns. "It seemed to work all right for you," she says tartly.

This makes me smirk. And that, in turn, makes her frown harder. I forgot how cute she can be. I tried to bury some memories so deep I practically dug a hole to hell.

She returns the cushion to the couch and smooths it down.

"How many guys have you been with?"

"Go to hell, Shane."

My brows rise, but she doesn't notice my bemused expression because she doesn't look at me. Instead, she goes to the closet, grabs one of my coats and puts it on.

Does she think she's leaving? It's late, never a good time for a girl to walk around alone. The whole point of her being here is so she'll be safe. I guess she's not thinking straight after what just happened.

My body moves toward the front door, prepared to block her exit. Instead, she heads the other way. It isn't until I hear the door to the back porch open that I remember her laptop's still outside.

Avery's not trying to leave. She just wants to be left alone.

I'll give her that. At least until the next time.

AVERY

Fuck Shane.

As I stalk away from him, anger isn't the only thing I feel though. It's supposed to be, but looking up the lines of his body while on my knees brought so many things rushing into my head. Physically, it was shockingly intense how attracted to him I was. The way he looked as his chest strained his t-shirt with his deep breaths, the way his head tipped back in concentration, the rough sound of his voice as he cursed from the sharp pleasure. All of it seeped inside me, calling for my own body's involvement in what was happening...into what I was making him feel.

In my core, I still feel the reverberations, the ache between my legs where the cock I tasted is really supposed to go.

Shoving open the door to the back porch, I practically stumble outside. The cold strikes me like a slap, making my breath catch and then fog the air.

The frosty night is bracing and will hopefully help clear my head.

I look over my shoulder, but he's not in the doorway. If I'm being honest, I'm sorry he didn't follow me. But weirdly I don't feel any longing the way I once did, because providing him with oral sex was an interaction that actually had a resolution. One he seemed to very much enjoy.

It's such a change from the past couple of years of seeing him across a room and watching him turn and walk away. Tonight, I wasn't ignored or dismissed. And that was satisfying for me in its own way.

For the past two years, Shane's cold attitude never failed to frustrate me to the point of wanting to scream because it felt so like my childhood when my dad failed to show up, failed to call, failed me period. Apathetic silence from someone you want to be close to is the worst.

The run of my thoughts causes me to shake my head at myself sharply.

"What the fuck, Avery?" I murmur under my breath, willing myself to get my head together and stop thinking of that blow job as anything other than a transaction.

I serviced him the way a prostitute would, for a price. His own emotions were not engaged.

As I grab my laptop, it almost slips from my hand. My jerking movement to catch the computer causes my knee to bump against a plastic chair, which topples and bangs to the ground. I stiffen, my heart thudding.

Jesus.

Normally, I'm not clumsy. Everything seems to have me a little off balance these days. Ever since I came to Granthorpe, I've slowly descended into darkness. Partly because of the threat of Casanova, but also from the threat of facing Shane on his own turf again. Since the rift, he's been quite good at bringing me to my knees, though usually just mentally. He's the prince. I'm the peasant. Logically I know that isn't true, but he can make it feel true with one look...or the lack of it.

Right now, I feel strangely better. Even though I know he doesn't care about me.

Don't care right back. Shane Moran doesn't matter. He's just the guy who's providing a safe haven so you can reach your goals. In a few years, you'll have moved on, and none of this will mean anything.

With a few slow deep breaths, I set the chair on its legs and walk to the door. It's strange how emotionally steady I am right now. Being a sex slave should be completely humiliating, and yet...

I lick my lips, and for a second, I taste him all over again.

If I'm being honest, I liked the feel of him in my mouth because it gave me some power, especially when he came. In that moment, the walls came crumbling down. We weren't at war. For that brief time, the rest of the world fell away and so did the past.

When I go inside, he's nowhere around. It doesn't matter. We each got what we needed from the other. Soon we won't need anything at all.

I'm looking forward to that day.

I can almost taste freedom. It's sweet and salty and sensual.

Like him.

6

AVERY

In the morning I come down from the guest room dressed and ready to go to campus. Even though it's seven thirty and my first class isn't until ten, I want to get out of the house. I can head to my dorm room and study there until I need to get to class.

My steps toward the kitchen falter when I smell coffee and hear sizzling. I'm barely breathing as I creep toward the entry way. Shane's standing at the stove, and he's shirtless.

My God.

His chest muscles make my tongue want to explore his body's texture, which reminds me of the way I got intimately acquainted with a certain part of him last night.

I should probably have mixed feelings about what I did with him, but so far, I'm still fine with it. I felt his anger change into lust when I dropped to my knees before him. And, for the first time ever, it felt as though *I* had the power to change the dynamic between us.

Even now he seems more relaxed than I've seen him look the past couple of years. It could be wishful thinking on my part, but I swear that blow job—the first I've ever given—was more effective in cooling his anger than two years of attempted apologies and carefully polite interactions ever were.

I drag my eyes away from his chest, but my gaze doesn't get far before it's transfixed on the black and charcoal gray tattoo on his left shoulder and upper arm. He didn't have that in high school.

Before I realize it, I've walked up to him to get a closer look.

It's a knight in full armor. The head gear reminds me of the Mandalorian's helmet. The breast plate has warring serpents. The details are stellar.

His bicep flexes, and his low voice says, "Go ahead."

That voice does things to me...between my legs. "What?"

"Give him a kiss." He raises his arm slightly, moving it toward me. "You know you want to."

So damned cocky.

"I'll give him a kiss when he flips his helmet up." My tone's smart-assed to match my words.

Shane gives me a speculative look that probably sees more than I wish it could. Retreating to the counter across the room, I give him my back. My lips purse together, still tingling at the thought of pressing against his tattoo.

I open cupboards looking for mugs. "Coffee cups?"

When he doesn't answer, I look over my shoulder. He doesn't point me to the right place, or even bother to turn toward me. *Jerk*. When I find them, I yank a cup from the shelf and set it on the counter with a thwack.

"You break it, you buy it."

"Deal." I raise the mug and smack it down again. The loud sound startles even me.

When I look over my shoulder, he's turned to face me. I stare at him with narrowed eyes and lift the cup again.

"I dare you." His voice is stern in its challenge.

My hand falters a second, then I bang the bottom of the mug against the counter. He stalks over, jerks the cup from my hand, and sets it aside. Then I hear a crack and warmth spreads over the seat of my jeans. It takes a second for me to realize he swatted me on the ass.

I suck in a breath, my eyes widening. "What the hell?"

"More?" he asks.

Maybe, my body says. But I rail against that crazy thought.

My hand presses against his chest. I mean to push him back, but the touch is electric and causes me to pause. When I do remember to shove him, it's anti-climactic because he doesn't so much as sway.

Big. Strong. Unbelievably good-looking. If there's a God, he hates me.

"All right," I say. "You've made your point."

His expression is surly. I think he might smack my ass again, but then the ham starts to smoke, which gets his attention. Thankfully, he moves back to the stove.

I check the mug to be sure I haven't cracked it. Fortunately, it's heavy stoneware and can take a little counter-banging. As I fill the mug, I chew the corner of my mouth. I want to start a civilized conversation with Shane to keep us moving in the right direction, but I have no idea what to say to him.

He sets the frying pan on a cool burner and then goes to the table with his plate. I watch him over the rim of my mug.

What is topping the ham on his dish? I'm not sure it's a good idea to get close to him right now, so I go to the stove instead. There is something caramelized in the small skillet. After a beat, I realize it's pineapple. I dip my finger in and bring it to my mouth. *Oh, my God.* It's brown sugary and seared in something—maybe butter. My feet carry me quickly back to the cupboards containing the dishes.

When I have a full plate of glazed ham, I sit at the table. I don't speak. My mouth is too busy.

Shane rises, leaving his dish. As he walks away, he says, "When you're done, clean the kitchen."

Sure. I'll start by licking every drop from these plates, I think, dragging my tongue across my lips. To his broad, retreating back, I say defiantly, "If I have time."

He doesn't rise to the bait. Such control. Shane could teach a master class in defending his walls. Maybe that's why he got a dark medieval knight tattooed on his arm.

⬩❧⬩

44

ON CAMPUS, MY NERVES ACT UP WHEN I THINK ABOUT ATTENDING my entrepreneurship class. I'm sure Todd and Daniel will be gunning for me like never before. I've had a taste of that in class. In the second week, I'd been speaking and Todd cut me off, claiming I had my facts wrong about big data being more valuable than fossil fuels.

When I looked things up later, I confirmed my facts were correct. But it was too late. He sounded so confident when he challenged me, I'm sure the class believed he was right.

I wonder whether Professor Smith-Hall took my falling silent as a sign of weakness. I wish I'd argued my position harder back then. I will now because I can't afford to be shown up in class with the internship recommendation letter on the line.

As I approach the door to the lecture hall, I spot Erik Sorensen standing a few feet away. He barely seems human. Cross a lion with a giant stone tower, and you've got something akin to Erik Sorensen's presence. People in the corridor literally stop and stare at him. The shoulder length blonde hair appears wildly uncombed. Like he rampaged across campus all night then decided to stalk over.

When I reach the door, he steps forward and opens it. I glance up at him. He doesn't speak but does incline his head ever so slightly by way of a greeting.

"What are you doing here?" I ask.

He doesn't answer. Instead, he follows me into the lecture hall.

My heart thumps wildly. *What* is going on? Did Shane send him?

Partway down the steps, Erik takes my arm into his massive hand and stops my progress. I glance up in time to see him nod toward an aisle. I look down it and spot the guys from my project group. I stiffen.

"Walk," the Viking giant says.

I don't move.

"Need me to carry you?"

"What?" My head jerks up to look at him. His face appears unchanged. There's a scowl, like he's set to murder someone. I decide he's serious about carrying me bodily to sit with Todd and Daniel. So, with dread drilling a hole into the pit of my stomach, I head down the aisle.

With every step, my feet feel heavier. By the time I'm a few feet from them, I'm shuffling.

In a low voice, Erik commands the men with one word. "Stand."

The guys clamber to their feet. Todd has a black bruise around his eye. *Jesus.*

"Morning, Avery," Todd mumbles.

My jaw drops open.

Daniel greets me as well without meeting my eyes. Then they look over my shoulder at Erik. Only then do they retake their seats.

Following suit in this odd tableau I've found myself in, I lower myself into a seat, trying to remember how to breathe.

Erik sits next to me, barely fitting in the seat. Other students file in and cluster around us.

"Hey, Erik. Great game, man!" one guy in a Granthorpe Knights t-shirt says.

Erik nods.

The guy thrusts out a hand and introduces himself. Erik shakes it, then inclines his head to the side toward me, saying, "Avery Kershaw. Shane Moran's stepsister."

The guy smiles at me and raises a hand in a wave. "Hey. Nice to meet you."

I nod, my mind racing.

There is no reason for Erik to be here unless Shane sent him. And given Todd and Daniel's shrunken appearance ever since we arrived, it doesn't take a genius to know Todd's black eye is somehow related to my newfound campus adoption by Shane and his friends.

It's the why I can't fathom.

"You don't have to stay," I whisper to Erik when Professor Smith-Hall approaches the podium.

In a Shane-like manner, Erik doesn't answer or even acknowledge that he's heard me. Instead, he leans back and folds his arms over his massive chest, settling in.

I glance around. People are looking at us while pretending not to. It's the opposite effect of what happened in high school when Shane and Declan froze me out. In high school, I went from being popular to being non-existent. Now I've gone from invisible to visible. That's the power Shane and his friends wield.

When I open my laptop, I find an email message I've been cc'd on from Todd. It's to our professor.

Dread curdles in my stomach. But when I read it, my fear drains away.

I read it again to be sure I'm understanding it correctly. The bottom line is that our team has decided that as the biggest contributor to the project, I'll be the one presenting.

Oh, my God. Unbelievable. I finally exhale.

Two different feelings war within me, like those serpents on Shane's tattoo.

One is elation. The other fear. I've got my shot at showcasing myself as team leader, but I owe it to Shane.

And owing him a favor puts me in an even more precarious position than before.

7

Erik comes with me to Café Ramen. People turn and stare at him, which I guess is normal for him. I wonder if he feels like a celebrity or a freak. Maybe both.

"It was cool of you to come to class. It made things easier for me, and I appreciate it. But you don't have to have lunch with me," I say softly.

He glances down at me for a moment, then continues walking with me to get in line. On the walk over, he said zero words. *Zero.*

I guess he's going to continue the trend.

"Okay, stay and have lunch with me." I blow out a breath. I've never seen Shane or his friends here, so I don't think low-key and cheap is their scene. "Where do you normally eat?"

"The team dining room."

Wow. He answered.

And, ah, of course it makes sense that GU's superstar athletes have their own place. I frown, thinking of Shane. He's not on the football team.

"I never see Shane here." Actually, it's not just the cafes and dining halls where I don't see him. I'm not sure I've ever seen him walking on campus either. "Does he usually eat at home?"

Erik shrugs his massive shoulders.

"You're a regular fountain of information, but try to give other people a chance to talk." If the snark registers, it doesn't bother him.

Once we have our food, people who know him or know of him circle around us. He nods for people to take the empty seats, and, within a minute, our table's like an ant colony teeming with life.

Even though I can barely move my arms because we're so squeezed together, it's nice. It's a welcome change of pace from the solitary life I've gotten used to.

Erik introduces me exactly as he did in class. It's the opening people seem to need. Suddenly I'm bombarded with questions about myself. I answer between bites.

When we're finished, he leans toward me. "I have practice."

"Sure," I murmur with a nod. "Have a good time. I mean...work-out?" Awkward. But I decide it's fine because stellar conversational skills clearly aren't something he values.

He rises, nods at the table, and then heads toward the door.

A stunning blond girl who's coming in stops to say hello. He speaks to her for a moment before he leaves. She's joined a minute later by another gorgeous girl. This one's more petite and looks Latina, with skin the color of a latte. They come to my table, and their glinting gold-and-diamond javelin pins mark them as members of the dance team, the campus's female elite.

Both young women have super precise cat's eye liner, high pony-tails, and short skirts. I wonder whether they've come from a performance.

The blond leans in, giving me a friendly smile. "Hi. Avery, right?"

"Yes."

"I'm Eden. This is Arya. We eat here at this time every Wednesday. You should join us next time."

Arya winks at me, like we're all sharing some friendly secret. I'm at a loss for words and am not remotely cool enough to pull off winking at these girls. Fortunately, they don't wait for me to respond before walking off.

All right. *What* is going on? Is this a *She's All That* bet Shane's made to see if he can make me popular in two days or less? If so, mission accomplished.

Uneasily, I grab my phone to text him that I'd like him to desist. Then I realize I forgot to get his cell number. For reasons unbeknownst to me, he changed it after high school.

I text my stepfather Ethan asking for Shane's number. My table's mostly empty by the time he responds.

> Ethan: Hey, kiddo. Glad to get your texts, but why only text messages the past couple of days and no phone call? We want to hear your pretty voice. You ok?

> Avery: Yeah, sorry. Just busy.

I'm lying. I've hesitated to call because there are some topics I don't want to talk about, and it's so much easier to avoid them in a text exchange. After the lavender rose, I nearly went home. Now I'm so glad I didn't.

That makes me think about last night and the way Shane's fingers felt against my hair as his hard cock glided into my mouth. Which is all I thought about last night in bed, too. So much so that it turned me on, and it was only after fingering my clit for an hour in the guest room bed that I finally managed to fall asleep.

Jesus.

Right. Obviously, I can't talk about what I've been up to or the fact that I'm staying at Shane's place. Or the reason I went to see him in the first place. If Mom and Ethan found out about the rose, they would lose their minds and drive straight to campus to pick me up.

> Avery: So, can I have Shane's number?

The phone rings. Ethan. *Shit.*

I glance around. With Shane as the topic, this conversation could be strange and awkward and not the kind of thing I want anyone at GU to overhear.

All four of us know Shane blames me and my mom for wrecking his relationship with Ethan. My mom claims the reason Shane's unwilling to forgive her and Ethan for the misperception and the secret video cameras is because Shane's jealous of her place in Ethan's life. I partly believed that because he held *such* a grudge. Now though, I don't think that's his reason at all.

From what Shane said yesterday, from the time we moved in, they basically told him they didn't trust him with me. I, on the other hand, was told to leave Shane alone in the basement so he could have his privacy. That was obviously a huge lie since cameras were pointed around the basement, including right at Shane's bedroom. There were no second-floor cameras except one that was directed at the stairs, presumably watching to make sure he didn't come up to my room?

That's crazy, and it's creepy that they put all those cameras in place. Why would they go to such extreme lengths? Especially Ethan.

I kind of understand it where my mom's concerned. She's always been insanely paranoid that something will happen to me. And when we moved into Ethan's, I was fifteen and only five-three and a hundred pounds. At seventeen, Shane was a full foot taller than me, ninety pounds heavier, and solid muscle. Of course, if you put us side-by-side, one of us was a physical threat and the other was not.

But Shane was never a bully back then. In fact, before things went sideways in that house, if anything, he was protective of me and used his size and strength to cater to me.

Ultimately it was my wandering downstairs, which I often did despite the rules, that caused the trouble. If my mom and Ethan hadn't overreacted to what they saw that morning, things could have turned out so differently.

After Ethan's call goes to voicemail, I send another text.

Avery: What's up?

Ethan: 😟 I'd appreciate a call back. Now, Ave.

I purse my lips nervously. Ethan never gets sharp with me. He's a better dad than my bio dad by a factor of ten thousand. And lately, I've been a lousy daughter to him, leaving his calls and texts hanging while Casanova prowls around the campus. It's unkind.

I hop up, grab my bag, and leave Café Ramen. As soon as I'm outside, I call him.

Ethan picks up immediately of course.

"Hi, Dad. How are you?"

"Hi, honey. Good here." He clears his throat. "We got a Granthorpe email saying that any female student who's feeling anxiety about being on campus right now can petition to finish the semester online from home."

My lunch suddenly feels like rocks in my stomach.

"Why don't you do that?" Ethan's voice is light but cajoling. "You said your chances of getting the internship are slim anyway. I can arrange for movers to empty your dorm room tomorrow."

"No, no." I take a fortifying breath. "Things have changed. I have a chance of getting a great letter of recommendation from Professor Smith-Hall."

"Oh? How did that happen?"

"Nothing's certain yet." Stepping off the walking path causes my shoes to sink a bit into the soft grass. "I'm going to present our group project. If I do well, I'm sure he'll recommend me. I've done well on all the other metrics."

"That's great, honey. Congratulations! See, I told you if you continued to do stellar work it would pay off."

"Mmm hmm."

"Listen, about Shane. I don't think your trying to contact him is a good idea. He's been hard to reach lately. I think he's really busy with school himself. I don't want you getting your feelings hurt if he doesn't answer your texts."

My heartbeat kicks up a notch at that.

Obviously, I can't tell Ethan everything, but I wonder if I should at least tell him that I've already been talking to Shane. It feels like the right thing to do, since I don't usually lie to Ethan. But if I tell him, it could start a whole conversation I don't want to get into.

"About that..." I murmur.

"Yes?"

"I actually spoke to Shane in person."

"At the party?"

I blink, confused. "What party?"

"He said he saw you at a party."

My skin prickles with unease. Shane and Ethan have talked about me?

"He did? What else did he say?"

"Nothing." After a pause, he adds lightly, "It's Shane. Since he moved out, he's never exactly talkative, is he? The best I hope for with him is four-word phrases."

I grimace. Oh, so not really a conversation then. I'm relieved, but also sad for them. Once upon a time, they were close. "Maybe things will get better," I say brightly. "He was actually okay to me. He may finally be letting things go."

"Maybe," Ethan says, but his tone isn't hopeful.

"So can you send me his number?"

"I think it's better that you don't push him. Why don't you wait until you bump into him again and play it by ear?"

Normally that would be good advice. Shane crushed my feelings under the heel of his boot every time I tried to reach out to him during his senior year. And my mom and stepdad had to watch me crumble into tears on more than one occasion.

Things are different now, though. I don't expect to be his friend. I wouldn't even want to be after the filthy deal he pushed me into making. Sex for a safe place to stay? It's pretty vile.

"Okay, Dad. No worries. I'll probably see him soon. I've been getting out more lately."

"Not alone though, right?"

"No. I'm—um—trying to make some new friends. I'm being careful."

"Good." He exhales. "I know you're a level-headed young woman. I just remember when you were a whimsical fifteen-year-old. Not that there was anything wrong with that either," he adds hastily.

Ethan is never anything but completely supportive and wonderful to me. At the moment, it makes me feel guilty. Ethan lost Shane because of my mom and me. In his place, I doubt I could be so nice.

"I wish the world wasn't such a grim place," Ethan continues. "You should be able to walk anywhere you want at any time of the day or night without having to look over your shoulder."

I change the topic. "I saw the verdict on the Palmer case. Congratulations!"

"You saw it at Granthorpe?" he asks, surprised. "I wouldn't think alumni news would make the front page, considering the story they're covering right now."

He means Casanova. I do not want to talk about that psycho since that's another secret I'm keeping.

"It wasn't on my home page. I looked it up. How did you win it? It seemed so impossible."

That's exactly the right opening. Ethan immediately launches into his trial strategy.

I smile. This is part of what I miss about living at home. I don't want to be a famous defense attorney myself, but I love hearing about the way Ethan attacks cases. His work fascinates me.

I sit on a bench and chat with him for an hour. It's not until my battery starts chirping that I stand and tell him I have to go before my phone dies.

"It's so good to talk to you, Ave. We'd love to see you. I can drive out and pick you up if you want to come home for the weekend?"

"Not this weekend, but soon. I miss you guys, too."

"Okay. Be careful. We love you."

My eyes sting. Ethan's the goddamned best. No matter how misguided those cameras were, Shane's a jerk for not forgiving him by now.

"Love you too," I say before I end the call.

As I head to the off-campus bus stop, I try to devise a strategy to convince Shane to reconcile with Ethan.

My attention's occupied, which is why I don't see or sense anything before something splashes me in the face. My scream comes several seconds late because I'm so shocked.

My eyes sting, and I throw my hands up in defense.

I can't see.

Who did this? Is he still nearby?

There's a sickeningly sweet scent. I drag the neck of my shirt over my eyes and face, terrified I won't be able to see.

My vision is blurred for a moment, but blinking helps clear it. The sting continues. I think about the acid attacks on Muslim girls and freak out. I look around wildly, but the only person I see is a jogger in a hoody sprinting down the path away from me.

I drop to my knees, dig a half empty water bottle from my bag and dump it over my head. Then I use the dry bottom edge of my shirt to wipe my eyes and face over and over. My vision clears, and the stinging goes away.

I'm shaky and disoriented as I wobble to my feet. *Jesus Christ.*

I look around again, but I don't spot a sneering aggressor anywhere nearby. There are just normal-looking people who watch me curiously. I'm half-drenched, and I must look wild with my smeared makeup and matted hair.

I move quickly to the bus stop, still trying to process what happened.

The jogger wasn't carrying a bucket. I'm not even sure he was the one who threw the liquid at me. It wasn't a big splash though. I wonder whether it may have been from a squirt gun.

What's that smell?

I touch my face. It itches slightly but doesn't sting or burn now. I pull my shirt up and sniff. Then I recognize the lingering scent.

Oh, God. Roses.

8

SHANE

Her last class has been over for a while, and the sun's setting. I scowl as I look out the window. The whole point of her living here is so she won't be a target after dark. What's she doing screwing around on campus this late?

I fire off a text.

> Shane: Where are you?

I tell myself it's not my problem if she's being reckless. That's her goddamned M.O., after all. She was at the fucking Beta House frat party all alone after dark, too.

I glance at the clock, and then catch myself pacing. Fuck this. If she's not back in ten minutes, I'll go to campus to get her. And if I have to go, she's going to be punished for it. At that thought, temptation snakes through me. Below the belt. My lust for this girl is endless, against my better angels.

Finally, I spot her coming up the walkway. I'm both relieved and pissed.

She opens the door and stomps in and right past me.

My eyes don't miss that her hair's damp, loose and matted to one side of her face, and her shirt's wet. It's stretched, too, like someone tried to tear it off.

What the fuck?

I follow her up the stairs. She reeks of sickeningly sweet perfume.

"What the hell happened to you?"

"What do you care?"

On the upstairs landing, I grab her arm and turn her to face me. "Answer me."

"Let go!" she screams.

She's only ever screamed at me one other time in our lives. The time she wanted me to turn around because she was naked. Screeching is not typical of Avery, so it gives me pause.

"Hey," I say in a low voice, trying to instill some calm. "Lower your voice, and tell me what happened."

Her expression shifts. One second she looks angry and harassed, the next her chin's wobbling.

Jesus. What the hell's up with her?

She looks away, and I watch her face crumble.

No. Inside, my muscles lock up. Something—or someone—happened to her. Even after I sent Sorensen to watch over her during her class. I should've gone myself.

"Avery," I say, leaning forward. "Hey, what's going on?"

"Can we just not?" she asks, her voice cracking. "I need—let go, Shane. Please?"

For a year, all she did was beg me to talk to her and watch me with puppy dog eyes when I wouldn't. Now when she seems to really need someone to talk to and I'm offering, she won't. I will never understand Avery Kershaw.

Tears spill over her lashes. I pull her against me before I realize what I'm doing. And she leans in, letting me hug her.

If that asshole Todd Bardoratch made her cry, I'm going to beat him to a bloody pulp.

"I need to take a shower," she mumbles.

"No argument about that. What happened? Overactive perfume sprayer in the quad?" My attempt at levity seems to work.

"Fuck," she says on an exhale. Then she pulls away and scrubs the heel of her hand over her eyes, smudging her mascara all the more. She's like a raccoon, except beautiful. "Can we talk *after* I take a shower?"

"Yeah, go."

She taps my fingers, and I realize I'm still holding her arm. Her eyes study my face, and something passes between us that is not anger or hate.

I let go.

Avery turns and hustles down the hall and into the guest bathroom.

Standing in the hallway seems pointless and stalker-ish, so I head to my own room. I sit in my desk chair, facing the open door.

From my position, I hear when she leaves the bathroom and goes into her bedroom. When I decide she's had enough time to dry off and dress, I start thinking about going in after her. I'm impatient to know what's going on.

Last night during our discussion of ground rules, I claimed I wouldn't walk in without knocking, but today I decide that might have been a lie.

My phone rings, and I check it. Ethan again. I swipe red, sending the call to voicemail. I'll talk to him later.

"Hey," Avery says.

Glancing up, I find she's standing in my doorway. Wet strands of silky dark hair spill over the shoulders of her t-shirt. If she's wearing a bra, it's not very thick because her nipples are poking against the front of the shirt. She's got blue yoga pants on that are thin enough for me to bite through.

Jesus Christ. This is not the moment to be focused on her body. But the outfit calls to me like she's wearing nothing.

"Come in."

From the doorway, she looks around the room, her eyes pausing on my king-sized bed. I can't help but wonder what she thinks of it. And whether she'll spend a night in it sometime.

"I thought you didn't want me in your room," she says.

That was another part of our agreement. She wasn't to come into my room, period. Yesterday I wanted there to be clear boundaries. Today, boundaries aren't looking so good.

"Get in here," I say, nodding toward the wooden chest at the foot of my bed.

She comes in and sits cross-legged on the chest, leaning her back against the footboard. With a makeup-free face and dressed in a t-shirt and yoga pants, Avery's back to looking like the beautiful teenage interloper who makes my cock so hard it's pure pain not to deal with it.

"What happened today? Who made you cry?"

She exhales heavily, and I'm hoping I'll just hear about some girl drama that will be easy to distract her from. Instead, what I hear causes me to sit forward and clench my teeth so hard I'm close to snapping my jaw.

I try to keep it together as she tells me someone sprayed her with something that included rose water. She doesn't know if it had another chemical in it or not. It got in her eyes and brought her to her knees on the sidewalk. She was scared it might be acid, so she diluted it by dumping spring water over her head. And after all that, she had to ride the bus home alone, scared and crying, and covered in whatever the hell the guy splashed her with.

That son of a bitch. If I get my hands on him, I will fucking end him.

"It really sucks," she says. "Why do there have to be psychopaths in the world? And why do they have to find me? Especially when I was having the best day." She shrugs and stands, hands shaky. "Sometimes I don't know if I'm going get through this shit," she whispers. Then she seems to pull herself together. "Anyway, that's what happened."

This is the Avery of old. The one I wanted to make mine. The one I would've spilled blood to protect.

My anger at the asshole who splashed her is still a blazing bonfire, so I don't really process her standing to leave until I circle back to it in my head. "Sit back down," I say. "Actually, no, don't."

She tilts her head with a look of confusion.

I stand and put my arms out. "Come over here."

Her big blue eyes get bigger. Then she walks closer, but not close enough.

I pull her to me and wrap my arms around her.

She melts against me, which doesn't help me remain sensitive to her stress. My cock only has one kind of objective where Avery is concerned, and the fact that she feels so fucking soft in my arms is a distraction.

I cup the back of her head. Her hair's silky against my fingers.

"I'll find him, and when I do, I'll make him sorry he's alive." My voice is rough in all the ways there are for it to be that way.

"I wish you would," she whispers, her fingers stroking my back.

If I don't let her go soon, I'm going to kiss her and then fuck her all night. There is no other possibility for how this moment ends. Until she speaks.

"You have to talk to Ethan."

"What?"

She pulls back, so she can look at me. "I want you to call him. Maybe tonight?"

My arms drop, and I step back. The moment's over. "Whether or not I talk to my dad is none of your business, Avery."

"The rift is hurting him so much. It's time to repair it, Shane. If you can forgive me, you can forgive him."

Christ, not again with this bullshit where they act as though they're the victims of undeserved neglect. Walking out of that house and limiting my interactions with the three of them was the only way I could stop her mother's constant, warped paranoia and its fallout from shredding me to ribbons.

"Who says I've forgiven you?"

Avery's eyes narrow on my face, and she looks much older than eighteen. For the first time in my life, I understand how my father becomes such a pussy when his wife wants something. The way Avery looks at me gives me pause. Fiery and beautiful. She acts like she's got the right to make demands. She almost makes me believe it. *Almost.*

Her hands reach out and slide over my forearms, clutching. The smell of shampoo and beautiful girl hits me all over.

"You can't tell me that things haven't changed, Shane. I know they have." The blue of her eyes from under her lashes is like the Colorado sky, endless and fucking breathtaking.

Careful, I tell myself. This is how one little siren takes the whole ship down.

"Some things are different," I say with as much neutrality as I can muster.

Her slim hands move in to rest against my chest. The touch is deceptively light, but it packs plenty of power behind it, causing sensations to hum through me, making my balls ache, and making me want to touch her the same way.

Time to change gears.

"Let's revisit how things are different." I unbutton my jeans. "Grab a pillow from the bed."

Her eyes widen in surprise. "Right now?"

"Right now," I say, lowering my zipper. I grab her hand and draw it to me so she can feel how hard I am.

She tugs her hand away. "How about after?"

After? I stare at her blankly, unable to piece together what she's asking for. Does she want me to give her an orgasm first? If so, I'm down for that. My fingers catch the tie on her yoga pants. "After what?"

She brushes my fingers off her drawstring. "After you call Ethan," she says in an imploring tone.

Jesus Christ. Is she still on that?

And did she put her hands on me just now to soften me up, so I'll do what she wants? Clever. Unfortunately for her, at the moment, soft is the last thing I am.

"I had a rough time today, Shane. You could do something nice. To restore my faith in humanity."

I almost laugh. "That's not what you really want."

Her brows knit together. "Yes, it is."

"This isn't about proving there's kindness and goodness in the world. What you want is to see if I'll give you your way. The fluttering eyelashes are a nice touch, by the way. Wanna know what will work better?" I point at the floor in front of me.

She glares at me.

"Don't keep me waiting."

"When they talk about toxic masculinity, this is what they mean."

"No doubt." I snap my fingers and gesture to the bed's pillows.

Her tight nipples and parted lips tell me she feels more than frustration right now.

Her hips sway as she walks to the bed, and my eyes drop to her perfect peach of an ass. I want to sample all of her, and soon.

Scooping up a pillow, she looks over the mattress. Is she thinking about what it would be like to be pinned to that bed underneath me?

Returning to me, she drops the pillow between my feet and lowers herself. My breath is stilted. She takes my cock out and breathes on it.

Jesus, that feels good.

"What did I do wrong last night?"

I don't understand what she means, partly because my brain's lost most of its blood supply. "Wrong?"

Her cool fingers wrap around my cock, and my neurons forget how to fire.

"Just tell me how you want me to do this, so it can be over as fast as possible."

Damn, that's cold. Practically ice water on my groin, but my cock soldiers on, standing stubbornly at attention.

My brow arches. "You want advice? Your telling me you want this over quickly means I'll make sure it isn't." My fingers grip her hair, twisting to make her head tip back. "Now open that smart mouth, little girl."

Her expression's startled a moment, then she opens her mouth obediently.

My thoughts distill down to one thing. I need her to blow me right now more than I need my next breath.

I'm rough when I plow my cock between her lips. Her teeth scrape me, which I know isn't her fault. I still tap her cheek in warning. "No teeth."

She looks up at me through the fringe of dark lashes. Her eyes say she wants to kill me. Which I like. Then her lips close around my cock like a velvet ribbon, and she suckles me.

Fuck. She is going to get her wish to make me come in record time.

I drag her off my cock by pulling her hair.

"Hey," she says, slapping my thigh.

"You'd better not slap. Or you'll earn some slaps of your own. Right on your pretty ass."

My eyes trap hers. She doesn't look scared. She looks intrigued. It's almost too much to resist. Fisting my cock, I raise it and pinch the tip. "Start lower."

She looks at me curiously.

Again, I've got the sneaking suspicion I'm only the first or second guy she's blown. I can't imagine how that could be the case when she's so pretty.

I let go of her long enough to push my jeans and boxer-briefs down to mid-thigh. I pull her forward, raising my cock again.

She gets it, finally licking my sac.

I watch her, giving her instructions on and off. It feels amazing to have my balls in her mouth, but half of my attention is on the way she moves, squeezing her thighs together and circling her hips as she works. Turning me on is turning her on, too.

I step back, pulling free of her insanely soft mouth.

"Stand up."

"What's wrong?"

"When my cock's a lead pipe, nothing's wrong."

She licks her lips and then stands, watching me intently.

"Take off your pants," I say.

"What? No."

My thumb strokes her tight nipple.

She takes a startled step back. "That's not part of the arrangement."

"It could be," I whisper in a husky voice.

I want to go down on her in the worst way. I want to taste her. I want to make her legs shake. I want to make her come until she screams my name.

My balls ache, reminding me that I also want to fuck her until she's so sore she has trouble walking.

Her flushed cheeks blush harder. "It's not a good idea." She lowers herself back to the pillow.

Now, what's this about? I can tell she's turned on. Why wouldn't she want me to give her an orgasm?

Then she takes my cock in her mouth, and I forget to wonder about anything.

She works the length of me with her tongue, stroking my balls for good measure. I couldn't fight the explosive orgasm she conjures even if I wanted to. And I don't.

I let myself come, and my little princess swallows every fucking drop.

AVERY

BETWEEN MY LEGS, I'M HOT AND STICKY. IF SHANE DECIDED TO pull down my yoga pants and panties right now I wouldn't even resist. He's gorgeous and something about the feel of him in my mouth makes me ache to have him inside me in other places.

I also keep thinking about being in his arms and how tight he held me when I was upset. He promised to deal with the splasher guy. That was when I started down this dangerous path of wanting him so much it hurts.

While his head is still tipped back and he's breathing hard enough to show off his outstanding pecs, I mumble something about leaving. Then I get to my feet and toss the pillow on the foot of his gigantic bed before I retreat from his domain.

In my room, I close the shades, turn off all the lights, and get under the bedcovers. With my eyes closed, I picture his face and the way it felt to have his hand on my breast.

My hand snakes down the front of my yoga pants. I rub between my thighs, the fabric of my panties warm and damp. My fingers find their way into them, parting my soft folds, searching for the spot that will get me to orgasm fastest.

I hear his voice, husky with arousal, when he told me to take my pants off. That voice was like being dragged over gravel and floating through clouds at the same time. It makes no sense that something can be both rough and tender.

There's a tap on the door that startles me. *Speak of the devil.*

It opens, and I freeze, lying perfectly still but blushing furiously.

"Hmm. What's going on in here?" His tone makes it clear that he knows exactly what's going on.

"What do you want?" I ask, half-embarrassed, half-excited by his presence.

"You know what would feel better than your hand between your legs?" The corner of his mouth curves into a sexy smirk. "Mine."

I don't turn my head to look at him. I don't dare.

"Or my mouth," he adds. "Or my cock."

I'm starved for breath by the time I let myself breathe.

"No thanks," I say in a raspy whisper, then I finally risk a glance.

Light from the hall makes him glow in the doorway as he leans against the doorframe. He's golden and gorgeous, like a lion on the African plains, effortlessly powerful with an animal grace. How does he make love? Is it the same as when he's sucked? A tantalizingly slow burn that gives way to hard thrusts?

My breath catches again. My body wants to know how his would feel sliding against it. If he ignored what I said and climbed into bed with me, I wouldn't be able to stop him. Not on any level.

"You know what happens when you tease a man by claiming you don't want him when you actually do?"

I'm silent, hanging on his next words.

"He takes it as a challenge. It's been a while since anyone pretended to run from me. Do you want me to chase you?"

I lie because I know I should. "No."

"Sure, you don't."

Several moments of charged silence pass, making me want to squirm, making me want to beg him to crawl into bed with me. I don't. Because I don't trust him not to hurt me.

Finally, he speaks. "The thing I came to say was I'll take you back and forth to school from now on."

That earns him another look. "Really? Until when?"

"Until I find the rose guy and deal with him."

Yes, please. The police can't seem to do anything. Granthorpe is Gotham City. It needs its Batman.

"Deal with him how?"

I want to hear that he'll smash him to pieces for scaring me and every other woman on campus. I want Shane to promise he'll pay Casanova back for every girl he ever hurt. Then I wonder what's wrong with me. Why do I want violence on top of violence? What I should wish is for the police force, not my stepbrother, to find Casanova.

He doesn't answer my question, which is probably a good thing.

Instead, the corners of his mouth tug into a small smile, and he says, "Night, Avery."

❧

I WAKE FROM A NIGHTMARE WHERE A FACELESS MAN HOLDS MY HEAD under rose-scented water.

I hear creaking steps, and I'm paralyzed with fear. Someone's right outside my door. My heart slams against my ribs, and my mind races. Casanova's gotten into the dorm again. If I scream, will he go?

All of the sudden, I realize I'm not in the residence hall. The creaks are coming from the old wooden stairs in Shane's house.

My pounding heart slows. I'm not in danger. Shane's here. In fact, it's probably him on the stairs.

I roll onto my side and read the clock. Three in the morning.

Waiting silently, I listen as the stairs continue to quietly creak. I'm confused because it sounds like he's going up and down over and over. Is he exercising? Did he wake from an unshakeable nightmare, too? *Of course not*, I think an instant later. What could possibly be scary enough to scare him?

I climb from my bed and open the door a crack.

There's definitely a light on down the hall. Pushing the door open a sliver more, I look out. That's when I see Erik Sorensen carrying crates up the stairs and into the usually locked room.

The men speak in low voices, and then Erik goes back downstairs. A moment later the light flicks off and, after my eyes adjust, I see the outline of Shane's body. He locks the door to the middle room and goes down the stairs, too.

I glance at the clock again. Seven minutes after three.

At fourteen after, I hear the front door close. Moments later, there are footsteps on the steps. Ones that eventually reach the second floor and head down the hall to Shane's bedroom. I close the door silently, staring at it for a moment.

As I climb back in bed, I know one thing for certain. Nothing legal is delivered at three in the morning.

9

AVERY

Shane's car is a perfectly maintained fifteen-year-old silver Porsche Carrera GT. It's a two-seater roadster that's so beautiful I want to give it a kiss. I don't care about cars, but no one alive wouldn't admire this one. The motor purrs like a cat, and the stick-shift is topped with a golden-brown piece of wood varnished to a high gloss.

"What are you doing for dinner tonight?" Shane asks as he pulls out of the driveway.

I shrug, glancing at his hand on the gearshift. He has great hands.

"Do you have a dress and some heels on campus? Or just at my dad's?"

"Yeah, I have a couple dresses. Why?"

"After class, I'll take you to the dorm to change, and you'll come with me to dinner in Back Bay."

"What's in Back Bay?"

"My grandfather's house."

"Since when? Ethan's dad lives in Connecticut."

"Yeah. It's my other grandfather."

I cock my head, confused. "I thought your mom's dad passed away?"

"I guess that makes the old man a zombie. Imagine that."

What in the world? Why did I think his maternal grandfather had passed? My mind scours its memories. I can almost swear—yes, I'm sure my mom told me that. She obviously believes that to be the case, which means maybe Ethan gave her that impression for some reason.

My eyes are glued to Shane's handsome profile. He's not quite clean shaven, but his stubble is much shorter and neater than it was yesterday. And he's wearing a white button-down shirt with his jeans. Apparently, he's dressed for dinner, too.

"Are you saying Ethan lied?"

"I'm saying your mother lied, and my father didn't contradict her."

I stiffen. My instinct is to be outraged on Mom's behalf, but listening is important. There are things I should've known that I didn't until Shane confided them. "Why would she lie?"

"You'll have to ask her."

He always makes it difficult to get information from him, which is frustrating.

"I think you have a theory, Shane."

A strand of his hair comes out from behind his ear. Without thinking, I tuck it back for him, my thumb grazing his jaw in the process.

Shit. Do not touch him.

His head turns briefly to look at me speculatively.

I give my shoulder a penitent shrug. "Sorry."

"It's fine."

It's definitely not fine. We're not dating. When I tried to get him to mend fences with Ethan, Shane ordered me to my knees. That's our relationship. I'm servicing his needs, like a sex worker. My arms fold across my chest, closing me down.

Then I think about the way he hugged me when I was upset, and it causes an unwanted warmth to spread through my chest again. I liked that he did that. I'm sure that's not the way a man touches a prostitute.

We're in uncertain territory.

"Well?" I ask, trying to get back to the topic of his not-really-dead grandfather.

"I think your mother wants to pretend there was no first Mrs. Moran. And she's definitely not interested in going to Back Bay for the holidays with my mother's family. Before you guys showed up, my dad came with me at least once a year."

"Ethan wouldn't let a new wife keep you from seeing your grandfather. He's too good a dad."

"Father of the year."

Rubbing the bridge of my nose, I look away. "He never meant to hurt you, Shane. You must know that. I'm sure everything he did was to put my mom—his new wife—at ease and convince her I was safe. Was it so wrong for them to try to protect me?"

"Seems to have worked out, princess, with you trading blow jobs so you can live with me."

I wince and then purse my lips. *There, see...*we're definitely not heading into a real relationship. "And who demanded blow jobs as rent? Seems like our parents were right all along to worry you'd exploit me." I wait for the explosion.

"I guess they were." His voice is calmer than I expect, but the dangerous undercurrent is there. "Ethan should've let Sheri castrate me with the garden shears when she asked him to."

I sigh and roll my eyes, staring out the windshield. Despite what happened, I don't believe things were ever as bad as he seems to think. Yes, my mom was probably cautious, but she doesn't go around trying to emasculate men.

If Shane made her extra paranoid, it was probably because she sensed there was something brewing between us. And she knew my level of experience back then was nil, when his certainly wasn't.

"Answer something seriously," I say. "When they told you to stay away from me, did it make you want things more? Did you plan to defy them?"

"He didn't say I had to stay away from you. She's the one who said that."

Did Mom really say that to him? So baldly? Because that would practically be an accusation in and of itself. No matter how worried she was about me, she shouldn't have spoken to Shane that way. He'd been abandoned by one of his parents, just like I had. Mom knows how tough that is for a kid. If she'd tried first to be a good stepmom to Shane, their relationship might have been so different.

Sunlight drives through the windshield like a golden white laser. Shane takes aviator sunglasses from the console and puts them on.

"My dad wanted me to treat you like a little sister."

"Mmm. You tried at first, didn't you?"

"You were there. You know exactly what I did."

Tucking my hair back, I glance at him and then at the road. "You did try," I say, remembering how kind and generous Shane was with his attention that first year. "I was flattered...I milked it," I admit. "'Can you open this jar for me, Shane?' 'Can you reach the lemonade pitcher on the top shelf for me?'"

The corners of his mouth twitch. "'I need four sandbags for my science project. They're really heavy. Will you help me?'"

A small smile forms. "Yeah, those." He never even let me touch the sandbags. For him, carrying them was nothing.

The car hums along the highway.

"This car is a stick of butter on four wheels," I murmur.

"True statement."

"Growing up, my dad was barely ever around, and my mom's boyfriends before Ethan...I never got to know them all that well. When we moved in with you guys, Ethan was so nice. It was like he loved doing things for us."

"What he loves is having a trophy wife who strokes his ego, among other things."

I roll my eyes. "She's not a trophy wife." I press my back into the seat, staring out. "He loves us, and we love him." My thumb rubs the knee of my jeans, smoothing the fabric. "I should've asked *him* to help me with the science project sandbags."

"Sure, when the heaviest thing my dad lifts most days is his gold-plated pen."

"You act like he's not fit. He jogs."

"For the endorphin rush. If you'd asked him to move sandbags, he'd have said sure and then paid the gardener to do it."

I chuckle. "Probably." I glance at Shane's profile, then back at the road. "Looking back though, I still shouldn't have asked you. I knew there was something wrong about it. Other girls mentioned their dads or brothers doing things for them. Moving furniture. Hanging shelves. It seemed normal...on the surface."

He's silent.

"You never acted like it bothered you."

"Because it didn't."

"But the only time I asked you to do things was when no one was close enough to overhear me. That's what made it sketchy."

"It's one of the things." There's a teasing note to his voice, which makes me smile.

"You could've stopped it any time. If you'd said no, even once, I wouldn't have asked again."

"There was no need to shut it down. It was innocent."

"It was flirting." My gaze slides to his profile, assessing him. As per usual, his face is unreadable. "I was fifteen. I didn't realize it at the time."

"That's why it was innocent."

I wait, but he doesn't say more. As usual, no conversation with him feels like enough.

"You just admitted you understand I was too innocent to know what I was doing around you, Shane. But you still blame me for not being experienced enough to instantly realize you didn't touch me while I was drunk?"

His jaw works, and he shakes his head. "Do you need me to spell it out for you?" he asks as he pulls into a GU parking lot.

"Yeah, I guess I do."

"First of all, if I'd wanted to touch you, I didn't need to wait until you were unconscious. You had a crush on me. If I'd wanted to fuck you, I wouldn't have needed to get you blackout drunk to do it. And I definitely wouldn't have left you naked on the couch for our parents to find. You were the virgin, not me. I knew where to take a girl if I wanted to get laid."

My stomach knots at the thought of him with other girls. "All right. But I didn't know you knew about the crush, and I didn't think about the fact that you probably knew where to take girls so you wouldn't get caught. I—"

"Aside from that, you're living in my house right now for a reason, Avery. What is it?"

"What?" My head tilts in confusion. "I'm afraid of Casanova."

"But why did you come to me? *Specifically?*"

"Because...I feel safe at your house."

"Exactly. Deep down you know if Casanova—or anyone—is stupid enough to try to hurt you when I'm around, it will end badly for him. You know I'll protect you, even when I hate you. If you know it now, then you definitely knew it at sixteen when I gave you anything you wanted.

"The second Sheri started spewing her bullshit that day, you should've put an end to it. I needed you to set the record straight, Avery. I *asked* you to. Instead, you were quiet, then you bolted, leaving things to spin out of control. The cops were ready to arrest me for rape. They came close." His voice is a growl, and he shakes his head, his mouth a grim line as he relives the moment.

I'd do anything to be able to make him forget it.

"That wasn't the first time a self-centered woman broke my heart," he says softly, making my own heart break at the reference to his mom's desertion. "But it's the closest anyone's come to destroying my *entire* life."

10

SHANE

She's upset and needs a minute, so I get out of the car and leave her to pull herself together. The truth is I need a minute, too. Until she got to Granthorpe, I thought I had all this shit in a locked box that I never needed to touch. Now we're fucking unboxing all over again.

As I wait, a part of me wants to get back in the car to comfort her because, for once, she's not trying to rationalize or excuse anything, and, for once, I actually believe that it *really* didn't occur to her how bad things could get if she didn't speak up to defend me. Sheri sounded as though there was no doubt about what happened, and I guess Avery wasn't capable of piecing the truth together and reacting fast while she was so hungover.

I wonder whether Ethan could've convinced me of a lie under those circumstances. Definitely not at sixteen. But when I'd been younger and as innocent as Avery was? Maybe. At thirteen or fourteen, I might've confused a lie for the truth for a few minutes.

I do know one thing. Even if I'd been fourteen and believed a lie in which Avery betrayed me, if she'd begged me to rescue her I would have. And I'd have covered for her in a heartbeat when the police came. There is zero chance I would've let them take her away in handcuffs. *Zero.* Protecting her back then was pure instinct. Anywhere. Anytime. I couldn't have stopped myself if I'd tried. That's what eats at me. That morning I was drowning; I asked her to save me, and she let me sink.

Maybe over time she'd have stepped up to defend me more forcefully. We'll never know because of my father.

As fucked up as being spied on by my dad was, it did save me. I haven't forgotten that. As any good lawyer will tell you, having ironclad documentation of the truth comes in handy...if you're innocent.

The door opens, and she emerges from the car. Her eyes are red, and she doesn't look at me.

"Let's take a walk to the bus stop," I say, wanting to move on from the topic that keeps coming back to haunt us. "I wanna see where the guy splashed you with the rose water."

She leads the way, and we walk in silence.

The task at hand helps to distract me. I look for anything that looks wrong. Trampled plants, a snapped branch, footprints in the dirt. I spot nothing.

From the layout, I agree with her that it was probably the jogger in the hoodie who splashed her because the tight row of bushes along the path would've made it hard for anyone to approach her from the side. Since the guy splashed her face, it had to be someone who approached her head-on. Which is ballsy as hell.

When I ask if he could've been wearing a mask, she shrugs.

"I was looking down."

"Who knows you're staying with me?"

She flinches, and I realize maybe my tone sounded rough to her. That's not how I meant it to sound.

"No one." Avery's arms cross over her chest, her hands rubbing her upper arms.

My tone is intentionally lighter when I speak again. "You didn't mention it to anyone? You're sure?"

"I'm sure."

MARLEE WRAY

"The bus you took to get to my house has an off-campus route. Not a typical bus for you?"

She swallows, glancing at the path thoughtfully. "Not normally, no. But I walked to this stop several times when I was bringing clothes and books to your house. Anyone watching me could've seen me and figured out I was moving off campus."

"All right. Let's go take a look at your dorm room."

We're again silent on the walk, and she's subdued. I decide that today's conversation is the last one she and I are ever having about that morning two years ago. We understand each other's perspectives now. It's enough.

At her residence hall, I look around outside. Nothing unusual.

Then she takes me in and shows me where she found the purple rose. A random event is easier to figure in the dorm. All Casanova had to do was walk in during the party, wait until the hall was clear, pick the lock and walk into her room.

There's no way to know whether he targeted her specifically that night, or if his time in her room was what triggered him to start stalking her.

If it is Casanova, he's being more brazen than he's ever been. In some cases, serial killers and rapists do get bolder and more reckless over time. Some even make calls or send notes to the cops and news media as a taunt. But announcing a *specific* target *before* an attack is crazy. For all the guy knows, the whole police force could be watching Avery and waiting for him to strike. That piece of things feels off. Of course, anyone who hunts women the way he does *is* off.

He left the rose in the bed. Maybe he planned to take her that night. He could've planted the rose so it'd be found in the morning after she disappeared. But he wasn't waiting in the room. Why not? Maybe because it would have been difficult to take her out of the building without being seen. Lit hallways, girls coming and going. He could have been watching her for a while and known there's no boyfriend or roommate and that she often walks around alone.

That night, he could have planted the rose and then waited somewhere along the path. Maybe near a parking lot where he has a vehicle on nights when he takes them.

But on the night of the Beta party, Avery didn't walk home alone. Declan was with her. Maybe Casanova planned to take Avery but changed his mind. And it was too late to get the rose back. If she's "the one that got away" and he's angry about that, it could be why he's still stalking her.

Avery sits on the edge of her bed, rubbing her arms. "I don't want to go to dinner. Can you drop me off at your place?"

"So you can stay there alone? Absolutely not."

She looks away, biting her lip. "I'm not feeling like a night out."

Is she serious? We've just taken a tour of Casanova's greatest hits. Is she really so uncomfortable around me right now that she'd risk her life?

Her blue eyes practically bore a hole in the wall. Apparently making eye contact is also off the menu.

"If I skip dinner, it would give us both some breathing room. We could use it, don't you think?"

"No." I sit down next to her. "I believe you. You couldn't see the truth."

"Shane, I did defend you. I just wasn't as forceful as I needed to be. I didn't understand how things could escalate even in the absence of evidence. If I'd known—"

"Okay. That's enough about that. Let's talk about tonight. I'm not leaving you alone at my place or anywhere else. It's not safe."

Her brows pinch together, and she rubs the back of her neck, exhaling a frustrated sigh. "If you hate me so much, why are you helping me?"

I shrug, mock perplexed. "Maybe I like seeing you on your knees with my cock in your mouth."

Avery sucks in a breath and turns her head to look at me, a spark of outrage lighting her eyes.

Good.

"Goddamnit, Shane."

A smirk threatens, but I squash it. She's not ready to joke yet.

"Look, I've said all I need to say about the past. I've also heard what I needed to hear from you. Let's turn the page on that chapter and call it over."

"Can we?" she asks hopefully.

"Yeah."

Her fingers pick at her jeans. "We can't start fresh if we hate each other."

It's the second time she's mentioned the word hate, which tells me it's bothering her that I used that word. She's angling for me to take it back. I don't want to get pulled down a rabbit hole into another deep dark conversation about feelings. Once was more than enough. But I can't resist telling her what she seems to need to hear.

"I don't hate you, Avery."

Her shoulders turn toward me, and she looks relieved. "Let's try to wipe the slate clean, all right?"

My brow cocks. "How clean?"

"Completely."

I lean my mouth against the shell of her ear and whisper, "If you're asking me to give up the dirty way you're paying me to protect you, my answer is no."

She shudders, her nipples puckering like arrowheads through the fabric of her shirt.

"You're a monster," she says, but her tone's mild.

"You're right. But that suits you and always has."

"What?" Her brows crinkle. "No, it doesn't."

"It did when I was the monster obsessed with you."

She blows out a breath but doesn't try again to deny that she likes my dark side. Good for her. We're all about the raw truth today.

Raw truth seems to suit us, too. Even the pain.

"Get out while I change," she says, glancing around the small room.

I raise an eyebrow. I've seen her naked. She's been eye-level with my cock and sucked it twice. Bouncing me so I don't see her bra and panties seems a bit much.

She pushes on my shoulder. "Come on."

I rise and step out into the hall to wait.

Avery can have her moment alone. For now.

11

SHANE

When the door opens, I lose my train of thought. Avery's wearing a sapphire blue dress that wraps around her body, hugging her in all the right places. Her hair's falling in fuck-me waves over her shoulders, her eyes are smoky with indigo powder, and she's traded her glasses for contacts. From Diana Prince to Wonder Woman in less than an hour.

I stare at her with the kind of hunger wolves reserve for a fresh kill.

Avery checks to be sure the door's locked and then turns. "Ready."

"So I see." Does she know she looks like she tumbled off a Maxim cover?

The day's been rough. Maybe the outfit is her idea of revenge, her way of making me burn for her all the way to Back Bay. If it is, so be it. The burn will be my appetizer.

We head down the hall and into the elevator. The temptation to stop it so I can pin her against the wall and do dirty things hits me hard. Unfortunately, we don't have that kind of time right now. I'll have to wait until I get her home for that.

When we reach the car, she strokes the door while waiting for me to open it. My cock is suddenly jealous.

Once we're on the expressway, I drive seventy to Back Bay. Half my attention isn't on the road; it's on Avery in my passenger seat. The wild, sexy hair makes me want to wind it around my hand later, so I can pull her head back as I fuck her.

When we reach my grandfather's house, I punch in the code to open the gate. Security is always a priority at his place.

Avery's eyes widen as the mansion comes into view. The row of five domed cut glass windows that are topped with offset clover-shaped ones are reminiscent of a medieval castle in Ireland. They never fail to impress.

When we get out, I come around and open the door to escort her to the front step.

My hand can't resist touching her lower back, like she's mine to guide. *Like she's mine.* It's a bad idea to think of her that way. But I'm a man who goes for bad ideas like they're covered in chocolate.

My grandfather opens the door, and my brows rise. The old man's seventy, but he pumps iron regularly and looks about two decades younger than he is. I told him I was bringing a girl to dinner, and he apparently decided to dress for the occasion. Normally when I come over, he's in khakis and an oxford. Today, he's wearing pressed black dress pants, a white shirt, and a blue silk tie. And damn. The tie matches her dress almost exactly.

"This is Avery," I say. "She's Sheri's daughter. Avery, this is Joe Sullivan, my grandfather." I wait for either of them to have a startled reaction, but all they do is smile at each other like they've just spotted their long lost love.

My eyes narrow. Apparently, she doesn't recognize his name, and apparently he's not going to hold it against a pretty girl that his former son-in-law married her mom.

The entryway is all black and white Italian marble and would look more appropriate in a hotel lobby in Vegas, but Avery marvels over it. She stares up at the black crystal chandelier for at least twenty seconds.

"You like it?" Pops asks. "My Riona picked everything out."

"I love it. Riona's your wife?"

"No, my daughter. Shane's mother."

"Oh! My gosh. I should've known her name. I'm so sorry."

"Shane, you don't talk about your mother?"

Definitely not, I think grimly.

"Shane doesn't talk about anyone," Avery says quickly, with a conspiratorial smile. "Becoming a talk show host is not in the cards for him, I'm afraid."

Pops laughs and puts out his arm to escort her inside. She slides her arm through and holds his as he takes her on a tour. I follow behind them, looking at her peach of an ass and biding my time.

In the living room, he shows her pictures of celebrities and tells stories. She laughs at all the right places and jumps in with her own one-liners. I haven't seen her this relaxed and animated in a long time. The underlying irony isn't lost on me, but I still like it more than I should.

"Do you look like your mom?" the old man asks her.

"A bit. I got her lips and her nose," she says, touching her face. "But her eyes are brown."

"You know who you look like?" He walks her over to a picture and points. "That's my wife, Siobhan, God rest her. She got a bit of the black Irish with the hair, and she had eyes as blue as the sea. Like yours."

As blue as the sea? Seriously?

Avery doesn't bat an eye, so Pops sails onward, talking and showing off more family photos. He always claims he was a "ladykiller" in his day. As a kid, I had an entirely different impression about what that meant until he explained the slang. At the time, I didn't really buy that he had a way with women. Now I see I misjudged him because Avery's hanging on his arm and his every word.

"Siobhan walked into a room and took every man's breath away," he announces. "That's Ri, too. Just the same." He points to a picture of my mother sitting at a cliffside café.

"Beautiful," Avery agrees. "She looks like a movie star. Where is this?"

"Portugal. She lives there, with a useless husband and two ugly cats."

Avery laughs.

His smile widens. He likes all pretty women, but especially the ones with a great sense of humor. "Come. Let's get to the kitchen where I've got the treasure stashed."

Her eyes twinkle. "Sounds perfect."

The old man takes us into the white marble and silver kitchen and pours himself a whiskey and us some iced chocolate concoction.

"If you dare, lad," he says, raising his glass.

I cock an eyebrow and sniff what's in my glass. Smells like cocoa and maybe—*damn him*—cherries. As a little kid once, when I stayed the night, I snuck an unopened box of holiday chocolate-covered cherry cordials into my room and ate the entire thing. Then I rolled around my race car bed with a stomach ache for the rest of the night. I was three, but he has not let me live it down.

Avery, all innocence, takes a healthy swig and then practically moans with delight. She drinks her entire glass before I've taken a sip.

When I get to drinking, I confirm the worst. It's cherry liqueur buried under so much chocolate and cream it's almost unrecognizable. Fucking hell. I have not touched a chocolate-covered cherry in almost two decades, which from the glint in his eyes, Pops probably realizes.

Tapping his glass, I shrug. "Slàinte."

"Slàinte," he says cheerfully with a wicked smirk.

I turn half away and down it quickly with no ill effects. My stomach's been iron clad since puberty. A chocolate cocktail is not going to come back up, no matter how nauseatingly sweet it is. When I'm done, I put the empty glass in the sink, signaling that one's my limit.

"That's a concoction my new girl made me special, she did." There's a teasing note in his voice, the Irish accent kicking up a notch. "I told her my lad has a bit of a sweet tooth for chocolate cherries."

"For fuck's sake," I murmur, but I laugh in spite of myself. "And what new girl?"

"*The very one*," he says with mock reverence. "Finally managed to get her on the line, so I could reel her in. I've been after a date for ages. She's a younger woman, dontcha know."

No, I definitely don't know, I think grimly. "How young?"

"Fifty-two," he says with a shrug of his brows.

"Cradle robber," I deadpan.

This brings on a riot of laughter from both him and Avery. Then I notice he's poured her another drink, and she's finished most of it.

"Avery," I say, circling the counter.

With a quick gulp, the last of it is gone, and she's licking her lips. "Yes?"

"You know that's got liquor in it?"

Her head jerks down at the glass like I've said it was full of hemlock.

"Oh, just a touch," my grandfather says dismissively. He's full Irish and, even at seventy, couldn't be brought low by a whole bottle of Bush Mills, let alone a cherry cordial.

In this case, his opinion doesn't factor, and sure enough, Avery looks warily into her empty glass.

"I don't really drink." Pouty lips purse, and her head tilts. "It was delicious, though." She takes her glass to the sink and sets it there as a companion to mine.

"No worries. The food will be ready soon." The old man peeks in the oven. The smell of bubbling gravy escapes, making my stomach growl.

Pops pours himself another whiskey and regales Avery with tales of my boyhood shenanigans. Low chuckles from her sound like purring, which sends my mind in the direction of sex.

A glance at the oven reminds me we're here to eat. "Is the Shepherd's pie another thing from the girlfriend?"

"Yes." Pops grins. "She claims she's no grand cook, but I call it false modesty. She's dead brilliant at Shepherd's pie and potato hash and every other thing she's made me."

"Pretty?"

"Gorgeous. Since the day she was born, I expect. I've known her going on twenty years or more, and she's always been."

"Surprised you found her single," I say.

"Well, she's widowed, you know. Wasn't very keen on taking up with anyone. And she has a notorious son, which keeps some away. I like the lad."

Hmm. "Do I know him?"

"You'll know of him, I expect. Name's Scott Patrick. Goes by Trick."

Christ. Trick Patrick's notorious, all right. Before I can comment on that bit of news, my attention shifts to Avery who sways as she takes a step.

"Whoa," she mumbles. Avery's hair falls over her shoulder when she looks back at me. "I didn't eat lunch...that spiked cocoa's hitting me, I think." The tip of her tongue traces her lips, as if checking their general disposition. My guess is they're tingling from her buzz. When she turns she teeters slightly. "My shoes are tall."

"And they've grown a couple inches in the past hour," I say with a sympathetic smirk.

Perfect white teeth nibble her lower lip. It is dead fucking sexy. Then a delicate hand reaches out for me, like I'm exactly what she needs. And that's an entreaty that will never fail to land. Without even thinking, I step forward, so she can grab on. Her hand slides up, past my elbow to my bicep. Her fingers are cool, but the touch is anything but.

"You're strong," she whispers. "It's a good thing."

She has me, a hundred fucking percent.

"How's it going, Ave?" I whisper back.

A breath escapes like a whistle through puckered lips. "I don't know. I feel very strange."

She wobbles, and my hands shoot forward to catch her. I lift her, setting her on the island's countertop so I can pull off her slinky heels. "Easy there, Cinderella."

"I think I'd better eat soon."

"Agreed," I say with a wink.

"I'm sorry. I shouldn't have had a second glass. I never drink—"

Her worried look hits home. Drinking alcohol scares her. Has she not been drunk since that time two years ago?

"Hey." My voice is as soft and reassuring as I can make it. "You're all right, Ave. I've got you."

"Yeah, I'm all right." Her head bobs a nod, but it's as if she's trying to convince herself. Avery crosses one leg over the other, and the panels of the dress separate enough to give me a view up her thighs almost to the promised land. The alcohol has hit her hard, which speaks to her lack of drinking experience. I don't even have a buzz.

Her head tilts, noting the direction of my gaze on her bare thighs. "I should get down." She tries to keep her skirt from riding up as she inches toward the counter's edge.

"Here, baby." I pluck her off the counter and carry her to kitchen table. Setting her in a chair, I say, "Just relax. Food's coming."

On the island, her abandoned phone chooses that moment to buzz. She starts to rise, but I put a hand on her shoulder.

"Nah, I'll get it for you."

I walk over to retrieve the device and am treated to a grin from my grandfather. I roll my eyes at his amusement. The old man's been waiting for me to get serious with someone. He might think that's what I'm finally doing. But this thing with Avery is complicated and unlikely to last.

When Avery opens the message, she exhales an annoyed sigh. "They are so ridiculous."

I glance down and see Declan's name in the thread. Leaning over, I see it's a message from Sheri.

"What's that about?" I ask.

She wrinkles her nose, and it's cute as fucking hell. "Nothing."

"Seems like something," I counter. "Spill."

"A ridiculous matchmaking scheme."

That's a complete sucker punch. When I speak, my voice is a low growl. "What?"

She shrugs. "My mom and Declan's think because we have similar dark hair and blue eyes, we'd make a cute couple. Black Irish all around I guess," she mumbles vaguely. Her head tips forward so her wavy hair falls around her face.

What the fuck?

First of all, Declan's not Irish. He's a fucking Mayflower blue blood. But more importantly, since when is matchmaking Dec with Avery a thing her mom and Dec's stepmother engage in?

"When did they say that, Avery? When we were in high school?"

"Yeah." She tilts her head to the side, and the black velvet strands fall away from her stunning face. "And on and off since. We're supposed to ski with them...or something? Winter break."

Jealousy grabs me by the throat, unleashing a tidal wave of testosterone and adrenaline. My heart thumps like a gorilla stomping through the jungle.

My dad invited me for a ski trip over winter break, which I immediately nixed as a possibility. A family trip for the four of us? Hard pass. But Ethan never said anything about the Heyworths being part of the trip. Declan didn't mention it either. Is Dec trying to keep details of the trip from me? He should know better.

An instant later, I reconsider. Declan's a brother to me. A girl has never come between us, and if one did, it certainly wouldn't be Avery Kershaw. Dec distrusts her even more than I did. He's the one who floated the theory that she knew all along we hadn't had sex but stayed quiet so the focus wouldn't be on her night of wild underage drinking.

Declan suspects most women of cunning ulterior motives. Over the years, there's been an endless parade of gold-diggers after the Heyworth family fortune. Dec says he was about five years old when his grandfather began impressing upon him the importance of a prenuptial agreement.

"It's like they've never met Declan." Avery holds up her palms in a "what the hell" gesture. "He doesn't see me that way. He actively dislikes me...although, the other night he did make sure I got home safe. I guess that time we were cool."

I'm speechless. I'm the one who sent Declan to walk her back to her dorm. Which she knows. What she doesn't know is that I had to talk him into it. In the end, he only did it to keep me from having to get near her. The memory helps cool my blood a bit. I hate the idea of Dec with Avery, but not because it's Declan. I've never been able to stand the thought of anyone other than me touching her.

"She's Ri all over," my grandfather warns in a whisper, like a devil on my shoulder. "Ethan never knew how to handle your mother, and she slipped right through his fingers."

Avery rubs her eyes, smudging the smokiness under her lids, oblivious to our side conversation. She shakes her head as if she's trying to clear it.

If I spend another second imagining her with Declan, I may put my fist through the wall. Time for a change of subject. "You need to eat something, Avery."

Pops opens the oven and removes the pie. The crusted potato peaks are golden and perfect.

"Yes, I do need to eat." Avery's fingertips press against her lips as if to lock her words away. "Can I just be alone a few minutes? I need that, too."

"Sure," I say, studying her as she tries to sit primly. When the steaming food is plated, I deliver it to her. "It's hot," I warn. "Give it a second."

Once she's settled and focused on her food and her phone, I return to the counter island where I can have a quiet word with my grandfather.

He stands there, shrewdly assessing me. In a very low voice, he says, "She's after talking about your friend Declan, is she?"

My nod is curt. This isn't a conversation we need to have.

"The heir to billions?" Pops shrugs his gray brows. "That would suit the new wife, I'd imagine. And Ethan, too. No problem with *those* family ties."

"Whatever." Declan's family has plenty of skeletons. His are just the high society variety.

Pops pulls out a bar stool and sits at the island, then takes a bite of the pie and smiles down at it. "She's a rare talent, my lovely widow is." His sharp gaze cuts to the table where Avery's temple is propped against her palm. "Now that one. You said, 'whatever.' Why's that? You're planning to stand by and watch her go? Like father, like son?"

"Avery and I are not married. We're not even a thing. I brought her here because I'm doing her a favor."

"Since when is it a favor to bring a girl here?" His green eyes bore into me, revealing the same eyes and the same knowing expression I face in the mirror every day.

"Someone's stalking her. She's scared."

A dark expression passes over his face as he leans forward. "What will you do about it?"

"When I find him, you can imagine what I'll do."

He leans back and licks his fork, then nods, looking satisfied. "So this is an opportunity with her. Your strength and her gratitude is a good combination."

I nod.

Pops washes down the shepherd's pie with milk. He raises the carton in offering, but I shake my head. He pours a second glass and nods in Avery's direction.

I take it and set it on the table near her plate.

When I return to him, he asks in a low voice, "Why aren't you and she a thing already? What do you think is wrong with her?"

"She's got a problem mother for one."

"Because the woman took one look at you and thought that, given the chance, you'd eat her pretty little daughter alive? I call that smart." He taps a finger on the counter. "Little Sheri outplayed you. She got her hooks into Ethan, and he did not have the stones to back her down when she wanted him to betray you. Don't blame *her* for that."

My grandfather heard the police were summoned to our house. I had no choice but to share some details with him, and at the time, his anger was nearly a match for my own. As someone who always spots an opportunity, he used it as a lever to get into my life in a way he'd never been before.

"Sheri's unhinged," I say coolly. "But I don't blame her for the things Ethan does. He lets women get the best of him. He's a killer in the courtroom, but that's it."

The old man points at me for emphasis and nods. "This one, Avery, I peg her as a good girl. Is she?"

"Seems like it. Most of the time."

"And pretty."

"Beautiful," I agree.

His eyes narrow again before he looks down at his plate. "Are you really gonna let your friend have her?"

"I never said that."

His head's tipped over his dish, but his eyes rise at the tone I use when saying the words. Hard. Resolute.

"Hmm. If you let her go alone on some ski trip, and she's like this —like champagne that sparkles and bubbles, he'll see it and he'll want it. You may not get a second chance. In life, timing is everything."

"She's not going anywhere with Declan. Or anyone."

"No?"

"I'm not my dad at twenty, Pops. I'm you."

This brings a smile to his face.

At the table, Avery gasps. Our heads swivel toward her, and I stalk over to see what's wrong.

She tries to cover her phone, but I pull it away from her and stare down at the screen, reading the text exchange.

> Avery: Why did you say Shane's grandfather is dead?! He's not dead! I'm having dinner at his house. he's lovely. I like him a ton.

Mom: Where are you?

Mom: Ave, where are you???

> Avery: Boston. At Mr. Sullivan's house in Back Bay.

Mom: OMG. how did you get there??? Leave right now. Do you need Ethan to pick you up?

> Avery: no. I'm with Shane. he drove

Mom: we're coming to get you

> Avery: why?

Mom: Joe Sullivan is the head of the Irish Mafia.

12

SHANE

Staying overnight in Back Bay wasn't the plan until our parents pulled the trigger on driving over. I figure if I take Avery back to Granthorpe, they'll show up there and discover she's living with me, which will lead to even more drama. Yesterday, someone trying to get her to leave my house would've been fine. Tonight, it's not.

I put Avery in a guest room, claiming I'm too buzzed to drive. She tries to ask questions about Pops, but I shut that down, saying we should talk about it in the morning. I also convince her that it'll be better for everyone if Ethan and Sheri don't find out she's been drinking. Avery agrees and lies on the bed on top of the covers. She's out in about five minutes.

Pops heads to the media room to watch sports recaps, leaving me to deal with Ethan and Sheri. That suits me fine. The less people involved the better.

I'm back in the kitchen by the time my phone rings with the third call from my dad. This time, I pick up.

"You at home? Or nearly in Back Bay?" I ask calmly.

"What's going on, Shane?" He's calm, too, but his tone is grim. He's not using his lawyer voice. This is his disapproving dad voice, one he hasn't tried to use on me in a long time.

My fingers drum a staccato beat on the island's marble top. "Nothing's going on. I came to Back Bay for dinner."

"With Avery? Since when do you hang out with her? When I tried to get you to have dinner with us when we brought her to Granthorpe, you flat-out refused."

"Our talking is recent."

Sheri pipes in with high-pitched agitation that grates on me. "And the first thing you do is tell her your Sullivan grandfather is alive and take her to meet him? Why would you do that?"

"It came up."

"Because you brought it up!" Sheri snaps.

My muscles contract hard enough to tear from the bone. I never tolerate it well when someone gets sharp with me, and from her, I'll tolerate zero abuse.

Pulling the phone from my ear, I decide I'm done. My finger is a millimeter from the screen when my dad interjects, and I pause.

"Sher, calm down," he says. "Shane, why did Avery reach out to you? Is something going on with her?"

I want to handle most of the drama before they get to the house, so I raise the phone again. "Casanova being on campus is the thing that's going on with every girl right now."

"Is that why she texted you? She's scared?" Ethan asks.

"They're all scared. And yeah, that's the reason."

"She can come home right now," Sheri says. "The school said there will be no consequences for finishing the semester online. Let me talk to her."

"Avery crashed. She's in a guest room sound asleep."

"We'll wake her when we get there," Sheri says primly.

"Not sure who you think you're talking to right now," I say in a low voice. "If you come with that attitude, you won't get past the gate."

"Ethan!" Sheri says.

"It's all right, honey." The placating tone he uses with her shifts to a neutral lawyer-mediator one when he addresses me again. "Shane, listen, I'm happy you're talking to your sister."

I roll my eyes. He's been floating that description of Avery for the past three years. It's never taken, and it's never going to. No need to say so though, especially with the wicked stepmother on the line poised to get shrill. I catch my feet pacing a hole in the floor and stop next to a countertop.

"Let's not turn this into something negative," my dad continues, trying like hell to be the peacekeeper. "It's a good thing."

"You're the one storming the gates in a panic. Seems like old times. I say she's all right, but you won't take my word for it."

There's a prolonged silence. He knows better than to come at me hard after I've tossed that down on the field of battle.

"You know this is complicated," he says gently and then sighs. None of us wants to tread too deeply into the past. "Why take her there of all places?"

"I brought her because she was with me. I come to Back Bay almost every week." I can predict how that will land, and as expected, there's a stunned silence on their end.

Keeping my visits here on the down-low was very much the standard from the time I was about fourteen years old. I'd ride my bike to the park, and one of my grandfather's guys would show up. They'd throw my bike in the back of a truck and deliver me to wherever he was. When I turned sixteen it got easier to see him because I could drive myself.

When it comes to my relationship with my dad and grandfather, the tables have definitely turned. I've been to my dad's house once in the past year, at Christmas. The couple of other times I've seen him have been when he's come to Granthorpe alone, and we had dinner out. That was before he sent Avery to GU and caused me to reinstate the cold war where I don't see him at all. I'm sure hearing that I'm making weekly trips to Back Bay is tough for him.

"What if we don't come by tonight?" he says finally. "Would you consider meeting us for lunch tomorrow? Or letting us take you both out to dinner? It would be great to have the four of us together."

I wait for Sheri to erupt, but for once she's quiet.

"We've gotta be on campus tomorrow. Avery's got a class that's important to her. Maybe we'll come your way on the weekend." A beat passes. "One of us will let you know."

"That'll be fine," Dad says. I'm about to end the call when he adds, "Shane, thank you for seeing Avery and for looking after her. Hearing the news about what's happening on campus has us worried about her being there alone. I know if she's with you, she's safe."

There's a sarcastic reply on the tip of my tongue, but I swallow it. I remind myself I'm putting the basement incident behind me for Avery's sake. That means I have to put it behind all four of us because Avery loves her mom and Ethan.

It's too bad her mom's been alerted to the fact that Avery and I are associating with each other again. I'd love to keep Avery just to myself for a while, but I know that won't play. And if there was a real tug-of-war over Avery right now, I'd lose. So there can be no ultimatums. No forced choices between me and them.

I need to play nice. At least until I'm sure I'll win.

AVERY

I WAKE AND ROLL FROM THE STRANGE BED. I'M STILL WEARING MY blue dress and adjust it so my bra's not showing before I creep out into the hall to find a bathroom. An open door nearby reveals an elegant powder room in cream and gold.

A look in the ornately-framed mirror reveals my makeup's badly smeared. *Good grief.* My face belongs on the cover of a horror comic. I use the restroom and then wash my hands and face.

My buzz is gone, thankfully. I'm embarrassed that I got intoxicated in front of Mr. Sullivan. *Mr. Sullivan.* Is Shane's grandfather really the head of an Irish Mafia organization? He doesn't seem like he would be. He's so charming. I felt an immediate connection with him. Maybe that's because his brand of charm reminds me of Shane's, from the old days. They're both good storytellers.

Last night, Shane picked me up and called me baby. A wave of heat courses through me at the memory. I hug my arms to my sides. The vibe reminded me of the way he was when I first moved into Ethan's. Though of course he never touched me or called me baby back then.

The sexual current between us is new. Just thinking about it causes prickles of desire between my legs. I shake my head at the way my attraction to him threatens to rage out of control over something so small. *Dangerous*, on so many levels.

I finger-comb the tangles from my hair and then sneak back to the guest room. It's toasty warm, so I push the thick comforter back to climb in bed. Which is when I realize I'm not alone.

"Shane?"

I sit on the edge of the bed, and using a fingertip, I press his bare muscled shoulder. Is he completely naked? I don't reach down to find out. Having him pull out his cock while I'm on my knees to service him is different than touching him while he's in bed asleep. The latter's definitely more intimate. Another round of desire curls through my lower belly and into my core.

Jesus.

I squeeze his shoulder gently, marveling at how great it feels. His whole body is ripped. He may not be playing football anymore, but he's clearly not missing workouts.

Shane stirs and rolls toward me. When he takes a deep breath, his chest expands.

He. Is. Beautiful.

"Hey," he murmurs, his voice gravelly with sleep. "You sober?"

My nose scrunches as I cringe. "Yes. Sorry about earlier."

"Nothing to be sorry about. Not like you danced naked on a table." He stretches and smiles. "You're cute as hell drunk."

Somehow I doubt that. A small frown threatens. "I bet your grandfather didn't think my getting drunk was cute."

"Sure he did. The old man thinks everything about you is cute. He's pulling hard for me to keep you, so he can see your pretty face again."

A small smile tugs at my mouth. It's nice that Mr. Sullivan likes me.

Of course there's no possibility of Shane "keeping me," since this isn't a relationship. And if Shane's grandfather understood the bargain

I struck with Shane, I'm sure his impression of me would change drastically.

"Hot in here." Shane shoves the covers down, exposing washboard abs and black boxer-briefs. He pushes up on his elbow and looks me over, then grabs the tie around my wrap dress and tugs. The loop disappears, and the tie slackens.

My hand darts up to cover myself. "What are you doing?"

"Unwrapping you." He pushes the fabric, which slides over so my silky blue bra's exposed.

Fortunately, the dress's internal tie keeps it from opening completely. Shane pulls at the dress, making the fabric stretch and strain.

"Shane, no. You'll rip it."

"Take it off."

"No," I whisper, bending forward so my face is closer to his groin.

He grabs my shoulders and lifts my mouth away from his cock. "Let's make it mutual tonight. Get up, and take off your dress."

A halting breath is trapped in my throat. I want to listen to him but know I shouldn't. Shaking my head, I whisper, "It's not a good idea." I mean for my voice to be firm, but the end of the sentence rises like I'm asking a question.

Shane arches a brow, and the corners of his mouth curve. "Hmm. Do you need me to make you, princess? Because I can."

That sends a ripple of lust through me, my nipples tightening to points that strain against the fabric.

He's right. I do like him as a monster.

His expression darkens. "But first, I'll spank you."

My breath catches. "You can *not* do that. Not here."

"I can't?" he muses. Then his body moves with panther-like speed, shifting both of us to the edge of the bed and dragging me over his lap.

"Wait—!"

He does not wait.

His leg scissors over mine, trapping my thighs between his. His hand drags the dress upward until it's at my waist, and then his fingers toy with my panties. "If you're a good girl and stay very quiet, I'll let you keep these on."

I press my lips together between my teeth, my muscles rigid and my core clenching with excitement. He could be teasing me, trying to get me to beg him to let me up, so I'll undress as the lesser of two evils.

Even though I know it's coming, when his hand comes down on my ass, I freeze. It's a slap and doesn't cause more than a sting, but it's still shocking.

Then his heavy palm comes down over and over with successively more force. It's gradual, so I don't realize how hard it's become until I'm gasping for breath.

Oh, my God. The moment's so darkly sexual my mind almost can't believe it's happening.

He pauses, rubbing me slowly, squeezing my warm ass. "Are you ready to behave?"

"What?" My voice is so breathy it's barely audible.

"I asked you to do something. Are you ready to obey?"

Obey. Shivers of fear and lust cascade through me at his use of that word.

"Let me go," I whisper as my body starts to tremble.

"That's not the right answer, baby." His fingers graze my spine, sending a riot of lust and new shivers through me. "But the way you squirm and squeeze your thighs together is."

The spanking continues until heat blossoms through my ass and between my legs. My core aches from something other than pain, and the burning in my backside intensifies. Tears sting my eyes, and my lip throbs from where I'm biting it.

My feet kick, and I try to twist free. It doesn't work.

He pins my arm against my back until I'm helpless and can't move without hurting myself. Once he has complete control of my body, he punishes me some more.

"Okay. Please, Shane. Okay!" I hiss.

Strong fingers squeeze my ass and dip between my legs to stroke the damp panel of my underwear. I gasp, my face flaming.

His grip eases enough for me to slide from his lap onto the floor. But as I try to crawl away, Shane leans forward and grabs a handful of my hair, making me gasp anew. He doesn't pull, but his hold makes it impossible for me to move another inch without having my head pulled back.

Trapped again.

"Stand up," he commands in a firm tone that brooks no defiance. "Right in front of me." He releases his hold on my hair, so I can obey.

I lurch to my feet but hesitate to move.

Do I run for the door or shuffle the few inches to stand in front of him? I tell myself that if I run, he'll catch me, but that's just an excuse to do what I really want to do.

When I'm standing before him, he puts his hands on the backs of my thighs and slides them up to cup my ass. "You all right?"

My face flames. "No, of course not."

His grip tightens on my warm flesh, causing my core to clench. My body's a sexual instrument, and he's the virtuoso who's taken it in hand.

"Are you sure?" His intense gaze leaves me feeling naked. "The way you move...a part of you seems to enjoy having your pretty ass spanked."

I glance down at his strong thighs, where I was just lying and the waves of lust crash over me again. My hair falls around my face, shielding me from his scrutiny. "I think you're saying that because you liked doing it," I counter in a whisper. Looking tentatively through my lashes at him, I'm breathless.

A slow smile curves his mouth. He's totally unabashed. "I did enjoy it," he says in that sexy voice. "I like when you're sweet and smile at me. But I'll like it just as much when you're not if that means I get to punish you in ways that make you wet for me. You are wet, right?"

I don't answer. We both know I am.

He moves one of his hands so it's against my panties, then a finger snakes under the fabric to touch me. All the blood seems to pool below my waist, making me lightheaded.

Drawing the finger out, he brings it to his mouth and sucks on it. His eyes close for a moment, and he exhales a heavy breath. "I need more of that."

Opening his eyes, he tilts his head, appraising me. "I won't force you, even though I really want to," he whispers in a husky voice. "Tell me what you want. Should I act sweet? I can do that for you." He takes my hand and slides it over his pecs, bringing it to rest over his heart. "If you want things to stop for the night, say so." His left hand is still cupping my ass, and he squeezes harder, resurrecting the soreness and the sexiness of having my ass spanked. "If you're quiet, Avery, I'll keep going."

The anticipation is excruciating. When I finally speak, my voice is as soft as feathers. "I'll undress if you promise we'll only use our mouths on each other."

Shane stands, and our bodies touch, causing electricity to spark between us as he towers over me. His eyes are dark and knowing. "I don't have a condom here, so I promise not to put my cock inside you where it belongs." His fingers grip my hair and pull my head back. He kisses my neck and then whispers in my ear. "Otherwise, no promises. I'm going to get you off and that will involve my fingers stroking your clit until you're begging to come."

I shudder at the raw way he talks to me.

"Now get undressed." More and more darkness enters his tone. "Unless you want me to do it for you."

When I don't move, he reaches inside the dress where it's tethered and jerks the inner tie. My eyes widen as the fabric separates, framing my body.

My hands catch his upper arms, squeezing his hard biceps. "If you're too rough, I won't enjoy it."

A sinister smile resurfaces. "I'll be just rough enough, and you will enjoy it."

He shoves the dress off my shoulders and grabs my hips, pulling me against him. His erection strains to free itself. His fingers play with my hair, then his thumbs hook the lace at my waist and slide my panties down to my thighs as he lowers himself to his knees.

His exhalation of breath is a sigh against my hot flesh. "Beautiful."

Leaning forward, he slides the tip of his tongue into my belly button. It's a small penetration, but a meaningful one. Then he grips my hips and slides his mouth lower, to between my lower lips. He licks me there. My whole body vibrates with pleasure and anticipation.

A shuddering breath escapes, and my shaky fingers clutch his shoulders.

He stands, towering over me again. "Lie on the bed and spread your legs."

I shimmy until my underwear drops to the floor. Stepping out of them, I resist the urge to cover myself. As I lie on my back on the bed, I'm more nervous than I've ever been. Easing my knees apart, I try to relax.

Shane's still wearing his boxer-briefs, and the hard line of his erection is obvious and makes my mouth water to taste it again.

He joins me on the bed and positions himself so he's kneeling on the mattress between my legs. Then he drops forward onto his palms, lowering his mouth to within an inch of mine. "You'd better kiss me now. In case you don't want to later."

My body shudders again. I can't seem to control my involuntary reactions to him. I press my palm over his lips. "Don't make me kiss you. That's the kind of thing I could hold against you if things go sideways."

He turns his head a fraction, freeing his mouth. "So I'm only allowed to kiss the dirty places?" he asks with a wicked smirk. "For someone who's nervous, you sure do like to taunt the beast."

He stares down into my eyes, then bites my skin, gently at first and then as a little threat. He's dangerous, the kind of dangerous that seduces. I'm vaguely aware that I want him to make me kiss him. And then to make me regret it.

Instead, he moves lower, kissing my breast where it swells out of the bra's cup. He slides his tongue under the fabric to lick me. It's sexy and slightly sinister, like a serpent slithering through a garden. He works his way down my body, not kissing me again until he's just above my hips. In the hollow of my belly, he tongues my belly button and kisses me once just below it.

"Earlier you asked if I knew about your crush, but you didn't ask if I had one too. The answer is no."

I stiffen, resisting as he pushes my legs farther apart, opening me. The vulnerability is almost too much to bear.

"What I had for you was lust. The raging kind that made me want to pin you to my bed and fuck you hard, then turn you over and start again." He says it slowly, like he wants the words to sink in and saturate every inch of me. It's a wicked confession that shocks me, and makes me hotter and wetter for him.

"Our parents were wrong to make me live in the basement like I lacked self-control. The truth is controlling myself around you is what I did all day, every day, and through the night. If I hadn't, I would've cornered you in dark places where we'd be alone and uninterrupted, and then I'd have done things like what I'm about to do now. I'd have tasted you, in all your innocence, until you weren't anymore."

Oh, my God.

He lowers his head, and his tongue slides between my lower lips. There's plenty of me to taste because I'm so aroused by this. His hands push my thighs wide apart and pin them to the mattress. Just being opened for him makes my body thrum with lust. My breasts ache, and my nipples tingle. I breathe deeply, trying to get enough air.

His mouth is open when he kisses between my legs, his tongue stroking and tasting until I raise my hips. My body wants a quick release. I'm desperate for it.

When he tries to push his tongue inside me, it meets resistance.

The pause is electric, a live wire sparking between us. He looks up the length of my body. I don't make eye contact.

His head lowers again, and he licks above my opening, sending shattering sensations through me. He chases the arousal by rubbing his thumb over the bead of my clit. It needs pressure and friction, and Shane knows exactly how to give me both.

I groan and hope I wasn't too loud. My breath leaves my lungs in gasps and pants. Writhing under his mouth, I try to keep myself from begging.

He's relentless with his sucking and licking until my body's on the very edge of orgasm. Finally, his thumb rubs back and forth over me with so much pressure I explode. The waves roll over me like ten-foot swells.

It's better than it's ever been when I've done it to myself.

My heart leaps in my chest as the ripples continue through me, making my core clench and release over and over. The spiral of plea-sure eases slowly, and I melt back into the mattress.

Shane crawls up my body and stares down into my eyes, searing my mind with his intensity. "You're too tight for me to tongue-fuck."

I turn my head to look away. Virgin is a word I don't want to say. I decide instantly I won't admit it unless he forces me to. For me, still being a virgin is synonymous with my pariah status in high school, which persisted even after Shane and Declan were long gone.

He lowers his body onto mine, so we're skin-to-skin and his hard-on presses between my legs. He shifts so it's resting right in the seam, cradled there by my soft lower lips that are wet and sticky from his mouth and from how much I want him.

"Still a virgin." He grinds against me, making my traitorous hips circle. "It's mine to take," he husks. "From now on, don't even look at another guy. No one touches you between your legs, Avery. Not even you."

13

SHANE

I wake at seven in the morning, and my first thought is I want to take Avery's virginity.

Finding I'm alone in the bed is probably a good thing because this is not the place I should do it. I get up and throw my clothes on, hitting the bathroom before I head downstairs to find her.

In the kitchen, Pops sits at the table as Avery pours him coffee. Her face is washed, hair combed. Pretty, pristine, perfect. She's back in the blue dress, of course, but her heels are still in the corner where I tossed them.

Pops and Avery seem cozy as they have coffee. She's smiling and polite, but the abandon she had while laughing last night is gone. I wonder if he notices. Probably does. Pops doesn't miss much.

When she sees me, she smiles, and that hits me in a way I don't expect. For an instant, I'm struck again by the magnetic pull between us. No matter the history, our chemistry does not die. In response to the smile, I wink, trying not to give away the thoughts circling my head.

I pour myself coffee, just to give myself something to do until I can get my shit together. She continues talking to Pops about some class she's got. He's acting like he's a dinosaur when it comes to tech stuff, which he isn't. This is his way of drawing her in. He asks her questions and acts impressed. In return, she's charming. It's a dance.

In reality, he's got people to do all the business things that need to get done, including the tech side of things. She seems to be under the impression that his billion-dollar empire is being run from the docks and the backs of warehouses. A fraction definitely is, but any kind of business, even an illegitimate one is high-tech or it wouldn't survive a week these days.

She talks about creating the optimal customer experience through a cascade of automated emails. "The person gets different ones depending on what he clicks." she says. "It's 'choose your own adventure' in email form."

"That's quite a thing, it is," Pops says admiringly.

I smirk down into my mug, thinking about Pops sending out a canned selection of emails, or any emails at all. What might they say? Last week, we broke a guy's hand for skimming. Click here if you want to read the terms of service for our enterprise and how theft will cost you more in the long run. Click the second button below to update your health insurance in case there's an emergency surgery in your future.

I chuckle, and when I turn, they're both giving me a questioning look. I shake my head. "Nothing."

Pops leans toward Avery and says, "I'd like to know more about newsletter businesses."

My eyebrows rise at this.

She smiles, ever the teacher's pet. "I'd be happy to forward you some things I designed for my e-commerce class. They're not as sophisticated as what giant companies have, but it would give you a feel."

"Hey," I say, inclining my head at the window. "We've gotta table this for now. If we're going to make it back to school in time, we need to hit the road."

"Right," she says, standing. "Mr. Sullivan, thank you again. I had a really great time. And I'll send the emails to Shane, so he can forward them to you."

Pops stands as well. "No need. Shane will bring you when he comes for dinner next week, and you'll show me yourself."

"Oh, yes, maybe," she murmurs vaguely, putting on her shoes.

I chug a few more swallows from my mug and dump the rest into the sink.

Avery does the same and washes both mugs quickly and puts them in the drying rack. Pops watches her with a smile and winks at me. He has very definite ideas of the way men and women should take care of each other, so of course he approves.

He'd also approve of the fact that she's still a virgin at eighteen. But that's a fact he's never going to know. No one is. That's between her and me.

We all walk to the front door, and I shake his hand. She gives him a brief hug and then slips out as soon as the door's open.

Outside, our bodies brush against each other as I open the passenger door for her.

Her cheeks are flushed from the cold and possibly more. Last night when I discovered she's a virgin, it was like stumbling across buried treasure. Rare, unexpected, hidden and secret. I wanted to know why she's got such little experience. But Avery was hesitant to talk about it. Instead, she gave me a blow job to reciprocate for the orgasm I gave her, and then we both crashed.

Today, her persistent innocence is the only topic of conversation that interests me. I love everything about the fact that I've got a second chance at being what I always wanted to be. Avery's first. The one who teaches her about sex. The one who makes her come for the first time when a cock's inside her. I want her to learn how good sex can feel, and for the sex between us to be the best she ever has. Where Avery's concerned, I basically want to be all things...first, best, and—if I'm being completely honest about my fantasies from back then—the only one ever.

As I pull out of the drive, I say, "You didn't answer me last night when I said—"

She cuts me off in a tone that's low but accusatory. "Are you working for him, Shane?" The sweet girl from the kitchen is suddenly nowhere to be seen. This version of Avery is clear-eyed and sharp. "Is that why you need a locked room in your house?"

Her tone leaves a lot to be desired, considering she's asking questions I've already said aren't open for discussion. "My business is none of yours, remember?"

She stiffens and turns her head to stare out the passenger window.

"Now you're upset?"

"No." Her voice is cool, and very clearly upset. "As you said, it's none of my business. Thanks for reminding me."

I blow out a breath as I enter the expressway. "What's between you and me is—" I'm about to say new when she cuts me off again.

"There's nothing between us." She continues to look at the road instead of me, which I don't like. "Last night was fun."

Fun? My lip curls in distaste.

I don't like the pattern that's emerging. My fingers tighten on the steering wheel when what they'd really like would be for me to pull over, yank her dress up and spank her gorgeous ass on the side of the road while cars pass. My cock hardens at the thought of owning her that way.

"That's as far as I go, by the way," she adds, not helping me talk myself out of punishing her for real. "No more pushing boundaries."

When I reply, my voice is level, even though calm is not what I feel. "What do you mean by that?"

"I mean, let's stick to the agreement. I'll do what I promised and that's all. No more sex-capades or falling asleep together in the same bed."

This is not the day we're supposed to have after last night. "Why are you still a virgin? You planning to save yourself for marriage?"

"No." She blows out a breath like she's impatient with the conversation. "But I don't want my first time to be with you."

My temper's fuse burns to the end, sparking into a full-blown flame instantly. I manage to keep my voice neutral, but it takes serious effort, and I'll be surprised if my steering wheel's not bent in the process. "Why is that?"

Her voice softens when she speaks, like she's a little wistful. "I want to be in love with whoever it is."

Love. That's not something I can deliver like flowers or a gold bracelet. I shift into third, glancing over at her. She seems serious, which I find strange. If she's such a puritan about sex, why did she agree so quickly to barter oral sex for protection?

"So how does that work?" My tone is genuinely curious. "If you don't fall in love, you stay a virgin forever? And all your boyfriends have blue balls till they give up and end things with you?"

She rolls her eyes, but her gaze flickers toward me for a moment, possibly recognizing that her plan to withhold sex until she's in love may interfere with her ability to find it.

"I don't know." Her fingers smooth down her dress, which causes me to catch a glimpse of her bare knee. Those legs were spread for me last night. I want them to be again.

"Maybe I won't wait till I'm in love," she murmurs. "I haven't been in a serious relationship yet. I guess I'll see how I feel at the time." Avery pushes her hair back over her shoulder and shrugs. "Anyway, it's college, and I'm a normal person with normal feelings. I'm sure I'll be able to find someone to fall in love with."

She says this casually, but for me, it's a dark veil descending on my plans. I put her in a box, one she's apparently been in since high school, and now she's trying to climb out of it.

In high school, when she was fifteen, I made it known that touching her would lead to bloody consequences. Then after the basement incident, when she was frozen out socially at school, she went through some sort of meltdown. She buzzed off her hair and dressed in jeans and black hoodies every day, like a subversive punk singer with a grunge singer wardrobe. High school, not known for its tolerance of anything weird, doubled down on keeping her isolated.

I figured after I graduated and wasn't around, she'd go back to normal and start dating. She did grow her hair back, but then she adopted a studious, no-nonsense style that was not exactly begging for male attention. The status quo of her being single continued. Which suited me. I may not have wanted her in my life, but I still never wanted to imagine her in another guy's bed. Even so, until last night, I'd assumed she'd been with *someone*.

Now she's pairing the 'girl next door' look with her diligent smart girl ways. Some guys will miss the point, but plenty of others won't.

I think about the old man's warning that she's an irresistible draw. In the sapphire dress, she was for me last night. Breasts threatening to slip out for a peek at the room, overlapping folds of her skirt separating to flash smooth thighs, practically begging for my hand to reach in to stroke her pussy.

Yeah, no. If I want her, I need to build new walls around her. And I do fucking want her. More than ever.

Her phone buzzes, and she looks at a text.

"What in the world?" she murmurs. Her brows pinch together, and her head turns in my general direction. "Why are members of the dance team inviting me to a party?"

Yeah, the Platinum Party. I need to make an appearance behind the scenes, since I'm supplying the liquor. I could skip the main event, though. Blowing it off would give me more time alone with Avery at my house, which appeals to me way more than any party. On the other hand, I could use it as an opportunity to raise the walls.

"Right, the party." I force a casual tone. "I forgot about that. We're going. After class, I'll take you shopping and buy you a dress."

"You're not buying me clothes."

"You're not staying home alone at my place, and the party's got a theme. So, unless you've already got a platinum-colored dress, you need one."

She frowns, then nibbles on her bottom lip. My mouth really wants a chance to do that.

"I don't do that kind of dress-up anymore."

I'm not sure what she means, but I don't want to get mired down. "Tonight you do, since you're coming with me."

Her sapphire gaze slides over to my face. "I *can* stay home alone."

"Not in my house you can't."

"Are you worried I'll break into your secret room?"

That hadn't even occurred to me. "I'm not worried about anything."

She wrinkles her nose. "It's not the kind of thing...I'm not good at those kinds of events."

"Sure, you are. In public, you're always on. Just like you were this morning with Pops. You've got a game face that you wear when necessary."

Avery's cheeks hollow as she sucks them in, pursing her lips. "I don't like being forced to wear it."

There's something deeper. I'm about to ask her, when she shifts gears like it's her hand on the stick.

"The dance team, how are they texting me?"

"Yeah, we mentioned you to Declan's ex, Eden. You're alone too much," I say.

Not that Avery needs Eden and her squad for company on campus anymore, since I've taken up bodyguard duty.

"It was a nice gesture, but you didn't need to do that. I have friends. I just haven't had time to cultivate those relationships. My schedule this semester is crazy." Her voice is soft, but also a little defensive.

"Nothing wrong with working hard. I just figured it couldn't hurt to have some female upperclassmen take an interest."

She licks her lips and nods, her expression softening. "I appreciate it."

"So tonight? That's settled?"

She grimaces. "I guess so. Yes."

There are layers to her that I don't understand. Yet.

I wonder if she realizes she's thrown down the gauntlet by claiming she'll only give up her virginity if she's emotionally invested. Rising to the occasion isn't just something my cock does. It's one of my defining characteristics.

❧ 14 ❧

AVERY

My world is officially spinning out of control.

Shane will neither confirm nor deny that his grandfather is in charge of the Irish Mafia, which almost certainly means he is. This is a terrible development because it means the darkness inside Shane, that he's often alluded to, is much blacker than I imagined.

Pieces shift slowly into place. The gun. The fights. His calm confidence when promising to deal with the man who splashed me with rose water. The Shane I've known is an illusion. The handsome, quick-witted boy who carried my science project sandbags seems to have been a cover for who he really is. I can't even wrap my head around that. Mafia is synonymous with murder-for-hire, right? Has Shane actually killed someone?

My mom texts several times. I assure her I've left Mr. Sullivan's and am safely back at school. Beyond that I don't know what to say to her yet. I'm noncommittal in my texts. I need to talk with her and Ethan. Like Shane, there's a lot they've been hiding from me.

Meanwhile, I'm having an off-the-rails shady Cinderella day.

MARLEE WRAY

Shane has a personal shopper waiting for me at an upscale department store. She seems to understand her assignment better than I do because within forty minutes, I've tried on five dresses in silvery shades, and one has been charged to Shane's account.

Next, he drops me off at a spa appointment that some unnamed assistant made for me. I'm exfoliated, waxed, and covered in nourishing body butter. My skin feels amazing, and my pussy feels very, very bare.

As I'm leaving the spa, I recognize some trust fund girls from school. For them, it's a day of pampering. For me, it was something else. I feel like a harem girl who's been groomed for her big night with the sultan. Which isn't to say the scalp massage wasn't fantastic. I might start donating plasma to afford another one.

When I emerge, Shane's leaning against his car, waiting. His gaze rakes over me, seemingly taking inventory of his property.

Give some men an inch, and they take a mile.

"It was one orgasm," I whisper, giving him a salty expression.

"Pardon?" The word is prep-school polite, but his tone holds a dangerous challenge.

In return, my tone is 'you need to take me seriously' firm. "Don't treat me like your trophy wife, Shane. I'm not that girl."

My hand reaches for the car door's handle, but his catches it. His hand is so much bigger it closes over mine entirely.

"That's a shame." From his tone it's clear my accusation doesn't trouble him. "I've never been in the market for a trophy girlfriend before, but you'd make a good one." He leans forward, so his mouth is near my ear. When he speaks, his voice is low and teasing. "Did you let them wax it? Or did you keep your curls?"

I want to kill him, but for some reason, I laugh softly, even as my face flames with embarrassment. So that wasn't just part of a generic spa package he bought; Shane actually told them he wanted me waxed. Unbelievably high-handed.

And his implying that I could've said no increases my discomfort. It didn't occur to me to refuse. Why didn't it? Maybe because a part of me is starting to feel like I *am* one of Shane's possessions.

I purse my lips and give him a little shake of my head. "That information is need-to-know, and you don't."

It's his turn to chuckle. "Challenge accepted."

SHANE

"Avery! Let's roll."

What the hell is she doing for over an hour? Stalling so I'll leave without her? Not going to happen.

I flex my wrists impatiently. I need time to supervise the unloading of the liquor, and the clock's ticking. Plus, I'm losing interest in the big reveal. The only outfit I really want to see her in is nothing.

My phone buzzes with another agitated text from the frat's high-strung treasurer. Is he wired on coke or what?

I send a text to see where Sorensen is. He can take possession of the crates and bring them in. I'm the only one who'll be unboxing the bottles for the VIP room, but the second and third tier stuff is good to go. Letting the asshole treasurer get his hands on those lesser bottles would probably settle him down.

Heels clicking on the stairs brings my gaze up instantly. The platinum dress is a goddamned ball gown, and it's sexy as fuck. There's a deep plunging neckline that a man could reach inside to squeeze a breast. The skirt's loose and made of two panels that allow high slits to open practically to the hip. I could reach inside the skirt too, to stroke her pussy.

The dress is worth every penny I paid. My tongue touches my top lip. My face could get into the skirt in a heartbeat too, to give my tongue what it's dying for. Another sweet taste of her and another shot at pushing deep into her virgin pussy.

I drag my eyes up to her face and pause. She's done something with her makeup that hits me below the belt as well. Shimmery silver and charcoal on her lids and lashes so thick they must've been glued on. She looks like a doll. A very, very sexy one.

I think I know why she looks so flawless. She's put on pageant makeup, which is something I've never seen her wear. She doesn't need makeup at all, but I like that she's gotten so dolled up for a night out with me.

"So, you're lucky," I say, raking my gaze over her slowly for emphasis. "It was worth the wait."

She flashes a smile, her lips a shimmery pink and paler than usual. They're innocent-looking lips, which makes me think about other innocent lips. My cock is rock fucking hard.

For the first time in my life, I understand why men buy trophy wives. I want to own Avery, from the roots of her glossy hair to the tips of her polished toes. I want an all-access pass to her body, so every pretty little hole has to surrender to my cock.

My muscles clench, and my gaze flickers to the couch. I could fuck her on it right now. Or bend her over it.

In my pocket, my phone buzzes, making me think of vibrators. Teasing her with one could push her over the edge into letting me do *really* dirty things. That's a temptation I won't resist forever.

Another buzz from my phone. I don't have time for sex now, but later...

I reach into my pocket to adjust my aching dick before I pull my phone out. Glancing down, I read Sorensen's text. He's walking over and is about three minutes out from the frat house. Good.

Avery passes me, and I fall in step. When she reaches the front door, I move forward to pull it open for her. Outside, I guide her to the car and put her in the passenger seat.

As I walk around the car, I call Sorensen and ask him to do me the favor. He doesn't speak until I'm finished. Then all he says is, "Sure." Often, the guy's only slightly more verbal than the monolithic rocks he resembles.

When we arrive, cars are lined up at the Lambda Delta house. I skip the line with a wave at the valet. "Moran. I'm parking in back."

He moves the orange cones, so I can drive through to the rear.

My hand drops to Avery's thigh and squeezes. "You made us late. How are you going to make up for that?"

Avery's head turns, causing the loose strands of her hair to sway.

Her eyes search my face, her expression dubious. After a moment, she says, "What did you have in mind?"

My smile's wicked. "I don't think you want my advice on that. You remember last night, right?"

The rising color in her cheeks tells me she remembers plenty about the way I forced her over my lap for spanking.

Her fingers lace together, hands clutching each other. "I believe I said no more games like that."

"If you don't want to be punished, you shouldn't be a bad little girl."

Her lips part, and she licks them. "Being late to a party is not a big deal."

My mouth curves into a smirk as I note she doesn't tell me not to call her a bad little girl. By day, she pretends to be a straight A, strait-laced coed, but with me, she's something else entirely.

"You'd think being late is no big deal, but sometimes it is." I pull in and spot Sorensen in the doorway. The truck's gone, so the crates are inside. "Stay in the car a minute. I'll take you in the front door so you can make an entrance."

Her brows draw together in consternation. "I don't want to. I'll just come in with you."

I'm surprised. Why wouldn't a girl who looks like she does tonight want a big entrance? "Not through the back. But if you want a low-key arrival, that's fine."

The tension in her shoulders eases, and she nods.

"You don't like parties?"

Her gaze shifts away from me, staring into the middle distance. "Depends," she murmurs.

I stroke her jaw with my thumb. My girl has secrets. I want in on them. "Wait here. I'll be right back."

AVERY

SHANE LEAVES THE CAR, BUT HIS PRESENCE LINGERS. THE FAINT scent of soap and spicy cologne, the memory of the timbre of his voice when he implied I owe him a sexy payback for taking so long to get ready. It would be easy to get swept up in the moment.

But the night is a ticking time bomb that could lead to an explosion of bad memories. I flick a finger against the inside my wrist. The pain helps distract from anxiety.

Let it go, Elsa.

Maybe this party is exactly what I need. Immersion therapy, of sorts, with Shane's larger than life presence creating a different focus.

As he emerges from the doorway, I admire the cut of his suit and the way he looks in it. Handsome. Powerful. Rich. The suit must have cost ten times what my dress did. Shane seems to have plenty of money, probably from shady deeds done for his grandfather. Monster, indeed.

He opens my door and holds out his hand. I take it, and my stomach flutters. Every time he touches me, I feel it to my core. Gooseflesh rises as I ease out of the seat and feel the heat of his body as I come into contact with him.

The night is pretty, but cold. The smell of smoke from a grill and the more subtle scents of fallen leaves being churned into soil waft by.

Shane slides an arm around my shoulders and pulls me against his side. The warmth of his body is welcome. "The side entrance isn't far."

We turn a corner and follow a narrow path.

He checks the side door and, finding it unlocked, pushes it open. I step in and onto a dimly lit landing. Behind us, he locks the door.

"Finally a dark corner I can use. I'll take a kiss." His voice is low and sexy and seems to curl right into my body from my belly down to the V between my legs.

I squeeze my thighs together, pressing the spot that hums with anticipation. "No kissing." I sound winded. "We decided, remember?"

"No." Shane's breath smells faintly of liquor, and I realize he must have had a drink when he was in the house. His lips brush against mine, soft and tantalizing. "Live dangerously."

Don't, caution whispers. But I do. When his lips press against mine, my mouth opens for him. The tip of my tongue touches his, and he strokes it slowly, penetrating my mouth and staking his claim.

He tastes of whiskey. Sexy and delicious.

Three years of wondering what this would be like finally comes to a close while we're cloaked in formal wear and darkness, standing in secret on a frat house landing.

The kiss is dangerously perfect.

One of his hands presses against my back, gathering me to him. His body is warm and solid, and mine melts against it.

The way we explore each other's mouths is unhurried and laced with lust. My arm snakes around him, too. A hand slips under his suit jacket, so I can feel his back through the soft fabric of his shirt.

Several moments pass, every one warmer than the one before, until I'm flushed and aching for him. His grip on me tightens, anchoring me against his hard body as the kiss turns deeper and more demanding.

The noise of heavy footfalls coming down stairs shatters the moment. Shane raises his head with a low growl.

Male voices, loud with excitement, are nearby and then recede.

Alone again in the darkness, we're hidden from view. He adjusts the front of his trousers, which I'm guessing are barely concealing his erection.

A little thrill of power courses through me, and I smile. "Was the kiss enough?"

"It was." He pauses, tilting his head so his eyes glint in the moonlight streaming through the window. "And it wasn't."

My chuckle is soft, not wanting to give away our position to anyone nearby. "I meant, was that enough to make up for keeping you waiting?"

"Yeah, it'll do."

His casualness dims the joy of a moment ago. I don't know what else I want from him. More charm? More romance? More...something.

A light flicks on nearby, illuminating our nook. We're still hidden, except from each other's eyes.

More footfalls on the stairs. "I say we should do a shot of that Rebel-knock 45 from Moran before we're too drunk to know the difference." By the sound of the guy's voice, I'd say he's already past the point of "too drunk."

"No, that's for tomorrow night." This voice sounds sharper. Or at least less inebriated. "We'll fire up some Cubans and each have a glass to celebrate."

"You locked both bottles in the safe?"

"Yeah."

When they leave the stairs and move away, I raise my brows at Shane.

"Are you dealing in liquor? You're not even twenty-one."

"Must be another Moran," he says casually.

Liar.

He takes my hand and starts to thread our fingers together. I draw my arms back, hugging my waist with them.

"Rebel Knock is whiskey?" I ask.

"I think what he meant to say was reibiliúnach."

"Which is Irish for?"

"Rebel." His smirk is irresistible.

I want to know his secrets. I wish I didn't.

He leads me into a small room with an archway entry into the main one. In the brightly lit space, there are lots of women in platinum-colored dresses and men in suits. None of the dresses are as formal as mine. My mom would say it's better to be overdressed than under.

"Wait in the shadows until I signal," Shane says.

"What?" My heartbeat kicks into a gallop. He promised no grand entrance.

Before I can ask what he intends to do, Shane steps out into the main room, blending in immediately and disappearing from view.

As moments pass, anxiety ticks up within me. This feels very much like waiting in the wings to take the stage during the pageants of my childhood. Lots of effort spent so I'll look a certain way, and now every inch of me is about to be judged.

My fingers come up to make sure my lipstick isn't smeared around my mouth. Mom's features always grew so pinched over makeup smudges. Her voice echoes in my memory. "Don't lick your lips. Don't touch your face."

On the most terrible of nights, six-year-old me looked flawless. At first.

My dad finally came to a pageant, took one look at me, and started raging. He used words I'd never heard. Pimping, whore, pedophile bait. Everyone began whispering and staring.

It was my turn to take the stage for talent, and I did, only to freeze up as I watched him storm out in disgust. Red blotches of angry, embarrassed color stained Mom's cheeks. She nodded sharply for me to continue. The opening bars of *Defying Gravity* started three times before I fled the stage.

That was my last pageant, and the last time I saw my dad in person.

As the memories consume me, my heart thumps uncomfortably, and my hands grow shaky.

Mom claimed by not competing again, I was letting him "win." But for me, being dressed and made up for another pageant wouldn't have felt like a triumph. I'd never loved it, and now, under my dad's ferocious criticism, it was tainted with shame.

Mom relented and let me quit. But we would never spend as much time together again. I went to science camp, and she went on to create lots of other little beauty queens as a consultant. That was better for both of us. Mostly.

A fleeting thought of taking a picture of myself to send to Mom and Ethan passes through my mind. My mom still loves to see me dressed up, and he'd enjoy it, too. Senior year of high school, they were disappointed I didn't go to prom. The lingering effects of being frozen out socially. Boys were wary of me. And girls were icy, lest the boys think they were sympathetic. I reacted to their scorn with some of my own, sheering off my hair and dressing as an outcast. Shane asked why I'm still a virgin. How could I be anything else?

My tongue traces my lips and recalls our kiss. I dressed for him tonight. I kissed him because it's what he wanted. In high school, I'd have given anything for a kiss like that with him. His senior year, he wouldn't give me as much as a hello.

Things between us are moving fast now. A part of me loves feeling irresistible and can't get enough of it. Another part knows this could end badly. And that he shouldn't get every piece of me now just because he wants it.

Shane appears in the archway, a couple of drinks in his hands. He nods for me to join him. "Come on, baby doll, let me show you off."

Baby doll. Let me show you off.

More shades of my pageant days, and of Shane's sudden tendency to treat me like he owns me. The straps of my shoes cut into my feet, which remain frozen to the floor.

You'll come to dinner in Back Bay.

You'll come to the platinum party with me.

Obey, or I'll spank you.

Your virginity's mine to take.

Dressed. Waxed. **Kissed.**

I'm like a pretty little puppet he controls with the pluck of a string. And his magnetism is so potent it's often irresistible.

Apparently noting my frown, his expression changes, shuttering away the warmth as his eyes narrow. He strides closer, watching my face the entire time.

"What's going on?"

"A doll's life...doesn't suit me. I shouldn't have come." I try to make my voice light, but I can't. The undercurrent is angry because I'm frustrated.

His brow arches. "Again I say, what's going on, Avery?"

"Things you don't need to know. I can have a locked room, too, right?"

Moss green eyes narrow farther, and his jaw ticks dangerously. Leaning down, he whispers in my ear, "Tell me."

My skin prickles, a wave of unease coursing through me. Shane's not just tough on the outside; emotionally, he's brutally tough, too. Am I prepared to fight this fight?

"We've hurt each other a lot in the past." I blow out a slow breath, steeling myself. "Let's not risk doing it again."

"You think kissing me is risky?"

"Yes." *Because it is.*

His lips brush the angle of my jaw. "You could be right. But it's too late to turn back now."

I shudder as the sensation of his lips on my skin spirals through me. Sucking in a breath, I step back.

Shane raises a glass. "Yours. Cherry coke. No alcohol."

A lime wedge bobs atop the fizzing liquid. As I sip, I watch him warily over the rim of the frosty glass.

"Seems like there's more we need to settle. All right. We'll talk when we get home." He tilts his head, looking down the front of my dress. Again it feels like he's taking inventory, admiring the way my breasts look in the ultra-sexy bodice. "We won't stay much longer, but you promised to wear your game face tonight, Avery. So put it on." He sets my empty glass on a ledge and takes my arm, pulling me into the light.

I'm startled by the suddenness of being in the more public space. I try to retreat, but in an instant, his left arm slides around my waist, encircling it. He maneuvers my body, so my back presses against his torso. The way he's holding me is overtly possessive, and covertly oppositional.

Shane raises his glass and then his voice. "Here's to Lambda Delta Kappa being nothing but platinum."

The room erupts with cheers, and suddenly hundreds of eyes are upon us. I try to move forward so we're not touching, but his grip is firm. I'm anchored to him.

I reach down instinctively, my nails digging into his forearm. Turning my head, I study his profile.

"Shane," I whisper, the one word a warning.

"Stay still. I'm doing something. I'll explain later." Then he smiles, but not at me. He's watching the room. "Hey, send me that."

My head jerks forward, and I realize people are snapping pics. I stiffen, forcing myself not to scowl because our personal war should not be for public consumption. As I smile, my nails dig deeper. I know I must be hurting him. Under all his hard muscles, he's still flesh and blood.

His mouth moves to my ear, the whisper excruciatingly intimate. "Are you a kitten? Because only kittens get to dig their claws into me."

That's a strange thing to say since he doesn't have a cat.

His cock presses against my ass, the thin billowy chiffon not able to protect me from the feel of it. Something in my core clenches and throbs in a traitorous primal response. My body wants his. Full stop.

My mind, on the other hand, rebels, horrified that my nipples have puckered and my hips want to press backward against him. My face heats until I feel like I'm about to burst into flames. I tell my fingers to let go of him, but they won't. I'm holding on for dear life.

"You have three seconds to stop, Avery."

His soft breath caresses my ear, and I can't think, can't move. My mind is trying to convince my body to listen to me.

"Three, two, one...you're in so much trouble. *Kitten*."

He pulls me a few feet to a table and sets his glass down. Then his right hand grabs my wrist and yanks my hand away from him.

When he turns me to face him, I avert my eyes. Too many emotions churn inside me. His left hand slides down to my ass. My eyes widen, and I start to reach back.

"I wouldn't," he warns. "It won't move until I decide to move it. All you'll do is draw attention to us."

My arm's motion stutters mid air, and I let it drop to my side. "Move your hand."

"I will in a second. But my hand's not what you need to worry about."

It's hard to contain everything I feel. A part of me wants to fight with him until he either lets me go or wins so unquestionably that the war waging inside me ends. My whisper is agitated. "What do I need to worry about?"

"The things I'm going to do to you when we're alone tonight."

My breath catches in my throat. I can't move or even breathe.

"Damn," a familiar voice says. "That's some brutal shit."

Shane's green eyes hold mine for a beat, then he directs his attention to the voice's owner.

As I start to turn, my gaze lands on Daniel's face. It was his voice, but he's not looking at us. He's looking up.

I follow the direction of his stare. On the second floor, a row of men stand at a half wall. Todd Bardoratch is among them. They're facing forward, studying the room below them like kings at a banquet. Each has a lavender rose in his button hole.

"What?" I murmur, confused.

"It's a salute?" Daniel sounds bemused.

"Yeah, seems like it is," Shane says grimly.

My head swims, realization dawning. "A salute...to Casanova."

15

SHANE

As soon as Declan approaches, I let Avery slip from my grasp. My eyes track her as she joins a line for the bathroom, but then Dec's deep frown demands attention.

"What the hell is going on?" His disapproving tone is no surprise.

For two years, my stance on the home front was unchanged, and he backed my play every single day. Which at the beginning, when I moved in with him, was the only thing that kept me from feeling completely isolated.

"Pretty much what it looks like," I say. My tone is mild, almost joking, though if anyone deserves a serious explanation, it's Declan.

Movement upstairs causes my eyes to shift. To his left, Todd Bardoratch has a pit fighter who goes by the nickname Cyborg. Is the guy here on bodyguard duty, watching Bardoratch's back? If so, I have to give Bardoratch credit for his countermove.

Dec leans closer, and light glints off his white gold designer tie bar. It retails for five grand, which I know because it was the gift I included when I paid him back the seed money he gave me to start our joint venture. The white gold complements the black and platinum silk tie he's wearing to conform with the night's theme.

Declan lowers his voice so he can speak without others overhearing. "I meant what's the deal with Avery Kershaw?"

"Yeah, so did I. She's with me tonight." *And for the foreseeable future*, I add in my own head.

His brows rise. "When did the goal of staying away from her change?"

"Yesterday."

"Because?" He's using his chairman-of-the-board voice, which demands answers. If anyone else took that tone with me, I'd shut the conversation down in a heartbeat, by force if necessary. But Dec gets a pass.

My gaze flickers up to the purple rose guys for a second and then back to Declan. "Is your stepmother trying to set you up with Avery?" It's my voice's turn to use a Heyworth chairman-of-the-board tone.

A groove appears between his dark brows as they draw together in confusion. "Not that I know of. Why do you ask?"

"You don't know a thing about it? What's the word on the home front? Is your stepmother in touch with mine?"

"My stepmom and yours are BFFs, which I saw coming from the first time they met." He rolls his eyes and shifts his weight. "But I've made it clear that Avery Kershaw is not welcome company. My dad and his wife know I don't want her around."

"So why would the stepmothers think matchmaking you guys would work?"

Declan frowns, leaning back defensively. "Who says they do?"

"You haven't heard about a Moran-Heyworth ski trip?"

He looks genuinely confused. "A Heyworth-Moran ski trip? No. *My* family is going to the house in Aspen for Christmas." He nudges me with a fist. "You're welcome to come, of course. I'd be glad if you did. Since it's before the championship game, I won't be skiing."

I smile at Declan's giving the Heyworth name top billing when he answers. His family always thinks about whose name is highest on the door. "Your dad uses the Aspen house more than you do these days. Probably doesn't always give you a heads-up on who he's invited."

He shrugs. "I'll check—"

"Nah, it's all right," I say, waving that off. "You'd never try to hook up with Avery." I watch him closely for any flicker of doubt on that score. None comes.

His hand smooths his suit lapel. "Last I checked, neither of us would."

I shrug.

"What are you doing, brother?" His tone is concerned now and trying to make me see sense. "You know you can't trust her."

After a beat, I nod. "I've taken some precautions. I have an insurance policy."

"But why waste your time with someone you know you need one with?"

"I'm not sure I know that about her."

"What?" He leans forward. "I mean...*what?*"

"What happened back then...I don't think it was ever malicious. She woke up from being blackout drunk. You know how that is. So do I. You can't even be sure what you've done, how are you gonna be sure of what other people did? She wasn't thinking straight."

Declan's brows shoot up to his hairline at my defense of her. I'm not bothered. It'll take Dec a while to stop thinking the worst of Avery, if he ever does. First, because his family's got the kind of money that leads to contested wills, messy divorces, and vicious custody battles. There have even been some mysterious deaths. The Heyworth family is like a *Game of Thrones* reality show, where blackmail and backstabbing are competitive sports. The unspoken family motto is *trust no one.*

And then there's the second reason he'll be skeptical much longer than me. He hasn't kissed her at a moment when she's trying like hell to keep her distance. If she was just out for what she could get from me, she would not play hard to get the way she is. And her mouth wouldn't taste the way it does under mine. So fucking sweet that I could make a meal of kissing her and nothing else.

There is something to us, the way there always has been, and now, after being dormant for two years, it's come back stronger than ever. Avery is meant to be mine. I don't know how long she'll belong to me, or if things will end worse than they did two years ago, but I know that right here, right now, she's mine and I cannot let her go.

I lean in, making sure I infuse some due respect into my tone because I'm about to disagree with Declan, which he doesn't get often from anyone. "I know you thought Avery let me twist because she was trying to keep attention off her own wrongdoing and because she couldn't resist feeding the drama, but that's not the way it was. It's not how she operates."

"Right." His skepticism carries some of the Heyworth arrogance, but not the full force of it because we're friends. "What do you know about how she operates?"

"Not as much as I'd like to," I quip.

His expression shifts to one of surprise. "What did she do for you yesterday?"

I smile. "Exactly."

Movement above us draws my eyes up, and time slows down because Avery is toe-to-toe with Bardoratch. From their expressions, I can tell neither wants to be friends. Then she reaches out and grabs his rose, jerking it and tearing his suit.

"Oh shit." I break for the stairs and fly up them.

By the time I reach the top, three rose guys surround her. Two of them are Lambda Deltas, which, since we're in their house, doesn't bode well for picking a fight with them.

Avery's way past the point of no return. She jerks another guy's flower from his lapel, throws it to the ground and stomps it to paste.

"How dare you?" she says, eyes blazing.

On Bardoratch's command, Cyborg reaches out to grab Avery.

I whistle, which causes Cyborg's attention to shift to me. I point at Avery and shake my head.

The guy steps back.

Todd swivels angrily toward his muscle. "I said to toss her out!"

I shoulder my way into the fray and shove Avery behind me.

"You didn't say your problem was with Moran," Cyborg says.

"What difference does that make?" Bardoratch snaps.

"Whatever he's paying you, I'll double it if you take a walk," I tell Cyborg, knowing my leverage isn't really about money. It's in the fact that he knows who I really am. Not only do I control the underground fight club where he makes serious bank, but I'm also Joe Sullivan's grandson. No amount of money from a limp dick college guy is worth taking on Boston's Irish Mafia.

Cyborg nods at me and lopes off toward the stairs. Bardoratch looks like his head might explode.

Wilson, the Lambda VP, steps forward, puffing out his chest. "Does this little bitch belong to you, Moran?" He leans close enough for Avery's hand to snake out and get his rose. She yanks it from his chest and throws it down, emerging from behind me to smash it in front of him.

She's out of fucking control.

But wild does look good on her.

Wilson's hand shoots out, like he thinks he's fast enough to put a hand on her while I'm standing right there. I sweep her back behind me so his hand gets air. Frustrated, he keeps coming. I let my fist have his nose. His head jerks back with a pop and a spray of blood. He goes down hard, landing on his ass with a thud that shakes the floor.

Bardoratch erupts with an angry challenge. "If you're not strong enough to get that little bitch under control then get out of the way."

If *I'm* not strong enough? I'm not the one whose suit she ripped. His taunt is fucking laughable. At the moment though, I'm not in the mood to laugh.

"Fuck off," I growl. "She's a hundred ten pounds and wearing high heels. Who you gonna brawl next? Some toddlers?"

Bardoratch is apoplectic with rage. "You fucking low life. You don't belong at GU, and neither does your white trash whore from the projects."

I answer that with my fist, and he takes it on the jaw and goes down flailing, knocking over a plant stand as he falls. The crash echoes throughout the upper floor.

Wilson regains his feet, and it's on. They rush me, and it's all fists flying. Declan swoops in from my blindspot and knocks a Lambda Delta flat. These guys know fuck-all about fighting, but they've got numbers on their side, so Dec and I have to dig in and let loose on them.

Then Sorensen's there, and it's over. He drives forward using his massive bulk, and the whole row falls like bowling pins.

A ton more guys come pounding up the stairs, including the LD president who barks for everyone to stand down. "What's going on, Moran?"

I'm breathing hard as I rub blood from my knuckles, but gangster rule number one is that violence is routine. When I speak it's with the casual ease of someone who doesn't worry about blood stains that aren't his own. "These guys tried to start a Casanova fan club. My girl, not a fan."

"A Casanova fan club?" The president's eyes narrow in confusion and dart to the pummeled frat boys who are trying to regain their feet and their pride.

"Lavender roses. Casanova's signature." I nod at a rose Avery's shoe hasn't met yet.

Bardoratch wipes blood from his mouth. "It was just a joke."

"Sure, missing girls, the perfect punchline," Avery says. "I don't know why there are True Crime sections in bookstores. Those stories should definitely be shelved in comedy."

"Shut the hell up, Kershaw!" Todd snaps, causing specks of his blood to tattoo the banister. "And just so you know, when Moran drops you, I'll be waiting."

"Naturally," Avery snaps back, taking a step toward him. "I'd expect nothing less from someone who'd wear a flower to gloat and glorify a sociopath."

Todd glares at her. "You have a problem," he hisses. "You'd better not go out alone."

If he knew me, my dead stare would shut him up. When I don't punch someone who needs punching, it's because I plan to catch up to him later when there are no witnesses.

Sorensen stretches out a hand and crushes first one and then the last of the two roses that were left standing. "There, Casanova Club," he says, his tone pavement flat. "Come for me, too."

Avery's eyes go from narrowed slits to saucers at Sorensen's unexpected defense. Declan just chuckles, grace under pressure as always.

"As much fun as this has been, I think it's time to go." Declan claps me on the shoulder. "Shane?"

"Yeah." I catch Avery's arm in my hand and guide her toward the stairs.

After a moment, she resists.

Stopping to look at her, I quirk a brow. "You made your point, and Sorensen put an exclamation point after it. What more do you need?"

"Nothing," she whispers, her expression fierce. "I just don't want it to look like a man's dragging me off for misbehaving."

Ah. I release her arm. "Want to pump your fist in the air while you jog down the steps in triumph? Go ahead." I smirk, though I know it'll go unappreciated.

An eye-roll is the lightest response she can manage. "No victory lap. That wasn't a victory." Avery clutches her skirt and lifts it a couple inches, so she can hurry down the stairs.

I keep pace, watching her in my peripheral vision. Declan and Sorensen follow us down. When Avery reaches the ground floor, there are several women standing in a row. As she passes, they fall in step behind her. The women are led by Eden Buchanan, the captain of the dance team.

A guy darts forward to try to stop the blond dance queen. "Eden, where are you going?"

For a petite girl, Eden has a knack for looking down her nose at others when the situation calls for it. "I'm going the same place every girl in this place should...away from here."

Her set-down is met with female applause. I doubt any of the Lam Delta's are getting laid tonight.

When we get outside, the dance team splinters off from us, heading toward the front of the house.

Eden turns and calls out, "Erik Sorensen, anytime you need a date for anything, call me."

"Or me," says another.

"Me," a third chimes in.

There's nothing flirtatious or cheerful in their tones. They're not talking to Sorensen the football superstar. They're speaking to Sorensen the flower-crusher. And doesn't that just make it sweeter?

Sorensen stares after them as their long hair and long skirts stream behind them. They stalk away like fucking Valkyries.

Once we're at my car, I open the passenger door of the Porsche. Avery hesitates, glancing at me as though she's not sure whether to make another stand, this time against the patriarchy that deems it chivalrous for a guy to open a car door for a woman. After a halting breath, she climbs in.

When I'm inside and pulling the car out onto the street, she finally speaks. "I want a gun and shooting lessons."

"No."

Avery's the last person I'd hand a gun to right now. She had no control over her emotions tonight.

Besides, guns do not belong in untrained hands, and having one might make her overconfident. Casanova undoubtedly has a way of getting in close before a woman knows to be afraid. Otherwise, someone would have heard a scream.

"Yes." Avery's voice is as firm as mine. "A gun. And lessons." Then she makes me the offer she thinks I won't be able to resist. "You can name your price."

🎎 16 🎎

AVERY

Rather than getting on the highway, Shane turns into a residential neighborhood a few blocks from the Lambda Delta house.

"Where are we going?" I demand.

"I need to make a stop on the way home. It'll only take a few minutes." His fingers drum on the head of the gearshift.

My gaze fixes on his knuckles, which are covered in dried blood that's as brown as steak sauce. I hope all of it is Todd's.

Digging through the small clutch I left tucked in Shane's car, I pull out the plastic sheaf of makeup removal wipes.

"I can't believe they wore Casanova roses." I jerk a cleansing wipe from the container and grab Shane's right hand. "They're such assholes!"

His fingers close into a tight fist as soon I start cleaning his scraped knuckles.

"Todd didn't even recognize their names. They mean nothing to him." Because Shane's silent, my gaze flicks up to his face.

His jaw is set, and he stares straight ahead at the road. Am I hurting him? The cleanser is gentle, but at the moment, I'm not.

I finish quickly and release his hand. "Well?" My fury continues to burst out in waves.

"Whose names? The missing girls?" Shane's tone is merely curious, which is much too calm to suit me.

"Yes! I know their names, where they're from, what they planned to major in. They're as important as Casanova. More so, in fact. There should be as much coverage of the missing women as there is of him."

"The focus is on Casanova because he still needs to be caught."

"No. When he's caught, which he'd better be soon, there will be endless hours spent dissecting his useless life and sharing every detail! To the media, only the man matters."

Shane grimaces, leaning his head away from me. "Lower your voice. I'm sitting right next to you."

My hand slaps the car door in frustration, and I turn my head away. "You don't get it." My voice is lower but still full of vitriol. "Of course, you don't."

Shane pulls into a driveway, and, for a second, I think it's so he can fight with me. My body goes rigid from shock and the anticipation of yet another confrontation.

When he speaks though, his voice is firm but not angry. "I do get it, Avery. I do." He turns off the engine. "I'll be right back."

He exits the car and goes to the door of a red brick house. After he knocks, the door opens, revealing the silhouette of a woman. She disappears from view and then returns, handing him a small gold gift bag.

After he puts it in the trunk, we finish the ten-minute drive home. I stay stonily silent, still stewing in my rage. Shane's countenance continues to be languid. Instead of calming me, that feeds my discontent.

Once inside the house, he sets the mysterious gift bag on the couch.

"Is it a gun?" I ask hopefully, standing a few feet away.

"No. You don't need a gun." His arms fold across his broad chest, and his gaze captures mine. "As the world saw tonight, you've already got a weapon. *Me*."

That's not good enough, I think defiantly.

Does Shane want me to stay powerless? A part of me wonders whether he wants to keep me feeling vulnerable so I'll need to stay with him and continue to be his sex toy. A little current of electricity runs through me at the thought.

But imagining Todd's smug face also makes me want to blow holes in the wall right now. Breathing through my nose, I try not to clench my teeth. "I've said I'll barter for a gun and lessons. Isn't there anything you want from me?"

His gaze rakes over me slowly. "You know there is."

My teeth grind at the thought of trading my virginity for a gun, but maybe that is what's meant to happen. All my innocence gone in one quick exchange. And good riddance to it. The world is not a place that rewards naiveté.

The next words catch in my throat, but I force them out. "So help me get a gun, and you can have it. I don't want to be reliant on anyone else's protection."

Arms folded across his chest, Shane looks impatient. "No. Guns are dangerous to their owners. Plenty of people have their own guns used against them."

"Is that the only reason you don't want me to have one?"

"Why else?" he counters, motioning with a head tilt for me to sit.

I walk over and lower myself onto the dreaded couch. Not because Shane indicated I should, but because my feet hurt from wearing heels all night. I circle my feet with a slow grimace.

Shane sits on the coffee table and rests my legs on his knee so he can unbuckle the straps of my shoes. With the straps slack, I'm free to kick them off, which I do with considerable force.

"Fuck Todd Bardoratch." A shoe bangs against the wall, leaving a mark as it drops to the floor.

"Easy. Let's not spend the night patching dry wall."

"Why was Todd's giant afraid of you? Because you carry a gun, right?"

"Avery," Shane says slowly, shaking his head.

The rage inside me makes my entire body vibrate. "Don't. Don't tell me it's all right for you to have a gun and not me."

"Listen to me."

"No." I shoot up and move around the couch toward the stairs. "If you won't help me, fine. I'll find someone who will."

"Wait," he commands.

I ignore him and hustle up the steps. Behind me, I hear his pursuit. I don't make it to the guest room before he grabs me.

"Do not manhandle me." My voice cracks from the strain of trying not to yell.

"Then control your temper."

The struggle I wage gets me nowhere, except deeper into my own frustration. Furious tears sting my eyes, and I have to blink them away.

"Enough now." His voice is louder than it's been as he lifts me from the floor and carries me into his room.

When he tosses me on the bed, I roll to the other side. I wish there was a way to knock him off balance. Tonight, I really want my own strength to mean something.

I must look ready for more mayhem, because Shane says, "If I were you, I wouldn't." His warning tone sends a shudder through me.

At the edge of the bed, I stop, looking back at him. I don't understand how he's not even breathing hard. His control pisses me off, even though I admire it.

Pushing wisps of hair behind my ears, I force myself to calm down. Shane's right. Enough is enough.

He drops the gold gift bag on the mattress. I can't believe he thought to grab it as he came after me.

His fingers pull the knob of the nightstand's top drawer, opening it. Retrieving a plastic bottle from inside, Shane tosses it on the bed next to the gold bag. As he looks at me, his expression is full of challenge.

What's this?

Leaning forward, I read the bottle's label, which reveals that it contains lubricant. It takes a moment for it to register that it's for sex.

My gaze jerks up to his face. He can't really be expecting to take my virginity right now.

"What the hell?" I push back until I'm on the opposite side of the mattress again. The skirt's billowing fabric tangles around my legs. I jerk it free, preparing for flight. My fingers crumple the fabric as I hold the panels together to keep from flashing my bare thighs.

Shane's pursed lips part, and he licks them, watching me the way a lion watches a gazelle. His expression seems to say, "Try to run. You're fast, but I'm faster."

What he actually says is, "Open the box."

Glancing at the white box that's peeking out of the gift bag, I'm still for a moment. Then curiosity gets the best of me. I slide the box out and remove its lid.

At first, I think the length of fur is a skinny stole. But when I lift it, I realize it's a faux fur tail with a tear-drop-shaped stainless steel knob on the end.

My confusion must show because he looks slightly amused as he speaks. "You wear it. The metal piece goes inside."

"Inside what?"

"It's a tail." He gives me a meaningful look. "For a kitten."

Oh, my God. My brows rise incredulously. "You're kidding."

He slides his suit jacket off and sets it over the chair. "You can go in the bathroom and put it in yourself. Or I can do that for you. Guess which I hope you choose?"

"Shane—"

"Yes?" He rolls up his sleeves.

"I'm not in the mood for games."

"You don't need to be in the mood. It's your punishment. You're going to crawl around my bed, naked except for your tail. If you're good, I'll pet you. If you're not, you can get spanked with the plug in your ass."

My heart thumps wildly. "Are you doing this just because I scratched you? Or is this because I made a scene and destroyed those purple roses?"

"It's ninety percent because you dug your nails into me and ten percent because your ass felt so good pressed against my groin *while* you were digging your nails into me. It's zero percent about anything else. The last thing I'd punish you for is crushing those roses underfoot like they were Bardoratch's balls."

"I wish it had been his balls. I wanted to hit him. Aren't you glad you did?"

He nods.

"Why didn't you keep going?"

A breath escapes as a small laugh. "It's not a movie, baby."

"I don't know what that means. You punched several of them."

"Yeah, I did." His left thumb strokes the knuckles of his right hand. "To keep them from getting their hands on you."

My head tilts, watching him closely. "What do you think they would've done to me?" It's only now that I'm even considering that.

"It depends." His expression tells me he can see in his mind's eye the exact possibilities.

I also realize I don't want to think about it. The situation began and escalated because I could not stop confronting them. I just *couldn't*. What difference does it make how they planned to hurt me? Even if I'd known, it wouldn't have mattered. My rage was out of control.

And Shane defended me, even knowing he was outnumbered. He could've left me to confront them alone, but he didn't.

I sit back on my heels, blowing out a slow breath. A lot of the anger I've been projecting onto him drains away.

"I have a couple things to say."

His palm turns up in a "keep going" gesture.

"I didn't want you to pull me into the main room the way you did."

"I know, but I had good reasons for doing it."

"Like?"

"Like I want people to think you're my girlfriend. That alone could make Casanova decide not to take you. And it will definitely prevent a lot of assholes from causing trouble for you." His green gaze burrows into me. "*Unless* you humiliate them, the way you did with the Casanova Club. Then all bets are off because when men feel humiliated, they don't behave rationally."

I stroke the fur and then put the lid back on the box.

"All right," I murmur. "I will pretend to be a sex kitten for you, but not as a punishment and not right now. I'll do it because you stood between me and five angry men. And because you didn't tell me to shut up or to stop grabbing roses, even though I was making a volatile situation worse. Why *didn't* you tell me to stop?"

The corners of his mouth lift. "Because."

I smile as well, realizing he understands exactly why it would've been wrong to stop me. I took a stand, and Shane made sure no one forced me to back down. It's why I fell for him at fifteen and why I'm falling all over again tonight.

"You should wear the tail now. It'll take your mind off how pissed you are."

"No, it won't."

"You sure you don't want to try? Anything else I do to you as punishment will make you sore."

My stomach does a little flip. "I don't...I'm not agreeing to a punishment."

"Yeah, well, when I told you to stop digging your nails into me unless you wanted to get punished, you should've stopped."

"You're not taking my virginity as punishment. I will never agree to that."

"There's more than one kind of virginity. I'll take the other one."

It takes several beats for me to realize what he's talking about. "Oh, my God, no." My heart hammers in my chest, and I shake my head. "Have you done it before?"

He smiles like the devil. "Sure."

Of course he has. "With which one? Which girlfriend let you?" I stare at his face and the way he cocks his brow shocks me. "More than one? No."

He's telling the truth; Shane's not prone to exaggeration. In fact, quite the opposite.

I don't like that he's been doing dirty things with others, but the realization reinforces everything I've always thought about him. In high school, Shane was worldly in ways other boys weren't. And that's only intensified in the past two years.

I glance at the box. He knows exactly which door to knock on to get a faux animal tail on a Friday night. Turning a girl into a pornographic cat woman is apparently par for the course with him. And whatever he does to me in bed will be something he knows how to do.

The way he spanked me comes rushing back. *Not* his first time. *Not* some random instinct he decided to indulge in. Shane knows exactly how to punish a woman to make her hurt and make her wet at the same time. It's very compelling, especially for someone like me who knows very little about sex but wants to.

Right now, he's calm and patient, reminding me again of a predator watching his prey. A shiver runs down my spine, from the nape of my neck to my tailbone.

Don't, I think, trying not to get caught in the erotic web he's spinning. I'm not supposed to be prey that's stalked and hunted. That's something I'm railing against in Casanova's case. And yet...everything is different where my stepbrother's concerned. He didn't kidnap me. I chose to be here, albeit under duress. And I'm still choosing it, for a reason other than fear.

As Shane takes his shirt off, I can't drag my gaze away. He's so gorgeous, so strong. It makes me want to touch him. I swallow against a suddenly dry throat.

"Come over here, Ave. Let me unzip your dress for you."

I rise from the bed but stand next to it. "I need to ask you a question."

"What's that?"

"Would this be between us? Our secret?"

"Yeah. I don't talk about my sex life."

"Not even to Declan?"

"Declan and I are way past the point of comparing notes, Avery. It's none of Declan's business what I do to you in bed."

I take a step forward, but my progress falters when he adds, "But there's something we need to get straight."

"Yes?"

"If you want to keep our relationship a secret so you'll seem available to Declan or anyone else, you can forget it. While you're living here, the only person you can have any kind of sex with is me."

I blink and then stare at him. "I wasn't planning to go from being a virgin to sleeping with a bunch of guys."

"Good. As long as you understand the rules."

"And you? Same rules? I'm the only one you'll be with while I live here?"

He nods and beckons me to him.

As I move closer, I draw in a shallow breath and release it. When I'm standing in front of him, I admit, "I'm nervous." My fingers tremble as I press them against his hard abs.

"Anyone would be."

"So much has happened...I think—"

"Don't think," he says, winding my hair around his hand and pulling my head back. His mouth claims mine in an all-consuming kiss that sets me on fire.

It takes a moment for me to remember my name, let alone my line in the sand. Jerking back, I shake my head. "No kissing."

"You're still trying to make that stick?"

After dragging a breath into my lungs, I say, "Yes, still. No kissing."

"But the way we do it...a kiss doesn't get any better than that," he murmurs, making me smile despite myself. His lips graze my temple as I attempt to take a step back.

My retreat fails because his hold is too strong.

"You're not gonna escape, baby." His voice is husky, driving lust into my pussy like a warm, thick lance.

My hands grip his sides, fingering his hot skin and broad muscles.

"There's a word I haven't used before now because, deep down, your body already knows. But it's time to attach the label, so you can stop fighting for control you're never gonna have." He kisses my ear before leaning back to look me in the eye. "In the bedroom—and elsewhere—I'm dominant."

I blink up at him blankly, and the corner of his mouth curves.

"So fucking innocent." His tone is soft and amused. The hardness slowly creeps back into his voice when he speaks again. "It means that in bed, you'll submit to my will."

My eyes widen as his meaning begins to dawn. "Are you saying...I won't have a choice?"

"You can set limits. But within those limits, the way I use your body is up to me."

Shane seems deadly serious. Between his sheets, I'll be his sex toy in every sense of the word, and not just because of our temporary arrangement. Exerting control is part of who he is.

Without giving me time to object, he reaches behind me and unzips my dress. His lips brush my neck as he lowers the straps. The bra falls with it, exposing me to the waist. His gaze burns as he looks at me. "Fuller than they were." His left palm cups my breast, and the sensation sends lightning bolts of need through me. "Still so beautiful."

Suddenly, all the things we need to sort out melt away.

Later. All of that can wait until later.

He picks me up, carrying me to the bed. I love the feel of his body when he moves. He sits on the edge and sets me on his lap facing him, so my knees are pressed against his sides.

"Are your nipples sensitive?" He bends his head and captures one in his mouth, sucking.

My head falls back with a gasp, and my hips circle so I'm pressing against his erection. It feels amazing.

He switches sides as I grind against his lap, suddenly frantic with lust.

"Tell me the truth." His voice is low and husky. "Two years ago, did you strip out of your clothes and lie on that couch on purpose? To see if you could tempt me into action? So I'd make you mine?" His whispers are rough against my skin.

"I don't know. I can't remember what I did, let alone why I did it."

With a small twist of his body, he repositions us so I'm lying on my back with him above me.

"That night wasn't the first time you came downstairs looking for me. You did that all the time." His big hands pin my wrists above my head as he licks my nipples. "You sought me out in a place where we'd be alone. Deep down, you knew you were looking for more than conversation."

I pull at my arms, testing his hold. His grip tightens, and freedom becomes an impossibility. Which is a relief.

Looking into my eyes, he shakes his head. "It's better that I didn't find you until morning. Your body wasn't ready to be used by a man the way I want to use it." He kisses me, sucking slowly on my tongue until

I writhe. "You're not too young now though. Over eighteen is fair game for any game I want to play."

My belly clenches, and my aching nipples bead.

He finishing unzipping the dress and jerks the billowing fabric down, practically ripping it as he does.

"Shane," I gasp.

The chiffon cloud lands in a mound on the floor, and he flips me onto my stomach, driving the breath from my lungs. I start to rise up onto my palms but a hand between my shoulder blades pushes me back onto the mattress.

"Lie still. When it's time to move, I'll tell you."

My body convulses, sinking into a twisted place of fear and excitement. He climbs from the bed and goes to his nightstand where he takes out a condom and a small black device. After he drops them on the bed, he unbuckles his belt and slides it free.

The belt falls onto the bed in a coil, like a sinister leather snake. It holds the promise of a different kind of punishment if I don't submit.

❧ 17 ❧

AVERY

It's difficult to catch my breath. Lying facedown on the bed, my thighs press together. I'm close to coming, just from listening to his rough, ruthless voice.

After Shane sheds his clothes, he rolls the condom over his cock, which looks huge. I lick my lips and then bite the tip of my finger, watching him. Pillows are stacked in the middle of the bed, a sexy and sinister pyramid.

"Pillows under your hips. Chest and face on the mattress."

My heart hammers like I'm running sprints. A part of me does want to run. Another part wants to know what every kind of sex with Shane is like.

"Need some help, Avery?"

"No." I rise onto my hands and knees and move into position. Almost as soon as I lower myself onto the pillows, a wave of fear and embarrassment hits me. Lying with my ass in the air, waiting for a taboo kind of sex, causes my face to flame. This isn't the sort of thing I ever thought about doing.

Shane puts a hand on my lower back, rubbing slowly, pressing me down against the pillows. Then he eases my underwear down and off, exposing me and making me breathlessly excited.

Sliding a finger between my lower lips, he husks, "So wet. Let's get you that way everywhere."

Something icy and slick drizzles between my ass cheeks. My hips twist. A hum fills the air, and my gaze searches over my shoulder for its source.

"Fingertip vibrator," he says, holding up his index finger to show me the dark gray device that covers the tip. "Put your head down, kitten, and close your eyes for me."

My teeth snag my lip and bite it. Then, slowly, I turn my head and lower it, letting my lids fall, plunging me into darkness.

The vibrator slides into position, buzzing against my clit.

"Oh, my God," I whisper, exhaling. The sensation's intensely good.

A different finger rubs the slippery lubricant around my ring and sinks its tip inside. I moan because it feels wildly erotic to have it there, teasing me. I raise my hips, and his whole digit presses into me. A hunger like no other grips me. My fingernails scratch the comforter.

"Knees farther apart. I want you open."

I reposition my legs, spreading wide for him. The buzz of the vibrator makes my insides hum and clench.

The back finger withdraws, and my moan gives way to a whimper.

"Mmm. Being penetrated there feels good, huh?" He bites the flesh of my ass, making it ache and throb until I squirm and try to escape. A sharp slap on the other cheek drives my belly down into the pillows.

Above me, he slides his cock between my cheeks, stroking himself in the channel. His arm slides under my hip, so his vibrator finger can tease my throbbing clit as I ride the hand beneath me. Arousal creams my lower lips as I burn with need.

"God," I groan. My hips press down, trying to help my pussy grind against his hand. "I almost want..."

"What, baby?"

"Don't do it...but, I really want to feel you inside me...in front."

"Mmm. Eventually." His breath ruffles my hair, and I quake, halfway to orgasm already.

More slippery fluid pools onto my little ring, and then his cock is there, rubbing and pressing. The broad head pushes into me, stretching me suddenly around it.

"Oh!" My body goes rigid, the pain like a lance. "No! Oh—" I try to lurch forward, but he seems to know what I'll do. One hand grabs my shoulder, anchoring me in place. His other arm tightens against my belly, his fingers cupping between my legs. There's no way to escape even an inch.

"Shane! Please, stop. Please," I whimper.

"Relax," he whispers. "Don't clench. Just stay still for me." His thumb strokes my shoulder, and he licks and kisses my shoulder blade, sending warmth through my back into my chest, even as a terrible ache radiates through my pelvis.

My staccato breath ruffles the sheets. "It's too much," I groan.

The piercing pain eases, but the feeling of being dangerously stretched remains, the burning pain making me afraid to move, or even to breathe too hard. I'm like a rubber band pulled taut and on the edge of snapping. "Please?"

"Listen to me." His voice is low, but stern. "It's intense, but you'll like it."

"How do you know?"

"I just do."

My mind can't work out whether he's just trying to convince me so he can use me the way he wants, or whether he's telling the truth.

"I'm scared."

"I know." He adds more lubricant to where we're joined, rocking his hips. Feeling him move inside me is agonizing, but also... compelling.

His legs push mine farther apart, and he activates the vibrator against my clit again. I cry out when I try to move, the friction of his cock inside me sending sharp pulses of pain mixed with sharp pulses of arousal. The sensations connect with each other in the most exquisite way.

Shane's hips move against my backside, driving his cock deeper. Having him buried inside me creates a pressure which rubs against the wall that's being seduced on the other side.

I'm helpless. And completely his.

He pulls back and thrusts again. A high-pitched cry escapes my throat, but the sensation of being impaled rips through me at the same moment an orgasm is triggered by his finger.

"Fuck," he groans. "So tight. It feels good when you clench around me as you come."

The thrusts begin slowly but are mercilessly deep. His strong hips pound against my soft, spread ass, the rhythm ruthless and gaining momentum.

My hands strangle the sheets, and my cries grow ragged, begging him to slow. He's not rough, but his body has demands it forces mine to fulfill.

It's punishment and possession, pleasure and pain. Perfect and perverse.

I spasm around him, my core clutching and relaxing rhythmically as I shriek into the mattress. He pumps in and out, his need for release like a snake coiling in my belly, sinking its fangs into me. It's so painful, but also maddeningly enthralling...and somehow exactly what I crave.

When the aftershocks of my orgasm fade, he's found his rhythm. A part of me desperately wants to escape, but that's impossible. Concentrating on the way it feels to have him surging into me, I try to hold on.

He lurches forward, lowering his body on top of mine. His forearms slide under me, one across my throat, the other beneath my breasts. I'm trapped and so, so helpless. My whimpers and cries are involuntary, almost animal.

His movements are instinctive, too. His hips grind against the delicate cushion of my ass as he drives into me. His arms squeeze me so tight I can't breathe. For a moment, it's like having a great python wrapped around me. I'm slowly being crushed.

My clit rubs against the pillow, also trapped and excruciatingly sensitive. Another wave of arousal hits me, making me dizzy. I gasp for breath. His hips jerk over and over in hard pulses as he groans and curses. His cock surges deep and throbs within me.

"Fuck."

The jerking thrusts hurt, but also intensify the surreal sensuality of being taken this way. I'm desperate for breath as the world falls away.

Shane's grip loosens.

I feel shattered and lightheaded, drenched in sweat that's both mine and his. My muscles shake and twitch, so spent they don't work properly.

"Mmm. Baby, you are unbelievable." He pulls his arms free and leans his face against the side of mine, kissing me as he pulls out.

It's over. The cool air chills my skin as he retreats.

He climbs from the bed, leaving me before I'm ready. I shift, falling off the pillows and burying my face in my forearms. My eyes brim with tears that spill silently over my lashes. Shock has me in its grip. The pain is still there, hidden and aching, but the emptiness isn't better. My tiny hole feels sore and soft and swollen, and also very well used by the hard cock I find so delicious. This orgasm was like nothing I've felt before. More soul-shattering and raw than when he used his mouth. More intense, in fact, than anything *ever*.

The bed sinks from his weight when he returns.

"Hey," Shane whispers, stroking my hair and the back of my neck. "Look at me."

The directive falls on deaf ears. I've started shivering and can't seem to stop. Communication is beyond me right now.

"Avery." He slides his arms around me and drags me to him, so my body's pressed to his side, my face and arms tucked against his chest and under his arm. Blankets are pulled into place, burying us in a warm cocoon. My shivering eases.

"Baby? You all right?" There's gentleness in his voice I've never heard before.

Tension seeps slowly out of me. "I think so."

"Do you want something to drink? Water?" His weight shifts, like he'll disappear again.

My grip on his chest turns fierce. "No. Stay here."

"I'm not leaving." He kisses the top of my head. And then kisses it again. "You were brave to trust me to do that to you." His slow caress of my lower back is soothing. "It shouldn't surprise me. When we're alone, you always trust me." His voice grows even softer. "I missed that. For two years."

His hand cups the back of my head and strokes my hair like he's petting me. Like a kitten. Like *his* kitten.

SHANE

AT TWO IN THE MORNING, I WAKE. I'M ALONE, WHICH IS EVERY kind of wrong.

The thought that Avery might have left the house makes me roll out of bed, my feet hitting the rug with purpose. I stalk down the hall, and as I pass the guest bathroom, the scent of shampoo and bath gel is strong. That's promising since if she took a long bath, she's probably still here.

In the guest room, Avery's safe and asleep, her hair still damp and smelling like coconut shampoo. My bed's the more comfortable of the two, so I scoop her up and carry her back down the hall. She's wearing a t-shirt and yoga pants that are almost as soft as her skin. When I set her back in the bed, she stirs. I climb in as she rolls onto her side away from me.

"Go to sleep," I say, spooning her with my nose practically against her scalp.

I guess I drift off because the next time I'm awake, her hands are pushing back against my ribs. I'm hard, and my cock's pressed against her ass until she scoots to the edge of the bed to escape.

I draw in a slow breath and look at the clock. Three thirty.

"Come back," I say, my arm snaking around her waist. I tug her to me.

She puts her hands back to create a barrier between us right where my cock is trying to nestle into the crevice between her ass cheeks. Her hands literally cock-block me, which makes me smile.

I roll onto my back, so the only part of me that's touching her is the arm that's under her neck. She rolls onto her other side to face me, and possibly to protect her ass from another invasion.

"My cock gets hard on and off all night. I'm not expecting you to do anything about it. It'll go down on its own."

"It's not like that because I'm here?"

So innocent...mostly. "Your being here definitely makes my cock hard on the regular, but you didn't cause this one."

My eyes close. I feel her sit up, the warmth of her skin against my arm suddenly gone.

"If you're thinking of leaving my bed, you're wasting your time. I'll just carry you back again."

"Why?" she whispers.

That's a decent question, but I'm too tired to get into the answer. "Come on, Ave. Lie back down and go to sleep."

Her cool hand comes to rest on my face. I kiss her palm, eyes still closed.

"Why are you really doing this?" Her voice is almost inaudible.

"Doing what?" I mumble, trying to get my eyes open since we're clearly not done talking. When I finally get my lids up, I find her sapphire eyes staring at me. "What?"

"I can't, Shane."

"What can't you do?" Sleep still hasn't let me out of its grasp, and her lingering touch on my cheek isn't helping me think straight. "Sleep in the same bed with me?"

"Yes." Her expression is grave as she pulls her hand back, crossing it over her chest to grab her upper arm. A defensive position if I ever saw one. Trouble is, her arm also does wonderful things for her breasts —pushing them up and stealing my attention.

"Can we have this fight after sunrise?" I don't want to have this fight at all, but if I can push it back until we've both slept, I'll handle myself, and her, better.

"Does it have to be a fight?" Her glossy hair falls forward, hiding her face. "I've drifted into the deep end of the pool. I don't like being in over my head."

That gives me pause. I may be a man who's half asleep, but, in this bed, it's my responsibility to take care of her, especially tonight. "Because of the kind of sex we had?"

Her teeth catch her lower lip again, biting down.

"Don't tell me you didn't enjoy it." Under the sheet, I nudge her with my knee. "You came twice with me inside you."

Her face flushes, and she looks away. "Yeah. Scary." Burrowing her toes into the covers, she shivers. "If I get too close to you, when you cut me out of your life, it could derail me."

When I cut her out? That's a certainty?

"What do you want me to promise, Avery? That we'll always be friends?'

"No." Her brows pinch together skeptically. "Look, I went to the guest room, *my* room. Why am I back here?"

"I wanted you in my bed. All night."

"So unfair."

Rubbing my eyes, I draw in a breath. "Come on. It's no accident you sought me out and gave in so easily to a bullshit proposal like sucking my dick for a place to stay. You want this, too. You're here to play out some Beauty and the Beast fantasy with me. And I'm here for it."

Her brows rise. "Beauty and the Beast?"

"Sure. She's innocent. He's angry. She enters his house voluntarily, gets trapped. Has to submit to his rule. That's us right now." My hand reaches out and fingers a silky strand of her hair.

"This isn't a fairy tale. I'm not your captive, Shane."

"No? Try to go." My hand catches her wrist and tightens around it.

She slaps my arm. "Don't play."

I'm not playing, but I don't say so. Instead, I continue to grip her wrist as I ask, "You don't like the analogy?"

"No."

"Liar." I smile. "Ask yourself this, baby. Who does the beast belong to?"

Deep blue eyes bore into me. "Beauty?"

I watch her for a moment and nod.

A small smile threatens to emerge, but she manages to suppress it.

"You're not going to tame me, Avery. But don't assume you're going to lose me either. For better or for worse, right now, we own each other."

"Own," she repeats with a grimace.

"I call it as I see it."

Sighing, she runs her fingers over my throat. I feel every fucking touch from her down to my bones, like pain and its cure at once.

I stroke her hair and pull until she's lying next to me. When we're curled up together under the covers, I start to drift off. She whispers something I don't catch, causing me to mumble we'll talk in the morning.

A loud alert sounds on my phone.

For fuck's sake.

Storm warning? At the second blast, I roll toward the nightstand and lift my cell.

Two words flash. Perimeter alarm.

I tap the camera feed. Sometimes a raccoon climbs up the house and sets it off.

My eyes narrow, focusing on what's moving. It's no animal. A shadowy figure—a man—carries something toward the house.

Intruder.

𝕾 18 𝕭

SHANE

My body jerks into action, sitting bolt upright and launching itself from the bed.

"What's wrong?" Avery asks, sitting up.

"Someone's on the property." I yank on jeans and grab my gun from the nightstand. "Stay here."

Flying down the steps and darting out the side door, I'm confronted by the cold night. When I round the house, the smell of gasoline hits me.

The guy's splashing gas from a can on my house. When the sound of my footfalls alerts him to my presence, he drops the can and bolts.

I chase him, stopping short of the fence as he starts over. I take aim and fire. His body jerks from my shot, and he falls into the neighbor's yard. But before I can advance, my shadow flashes on the fence, illuminated from a light behind me. Spinning, gun up, my eyes burn from the flames licking at the bricks of my house.

Motherfucker.

And Avery's inside.

I sprint to the house and turn on the hose. Spraying down the bricks and grass continuously dampens the flames but costs me time. I don't know how bad the asshole's hit. He may get away.

Flames out, I curse in frustration. I head toward the fence, pulling my gun again.

"Shane?" Avery calls from the side of the house.

Jesus. Avery came outside while things were burning and while my gun was drawn. Worse is that I didn't realize. I engage the gun's safety and tuck it away, circling to her.

"Get back in the house, baby," I say, careful to keep my voice level as I jog over to her and yank the side door open.

She precedes me inside, but I stalk into the kitchen right behind her.

"I'll be right back," I promise as I grab a flashlight from a drawer.

Back outside and shining the light, I survey the property. There's black soot on the bricks but the structure looks intact. I walk to the fence and climb up. Scanning the neighbor's yard as I sweep the column of light over it, I don't see a body. I'm pretty sure I hit him, but there's no sign of it. At first light, I'll go over the fence to see if I can find a blood trail.

He wore black clothing, including a hoodie, and some kind of Halloween mask on his face. Seemed to be average height and lean. Fast on his feet.

I interrupted the son of a bitch as he was pouring gas in a circle around the house. It would have left us with no way out.

When I go inside again, Avery stands in the bright kitchen where she's turned on all the lights.

"I smelled smoke outside."

"Yeah, a guy tried to light the house on fire."

She sucks in a startled breath, her eyes darting around the room. "I don't understand. How could he know I'm staying in this house? Do you think he followed me the entire way from campus?"

"Maybe. Or he could've seen us at the Lambda Delta party or heard rumors that we're dating. My address is known. When I first bought the place I had a couple of parties here. Or maybe you weren't the target tonight. We don't know for sure it was Casanova. I didn't see any roses. Even if it was him, he could've just wanted to kill me. I'm the one who's standing in his way now."

"If he's willing to burn the house down, we're not safe here."

"Did the house burn down?" I counter gently, shaking my head. "That's what the security system is for. The house's perimeter has motion-activated lights and cameras. An alert sounds on my phone when something triggers them to come on. I chased him over the fence. Probably could've gone after him and caught him, but I had to come back to deal with the fire he started. When the sun comes up, I'll canvas the neighborhood."

"How will you do that?"

Shivering, I glance around for a towel. The blowback from the hose got me, and I'm wet and cold as hell.

Avery notices and steps forward, touching my bare chest. Her grimace deepens. "God, your skin is freezing cold, Shane." Her hands rub my arms, trying to warm me.

The worry she directs my way is sweet, and it hits me in all the ways.

Her hands pause. "Go upstairs and put on dry clothes, okay?"

"Yeah, I need to." Taking her hand, I guide her toward the stairs with me.

"I can't believe this is happening," she murmurs. "Should we call the police?"

"No, not yet." Cops snooping around my house is the last thing I want.

In my room, I open a dresser drawer and find a Granthorpe sweatshirt. Putting it on helps. As the adrenaline wears off, my temperature's dropping. Crossing the room, I look out the window. No movement in the yard. All quiet.

Behind me, Avery's pacing.

I turn to look at her. "Need something to do, babe?"

"Please."

"Go downstairs, and put on a pot of coffee. Neither of us is going back to bed anyway."

"Okay."

When she doesn't leave the room, my head cocks.

Her voice is steady, but her brows pinch together with worry. She blows out a long breath. "Sorry. I need a minute. Someone *set the house on fire*." Her teeth sink into her lower lip.

She's rattled. Anyone would be.

I cross the room instantly and pull her against me in a tight hug. "Hey, everything's fine. I've got you, baby. Promise."

AVERY

I AM NOT OKAY.

Thick storm clouds choke the sky, cloaking the neighborhood in darkness even after dawn. When it starts to rain, Shane scowls and murmurs a curse. Then he grabs his flashlight and heads outside anyway.

There's a gas can on its side on the lawn near the house. He uses the flashlight to lift it, so he doesn't smudge any fingerprints that may be on it. After putting it in the garage, he walks around the lawn and looks into the yard behind his.

I trail after him, watching him scan the grass. "What are you looking for?"

"Clues," he deadpans.

"Seriously though. Did you see him drop something as he ran away?"

"Just the gas can, but you never know."

Shane hops the fence and walks through his neighbor's yard all the way to the gate. After what seems like a thorough sweep, he returns.

"I'm going to talk to some of the neighbors. You don't need to come. Go inside and get warm, Ave."

"I want to come," I say, convinced there are things I can learn from watching what he does. "About my getting a gun..."

He scowls at the horizon. "Listen to me," he says, his voice low and impatient. "Problem number one with your plan is the fact that you don't know how to use a gun and are therefore more likely to have it taken away from you than to defend yourself successfully. The second problem is that it won't do you any good to have a gun in your purse if Casanova tries to grab you. When he does it, he doesn't even leave the girl time to scream, let alone to go digging through her purse."

The evidence does suggest that Casanova is stealthy. "Maybe I'll wear my purse across my body and keep my hand inside on the gun while I walk across campus. How do you carry a gun? Do you wear a holster?"

"I don't carry on campus. That's problem number three. It's illegal to carry firearms on school property, and if the school catches anyone carrying concealed, it leads to expulsion and criminal charges."

"You're not armed at school? So if there was a school shooter...?"

"I'd have to go to my car, get my gun and double back. Or I'd have to take him down another way. It would depend on the situation."

"But if Casanova snuck up on you alone?"

"Look, if someone's going to come after me, it won't be by trying to grab me from behind while I'm walking across the quad. It'll be by doing something like the fire last night. Or just walking up and shooting me in the back of the head. He won't be trying to capture me. He'll be trying to kill me. And good luck to him on his approach. Any warning, any hesitation, will mean he's the one who's dead.

"You're a different type of target, baby. If someone comes after you, the motive will be sexual. And I promise you, this guy Casanova is smooth. I think he gets in close somehow before the girl knows she's in trouble. Maybe he even lures her to him or has someone else lure her."

"You've given this some thought."

"Of course. I'm your bodyguard."

"I only asked for a place to stay," I say quickly and a little defensively. "I never asked you to be my bodyguard."

"If you say so." Shane's tone is casually dismissive, but his expression isn't annoyed or impatient. He volunteered to drive me to campus and back, and he's never seemed put out over having to do it. If anything, I think he likes having me rely on him for protection, since it means he can push for things he wants as payment.

"What about a knife? It's not against Granthorpe rules to have one of those, right? And if there was duct tape to cut or whatever, it could be useful."

He pauses, and his head tilts back and forth as he weighs this.

"Easier to have that at the ready in a pocket," he concedes. "But you've gotta be within arm's length to use it. And again, if you pull it out to defend yourself, you have to be ready and able to kill with it. Otherwise, he could use it against you. The thing about all this is that you never know how you'll react in a real situation. I've seen big guys, ones who seem tough as nails, go into a ring to fight and after they take a few hits, they just fold. You feel me? If you pull a knife and then hesitate, it's more dangerous than being unarmed."

"If I come face-to-face with Casanova and he's trying to abduct me, I will not hesitate."

"You say that, baby, but until the fear and adrenaline hit you, you don't know what you'll do. I'll tell you what. I'll continue to play bodyguard till the end of the semester. If they don't catch him before you decide to come back to campus next term, we'll do some weapons training."

"Okay, yes. Good." I smile. "Thank you."

He frowns. "Don't thank me yet. I doubt you'll like training with me. It won't be fun and games. I will show you your limitations." His voice grows more grim. "If I'm not one hundred percent convinced you can handle yourself, I won't let you carry anything. You can just do class virtually next semester or come back for another round in my place."

"Probably virtual, then. My staying with you as a sex slave you get to punish is very much temporary."

That causes him to smile wickedly. "Yeah, 'cause you hate it so much when you come all over my fingers. Or against my mouth. Or with my cock buried in your ass."

A small gasp escapes, and my face heats, but I manage a scowl. "So crude. You never showed me this side of you before."

"We weren't having sex before."

I open my mouth to say we're not really having sex now, but of course we are. I originally wasn't counting my performing oral sex on him as a type of sex that truly involved me. In my mind, I saw it as separate. But when he started touching me back, things changed. And being brought to orgasm, being called baby, and definitely sleeping in the same bed is much more personal.

Spending time parsing out my complicated feelings doesn't seem useful at the moment. Instead, I silently join him as he goes up and down the street. When Shane spots a house where the lights have been turned on, he knocks on the door. Once someone answers, he tells them about the arson attempt and asks if they have any street-facing cameras, or if they've seen any strangers walking up and down the block or acting suspicious. I'm surprised at his tone, which is more conciliatory than I've ever heard it. He's friendly. He's charming. He encourages them to forward the footage from their security cameras to him.

People are concerned, acknowledging that, as Shane points out, a fire at one house could spread to others. His neighbors with cameras promise to look at their clips. Shane gives out his cell number to every person we talk to.

After twelve households, he announces we're done for the morning.

As we walk back to his place, I say, "Are you sure this was a good idea? What if the strangers on the clips include men delivering things to your house in the middle of the night?"

His gaze cuts to me, his expression suspicious. "What men?"

I've outed myself as a witness to Erik Sorensen's three-in-the-morning delivery. "I thought I heard people in the house one night. Bringing in boxes?"

"Hmm. Could've been a dream."

A frown tugs at the corners of my mouth. Keeping secrets is one thing; lying and gaslighting is something worse. "No, Shane. Not a dream."

"Avery, we talked about this." Unlocking his front door, he pulls it open for me.

"About what?"

"You digging into things that aren't your business." He closes the door behind us, and flicks on the living room's recessed lights.

"I'm living here right now, so it *is* kind of my business."

His palm connects with my ass in a light swat, causing me to suck in a startled breath. "Behave yourself, kitten."

My nipples tighten at his use of that pet name, which only makes me more annoyed. My eyes narrow, and my frown deepens. "Cut it out. I can't help it if I'm a light sleeper."

"No, but you can help whether you ask questions."

"Don't be a hypocrite."

He goes still, his expression darkening. "Come again?"

Standing up straighter, I look him in the eye. "One minute, you act like we belong together like fairytale characters. The next, I'm an interloper in your house who it's ok to lie to. Make up your mind. This is either a temporary situation, or I'm your girlfriend. You don't get to change the dynamic whenever it suits you."

His scowl deepens. "Don't act like you want to go back to when the only thing I did was order you to your knees. That's not how you want to be treated, and we both know it."

"I wouldn't like it, no. But I also don't like being lied to or kept in the dark."

"Even if you were my girlfriend, there are things I wouldn't talk about. Not just for my own sake. For yours, too."

My face clouds. Things are so murky because of his criminal connections. I want him to trust me enough to confide in me, but maybe there *are* things I'm better off not knowing. Though, how can I be involved with someone I don't really know? That's not a real relationship.

Shane walks into the kitchen, leaving us at an impasse.

So stubborn. And so heartbreakingly skilled at staying out of reach.

From the living room, I text my mom to say I'm not sure I can make it for brunch. She texts back, very insistent. Mom says they'll come to Granthorpe, which I don't want, so I relent.

I tell her Shane will be with me. It's obvious by her reply that she's not anxious to see him. Mom reiterates that I don't need to rely on Shane for transportation.

And I remind her I want her to be nice to him. I add that I'm much safer spending time with him than spending time alone on campus and that I hope she won't do anything to jeopardize my safety. Since she's so protective, I'm sure that tactic will work as well as anything could.

19

AVERY

When I come downstairs to leave for brunch, Shane's wearing a button-down shirt and modern dark gray sport coat with jeans. As is often the case, his style is the perfect marriage of casual and rich.

In a sharply tailored burgundy and ivory dress, I'm dressed more for a business meeting than a breezy brunch, but it's the only dress other than the blue one that I have on campus.

His gaze takes me in, pausing at a thin gold chain that circles my left ankle. It's a string of small X's and O's and was a Valentine's gift from my mom. Her favorite way of saying I love you is with presents.

After I step down onto the landing, I smooth the fabric of my skirt which rode up my thighs on the descent. "It's great that we're doing this. They're excited to see us."

Shane doesn't roll his eyes, but he comes close. "Sure."

"Hey, if they do anything that starts to make the conversation awkward, let me handle it, okay? I'll try to smooth it over."

He gives me a sideways glance as he opens the front door and ushers me out. "I don't need you to run interference, Avery. If they're cool, I will be, too. Otherwise, I'm gone."

The mood has been tense between us since I called him out over his lies. Now add in our parents, and this may be the shortest brunch in history.

On the drive, he glances more than once at my bare legs, but he doesn't touch me.

"So what's the deal with dressing up?" he asks, running his hand over the top of the steering wheel. "You wore a dress to dinner at my grandfather's house, and you're wearing one now. What was the problem at the platinum party?"

I stiffen, resting my hands on my knees. A quick glance at his profile reveals his eyes are fixed on the road.

"That kind of elaborate staging of myself reminds me of beauty pageant prep." A road sign announces we're twelve miles from Boston. Almost there. "My last pageant was a Dumpster fire. I developed...they say it's a mild to moderate case of PTSD. It makes events that require formal wear difficult."

My tongue darts out to moisten my dry lips. Just thinking about the triggers makes me cringe.

"Why the hell did Sheri force you into doing those?"

"My mom didn't force me. She'd won a lot of prizes and scholarship money in pageants. She wanted that for me, too. But when I couldn't do it anymore, she let me stop."

"What made the last one a Dumpster fire?"

I grimace and watch the trees outside my window whip by. "Just a bad scene with my bio dad. My parents fought about everything, but he'd never directed his anger at me before. I don't think he meant to that day either, but he was looking at me while he was yelling. It felt like Mom and I were both at fault."

Shane's angry scowl and the look in his eyes are dangerous. I recognize the expression from the night he put Todd and Daniel in their place for threatening me. "You were a little girl, Avery. Six, right? *Nothing* was your fault."

"No, I know. But logic isn't an effective shield."

"What did he say? Specifically?"

My throat grows tight, and my eyes burn. "Nothing I care to repeat." I realize my hands are crumpling the fabric of my hem and release it. "I couldn't tell you even if I wanted to. I was six. The memories are just fragments of rage and disappointment." I draw in a breath through pursed lips. "So, yeah, that was heartbreaking. And right afterward, he took an out-of-state job, so I never saw him in person again."

"He didn't even come to say goodbye?"

"No. After that incident, my mom sued for full custody and tried to file a restraining order, so he just washed his hands of us."

Shane's eyes are still on the road, but they narrow to slits. "Parents are immature assholes sometimes. They should really grow the fuck up before they have kids." His thumb taps the steering wheel. "I'm sorry that happened to you, and that you felt compelled to make yourself up like a pageant queen for the frat party." He shakes his head, and I can tell he's angry now with himself. "I'll never put pressure on you to look a certain way again. You have my word."

I love that he understands. He's unflappable, so I didn't expect him to be able to. In some ways, Shane really is perfect for me. Pulling slack into the seat belt, I lean over to kiss his cheek. Fortunately, I catch myself in time and stop before I do.

Christ. No kissing.

You accused him of being a hypocrite. Don't be one yourself.

Leaning back into my seat, I say softly, "Thank you for understanding."

And if you expect this brunch to work, Avery, you'd better not act as if you're at a funeral. Get your game face on.

Injecting a little sass into my voice, I say, "That's quite a sacrifice you're offering to make. I'm surprised."

"You overestimate the value I put on beaded gowns and fake eyelashes, Avery. You're at your most beautiful without makeup. Right out of the shower or in my bed completely naked, that's what I'd have a hard time giving up."

Heat washes over me. "The ball gown and pageant makeup weren't actually what I meant. Won't it be a sacrifice to refrain from making impromptu spa appointments to have your little pet waxed?"

His head cocks, and he glances over at me with a small smirk.

"Hang on. Don't conflate getting your pussy waxed with putting on false eyelashes for a frat party. Those don't belong in the same category of grooming."

My laughter is partly from amusement and partly from relief that I've been able to insert a little levity into our difficult morning. "If there's a loophole, you'll find it, huh?"

"Pretty much." His tone is remorseless, which, in the moment, actually feels reassuring. For better or for worse, Shane is decisive and consistent. Unlike a lot of people I've known, he doesn't waffle. When he promises me he won't pressure me to wear a formal gown again, I believe him.

We ride the rest of the way in silence, but the earlier tension is gone.

The upscale restaurant our parents have chosen for brunch is lovely. White linen napkins fashioned into blooming flowers are center stage in the waiting place settings.

Our table is next to the stone fireplace, which glows with burning embers. Ethan and Mom both stand to greet us.

My mom looks gorgeous in a royal blue blouse and blue and green geometric print skirt. Ethan looks handsome in his signature weekend trousers and polo shirt. He's wearing his tortoise shell glasses, which are his casual glasses. For court, he wears lightweight steel-framed ones that look serious and distinguished.

When Ethan comes around the table to hug Shane, I can't help but compare them physically. I never think of Ethan as small. He's five-nine but looks taller because he's rail thin from his addiction to cardio. Shane, on the other hand, is six-foot-three and made of solid muscle; he suddenly seems much bigger than Ethan. It's not just Shane's physique; his very presence dominates any space he occupies. Also, unlike his dad, Shane is never completely clean-shaven anymore, which makes him look rougher.

My mom says hello to Shane and gives him a kiss on the cheek, which I think is more than she has done in the past two years. To his credit, Shane doesn't look surprised or pull back when she embraces him.

As a precaution, I sit between my mom and Shane to act as a

buffer. The two of them are mostly silent, which is fine since Ethan and I can easily carry the conversation. I tell our parents about the preparations I'm doing for my presentation.

"For the internship letter, right? Now who's this woman Ethan says you want to work for?" Mom asks.

"Her name's Roxanne Keller. I started following her after I heard her on a podcast. Her background is in tech and finance, and she's amazing. The things I could learn from her, it'll be incredible." Realizing I'm doing a fangirl gush, I roll my eyes at myself with a small laugh. "Getting the internship is a long shot, but I *have* to try."

"Honey, I'd be happy to take a look at a dry-run of your presentation," Ethan says.

"That would be great. Mom, would you watch it, too? I'm going to try a couple of different professional styles. I want to look good onstage."

My mom's smile is worth its weight in gold as she nods.

Ethan and I go on to talk about his cases, which quiets my mom because it's not as interesting to her as it is to me. I ask a lot of questions, but toward the end of the meal, Ethan glances around the table and looks abashed. "Well, Ave, you and I should talk about this sometime when it's just the two of us because I don't want to bore Shane and your mom. How about you, Shane? Fill us in on your life. How is school going?"

"Fine," Shane says.

"Good, good. What plans do you have for winter break?"

"Not sure yet."

"We should sort that out soon," Ethan says. "We're going skiing during the break, but if you're not going to be with us, we'll have to figure out which day to come back to town, so we can all be together for Christmas. We'll probably fly the twenty-third."

"Oh, no," my mom says, her brows pinching together. "That's right in the middle of the trip, and that would mean missing the New Year's Eve party. I already got my dress. Besides, Shane said he had other plans for break. I'm sure he's planning to spend Christmas with his other family. In Back Bay, I guess?"

Shane leans back in his chair and looks at her for a moment. My shoulders tense.

"I do plan to be with the Sullivan side of the family on Christmas Eve, but I'll spend Christmas with you guys whether you're in Aspen or here."

"Really?" Mom's brows draw together. "That would mean you'd have to fly alone on Christmas day. That wouldn't be great, would it?"

"Avery can keep me company."

I freeze.

My mom's gaze darts to my face, which I'm sure looks stunned. "Why would Avery do that? She'd miss days of skiing before the holiday. And she'd be alone on Christmas Eve. No, Avery is flying with us. Right, Ave?"

Oh, boy. My gaze slides to Shane, wondering what he's playing at. He can't be planning to take me with him to a big gathering of his mom's family on Christmas Eve, so how would it work for me to stay behind?

With a lick of my lips, I admit, "I wouldn't want to be alone on Christmas Eve."

"I won't leave you alone. You know that," Shane says in a low voice that he usually reserves for when we're alone. The intensity of his gaze feels as intimate as if he'd reached under my skirt.

I shift in my seat.

Since we arrived, he hasn't touched me once or dropped any hints that we've been together as anything more than casual step-siblings. Right now though, the look he's giving me tells the story of us as we really are...we have private conversations. And plans that exclude other people.

Ethan clears his throat, and when I turn my head to look at our parents, I find that my mom's face is frozen.

Oh, God. I don't want her to worry.

Shane's phone buzzes, and he takes it out. Dropping his napkin on the table, he stands. "Excuse me a minute."

Mom lurches up from her seat, too. "I have to go to the Ladies' room."

Ugh. We almost made it to the end without incident. And things were going so well before the talk of Christmas break.

Ethan and I watch them walk away, then he leans forward and whispers, "What's going on, Avery?"

SHANE

ONE OF MY NEIGHBORS SENT FOOTAGE FROM A COUPLE DAYS EARLIER. It looks to be about midday. A guy, who's dressed in black with a baseball cap pulled low over his face, walks past my house twice in the span of five minutes. He looks at my place and into the yard. On the second stroll, he turns his face enough for me to recognize him. Todd Bardoratch.

Son of a bitch.

So Bardoratch cased the house even before the frat party. My shutting down his bullying on the video call and sending a message that he needed to let Avery take the lead on the project obviously infuriated him.

I don't blame him for coming after me. I stripped him of his power and made him look pathetic and weak in front of his friend and a woman who threatens the pecking order in the class. No guy like him wants to let that go.

But to try to burn me alive, especially when Avery was with me, makes me think he's a psycho. The only thing Avery's done to cross him has been to stick up for herself and the female victims of a serial kidnapper. Only a dickhead would retaliate against a girl for doing that.

Someone comes to stand next to me, which prompts me to look up. It's Avery's mom Sheri, and I can tell by her grim expression she's got something on her mind.

I slide my phone away.

"I know you hate me, but please don't hurt my daughter. It's such a vile, cowardly way to get back at me. I'll do whatever you want to make amends—just please don't hurt Avery."

Jesus Christ. Here we go with the melodrama.

"I don't know what you're talking about, Sheri."

"Why can't you leave her alone?"

"I did leave her alone. I didn't even want her at Granthorpe. Didn't Ethan tell you?"

"Ethan knows people at the school. He felt it was a good place for her to be, not too far from home and in a community that he still feels a part of. Then Casanova—" She blows out a breath. "The irony is not lost on us, I promise."

When I don't respond, she leans forward, giving me a whiff of her three-hundred-dollar-an-ounce trophy wife perfume.

"So, if you'd just give us a break," she says softly. "We'd really appreciate it."

"Avery came looking for me. You want her to stay away from me? Tell her."

"I'm talking to you for the same reason I always did. Guys are the ones who go too far."

Too far? Sheri is fucking unbelievable. My temper's a grenade where this woman is concerned, and she's tugging at the pin. "You can't rape the willing."

Her mouth drops open, and, once again, she looks shocked. "Are you saying that you've already—"

"I'm not saying a damn thing, other than that I don't get off on forcing myself on women. Which you should already fucking know."

She jerks back. "I was wrong about that night when she was drunk. I apologized to you."

"That apology was bullshit, and you know it. Deep down, you still think the reason nothing happened is because I didn't know she was out there."

"Can you blame me, Shane?"

"*Yes.*"

"With the family you come from? And the way you look at her? From the minute you guys met...I *know* that look."

Sheri's a complete lunatic. Of course, I was attracted to Avery. She was super cute. But I don't buy for a second that Sheri read anything sinister on my face when I looked at fifteen-year-old Avery. I protected her from everything back then, including my own urges.

There's something deeply disturbed about the paranoia Sheri

targets me with. I've had my suspicions for a while that I remind her of someone from her own past.

"How old were you when it happened?" I ask, taking a shot. "Fifteen? Sixteen?"

She recoils like I've slapped her. A moment later she goes from looking stricken to shuttering her expression. "Stay away from her."

"No."

Sheri's fury is palpable as she glares at me.

"If you don't think she's safe around me, tell *her* to stay away from me. I promise that's a better use of your time because you've still got influence over her. You've got none with me." There's a beat while I let that sink in. "*Zero.*"

Avery chooses that moment to show up to check on things. She swoops in and clutches her mom's arm. "Mom, everything okay?"

Sheri glances my way, and Avery turns to look at me.

"Shane?" Avery says.

When I answer, my voice isn't particularly friendly. "Yeah?"

Avery steps closer to me.

I'm pissed about Sheri's ongoing harassment, but my ability to be a hardass is seriously impaired with Avery's big blue eyes imploring me to be nice.

"Are you all right?" Avery whispers.

That takes me off guard. When has anyone in the core family unit ever asked me if *I'm* okay when something's going down? Honestly, I am all right. There were many days I was torn to shreds by having Sheri's paranoia targeted at me, but those days are long gone.

"Yeah, I'm fine. Your mom has concerns. As usual. I told her she should talk to you, not me."

"Okay, good." Avery's smile is sweet. "Thank you."

Her gratitude is misplaced, which I'm sure she'll hear soon enough from her banshee mother. For now though, I'll roll with it. I have bigger issues to deal with than Sheri Kershaw's hysteria. "Do you mind if we stop in Back Bay after brunch?"

"No, I don't mind," Avery says. "Wanna say goodbye to Ethan while I say goodbye here?"

After a moment, I nod, and I'm rewarded with another smile that tries to pulverize my defenses. This girl is all kinds of dangerous in her own right.

20

AVERY

"Please don't go, Ave," Mom says. "Come home with us instead. Ethan would be happy to drive you to school tomorrow. We can have a movie night and make Nutella protein balls for you to take back as a snack."

My mom, who wears sample size designer outfits, doesn't indulge her sweet tooth often, which means if she's talking Nutella balls, she's clearly in some kind of panic.

"Brunch went pretty well, right?" I try to make my voice cheerful. I already evaded Ethan's questions with light, casual replies. I want to do the same with my mom. "Why don't we try to do this again next week? I'll work on Shane to see if I can get him to agree to spend the weekend at home."

"At whose home?"

"Yours and Ethan's. That's Shane's home, too, Mom."

She purses her lips.

I sigh. "You do realize that not seeing Shane is hurting Ethan, right?"

Mom's sigh is much heavier than mine. "Ethan can see Shane any time he wants. He's had dinner with Shane at Granthorpe several times. I support that decision. I've encouraged it!"

"Ethan can't see Shane any time he wants because Shane isn't open to it. But he could be."

"It's not your job to fix Ethan and Shane's relationship. They need to go to therapy."

A surprised laugh escapes my throat before I can stop it. Neither of them would ever agree to therapy. Ethan's a workaholic who barely keeps up with my mom's crazy social calendar. Fitting another thing into his week is not going to happen. And Shane...I shudder at the thought of even mentioning it to someone like him. He thinks the best way to deal with a problem is to bury it under a thousand pounds of ice.

"Right, sure. I'll tell you what, Mom. If you can get your husband to agree to therapy, we'll circle back to this discussion." At this point, Shane reappears, so I give my mom a quick hug. "I'll talk to you soon."

"I love you," she says, hugging me tightly.

I pull away gently and head to the door that Shane's holding open for me.

He's silent as we walk to the valet stand.

"Ethan asked what's going on between us." I keep my voice light and cheerful for him, too. "I told him we're trying to be friends."

The corner of Shane's mouth quirks. When the car arrives, he opens the Porsche's passenger door, and I slide into the buttery leather seat.

"What?" I ask.

"Nothing. That resembles the truth, somewhat." He closes my door and goes around to get in the driver's side.

As we travel to Back Bay, I'm not sure how to breach the subject we need to talk about. I can tell my mom said something that dredged up the past for him. I want him to know that's not okay with me.

Watching his hand rest on the gearshift, I'm tempted to put mine over the top of it. But tender touches need to fall into the same category as kisses. Despite how tough it is, I refrain from reaching out.

"Can we talk about it?" I ask.

"About what?"

"Ethan wants to know what's going on with us. I'm sure my mom does, too?"

Shane's head turns slightly, not all the way to look at me, but enough to acknowledge he's heard me. Then his eyes return to the road in front of him, his expression neutral and unconcerned.

"I don't know how you do that," I say.

"What's that?"

"Pretend you don't care."

The corners of his mouth curve up. "Who says I'm pretending?"

I shake my head. "In your place, I would have to know exactly what was said between me and Ethan. Just like I hope you're going to tell me what my mom said to you."

He shakes his head. "I'm not gonna rehash it. If you wanna know what's on your mom's mind, ask her yourself. Leave me out of it."

"I think she would very much like to leave you out," I say lightly.

His expression turns grim. "She has a problem with me that has nothing to do with me. She needs to get her head examined."

"She's wrong to be as paranoid as she is. I think it's just that Ethan said that you had trouble controlling your temper after your mom left. You acted out and got in a lot of fights or something? And even when you learned to keep your rage in check, he worried it was always just below the surface. He thinks you never got over your mom leaving."

His fingers tighten on the steering wheel, turning his knuckles white. "He told Sheri that, huh?"

"They were planning to get married. Yes, they talked about us."

"And she said you were perfect, of course."

"No, I'm sure she didn't. She probably said I was stubborn and had a hard time making friends. Too tentative around new people."

"Why would she say that? It's not true."

"Yes, it is. 'Hesitant to try to connect.' Because of my unreliable dad, the counselor said."

"Kids don't get over being betrayed by a parent. Adults don't always realize that. Little kids are so trusting and willing to forgive. Parents forget that kids grow up, and the window closes. My mom has invited me to visit her in Portugal at least a dozen times." He shakes his head, his expression even more grim. "Like I'd ever go now."

I wince. This is how he copes with pain and loss. He ends the possibility of being hurt by someone a second time by cutting them off completely. No wonder his ability to freeze us out of his life the past two years was so profound. He learned and perfected the technique years earlier.

"How was Ethan when your mom left? Was he too preoccupied with his own loss to be there for you?"

"No, my dad was great. He cut back on his hours. Picked me up from school every day. Took me with him to his office if he had to work late. I'd sit and do my homework or watch videos while he worked. For months and months, he made sure I was never alone. If I wasn't with my friends or my grandparents, I was with him."

"So you knew he cared about you?"

"Of course."

"But we messed that up for you, huh?" I say gently. "You never seemed to resent us when we first moved in."

"Because I didn't. Look, I was nine when she left. By the time I was fifteen, I was long past wanting them to get back together. I told him he should start dating. It was time, and I was fine with it. When he met your mom, he'd been dating a couple of years. It was different with her. I could tell right away it was serious. He was happy, and I was glad he'd found someone. It wasn't until later that I realized she was going to become a problem for me."

His fingers tap on the steering wheel. "When he first talked about marrying her, he asked me if I was okay with it. I said yes. I never tried to interfere. I thought it would be good for him. I had my own stuff going on, so we weren't spending as much time together. Why shouldn't he spend his free time with a wife who'd be in his bed full-time? That's how life is supposed to be for a man in his forties."

"He loves you, and you obviously love him, too. I don't understand why you barely see him anymore. I know you were mad at him for misjudging you, Shane, but I think you know my mom was so upset and irrational that morning that Ethan didn't know what to think. And he very quickly showed you were innocent of the things she was saying. He apologized so sincerely, right?"

"Ethan's a good man. When I was young, no one could've been a better dad. But after Sheri's accusation, when he took her side against me, I knew I'd never be able to relax in that house again. Those cameras he installed...her paranoia infected him. That morning when she went off the deep end, he looked so gutted. That gutted me." He clenches his jaw. "He loves me, but he doesn't trust me. Now, that cuts both ways. I love him, but I *do not* trust him."

"He'd never make that mistake again, Shane. Neither would I."

He's quiet and clearly unconvinced. I think about the locked room, and the secrets he would never trust me with.

"Look, no one's asking you to share all your secrets with us. But if we all spend more time together, things will be less awkward. Can you stay in Aspen the whole week after Christmas? It's Declan's family's house. You'd feel comfortable in that group, right?"

"There's still a problem between your mom and me. It's not just about that morning. It's about how she treated me the entire time we were all living together and the way she still treats me to this day. Whatever it is about me that triggers her, it's always going to trigger her. And that is not my problem. I almost told her to fuck off this morning. I would not last days sharing a house with her. And if she tried to fix you and Declan up in front of me, I would end up showing her exactly what happens when I really lose my temper."

"All right. I guess things are still too complicated. We can work on it slowly over time. Why don't you skip Colorado altogether? You can come by the house when we're back after New Year's. You could see your Grandpa Sullivan and maybe go to Connecticut to see Ethan's parents. Low key. Low stress."

"You're not going to Colorado for two weeks without me, Avery."

"Why not?"

"I don't want you and Declan together when I'm not around."

My brows rise in surprise. "Now you don't trust Declan either?"

"I trust Declan one hundred percent to have my back in a fight or to take me at my word. But do I trust another man—any man—with you in a big house in the mountains? No."

That causes a shiver to run down my spine. He's got no right to act so possessive.

"I'm not interested in Declan, but if I was, it wouldn't be up to you whether I pursued something with him. When the semester ends, I'm moving out and our arrangement ends. Eventually there will be another guy in my life."

He's silent as he pulls up to his grandfather's house.

"Shane?"

"No." His jaw is set.

The car idles next to the security keypad with the gates looming above us, casting shadows on the hood.

"No what?"

"Even if you move out in a few days, this thing between us is nowhere close to being done. So, no, I won't let anyone else have you."

Heat washes over me at the rough and intimate way he looks at me, but no matter how sexy he is, I can't let him think he gets to control everything.

"You won't *let* them. How could you stop it?"

"The way I always do. I'll drive them away."

"How? By ruining my reputation the way Declan did in high school?"

"Of course not." He lowers his window, so he can reach the keypad.

"I don't understand."

"I make people assume you belong to me. Most guys won't risk a confrontation with me."

The memory of how tightly he held me while making the toast at the frat house comes rushing back. He wanted everyone to see us together and believe I was his girlfriend.

"I'll say we broke up. I'll just—"

"Try," he says calmly.

An uncomfortable flush washes over me. I stare at him silently, trying to decide what else to say.

"For you to convince them, I'd have to let you go. Which I won't." His voice isn't gentle. It's terse, as if he hates that he doesn't want us to end. "So, as I've told you before, no one touches you except me."

Our relationship is a spiderweb, deceptively fragile in appearance, but actually an inescapable trap. Maybe I've been naive to think I have control over what happens. Shane said he's a dominant personality. Clearly he wasn't exaggerating.

He punches in a security code. "We're here, so let's drop this for now. If you need to, we can talk about it later."

If I need to? I'm speechless. He's called himself a beast who's holding me captive, and suddenly I realize just how honest a statement that was on his part. So yes, of course, we're going to need to talk more about this.

The gate slides open, and we roll forward, curving around the tall hedges. The long driveway's clogged with cars, most of them expensive.

"Hell," he murmurs. "When I texted him, Pops didn't tell me he had people over." Shane parks the Porsche at the end of the row. "Wait in the car. I won't be long."

I tilt my head but say nothing. I'm not exactly anxious to fraternize with strangers at the moment anyway.

Shane gets out, and I watch him walk toward the door. He's only halfway there when he takes out his phone and stops to look at it. After he does, he turns around and comes back to the car. He opens the passenger door.

"What?" I ask.

With a small smile, Shane points at a security camera perched atop a metal post. "He saw you and texted me a message that said, 'Do not leave that girl in the car. I want to see her.'"

This makes me smile, too.

I take Shane's offered hand to climb out. He leads me to the front door where his grandfather waits on the landing for us. Mr. Sullivan shakes Shane's hand and cocks his head toward the hall, indicating Shane should walk on.

Mr. Sullivan gives me a side hug and draws me in the other direction, toward the kitchen. As we go, I catch a glimpse of the formal dining room where a whole group of men sit around a table. Gangsters? Some of them wear dress shirts and trousers, others are in jeans and sweatshirts. None looks especially sinister, but I suppose criminals don't always look shady in the light of day.

Shane steps into the dining room, and most of them stand to greet him, reaching across the table to shake his hand. He says a few words, and I hear their laughter. Then he steps back and closes the door.

"Do you want lunch, darlin'?"

"Oh, no. We just ate."

Mr. Sullivan pours himself a cup of coffee and offers me one. I nod and take the cup when he's filled it. Shane joins us in the kitchen a few moments later.

"Avery, sit down for a minute. I need to talk to my grandfather alone."

I nod as Mr. Sullivan gives Shane an appraising look that doesn't seem especially pleased.

They move to a nook that's off the breakfast area. Shane says a few words and then brings out his phone and shows his grandfather something. I wonder if he's telling him about the fire and showing him pictures of the house. Mr. Sullivan's attention to the screen lasts longer than I expect, though.

When I finish my coffee, I rinse the cup and move a bit closer to them.

Shane notices and puts his hand out to his grandfather, who gives him the phone back. Shane slides his cell away as they start toward me.

To Shane, Mr. Sullivan says, "Yeah, someone will look into it." When his grandfather reaches the counter where I'm waiting, his serious expression lightens, and he gestures for us to sit down at the island.

Even though Mr. Sullivan has a whole room full of men waiting for him, he doesn't appear rushed. Instead, he asks me how the weekend is going.

I tell him about the party we went to and show him a couple of pictures that someone posted of Shane and me.

His grandfather smiles. "Where are the close-ups of the two of you? Did you get one at the house before you left? Send me one of those."

"There are no shots from the house," Shane says. "It wasn't a high school prom, Pops."

His grandfather leans back, giving Shane an assessing look. It's exactly the same look Shane gives other people. "A pretty girl dresses up for you, and you don't get a picture? What's wrong with you? Your cousin Jack takes pictures of his cheeseburgers."

I chuckle.

"Idiot," Shane says with a smirk.

"Who? You or him?" Mr. Sullivan's expression is bemused.

Shane rolls his eyes.

"Tell me about the party, Avery love."

I scroll through images and find another slightly blurry shot of us to show. "We had a good time until I started causing trouble, and Shane had to get me out of there."

Mr. Sullivan laughs. "You caused trouble? I doubt that."

"No, I did." I glance over at Shane to see if it's all right to tell his grandfather what happened. When Shane doesn't move, I lean toward him and whisper, "All right to share the story?"

Shane's arm comes to rest on the back of my chair. "Little late to ask now," he says, but he looks more amused than annoyed.

"Come on," his grandfather says, beckoning me with his fingers. "You can't start a story and leave it unfinished. On you go." His Irish accent is charming, and I can't resist being charmed.

With a last glance at Shane's profile, I press my lips together, and then turn to Mr. Sullivan. I explain about seeing the guys with the Casanova roses.

Mr. Sullivan says darkly, "I've heard about Casanova. Someone needs to deal with him." That's the exact wording Shane uses. He has so many mannerisms and turns of phrase that seem to come from his grandfather.

Mr. Sullivan sips his coffee, and his expression remains grim. "You're sure the lads at the party wore those flowers as a tribute to Casanova?"

I nod. "It's the first thing I asked when I confronted the guy from my class. I wanted to know if he realized that color rose is Casanova's calling card. He smirked at me, making it very clear he knew exactly what he was doing. Wearing it was like a slap."

My teeth grind together as bitter anger hits me again. "To sneer and celebrate someone who stalks women and completely erases them from the world...those guys were trying to intimidate us. Again." I look away, scowling. "I wasn't in the mood to be intimidated, especially by a bunch of shitty fan boys." I exhale, trying to get control of myself.

"Sorry for swearing. I guess I'm still upset." After a hard swallow, I shake my head. "I tore off every rose I could get my hands on and smashed them."

Stealing a sip of Shane's coffee, I study Mr. Sullivan over the mug's rim, trying to determine whether his impression of me has changed.

His gray brows crowd each other, forming an angry crease. "So it was you who had to confront them? Then what?"

My voice is distant. "That's it. What more could I do?"

Mr. Sullivan looks at Shane. "And what did you do, my lad, while this went on?"

My gaze shifts to Shane's handsome face, which gives nothing away.

"Shane did the perfect thing," I say. "He stopped them from trying to squash my rebellion."

"Oh yes? How so?" Mr. Sullivan asks.

"They wanted to get their hands on me. To force me out of the spotlight, and then I'm not sure what they would've done. They never got the chance."

"There was a bit of a scuffle," Shane admits, his tone mild.

"You alone?"

"No, Declan saw and jumped in. And Sorensen came up and cast a big shadow."

His grandfather finally smiles. "He does that wherever he goes, so he does. Good, and...what kind of casualties?"

"None really." Shane shrugs his broad shoulders. "Some scuffed knuckles. Maybe a broken nose."

"The nose, their side or yours?"

"Them."

"Good." Mr. Sullivan's spoon drops to the saucer with a small clatter as he looks at me. "Did you warn Shane what you planned to do?"

I shake my head.

"You should have. Sullivans think fast on their feet, but it's always good to have a minute to plan."

"If I'd told him ahead of time, he might have tried to stop me. I couldn't risk it."

Mr. Sullivan flashes a smile at me. "Aye, sometimes there's no help for it, is there? Anger must have its way, and so it will."

"Exactly," I say softly.

"We should go," Shane says, rising. "We'll see you soon though, Pops. I'm bringing her to Christmas Eve."

Oh, my God. The beast strikes again, springing his traps.

"Right, good," Mr. Sullivan says as he stands.

Licking my lips, I draw a deep breath as I stand too. "Well, maybe I'll be able to come. It depends on the holiday flights to Colorado and...some other things."

"Oh, aye, but you'll make it work out so you'll be with us on Christmas Eve," Mr. Sullivan says confidently with a wink. "Since Shane's helping you stage your party rebellions, you won't want to disappoint him, I'd imagine?"

"I wouldn't, but—"

"Good girl," he says approvingly, cutting off the rest of what I planned to say about my mom and Ethan and plane tickets. Mr. Sullivan taps his cheek and adds, "Now let's have a kiss right here, and it'll set me up for life."

Unable to resist, I lean in and kiss his cheek.

"That's the stuff all right," he says with an infectious grin. He claps Shane's shoulder as he goes by. "We'll talk later, lad. When I have some news."

Shane walks me down the hall with his grandfather.

Mr. Sullivan stands at the door to the dining room but doesn't open it. Instead, he waits and then waves to us as we go out the front door and close it behind us.

"Cunning," I say softly. "You told him you're bringing me to Christmas Eve, so now there's added pressure on me to stay in town."

Shane nods. "You do not have to wear a ball gown."

"You think you're cute." My gaze cuts to him, and I wrinkle my nose. "I like your grandfather a lot, but not more than I love my mom and Ethan."

"If they want to see you over the break, they can either skip Colorado or see you when I bring you."

"The timing of my Colorado trip is up to me, Shane. Not you."

He opens the passenger door.

I pause, looking him straight in the eyes. "Tell me you understand that."

"Do whatever you want, Avery." His gaze is measured. "If you think it's a good idea to go straight to Colorado and spend the whole break there, do it."

"Really?"

He nods, closing the door. When he joins me inside and starts the car, he says, "I have a lot of experience ignoring people's reactions to my unpopular decisions. That means no matter where we are for the holidays, I'll be able to deal with the fallout. Let's see if you can say the same."

"Are you saying if I go straight to Colorado, you'll come too?"

"Of course."

I exhale softly, watching him out of the corner of my eye. "If that happens, will you ruin Christmas?"

There's a brief flash of a smile on his face. "Who am I? The Grinch?"

"I don't know. Your actions are highly suspect. You said you couldn't do the whole break with my mom. Now you say you will." Another thought occurs to me, a dark underpinning to his strategy. "If you miss Christmas Eve here to come to Colorado, your grandfather will blame me."

"I'd imagine he will, since it'll be your fault."

"You are unbelievable. Absolutely ruthless," I say, shaking my head.

His lips curve into a smile as he shrugs. "If you don't want monster trouble, stop baiting monsters."

21

SHANE

Downstairs where the light best mimics the lecture hall, Avery films herself practicing her presentation. I leave her to concentrate, going upstairs to watch a football game.

There's a heavy three-panel wood screen that hides the bedroom's sixty-inch flatscreen television, and I move it. Usually if I watch something in my room, I just stream on my phone, but I don't want to watch an entire game that way.

Sitting with my back against the headboard, I put on the sports network.

Periodically, my mind wanders to what I'd rather be doing in bed right now. I grab a pillow and lift it to my face. Regrettably, I don't catch the scent of Avery's coconut shampoo.

I picture her lying over the stacked pillows while I fucked her from above. My cock hardens at the thought. I want to do that again. And so much more.

In her current mood, she'll probably try to resist having sex unless all I'm after is a blow job. My gaze cuts to the doorway. I could take care of my erection myself, but that wouldn't be as satisfying as having her do it for me.

When I go downstairs, she's not filming herself. As I approach, I realize she's watching an online video about guns.

"Did you finish your presentation?"

"Yeah, I sent a couple of versions to my mom and Ethan. I also sent the one I think is strongest to Daniel and Todd, so they can review the content and make suggestions."

I lean over her laptop. "Guns, again?"

"Yes, just investigating for later in case I need it. The closest shooting range is just off campus. I could take a bus or get an Uber from the dorm."

I want her to stop thinking about guns, but Avery's stubborn. When she wants something, she doesn't let it go easily. She closes the lid of the laptop and looks up at me, all sea blue eyes and determination. Hard to resist.

"Granthorpe sent an email asking all the male students to give DNA samples," she says.

"I saw it."

"Do you think that means the police have a sample of Casanova's DNA?"

"Maybe."

"Should we give the gas can to the police, and let them see if there's touch DNA or fingerprints?"

"He wore gloves."

"Okay, so, last night he did, but maybe not when he filled the can or touched it at some other time?" She spends too much time talking to my dad about forensic evidence.

"I'm gonna hold off on turning the can over to the cops. I want to see what comes in from the neighbors."

"Are you going to give the police your DNA?"

"No."

Her eyes shift back to her laptop, and she unplugs it. She probably has something more to say about my lack of cooperation with the police, but if there's a tide of follow-up questions, she manages to hold it back.

"Dinner?" I ask as she stands. The sun's going down. Brunch was a long time ago.

She shakes her head. "Not hungry yet."

"Then we could do something else." I take the laptop from her and set it aside. My hand slides into her silky hair and tugs it to tip her head back.

I kiss her slowly, the taste like honey in my mouth. Her lips part, letting me have her tongue for a few moments.

When she draws back, she gives me an appraising look. I've broken the no-kissing rule again, and, by the downward tip of her mouth, she's trying to look unhappy about it. I'd prefer a smile, but I'm not ruffled by the frown. She's still here and still mine, whether she wants to admit it or not.

I rub my thumb over her lower lip. "On Monday, you should go to Student Health and get a prescription for birth control pills."

"Why would I do that?" she asks, her expression shifting to defiance. "I'm not going to need them anytime soon."

I fold my arms across my chest. "We're spending Christmas and New Year's Eve together. You don't think it'll happen?"

Her voice is breathy and gentle when she says, "No."

I'm not convinced, and I doubt she is either.

"You sure that's a line you want to draw in the sand, baby? Because some nights the sex will be rough, and that's easier for a girl to take the traditional way."

A flush spreads over her pretty cheeks, but she arches a brow. "The thing I let you do to me...that wasn't meant to be a regular thing we do. I just wanted to try it."

"Then you should get some pills."

Despite the blush, she looks me straight in the eye, and she's so fucking cute I want to kiss her again, but I know that would just set her off more.

"What's wrong with oral?" she asks, gathering up her laptop.

"Not a thing."

"So, for now, that's what you can have."

I chuckle dismissively. "You think so?"

Her eyes snap up to my face like she's ready to confront me the way she did the frat boys with the flowers. My unmoved expression must make her think better of it, because she just studies me, albeit with fire in her eyes.

It's unclear to me why she thinks an announcement from her will affect what I do when it comes to sex. Maybe because I said she could set limits, and she doesn't understand what hard limits are. The truth is I've already decided there are things I won't do while she's still so young and inexperienced. But I'm not looking to her for guidance on that score, since she's got no real experience to draw from.

"I need to ask you something," I say, sobering.

She circles around me in a wide arc, out of my reach. "Yes?"

"Besides the pageant PTSD, is there any other trauma in your past? Anything that triggers anxiety or depression?"

Her head tilts, and she licks her lips. "No." She waits a moment, but when I don't follow up with another question, she turns and heads upstairs.

We're not done for the night, but I'm not going to chase her until I've eaten. Heading into the kitchen, my mind's still on how sweet her mouth tastes even when it's frowning.

I chop some herbs to add to ground beef for burgers, listening for sounds of her. None come. The fact that she doesn't return while I'm grilling tells me she's either distracted, or she's avoiding me. I toast a bun on the grill and melt cheese on the burger before sitting down to eat. That earthy flavor suits me.

When I'm finished, I head upstairs and go straight to her room, passing the empty guest bathroom on the way.

Her room's empty, too.

Well, well.

I'm surprised she's in my room, which she must know is dangerous ground if she's trying to keep her distance.

As I pass the locked room, I check to be sure the door's still secure, which it is.

I enter my bedroom, and Avery's standing next to a nightstand with its top drawer open.

My eyes narrow, dropping to her hands. *Jesus Christ.* She's fiddling with my spring-action knife.

184

The worst-case scenario of what happens if it pops open explodes in my brain like a bomb.

"Drop that," I bark.

Her head jerks toward my voice, and her fingers release the weapon, which falls to the floor.

I stalk over and bend down to grab the knife. She managed to disengage the safety.

When I stand, I glower at her. "You're like a kid I've gotta watch every minute."

Her expression is mutinous.

"This blade is sharp enough to cut your fingers right off. And it's spring-activated to pop open." I hit the button, and the carbon blade releases from its sheath. With no force at all, I bury the blade in a pillow and, with a small movement, slice it open until its feathery guts pour out.

Her eyes widen.

I smack the pillow, which sends dozens of feathers into the air. They land like snowflakes on the dark carpet. I close the blade and re-engage the safety before dropping it into the nightstand drawer.

Exhaling some frustration, I shake my head. My heart's still pounding in my chest as though I've run a mile. There's not much in life that raises my blood pressure, but the thought of Avery getting hurt gets a rise every time.

For fuck's sake.

"Later, we're going to have a physical conversation about knife fights and hand-to-hand combat." I blow out a breath through my pursed lips, then I grab her hands and raise them. "These are beautiful fucking hands. I don't want you to lose a finger. If you want to examine a weapon, ask first."

"I was just looking," she says defensively.

I arch a brow and give her a stern expression. "The safety was on before you touched it, so you did more than look. You could've hurt yourself."

She needs to be punished, but she also needs me to teach her weapons safety. Everything's a delicate balance with Avery, especially now.

I glance down at the knife and shake my head before I close the drawer. "I promise I'll teach you. Don't get ahead of yourself, baby." Pulling her against me in a tight hug, I kiss the top of her head.

Her body relaxes a little. "You ruined your pillow," she murmurs against my chest. "Look at the mess you made."

"Made my point though, didn't I? That blade's razor sharp." Fisting her hair, I tug her head back so I can kiss her.

She tries to resist, but it only makes me kiss her harder. When I raise my head, we're both breathless.

"You're going to clean up the mess."

"Me?" she says skeptically.

My hand slides down to squeeze her ass. "Yeah, for being a bad little girl."

She clucks her tongue in protest, but I twist her arms behind her back and hold them there, trapping her.

"The other punishment, you get to choose."

Her wide eyes look up into mine. "Other punishment?" Trying to pull free, she leans back.

My grip on her arms is too tight for her to escape. "Three choices. Spanked and then on your knees to give me a blow job. Naked except for your tail until it's time for bed. Or bent over the footboard while I fuck you the way I did last night."

Her head shakes so strongly, her hair falls over her face.

"Ten seconds to choose, or I'll choose for you. Nine, eight, seven—"

"Tail," she blurts.

I smirk and release her arms. "Can I trust you to go in the bathroom to put your own tail in? Or should I empty the sink drawers of sharp objects first?"

"Jerk," she says. "Maybe I'll cut the tail right off its holder and destroy it."

"Go ahead. We both know I've got something bigger and better to put inside you where that's supposed to go."

Her stride falters for a second, but she doesn't turn around to argue. Smart, because at the moment my body wants the release it gets from rough sex that leaves a girl really sore.

22

AVERY

'm naked except for the tail. I've painted on cat's eyes and as I study my profile in the mirror of the guest bathroom, I have to admit it's really hot. Resting a palm against my fluttering belly, I draw in a breath and exhale.

As I pad down the hall to Shane's bedroom, I'm filled with warring emotions. I'm turned on by this game; I'm also unnerved by the slipperiness of the slope.

When I pose in the bedroom doorway, he's texting. His eyes catch a glimpse, and his head lifts. He smiles and raises the camera. I immediately dart out of the doorway and into the hall.

"No pictures! Jeeze."

"Just for me. I swear." His voice sounds amused by my pedestrian concerns.

"Absolutely not. Phones get hacked!"

After a beat, he says, "All right. Phone's in a drawer. Come back."

Peering around the corner through the doorway, I find he's standing in the middle of the room, smiling.

I step into view. Lifting the end of the soft furry tail, my manner is catlike in its challenge. With an arched brow, I say, "Well?"

"No talking." Shane hauls his shirt over his head, massive muscles rippling, and tosses it aside. "Get down on four paws and come over here."

Of course, he wants me to crawl. So twisted.

Of course, I did promise to do this as a reward for the way he stood between me and the five asshole frat guys. But crawling? Glancing down at the carpet, I wrinkle my nose.

"Come on, kitten." His voice is husky and cajoling, like he's coaxing an actual pet. "Come over here, so I can make you purr."

My nipples tighten and gooseflesh rises on my arms. Sexy talk from him is hard to resist, especially when he uses that tone of voice.

Finally, I lower myself to the carpet and crawl across it slowly with an exaggerated swing of my hips that makes my tail sway.

His breathing is audible as I reach him, which causes more shivers of excitement within my body. I love when his control slips because of me. Embracing the kitten role, I rub my cheek against his pant leg and lick his zipper.

"Fuck," he murmurs softly, adjusting himself.

His fingers tangle in my hair, gripping it tighter as I tease. Muscles contract making his abs as hard and flat as a washboard.

My teeth close on the zipper tab and tug it downward. His groan is deep when my tongue tunnels into his trousers. After a moment, he steps back and strips off his pants and underwear.

His cock is long and thick and hard. It's the only one I've seen, but I think it matches the rest of him because it's gorgeous.

I lick the drop of pre-cum from the slit with the tip of my tongue. He growls softly, his biceps flexing as he catches my chin in his palm. He draws me up to my feet, then picks me up and sets me on his bed.

He lies down on his back, running his hand down his belly before he grips his cock and strokes it. His head tips back, mouth open as he sucks in a deep breath. I watch greedily as his chest expands. Yeah, gorgeous.

Capturing my hips in his hands, he pulls me over and above him, so my knees land next to his temples. An arm around my waist drags my pussy down to his mouth. His lips and tongue devour me, and my body collapses onto his, my belly against the hard muscles of his pecs, his six-pack under my breasts.

His hand tugs the tail, moving the smooth metal plug inside me. That sends waves of arousal coursing through my pelvis, prompting me to rub my clit against his chin. My breath catches as my core clenches with need.

"Lick me," he orders.

Oh, right. I'm supposed to be pleasuring him, too.

Raw tingling engulfs my flesh. His mouth is so amazingly talented.

"It's hard to concentrate," I murmur.

A slap lands on my naked ass, making my body jerk.

"No excuses, kitten. And no talking."

I nip the soft skin of his scrotum, and he sucks in a breath. Then he slaps my ass twice more, and harder.

"Does my naughty kitten need to be spanked first? If so, I'm up for it."

My body shudders at the threat. I'm so wet and ready to come. What this kitten needs is *anything* he wants to do. Lowering my face, I lick his sac. He groans and raises his hips, beckoning me to give him more. I suck and lick slowly until I've tasted every inch of what's between his legs.

His tongue pushes deep into my aching core, and I groan. It's so soft and warm, so deliciously thick as it stretches me. My body throbs with pleasure and need. I want more than his tongue inside me. My hips circle, grinding my flesh against him. Then, to show him without words how I'm feeling, I take the head of his cock into my mouth and suck hard and sweet.

He moans against me. His fingers and mouth become rougher, which makes me squirm, until the undeniable sparks of arousal catch and burst into flames. I moan as the orgasm hits me, my legs shaking uncontrollably, my walls contracting around his tongue.

He keeps going, relentlessly, until I feel like I'll shake apart.

When the orgasm ebbs, I pull my body away from his mouth. It's too intense when he sucks my clit after I've come.

His head falls back, and his breath is short. His fingers squeeze my upturned ass. "My turn."

The tingling aftershocks continue inside me as I suck him into my mouth. Everything's wickedly intense, and I enjoy the feel of him. I like the way my body rises as he sucks in air. It feels like he needs something only I can give him.

His hips rise and fall, his cock jerking deeper and sliding back over my tongue. His hands slide down to grip the backs of my thighs. My head meets his groin over and over, letting him thrust as deep as he can reach.

"Fuck, yes," he groans. "Just like that, baby. Mmm."

I close my fingers around the base and stroke up and down while sucking the rest of his length. His hand plays with the tail, and his teeth bite the inside of my thigh. The bite isn't hard enough to leave a mark...it's just a tease. We're playing with each other, and it's so, so sexy.

When he comes, he fills my mouth. A little fluid escapes, spilling down onto him and the sheets below. This bed must have so many traces of us and our secret relationship.

His grip goes slack as he pants to catch his breath. I use the moment to slide off him. I land on my side, my mouth near his hip. My breathing's short and staccato as well.

After a while, I say softly, "It's pretty great, right? The way we are together?"

"It's exceptional." His voice is husky and confident.

Exceptional. That makes me smile. I *know* we're good together, but I like hearing him admit it. He's the one with experience.

We lie along each others' bodies for a long time, lips near hips, my toes tucked into the grooves of his headboard.

"You should tell my dad and your mom the truth."

"About what?" I scoff with a small laugh.

"This."

My head turns sharply, surprise jarring me out of my stupor. "What? No way." I sit up slowly, crossing my arms over my chest and bringing my knees together.

"I don't mean the details, Ave. I meant you should tell them we're in a relationship."

"It's way too soon to tell anyone anything."

He sits up and grabs me, pulling me toward the head of the bed. "Sure. Too soon." The teasing in his voice softens the sarcasm. He twists so I'm half-pinned beneath him. "Over the past couple days, you've swallowed a river of my cum." His hand slides down to my belly and presses, then his head drops so he can suck on my nipple.

I squirm, trying to escape. Though, I don't really want to.

He raises his head slightly and licks the wet nipple. "When is it time to make it official, baby? When someone catches us with my cock in your mouth in Colorado?"

I'm pretty sure he's being purposely crude to make it harder for me to argue with him. Shane brings his mouth close to mine, but I turn my head to avoid his kiss.

"Cut it out," I protest.

"No," he says, pinning my arms over my head. His green eyes hold mine, then he lowers his face and kisses my neck before he whispers in my ear. "You belong to me. I'll do what I want to you." He licks my throat slowly, and, God help me, it feels so sexy and delicious.

"I won't tell them. You can't make me." Sounding childish, even to my own ears, makes me roll my eyes.

"Doesn't matter." His unconcerned tone matches his words. "Deep down, they know."

My body stiffens. *No, they don't.*

The flat of his tongue grazes my nipple. "Anyone who sees us together can tell."

"Not true," I whisper, trying again to twist free of his grip, this time in earnest.

He pins my arms again easily and exhales a small laugh. "Are you really still so innocent?" His lips brush mine in a kiss that's more of a caress. "All right, stay a kitten as long as you want."

"I'm not playing games." I force some backbone into my voice. "They noticed our new rapport because it's so unexpected—and shocking, given how big the rift was. But they don't think we're together *like this.*"

A smirk persists as he shakes his head. "I'm telling you, they've got their suspicions. To keep it a secret, you'll have to lie. And lie *well*. That's what you want to do?"

"If I need to, yes."

An edge of dark unrest settles into his expression and his voice. "The innocent virgin princess for as long as possible?"

"I guess. What's wrong with that? You certainly liked finding out I'm still a virgin. Which is mostly your fault."

His head is bent over me, but it rises at my last accusation. Shane's sharp scrutiny makes me uncomfortable.

"I love that you're a virgin, Avery, but I'm not planning to keep you one. I'll enjoy your body even more when you're not, and so will you."

"Be that as it may, we're not telling Ethan and my mom that we're sleeping together."

"Lying will make it seem sketchy."

"It is sketchy! So far, it is." I snap my fingers and try to move my trapped wrists. "Trading blow jobs for a place to live? A cat's tail? Come on. Things are kinky and sketchy, Shane."

He shrugs. "Yeah, you probably shouldn't mention the tail." His smirk returns and is very infectious. I have to work to keep from sharing in the joke.

After Shane releases my wrists, he rolls onto his back and sits up. "The vacuum is in the hall closet. You clean up the feathers and then dress in school clothes and come down to the basement."

School clothes? On a Saturday night? What the hell?

Rising, I arrange myself so my nakedness isn't so exposed. "The basement? Why?"

"I'm going to teach you how to defend yourself with a knife."

23

SHANE

By the time Avery gets downstairs, I've got a paint marker and mat ready. She's wearing jeans and a sweater, which is a good start.

"Where's your jacket and purse?" I ask.

She studies my face for a moment and then starts toward the stairs with a look of determination on her face.

"Hey, bring me down a jacket, too, and the night-light from the guest bathroom."

Nodding, she disappears.

When she returns, I plug in the night-light and flick off the overhead one. It approximates the level of illumination on campus paths pretty well.

I pull my jacket on and smooth it down, assessing the thickness and how I feel about it being ruined if I can't get the impending marks out. I decide I'm all right with sacrificing it to the cause.

"All right. If you pull a knife, you cut to kill, right? Like we talked about. So, of the kill zones, which would be the easiest to go for on me?"

She doesn't answer at first, then says, "Neck?"

"Yeah, good, if you can reach it."

I grab the paint marker, but leave the cap on. "Here's what we're going to do first. Your objective is to get a red mark on my skin in a kill zone. A dot on the outside of my clothes doesn't help you."

Grabbing her hand, I pull it up to my jaw, helping her find my carotid pulse. Once her fingers are over my pulse near the end of my jaw, I drag her fingertips down at the angle I want her blade to make. I illustrate the movement a second time, then lean forward for her to make the motion on her own.

"Femoral artery is good, too." I put my hands on either side of my right femoral. "He won't be naked, so you'll have to get through his clothes. And your target is about the width of my finger. Less in someone smaller than me." I hold my pinky up and then lay it against my jeans approximately where the artery should be. "Unless you're very lucky with a single stab, it's just like the throat. You've got to stab and then drag the blade. You might meet resistance because there's a ligament."

Her brows crinkle as she watches me.

"The chest isn't a bad target for someone strong, but in your case, I'm not sure you could be effective. There are ribs to protect the heart and lungs, and there's thick muscle between the ribs. Power is something we can work on later, maybe."

Avery stands next to the mat, looking so small it makes me grimace. In fights, or even while sparring, I've only ever faced other men. I blow out a breath, my reservations mounting every time I look at her.

"Okay," she says, breaking the silence. "Thank you." Prompting me with a nod, she steps onto the mat. "What else?"

Reminding myself I was only eleven the first time Pops started to teach me to fight, I relent. "To try to mimic real-world conditions, sometimes when I come up to you I'm going to be playing Casanova and others I'm going to be playing an innocent student. You'll have to decide which I am. You don't want to stab a kid for stopping you to ask for directions."

Avery nods, chewing on her lower lip.

"But listen, when I'm Casanova, at some point, I'm gonna be rough. He can't afford to get caught, and he never has. He doesn't hesitate, and he could be as big as I am."

"Yes, okay." Very big, very beautiful blue eyes stare up at me. The ones that held so much innocence when we met that I would've happily torn the world apart to keep them that way.

"You may hit the floor pretty hard. Are you sure you wanna do this?" With every fiber of muscle in me, I want her to say no. *I* will protect her from Casanova for as long as it takes.

"Yes, I want to." Her voice sounds much less sure than it was upstairs.

"Baby?"

"Yes?"

"I asked you a question. Are. You. Sure?" I emphasize the last word in a loud voice, communicating that if we're doing this, I need her to toughen up.

She blinks, grimaces, and then grabs the marker. Her voice is harder when she answers, "Yes, I'm sure."

Fuck.

All right, you heard her.

I've told her over and over she can't fail to follow through once she pulls a weapon. That means I can't get her on the mat and then fail to pull the trigger on a real training session.

With that in mind, I put her through the paces.

And from start to finish, it's not great.

Once, she stabs an innocent student mid-thigh. And every time I'm Casanova, she ends up flat on the mat or carried off it. I put a forearm over her throat twice to show her how it feels to have her breath and voice cut off. After the first couple of times, I stop doing chokeholds because they make her so upset and panicked I can't stand to see it.

It's brutal on both of us.

Twice, she starts to cry in frustration and has to walk away to pull herself together.

I wait with my hands on top of my head until she comes back for another round. I tell her several times we can stop any time she wants, until she yells at me to stop trying to get her to give up.

Fucking brutal.

"Wait for your moment," I tell her repeatedly because she constantly telegraphs when she's about to strike, and because when she does make her move, she's always too wild and inaccurate.

She needs to be stealthy, precise, and committed. She also needs a longer reach. I'm too much bigger. That's just a physical fact. And a goddamned brutal one.

When she finally calls an end to the session, I'm the one who lies down on the mat for a breather. Not because I'm physically worn out. I just feel like shit because she tried so hard and I made her cry, and she still didn't kill me with the marker even once.

Avery surprises me by sitting down next to me, crosslegged like a kid. In her place, I would have gone straight upstairs to rethink my options.

"Shane." She waits, licking her lips. "There's one mark that might be on target." Her voice is thoughtful as she touches my jeans. "I didn't drag very far, but still...can we check how deep it goes?"

I rise up to examine my groin, and there is a red mark. I unzip my jeans and lower them and my boxer-briefs a few inches.

She leans over me, peering down. "There's paint on your skin," she says tentatively.

I look, and she's right.

I put my fingers on my groin and feel for the pulsation from my left femoral artery. "Pulse is here." Looking again, I move my fingertip. A dot of red paint is right next to my pulse. "Maybe." I nod. "You might have nicked it with that one."

For a moment, her face wears a small smile. It fades as she turns her right hand over. There's a lot of paint on her fingers and palm. "I was sweating. Does a knife slip as much as a marker does?"

"Yeah, especially when it's coated with blood. Good observation. It's not unusual for the fingers holding the knife's handle to slide down over the blade during an attack. The hilt becomes slippery when it's wet."

"Your knife had a handle the fingers went through. So they won't slip?"

She's so smart. That's good at least.

I nod. "But that knife's too big for your hand. If you want to keep going with training, we need to find one in your size."

"Or modify the grip."

"Yeah, or modify the grip." My hand catches hers and rubs. "You sure you want to keep going?"

"Yes, of course. How can you even ask when I did so well?"

Is she serious? If her earnest expression is anything to go by, yeah, she is.

My brows rise, and the corners of my mouth rise with them. "So well? You cried twice."

She cocks her head in challenge, a dark curtain of hair swinging. "So?"

I shrug. "Tough to take."

"No, it wasn't. I'm fine."

"I meant for me."

After a moment of surprise, her small smile re-emerges, then she lies down on the mat next to me, curling up against my side. "Tough on you, tough guy? Really? I thought you liked hurting me? Isn't that the point of your punishments?"

"Definitely not. Those are sex games." My palm cups the back of her head and strokes her hair. "This, what we just did? Not a fun game. I'm sorry we had to do it."

She kisses my jaw and then whispers, "The fact that you feel that way is why you're my crush, and Casanova is someone I want dead."

24

SHANE

It's been less than twenty-four hours since I talked to Pops when he texts saying to call him.

When I stopped at his place after Saturday brunch, I showed him my neighbor's footage of Todd Bardoratch and laid out my suspicion that Bardoratch is an arsonist and that I think I shot him while he was fleeing.

Pops promised to have a guy look into it, and apparently he's learned something. I go out onto the screened porch where there's no risk I'll be overheard by Avery.

When I call Pops from my secret burn phone, he skips the greetings and simply says, "That guy you mentioned? You were right."

"Yeah?"

"Got treated for a puncture to his arm. Said he fell on a ski pole, but an X ray showed bullet fragments."

I knew I got him. Sitting down, I lean forward.

"He's living dangerously," Pops says.

I wait a beat.

"But he's a rich boy, huh? With a powerful father? If anything other than an accident happens to him, it'll make a lot of waves."

A frown forms. If Pops advises me to let it go, I will not be happy. "Yeah, I guess."

"Specialty services are expensive."

Ah, that's more like it. I lean back, relaxing some. It's easy enough to read between the lines. Pops is telling me that there are plenty of men who could kill Bardoratch, but not a lot that could make it look enough like an accident to fool the cops and the coroner.

"In life, you get what you pay for," I say, tapping my thumb on the chair's arm rest.

"Speaking of that, payroll is costly."

Apparently my line of credit for being family is about capped out. I've already used one of my grandfather's guys to send a message to Bardoratch on the night he was a dick on the virtual call with Avery. I could have delivered that message personally, but Avery had just gotten to my house, and I didn't want to leave.

This time, I'd really like to deal with Bardoratch myself, but I know it's not a good idea. I'm many things, but a professional hitman isn't one of them. If I go after him, it won't look like an accident. Also, there are plenty of witnesses who can testify to the fact that I've been in fights with the guy. I'm sure I'll be Suspect Number One if he's murdered.

I don't expect my grandfather to foot the bill on a murder-for-hire operation though, when I keep insisting on running my own show at Granthorpe and haven't cut him and the Sullivan family in so far. I've done work for Pops in the past on a limited basis and that went well. He's ready to move me up in his organization, but I have my own plans.

So instead of asking for another favor, I say, "Yeah, I hear you, and I understand. The costs will be covered."

There's a pause, and then he says, "Good for you. What do you have planned for tonight? Maybe take your girl to dinner in Boston. Go dancing after. Does she dance?"

"I don't know."

Tonight's fast for a job like this. My pops must be pissed himself that someone tried to torch his grandson. I appreciate his heads-up that tonight's the night, since I'll need to establish an alibi.

"Don't take her to any of the family pubs," Pops continues casually. "She's only eighteen, and it sounds like the mother might pitch a fit if she gets tipsy. If anyone goes over the receipts later, we don't want the hassle."

That earns a smile he can't see. "I'm not twenty-one myself. You never bar me."

Pops laughs. "They'll never come after a Sullivan for underage drinking, lad. When it's my grandson, they won't bother to fish for minnows. It's a great white shark or nothing at all."

"I'll keep that in mind." After a moment, I say, "I appreciate the assist, Pops."

"It's what family does. I'll talk to you soon."

When the call ends, I glance at the burn phone speculatively. The old man still thinks he's going to pull me into his organization. Every favor he does for me means I'll have to do something in return. Speaking of fish, he's reeling me in bit by bit.

The side door opens, and Avery appears in the doorway, looking like she's ready for school. Even with the ponytail and the dark-framed glasses, she's fucking gorgeous.

I wish again I was the one going to deal with Bardoratch. He tried to burn her alive, and he's the reason she has bruises on her back from slamming into the mat during self-defense training.

"Everything okay?" Avery's concern hits me square in the chest.

"Absolutely." My forced smile turns genuine. "You ready to go out?"

She nods and disappears inside.

I stash my burn phone and retrieve my gun as Avery waits in the living room for me, sitting on the controversial couch. I kept it as a reminder of the betrayal, but now it's starting to remind me more of the way Avery used to come downstairs looking for me.

"Feel like taking a drive? There's a restaurant I've been hearing about that I want to check out. It's a couple hours away."

"Sure," she says, all casual ease now.

Last night, we argued over the sleeping arrangements. Once again, she wanted to sleep in the guest room. And once again, I waited till she was asleep to retrieve her from there to put her in my bed.

This morning though, she didn't hesitate to spread her legs so I could tongue-fuck her until she came. There was also no hesitation about sucking my cock until I got off just as hard. She was even down for taking a shower with me, which is how I saw the faint blue bruises from our basement training session.

When we were drying off, I told her I wanted to spend the day with her today, and she smiled and gave me the kiss I also wanted. I don't really understand what good she thinks her boundaries are doing, but whatever. I'll just keep working around them until they're gone.

My problem-solving skills are well honed, which is why we'll be a couple hours away with receipts to prove it when Todd Bardoratch gets what's coming to him.

If he'd only come after me, I might not have killed him. But he came for Avery, too, and that is not allowed.

Once she's in the Porsche, I run a hand through my hair and grimace at the horizon, knowing I'm back to the way I was in high school. And worse.

No one's allowed to hurt her. No one's allowed to touch her except me. But this time around, I'm pushing past her boundaries and fucking her in filthy ways she might not even be ready for.

This time, even when she hesitates, I can't make myself stop.

There's a word for what this is, and it's not a nice one.

❦ 25 ❦

AVERY

The restaurant Shane wants to try doesn't open until three, so when we reach Coynston, a city about an hour outside Boston, we go to a place called the Shamrock Café. It's newly opened as well and is being touted as one of the best places in the region for an upscale brunch.

We're seated at a window that looks out onto the back patio, which in summer must be gorgeous with the flower borders in bloom. At the edge there's a greenhouse, and our server tells us proudly that some of the menu's tomatoes and greens are grown there.

I want to order an Irish coffee but figure I'll be carded. Shane orders it instead and then gives it to me when it comes. If the waitress notices, she doesn't let on.

Partway through my eggs, my mom calls. I would let it go to voice-mail, but because she was upset yesterday, I don't want to leave it.

"Sorry," I say. "I need to take this."

Shane leans back in his chair, saying nothing, but looking displeased.

"Ave, good!" Mom says. "Ethan and I are coming to Granthorpe so

I can see you today. What's the best time to pick you up? I need to speak privately with you, so where on campus would be good for that? A park maybe? We could take a walk."

"Mom, I'm not at Granthorpe and won't be until tonight."

"Where are you?"

"Right now I'm having brunch in Coynston. Do you know it?"

"I think I've heard of it. You're with friends?"

My teeth sink into my lower lip for a moment. "I'm with Shane."

There's a long pause, and my gaze flicks to his face, which frowns back at me.

"Can you come by the house on your way through Boston? I really need to talk to you." There's something in her voice that causes me to go still. "Please?" she says. Her voice sounds on the verge of tears, which isn't like her at all.

"Yes, I'll try."

"It's important. And if you need us to come and get you—"

"I know. But, no." My voice is kind but firm. "We'll try to come. Right now, I have to go. I'm in a restaurant."

"All right. Text when you're on your way, so we know when to expect you."

"Ok." When I end the call, Shane folds his arms across his chest. "I need to stop by their house."

"Today?" The word is an accusation and a rebuke all rolled into one.

"Yes, today. Something's wrong. She needs to talk to me. If you really don't want to go, you can drop me off and either come back for me or Ethan can drive me back to campus."

"What's the emergency?"

"I don't know."

"I bet I do." He uncrosses his arms and takes a swig of his coffee. "There's something I need to take care of in Back Bay. Not urgent, but I might as well get it done. I'll drop you at Ethan's and then swing back later to get you."

He doesn't want to let me go to them, so I'm grateful there's no fight. Not that he really does that. With him, it's the silent treatment. Sometimes for years, I think tartly.

Thoughts of the rift come back whenever we have a disagreement. That's something I need to let go. As I finish my coffee, I slide my plate away. Shane eats his breakfast and then what's left of mine.

"Hungry, huh?"

"Worked up an appetite fighting for my life last night." He says this as if he's serious, which has the desired effect of making me chuckle.

"I bet you're shocked that I'm such a great training partner."

He looks at me over the rim of his mug, his gaze moving from my face down to my chest. "No, I'm not." With one heated look, he makes my mind flash back to the start of our day, to oral sex and the orgasm that made my legs shake almost as much as grappling in the basement did.

We have great chemistry. We always have.

My hand slides over, so my thumb can rub his.

His thumb moves on top to trap mine, and he smiles. "Parents twice in one weekend, interfering with our plans." He shakes his head, chastising me in that sexy, dominant way of his. "You'll need to make that up to me."

I shake my head with skeptical raised brows.

"Oh yeah, you will."

The battle to suppress a smile is lost. I'm not sure that trading sexual favors is the right way to manage conflict, but it definitely feels better than yelling or not speaking to each other.

WHEN MOM AND I SETTLE IN AT THE KITCHEN ISLAND WITH CUPS of herbal tea, her tone is full of false cheer. She's working hard to keep things light, and that feels false.

I reach over and squeeze her hand. "Mom, come on. Let's talk for real."

She blows on her tea and takes a sip. Then she frowns but nods. "Ave, when Ethan and I were reviewing the videotapes of your presentation to give you feedback, he told me he recognized the living room in the background. You made the videos at Shane's?"

"Oh. Yeah, actually." It didn't occur to me to mask my location. It probably should have.

"And the other day, Shane said he took you with him to his grandfather's because you were with him. What's going on? It seems like you're with him constantly lately."

I blow out a breath. Time to rip the Band-Aid off.

As soon as I start speaking, the words fly out of my mouth. "I'm staying at Shane's. Something happened on campus that scared me. I went to see Shane and asked if I could crash at his place until the end of the semester. He agreed to let me. And actually, it's been good in a lot of ways. We're working through things. Which is good for everyone."

She exhales audibly. "There are some things I need to say."

I wait, chewing on my lip. I can't tell yet whether this is going to be a productive conversation or not.

"There's something I should have told you a long time ago. After brunch, Shane asked me a question, and I didn't answer him. Did he mention it?"

"No." Warming my hands on the sides of my mug, I give her an encouraging smile.

"Here's the thing. When I was sixteen, a boy who was a year older —and who was dating someone I cared about—did something horrible." She looks down into her cup, swirling the contents. "I was at his place. Several of us were there, and his girlfriend was on her way, too. He pressured us into doing shots of cough syrup, which it turned out had codeine in it. The shot he gave me had a double dose. I passed out almost immediately. He convinced the others to leave and rescheduled with his girlfriend, without ever mentioning I was still there. He claimed he was tired and would call her later."

Mom scrapes the fingernail polish off her thumb, leaving ragged edges with bare nail showing from underneath.

"I woke up partway through the night. He was on top of me. I struggled and told him to stop, but I couldn't get him off. My body felt like Jello. Then I passed out again. When I woke up the next time, I was lucid but felt sick. I was also naked. He was in bed with me and just had shorts on."

There's a horrible silence for several beats while my heart breaks.

Her voice is low but steady as she forces herself to keep going. "He pretended he had gotten very intoxicated and passed out. He said nothing happened between us. I told him I knew something had happened. He continued to deny it. We argued, and he became irate and basically implied I was crazy for accusing him. Said that whatever I thought had happened was just a dream. He acted so outraged and sounded so convincing that I knew other people would probably believe him. I even started to doubt myself..." Her voice is strained with emotions and then trails off. She uses one fingernail to tear the polish off the nails on the opposite hand.

"I went to the hospital and had my mom meet me there. They did a rape kit and, of course, it proved exactly what I remembered. He raped me. I wish I could say the actual assault was the worst part, but it wasn't. My mom didn't want me to make a report. She didn't want me to talk about it period. She acted like it was just the kind of thing guys do if they get the chance. According to her, it would ruin my reputation and embarrass the family."

My mom's short, angry laugh is like breaking glass, and it makes me stiffen.

"She wasn't wrong." Mom runs a hand over the pale stone topping the island. "It's definitely the kind of thing some guys do if they think they can get away with it. Later when I saw him at school, he either pretended it didn't happen or made jokes about what happens to girls who get too drunk."

In the space between her words, I don't know whether to try to say something comforting or to stay silent. I'm afraid if I speak too soon she won't get through telling me the whole of it, and I think she wants to.

Mom takes a swig of tea like it's whiskey and blows out another long, slow breath.

"The other piece was that I told his girlfriend, who also happened to be my sister. She was outraged at first. Until she listened to 'his side of the story' where he claimed he couldn't remember anything. He said, if a test proved we'd had sex, we must have been flirting and then had consensual sex. He said it was a terrible thing to do *to her*, and he was sorry. He said I must feel really guilty, and that's probably why I was saying it was all his fault." Mom shakes her head. "He was *such* a good liar. My sister just kept saying things like, 'He doesn't need to rape anyone. He has a girlfriend to do things with. *Me*. And he's really good-looking and popular. Even if I wasn't with him, he wouldn't need to trick you or anyone into having sex with him. What you're saying just doesn't make sense, Sheri.'"

A cold harder than ice enters her voice. It matches her expression. "The truth is some guys just want more than they have. In the weeks leading up to the rape, I felt something shift. When we were alone, he flirted with me. I became very uncomfortable around him. I wish I'd never gone to his place. I thought it would be okay because there were other people there, and my sister was on her way. But he wanted what he wanted, and he manipulated the situation so he could do what he did. The hardest part was not being able to get justice, on *any* level. My family didn't want it to be true, so they acted like it wasn't. They moved on and told me to stop talking about it. He got away with it completely. Zero consequences."

Her voice is more broken now, and my eyes sting. I'm so angry on her behalf. No wonder we never see her parents or her sister.

"I did eventually find a way to cope," she says, biting a nail that's been stripped of polish. "I went to a support group and met a whole bunch of other girls. Not being alone, being believed, having people agree that it *is* a crime and *is* a big deal when a guy does that...it saved me. So many of their stories were like my own. 'I got drunk and woke up naked and no longer a virgin.' 'He gave me a pill, and I woke up naked and then was pregnant.' 'I woke up in the middle and couldn't stop it.' 'He got me alone at a party and held a hand over my mouth while he raped me. Afterward, he went back out and had beers with his friends.' 'He held me down. I couldn't fight him off. Too much bigger. Too much stronger. Against him, I had no chance.'"

I swallow against my dry throat. A tear spills over my lashes, and I wipe it slowly away.

"That's why I never, ever wanted you out of my sight. Not at pageants or anywhere there were strange men around. I kept my eye on you every minute. But when you got older, I couldn't always be with you. All I could do was warn you to be careful."

She draws in a shuddering breath and a little sob escapes. "I got involved with Ethan, who I just loved and trusted. He's the best guy. When I confided in him, he never, ever questioned whether I wore a short skirt or tight sweater or a million other things idiotic people ask you when you've been assaulted. Ethan never made excuses for the boy. What Ethan said was that he wished he had been my lawyer, because he would have made sure there were charges filed. No way would that prick have gotten away scot-free."

My mom's cuticle is bleeding. She gets up and grabs a paper towel to staunch the blood. "While we were dating, Ethan and I talked about his teenage son, who Ethan worried about. He said he was doing everything he could to raise his son to be a good man but confided that the boy had some troubling tendencies. After his mom left, the boy was never the same happy kid he had been. He got into a lot of fights. He had difficulty controlling his temper. And once during an argument, Shane admitted he blamed Ethan for letting his mother leave. Ethan told him he'd tried to convince her to stay and go to counseling, and that he'd started working less so he could spend more time with her. But in the end, it didn't work because she'd already fallen in love with someone else. He told Shane he'd been willing to try anything, but she wasn't. And Shane said Ethan should've forced her. Shane said some men wouldn't just let their wife leave like that. If another man was in the picture, they'd have gotten rid of him. Ethan said he knew that was coming straight from the mouth of Shane's grandfather, an Irish mobster."

I grimace, wondering whether what she's saying is true. Would Mr. Sullivan keep a wife prisoner? And kill her lover to eliminate the competition? Some of Shane's words come rushing back. *Other guys won't risk a confrontation with me.*

"I was scared of Shane's other family. I still am," my mom says. "Ethan said we wouldn't have to see them. He'd already taken measures to limit Shane's visits with his maternal grandfather. I thought everything would be all right. Ethan and I got engaged, and I flew to Boston to meet Shane. He turned out to be my worst nightmare. Charming, popular, handsome, star athlete, all the friends. He was great on the surface, but I knew that was his cover. He had scuff marks on his knuckles that he lied about. Ethan knew he was still getting into fights, but they weren't on school property, so there was no way to prove it. Ethan tried to talk to him, but by then, Shane was a very smooth liar. And if Ethan pushed too much, Shane became very cocky, saying he could handle his own business. Here was a kid who didn't think he needed to answer to anyone. And he was the biggest person in the house. It was terrifying."

She looks at me with sorrow in her eyes. "I watched him watch you, Ave. Anytime he thought no one was paying attention, his eyes followed you, like he was lying in wait. I love Ethan so much, but there were days when I just wanted to grab your hand and pull you out of the house. I felt, down to my bones, that if he got a chance to take advantage of you, he would. It was in my head all the time. I thought, 'If we're ever not here, my baby is not going to be safe.'"

I jump from my chair and go over to hug her. "I'm sorry you were so afraid, Mom. And I'm so sorry about what happened to you, and that you never got justice."

She hugs me tightly, silently, and a part of me twists into knots with grief at all she's been through.

"After the morning of the misunderstanding...the way he cut everyone off and made everyone feel so wretched. I get it. He felt angry and betrayed. But the ruthless way he got even with me was by hurting you guys, and that's how I know he can't be trusted. He destroyed your reputation at school and refused to see Ethan. It broke my heart for you both. And then I thought things were finally getting better, and you were going to get a fresh start at college. Until you and Ethan decided on Granthorpe. Now Shane is back in the picture, older and more dangerous than ever."

I'm torn between wanting to defend him and knowing I can't honestly deny that Shane is dangerous.

"Shane's a complicated person." My arms tighten around her. "But he wouldn't hurt me the way you think."

"Not the way I think? But in other ways, right? He already has. And now you're alone in a house with him." Her voice is so soft and so filled with dread. "I'm scared all over again. Please come home. I'm begging you, Ave. If not for your sake, then for mine."

I stroke her back and squeeze, my eyes stinging. "I'm okay. I promise. And I will be home in just a few days. I've got my presentation and a couple of exams and I'm done. Please try not to worry. Shane's not going to hurt me."

"You say that, but—"

"Mom, listen." I pull back and make my voice firm, leaning against the counter, so I can look her in the eye. "You've told me everything, and I'm so glad. Thank you for trusting me with your story. But Shane is not the guy he reminds you of. I know how to handle Shane." That's a huge exaggeration, but I make it sound true. "Please don't treat him like a criminal. Innocent until proven guilty, remember?"

"I'm not a lawyer. I'm just a worried mom."

"Keep an open mind, okay? For Ethan and me? Because when we treated Shane like he was guilty of something he didn't do, it hurt him just as much as it hurt you to be treated like a liar. Remember how you felt when your sister didn't believe you? To feel like your family betrayed you? That's how he feels. And in his case, the police came. He was worried he might get railroaded into jail because of your accusations. Ones that *weren't* true."

For an instant, she looks stricken. "I wasn't trying to hurt him."

"None of us were, but *we did*. And when you act suspicious of him now, it reminds him of the past and that he can't trust the people who are supposed to love him. I don't think you want to be a person who inflicts that kind of trauma."

"Of course not," she says quickly.

"Okay, so try to keep an open mind. I'm an adult. If I start to feel unsafe around him, I'll leave. But so far, his house is the only place near school where I do feel safe."

She squeezes my hand. "Just come home."

"I will. Soon."

My mom hugs me again, holding on so tightly I'm not sure she's ever going to let go.

✦ 26 ✦

SHANE

Throughout dinner at an Italian restaurant in Boston, Avery's quieter than usual. When I surprise her by saying we'll spend the night in a hotel because I'm too tired to drive back, she studies me speculatively.

"Why would we stay in a hotel when we have family in Boston?"

"I don't feel like dealing with anyone." That's the truth, but staying in an upscale hotel is also about my car being in valet parking all night, and there being lobby camera footage of me. My alibi needs to be well-documented.

I checked in online, so I just drop by the desk to grab a key. Avery stands near me with her hands clasped behind her. Out of my reach.

In the elevator on the way up to the room, I say, "Wanna talk about what happened when you went home?"

"Not really." Her expression is guarded as her interlocked fingers press into the hollow below her breast bone.

Impatience creeps into my voice, and I don't try to hide it. "Avery, come on."

She glances at me, shrugs and looks away. "My mom said you asked her if she was ever sexually assaulted. She was."

Hell. "I'm sorry that happened to her."

"Me too." Avery presses her lips together, and her eyes take on a teary sheen that she has to blink away. "Mom's not over it. I doubt she ever will be. He got away with it."

"Too bad she didn't have a monster to avenge her."

She looks over at me sharply. "What would a monster do?"

"Monster things," I say noncommittally. This is not a conversation I should have with her tonight while I'm covering my tracks.

Her expression softens despite my cagey reply. "Yeah, that's not our kind of problem."

The bait dangles. I don't take it.

The elevator doors open, and I extend a hand to usher her out. We're silent as we head down the hall. The other shoe has yet to drop.

Inside the room, there's a king-sized bed with a glossy navy bedspread and a thousand pillows. Avery barely gives it a glance as she walks to the far side. She sits in a thick-cushioned gold chair, with a distant look in her eyes.

I drop my duffel next to the bed and walk to her. Sitting on the bed's edge, I lean forward. "What's on your mind?"

"You said we own each other, but you don't really mean that, do you?"

My innocent smile is a cover.

She slides her shoes off and tucks her legs under her, leaning against the side of the chair as she looks at me. Her sigh is troubled. "I think," she begins, her voice as soft as feathers. "When people get wrapped up in the idea of ownership, things can go badly when one tries to leave."

The feigned smile vanishes as my eyes narrow. Seems like Sheri managed to plant a dangerous seed.

"Don't dance around it, Avery. Ask what you really want to ask."

"How far would you go to keep someone from leaving you?"

"Hard to say. In the past, when a relationship stopped working, I was always the one who left. But those girls weren't you." I shake my head, pressing my lips together. "Are you asking what would happen if you cheated on me and tried to take off with another guy? Yeah, that would not go well. If you cheat, you should not let me find out. There would be a fight, and he *would not* win."

She tilts her head, a small breathy laugh escaping. "That's not what I meant. At all." Her fingers rub her forehead, and the big blue eyes roll. "Cheat on you? Who with?" Her gaze locks with mine. "If I leave, it won't be for someone else. For me, no one compares to you."

My eyes hold hers for the span of a dozen heartbeats. "Same."

Her fingers flutter and then come to rest on my leg. "Crushing on other people...that's not our kind of problem. Our problem is trust. When my mom talked about Ethan today, it made me realize that she trusts him completely. He's her best friend. They tell each other everything."

"Maybe they do now. They're married. They've been together a long time."

"You have a lot of secrets—"

"Hey, I'm not keeping secrets about how I feel. I'm in this. It's not a game." My hand drops onto hers and squeezes, holding tight. "You're trying to hold back because you're scared, but that's a waste of time. Your fear isn't big enough to keep you away from me. I'd stake everything I own on that."

As she watches me, Avery licks her lips and nods. "You're right." She exhales, and it's almost a sigh. "I'm really bad at enforcing the boundaries I try to set. I think it's because I don't actually want them. They're a sensible precaution...but what I really want is for us both to be all in."

Fuck, yes. "Same."

Beneath mine, her hand turns over, and our hands clasp each other.

"After my presentation tomorrow, I'll go to Student Health." Her head tilts, her bright eyes studying my face. "Maybe on New Year's Eve...?"

Fuck, yes. "Yeah, perfect. Let's go somewhere special. I'll take you anywhere you want. Name the place."

"A hotel in Aspen would be fine, if we're still there from Christmas.

Or at your house, if we're back. It won't matter where we are. That never does when I'm with you."

Same.

The chemistry between us is a rare, perfect thing. Like a fifty-year-old bottle of Reibiliúnach that I wouldn't part with at any price.

"I know." I raise her hand to kiss it, brushing my lips over her soft skin. "That's the way it's always been for me, too. When you're in the room, the rest of the world falls away."

AVERY

LYING NAKED ON THE BED WITH MY CALVES OVER SHANE'S shoulders as he goes down on me is a revelation in just how skilled his mouth is. I come three times over the course of an hour and finally have to stop him before I pass out.

My legs quiver so hard I'm not certain I could kneel or even crawl into a position to reciprocate. When I admit this, he chuckles.

"Lie back and relax," he murmurs after he crawls up the bed and reclines against a stack of pillows next to me. His cock is so hard it looks angry and painful, but he's calm as he fists it and strokes.

"Don't you need me to help with that?" I ask curiously, rolling onto my side to watch him. His body is so gorgeous. His abs alone could star in an action movie.

He smirks. "It's not my rookie season, beautiful."

"Should I leave you alone to concentrate?"

"So I can fantasize about your naked body instead of actually looking at it? No."

That makes me smile.

He draws in a deep breath, making his chest expand and his muscles stretch. His hand pauses. "I thought you were tired, so I was giving you a pass. But if you're not tired after all, then yeah, put that pretty mouth to good use."

His practical hard-edged approach to sex is so foreign...and, I suppose, masculine. The way I think about sex with him is laced with so many delicate little feelings.

"Would that feel better? Or just different?" I ask, trying to match his blazing candor.

"What? A blow job? Versus using my hand?" His tone is incredulous.

"Is that a crazy question?" I try not to sound defensive. "I read something online that made me wonder. You're the only person I've ever talked to about sex. Couldn't really ask before…"

He exhales and licks his lips. His hand releases his cock, and when he speaks, his voice is low but earnest. "Anything that involves you feels better. Much better." He rests his hand against his ribs, like he's in no rush. "What else do you want to know? Ask me anything."

"I wouldn't be able to masturbate with you watching." My voice catches on the word masturbate, but I press on. "It seems like you could?"

"Yeah."

When I don't say anything more, he studies my face closely.

"Do you want to watch?"

I nod, barely managing to keep myself from admitting how many times I've fantasized about spying on him in the shower or in bed. "Will it ruin your concentration if I talk to you?"

"Not the way you do it," he says, sounding bemused.

That makes me chuckle. One of the great things about being with Shane is that he never implies that my inexperience makes me less adept at turning him on.

"Come closer, baby." His right hand closes around his cock, and he pumps up and down in a steady rhythm.

I press my body against his side, and he closes his eyes and husks out a breath.

For a while I just watch, memorizing every inch of him and the way his face looks when his mind's occupied with filthy thoughts.

When I put my hand on him just below his ribs, his abs tighten. My fingers trace the lines of his six-pack.

"More," he groans. "Slide your hand lower."

I press my palm against his stomach and slide it down until it's over his pubic bone and his knuckles are raking over mine.

"You're so beautiful," I whisper and then kiss his chest. "I could look at you forever."

"*Fuck*." His body goes rigid, and his cock erupts.

27

AVERY

We drive back from Boston early in the morning, and I rush to get ready so I'll have a few minutes to review my presentation before school. I dress in the simple royal blue pant-suit that my mom favored and have half a bagel with some jam while running through the key points in my head.

When Shane comes down he's dressed in jeans and a t-shirt with his hair still wet from the shower. The only reason he's up is to drive me, which suddenly strikes me as really sweet.

I pace the living room floor, reviewing the takeaways I want people to remember. Then I check my slides, of which there are very few. That was intentional, so the focus would be on me and my message, not the screen. It could be a miscalculation, though. What if I forget what I planned to say? I'll have nothing to prompt me.

Shane drinks his coffee, standing in the doorway, watching me.

I glance over and grimace. "I'm either going to kill this, or I'm going to crash and burn. There is no middle ground."

"Anything I can do?"

"Not unless you have a time machine."

He smiles, finishes his coffee, and sets the cup on the counter.

"Ready to drop me off?" I ask.

"You wanna go this early?"

I nod.

He gets our coats while I pack up my laptop.

I don't remember the drive to campus or if we talk about anything. My entire mind is focused, and my heart's started to beat like I'm jogging.

Shane walks me to the building. I stop at a bench a few feet from the door and sit.

"Too early to go in," I say, taking a deep breath of bracing cold air.

Shane sits next to me.

"You don't need to wait with me. It's daylight. There are plenty of people around. I'm safe here."

He puts his arm on the back of the bench behind me and settles in.

I glance at his profile and smile. "I appreciate your calm this morning. It's helpful."

He nods, and I turn to sit sideways on the bench to face him. My hand rises to rest against his face and rubs his whiskers.

"Last night..." I whisper.

That draws his gaze.

"Was really great."

"Agreed," he says with a smile. After a beat, he adds, "Unexpectedly didactic."

I laugh softly. "Next time, you could tell me to ask Google my questions."

"That falls into the category of *never*."

My hand drops to his thigh, and I squeeze his leg gently before withdrawing my hand and setting it on my tote.

When people start to arrive, I stand, and he does as well. "No PDA. Let's save the good stuff for when we're alone."

"As usual," he murmurs with a smirk. He walks to the door and opens it for me. "If I stay to watch will that rattle you or provide moral support?"

"I don't know," I say honestly.

"I'll sit in back. If you want me to leave, signal me by tapping your wrist like it's time."

"Okay." I squeeze his hand before walking past him and entering the lecture hall.

Professor Smith-Hall is already onstage, and he suggests everyone move down front. The class does, but Shane stays where he is. I glance back twice and decide I'm glad he's there.

Daniel sits directly behind me and leans forward. "Thanks for sending the latest version of the presentation. It's good."

"Did you hear from Todd? He's said nothing. Not even that he got it."

"No, haven't heard from him."

I roll my eyes. Radio silence from Todd for days. And now he hasn't even bothered to show up. Unprofessional, passive-aggressive bullshit.

Smith-Hall begins talking, and I immediately turn to face forward. We're starting.

He flashes the list of presenters, and I'm fifth of eight.

The first few presentations fly by. They're pretty boring, in large part because the speakers aren't dynamic. They all probably lack stage training. At least my pageant time should help with something.

When it's my turn to present, I stand onstage staring out at the dark auditorium. For ten seconds, my mind is blank, and my heart kicks into high gear. Then my slides load, and an old polaroid snapshot of a dandelion appears. The story I plan to start with comes flooding back.

There you are.

I face my audience but don't see them. When I speak, it's exactly as I rehearsed, complete with meaningful pauses and expressive gestures. My energy rises at the end, partly from relief and partly because I'm excited. I know it's gone well.

The applause is enthusiastic, but my attention goes to Smith-Hall. He's smiling as he makes some notes on his tablet.

When I leave the stage, I move to the second row and sit next to Daniel.

"That was fantastic! Well done," he says.

"Thanks." I want to look back at Shane but don't because the next presenter's ready to start.

The next two presentations pass quickly and are mostly a blur. People are restless and distracted by their phones, which is rude. I leave mine in my tote bag.

"Jesus," Daniel murmurs, glancing surreptitiously at his. "Well, that explains why he's not here."

"What?" I whisper.

"Todd was in a bad car accident last night. He's in a coma. They airlifted him to a trauma center in Boston this morning."

"Oh, my God," I murmur, my body going stiff with shock. "Alone in the car?"

"I guess."

"Drinking?"

Daniel shrugs.

The last presentation is over, and Smith-Hall dismisses us. I stay in my seat for a moment because a couple of guys turn around to talk to Daniel about Todd.

"Heard it was a single-car accident," one says. "Hit a tree. There's some speculation that maybe he did it on purpose."

"No way," Daniel says. "Must've hit a patch of ice or something."

Rising from my seat, I say, "I have to get going. I'll talk to you later."

"Yeah, me too." Daniel stands and motions for me to precede him down the main aisle. "Let's get together to finalize the project. Hopefully Todd will be back in commission soon, but we may have to finish without him."

I nod as we walk. "We should do it soon. Sometime tomorrow maybe. I'm leaving town before break officially starts."

"Home to Boston?"

"No, Colorado."

"Whereabouts?"

"Aspen. Declan Heyworth's family and mine are friends. The Heyworths have a house there."

"Of course. And here's Moran again, huh?" Daniel frowns as he eyes Shane waiting near the doors. "There's a guy who wouldn't hesitate to disconnect Todd's ventilator if he got the chance."

A prickling sensation runs through me. Of course neither Shane nor I will be visiting Todd in the hospital since we can't stand the smug bastard, but we wouldn't wish a coma-inducing car crash on anyone.

Daniel walks out the doors just before me and keeps going without looking back.

"Todd Bardoratch was in a car accident last night," I say.

"Is that right?" Shane's brows rise, but his interest is fleeting. As he holds the main door open for me, he says, "So the presentation, you were right about there being no middle ground. You killed it. Want me to take you to breakfast to celebrate?"

That draws a small smile from me, and I nod.

SHANE

When we return from breakfast and a trip to Student Health, Sorensen's on my front porch. I can guess what he wants to talk about. I sent some texts to get him off campus, but because it was a last minute move, I left him hanging in Boston on his own with no explanation. He and I will need to have our conversation out of Avery's earshot.

I park the car in the garage.

When she gets out of the Porsche, she spots the empty gas can that's still lying on its side on the floor. "Shane, is that from the other night? The one the arsonist dropped?"

"Yeah, don't touch it. You'll stain your clothes."

"We should give it to the police and make a report."

"Let's talk about it later. I've got company."

She tucks her hair behind her ear and nods. "I saw Erik. I didn't realize he was coming by."

I don't answer as I put a hand on her back and usher her toward the house.

When we get to the porch, Sorensen stands. "Morning."

"Hi," Avery says in return. "Do you want coffee?"

"No, we'll talk out here," I say. "You go in, Ave."

She glances between us, looking like she wants to argue. Instead she complies, disappearing behind the front door.

Once the door's closed, Sorensen leans his massive bulk against the bricks. "So, last night?"

"Yeah, thanks for coming to Boston to meet me. Sorry I had to cancel. The hotel room was all right?"

Sorensen's pale blue eyes study my face. "Why'd you keep me in play all night?"

Lowering my voice, I say, "I thought getting out of town was a good idea for both of us."

He glances around, verifying no one's nearby. "The TB accident?"

I nod.

I sent Sorensen to Bardoratch's class to intimidate him, and Sorensen stepped in to lend a hand during the frat party fight. If I'd realized that things would escalate to the point of my putting a contract on Bardoratch, I never would've involved Erik. I don't want him pulled in as a suspect if the police realize that what happened to Bardoratch wasn't an accident.

"If someone looks, the text chain is suspect," Sorensen says.

"No, it's fine." A police investigation couldn't do anything useful with my luring him to Boston and then blowing him off. Schedules changed. There's nothing remotely related to Granthorpe or Bardoratch in the texts.

"I don't mean the ones from last night. I mean the earlier ones."

Yeah, those early ones could've been a problem. But not with our alibis in place. "Should be fine. Sorry I didn't meet up to lay things out. Avery was with me."

He glances at the front door. "Seems like the girl's never out of your sight anymore."

"True statement." My gaze cuts to the window where the shade sways. Avery must have looked out.

"You've got her in your house. You trust her?"

I suck on my bottom lip a moment and then shrug again. His interests are tangled with mine, so I appreciate the mild tone with which he questions her loyalty. I wish I could tell him there's nothing to worry about when it comes to Avery being installed in my house, but I can't swear to it. "I can resist everything but temptation."

The corner of Sorensen's mouth twitches, and he shrugs his brows. "The most dangerous food is wedding cake."

That draws a chuckle from me. "Is that a Wilde quote, too?"

He shakes his head. "Thurber." His giant hands push against the brick, setting him forward on his feet. "The money was higher than expected this month. Profit sharing?"

Officially Sorensen's on my payroll as a shelf-stocker at a convenience store I own. It's one of the fronts I use to launder our money. After some careful vetting, I brought him into my illegitimate businesses a year ago as a minor partner. His cut is normally fifteen percent, but I paid him more this time.

"Of sorts. I gave you an extra ten percent from my share. The past couple of weeks you've gone beyond what we agreed to, so let's call it a Christmas bonus."

His light brown brows rise. "That help was for blood's sake." He runs a hand through his hair that's well into lion's mane territory these days. It's a good thing the football season ends soon. "For family, favors are free. So you've said and proved yourself."

Yeah, when he was strapped for cash as a freshman, both Declan and I floated him loans. For us, Sorensen started out as an investment. But that's not what he is anymore. Now he's a partner whose debts were paid long ago.

"Then don't consider it a bonus. Call it a Christmas gift."

"If you say so." Briefly flashing a grin, he shrugs. "I'll get going. Gotta contemplate all the unwise ways to spend that money once football's over."

Sorensen goes down the porch steps, and I nod my goodbye when he's behind the wheel of his SUV.

Once his truck is out of sight, I head into the house. Avery's waiting just inside, her eyes filled with kitten curiosity.

"What's going on?" she asks.

"Nothing. You gonna change clothes?" I catch her hips, drawing her to me. "If so, I'll help with the unzipping." My hand comes to rest on the back of her slacks.

Avery brushes my fingers away and steps back. "When will you trust me with the truth?"

How's never, I think. "The truth about our relationship? I told you, ask me anything."

Avery shakes her head. "C'mon, Shane."

I'm not just keeping secrets to protect myself and my partners. An equally important issue is that there's no way I want the things I do to end up on her conscience.

"Baby, listen. If you go to work for a tech company with proprietary secrets, I'm not going to ask you to open the corporate files, so I can read them. It's the same for my business."

Avery frowns. "Except my company won't be doing anything illegal."

"Who says mine is?"

She shrugs. "I feel like there are important things you're not telling me. Things I should know."

I don't respond.

She sighs. "Okay. I need to study. First final is tomorrow."

My arm corals her. "Give me a kiss first."

Avery moves closer and kisses me. Her lips are petal soft and sweeter than honey. I know her curiosity is a problem, but that innocence of hers is impossible to resist. *She* is impossible to resist.

Sorensen and Declan both question whether I can trust her. That's not even a consideration anymore.

The stage I'm at now is "ride or die."

28

AVERY

S hane's asleep when I slip from his bed in the middle of the
night.

I can't sleep because I've gotten wrapped up in campus
posts about Casanova, and I'm thinking about how shady it is that the
gas can from the arson attack is still sitting in Shane's garage. Casanova
could be the one who started the fire. If so, the gas can should've
already been turned over to the police, in case there's forensic evidence
that matches something collected from the abduction crime scenes. If
Shane's aversion to the police allows Casanova to remain free longer
than he should, I will not be all right with that.

Turning in the gas can is something I'd be happy to do on my own.
But the police would probably want to visit the house, at least to look
at the exterior. For multiple reasons, I really need to know how serious
Shane's criminal endeavors are.

On top of which, I'm annoyed because he's shamelessly creating a
double-standard. While Daniel and I were working online to finalize
our project for submission, I left my phone unattended. When I
walked into the kitchen to grab it, I found Shane going through it.

His claim that he needed to check my calendar to make holiday travel plans may have been true when he unlocked the phone, but at a glance, I could see he was reading my text threads, too. Which tracks with my suspicion that Shane thinks it's acceptable for him to keep secrets from me, but not for me to have secrets from him.

Scowling now, I take Shane's phone from the nightstand and tip-toe out into the hall. I don't know his code, but I've watched his finger move as he swipes a figure-of-eight pattern to unlock it.

It takes three attempts for me to get in.

I go into the text messages and immediately know that he must routinely delete his threads. There are only two open message chains. One with Declan and one with "Neighbor 8353." From the house number, I assume that's the neighbor next door.

I open the Declan thread. There are only a handful of messages, all from earlier in the evening tonight.

> Shane: what do u say to upping job description n pay for guy who stocks shelves? I trust him w/ inventory. u?

> Declan: yeah, agreed. y now?

> Shane: tell u when I see u

> Declan: sure // word came down date set on celebration. what condom brand u want there?

> Shane: hole in your schedule tomorrow to talk? 10a?

> Declan: 1130 all i got.

> Shane: Ill make it work. see u your place

> Declan: sure

I remain frozen for several heartbeats, re-reading Declan's second message. Why does anyone need to know Shane's favorite brand of condoms? For a moment, I try to believe it's about New Year's Eve and having condoms on hand for Declan's houseguests as some sort of creepy amenity. But I'll be on the pill by then, so Shane won't need to wear one, and I don't believe Shane would have Declan's staff buying his condoms anyway. Also, when Declan writes that "word came down," it makes it seem like someone else is calling the shots. *Date set.* What kind of celebration requires a supply of condoms. An orgy?

I open the neighbor thread absently. There are a couple greetings, and there's a video. After a second, I realize the clip was sent in response to Shane's request for security camera footage during the neighborhood-canvassing.

I watch the video, freezing and zooming in when I think I recognize the person being filmed. It's Todd Bardoratch. An icy chill runs through me until I remember that Todd's not a danger to us anymore.

I stare down at the video as it replays, then I lower the phone, staring at the wall.

Too bad she didn't have a monster to avenge her. Those were Shane's words about my mom's assault. And when I asked what a monster would do, he said, "monster things." Like causing a near-fatal car wreck?

No. It was a single-car accident, and Shane wasn't anywhere near campus at the time it happened.

Shane is so smooth though, and he has those ties to the Irish Mafia. On Saturday, he showed his grandfather a video clip of something.

I look at the time his neighbor sent the video. Saturday during brunch. Right after which, Shane announced he wanted to stop by his grandfather's on our way out of Boston. Could Mr. Sullivan have sent someone to deal with the man Shane suspected of trying to kill us?

I shake my head. It's too crazy. The fire just happened three days ago. They wouldn't have had time to retaliate this quickly, would they? And anyway, it was a one-car accident, not some hit and run.

Unless someone ran him off the road and kept going. Or tampered with his car...

No.

Then I think about Todd's black eye the morning after he threatened me on the video call. Shane never left the house that night. He sent someone to intimidate Todd and then had Erik Sorensen watch over me the next day to be sure I wasn't hassled. There were no delays. No long planning sessions. Shane dealt with that situation immediately. And, by doing so, he proved he doesn't need to hurt anyone directly. He can arrange for it to happen.

My mouth goes bone dry. I need a glass of water, but I can't seem to move.

The uncertainty is killing me. Was Todd's crash an accident? Or something Shane arranged? And does that mean that Todd is Casanova? We didn't find a flower on the night of the fire, but the arsonist was interrupted in the middle.

I open the gallery on Shane's phone. I want to see if there are any more videos of Todd from Shane's neighbors or anyone else.

I find a video of my project presentation, and a picture of me from the Shamrock Café that I didn't realize he took. I exhale a little sigh because it's sweet that he has these.

I pause, feeling suddenly awful for rummaging through his phone.

If Shane knows Todd tried to kill us and that he's Casanova, then Todd had to be stopped. Not just as revenge, but because he would've gone on to hurt other girls.

I lower the phone and almost swipe to re-lock it, but if there is any other evidence that Todd is Casanova, I want to know. I return to the gallery.

I discover some photos of Shane's house from the night of the fire and the next morning, but no more of Todd.

Switching to the download file folder, I look for videos. There's only one, and the file name is Insurance_AK. Maybe some video he took to file an insurance claim related to the fire?

No, because the date is from before Friday.

I click on the video and freeze. It's me...and Shane.

Someone took a video of us in his living room?

There's no sound, but the picture is clear.

My mind races, and my heart hammers as I try to piece together when this was. The shirt I'm wearing in the video is the one I had on the day after I found the rose in my bed.

I watch as I walk over and grab a pillow from the couch. I drop it at Shane's feet and then lower myself to my knees.

Oh, my God.

The roaring in my ears is deafening.

The clip continues to play until I jab my finger to stop it. I'm too slow. The last frame is one of me with his cock in my mouth.

My breath catches in my throat. I can't breathe.

I stumble into the guest bathroom, thinking I'm going to be sick. I drop to my knees at the toilet, my mouth filling with saliva as I break out in a sweat. I spit into the bowl over and over, but I don't vomit.

For several moments, I'm too sick to move, but my mind continues to race. It dawns on me that there was no one lurking in a corner filming us. We were completely *alone.*

There's a hidden camera somewhere in Shane's living room. *He's* the one who recorded me, and then downloaded the video onto his phone.

Goddamn him.

Was this video just for himself? Or did he forward it to other people?

I delete the video as tears fill my eyes.

Fucking asshole.

I check the gallery and delete the other video and picture of me. Scrolling back, I make sure there's nothing else. Of course, the video in the living room was downloaded. That footage could be in cloud storage somewhere, and probably is.

Another wave of nausea hits me. My very first time giving anyone a blow job, and the guy records it. He can use it against me anytime. If he posts it online with my name, it will be searchable by potential employers.

Saliva fills my mouth again, and my stomach heaves.

For several minutes, I wretch, feeling as ill as I've ever felt in my life. Suppressing a sob, I lie on the cold tile until stillness helps quell the nausea. Finally, I'm steady enough to wipe my face with a cold cloth.

Then another thought hits me. Shane could send the video to my mom.

See, Sheri? As I said, Avery's the one who chases me, not the other way around. She's eighteen, so I finally gave her what she's been dying for. A taste of my cock.

The phone drops onto the bathroom tiles as I stumble to my feet.

I have to get out of his house.

Right fucking now.

❧ 29 ❧

SHANE

When I wake before dawn, I'm alone in my bed. There's no light coming from my bathroom, so she's somewhere else in the house.

Come on, Ave. What are you doing?

She could be studying. If she is, I wish she'd just brought her laptop to bed.

I wonder if Smith-Hall posted a grade for the presentation. Avery wants to hit him up for the recommendation letter immediately, assuming he gives her a high score. He will. She killed it.

I smile. It was tough to see her nervous before the presentation when there was no way for me to help. But when she presented, I decided it was better she did it all on her own. More for her to be proud of.

"Ave," I call out.

There's no answer.

Raising my voice so she'll be able to hear it downstairs, I repeat, "Avery?"

The house is silent.

Uneasiness hits me like a splash of cold water. I reach for my phone to be sure there was no security system alert while I slept. The phone's not on the nightstand.

I roll out of bed and drag on a pair of jeans.

"Avery!"

In a matter of seconds, I'm scouring the house, but she's nowhere to be found. My phone is on the floor of the guest bathroom, and I check it quickly to be sure she didn't try to make a nine-one-one call.

No, the call log's empty.

I open my text messages. There's one from her that's waiting to be opened. Thank Christ. If she went out for coffee or on a walk by herself before dawn, I'm going to give her hell about it.

> Avery: Saw video of myself. Insurance_AK

For several seconds it doesn't register. Then it does.

Fuck.

It's a gut punch. I picture her watching it and feeling the exact same thing. I wish she'd confronted me immediately instead of taking off. Then I could've told her the truth. I kept it as insurance but planned to delete it after she told her mom we're together.

I try to call her, but she lets me go to voicemail. I don't leave a message.

Where is she now? Campus? Alone?

My fingers jab the screen as I type.

> Shane: where r u? call me.

> Avery: who else has seen it?

Who else has seen it? What the fuck? Like I'd show that to other people.

> Shane: no one. kept it as proof of consensual relationship. at beginning, i thought i needed it. just insurance. not for fucking show and tell. would not do that. u can't think i would

She doesn't respond.

> Shane: where r u? i don't want u outside alone in dark. let me come get u. let's talk

Avery: i don't want to. i'm safe. leave me alone.

> Shane: for how long?

Avery: don't come to Colorado. I don't want to see you

I call her, but again, she lets the call go to voicemail. Grimacing, I blow out a frustrated breath.

> Shane: it was from first day. swear I was gonna delete it.

Avery: but you didn't. u delete things every day. but u kept that over n over n OVER.

Shit. I stop walking and shake my head.

How does she know I delete my logs and threads regularly? That's a habit of mine in case my phone is ever compromised.

I back out to the main page of my messages. Obviously, she could tell I clear things away because there's almost nothing there. I erased old threads last night. The only things left are the video of Bardoratch from my neighbor and my last texts with Declan.

Oh, fuck. Another landmine.

There's that text about the party at the Dark Knights club where Dec talks about condoms. If she read it, she must be wondering why the hell I need a stack of condoms for a party I haven't mentioned.

Rubbing my forehead, I grimace. I was never going to fuck any random girls in the DK club, even if Avery wasn't in the picture. Running train is not my thing.

I check the thread to see what I said in response.

Yeah, fuck, nothing to get myself off the hook. That's the problem with playing my cards close to the vest in emails and text messages. If

I'd texted that my condom brand wasn't relevant, she'd have been clued in to the truth.

I head into the guest room and open the closet. A lot of Avery's stuff is gone. Probably as much as she could carry. I've gotta figure out where she went. No matter how pissed she is, she's too smart to have taken a bus back to campus in the dark.

It's still early as hell, but Ethan's sometimes up at four or five in the morning, working. I open my contacts to call him.

He answers immediately. "Morning, son."

"Hey, Dad. Where are you?"

"In my car."

"Headed here?"

"No."

"Have you already been here?"

"Yes."

Shit. He came and took her, and I fucking slept through it.

The silence stretches between us as I wonder what she told him.

"Is Avery with you?"

"Yes. Do you want to talk to her?" His tone is neutral, which likely means she didn't tell him much.

I want to talk to her more than anything in the goddamned world, but we can't have the conversation we need to have while she's sitting next to Ethan. "No, I'll talk to her later."

"Okay." There's a beat. "Is there something else on your mind, Shane?"

"No," I lie.

I don't like that Avery went running home to them instead of staying to work things out with me. I don't like that she broke into my phone. But more than anything, I don't like that she found that video and left me because of it.

I should've deleted it sooner. Or better yet, never downloaded it to my phone in the first place.

I GIVE IT A FEW HOURS BEFORE I TRY TO CALL AVERY AGAIN. SHE doesn't pick up, which is no surprise. I decide to leave a message, which means I get to hear her voice, soft and sweet, and insidious. I should be hearing that voice in person today.

After the beep, I speak, working to keep my voice level. "Hey, I know you're pissed. You have a right to be. I shouldn't have allowed that recording to exist. It's gone now for good. Source file erased. And just so you know, there's only one camera in the house, it's in the living room, and it's been off since the morning after you arrived. Today, I erased everything that was in storage, so there are no recordings of you. *Zero.*"

I pause, rubbing my thumb over the side of the phone.

"I would never have used that video to hurt you. It was insurance because I thought you might try to hurt me. I know you wouldn't, not intentionally, but I realized that later." I shake my head in frustration. "Come on, Ave. Call me back. We're not leaving things like this, and you know we should talk in private, not in the middle of my dad's house with both our parents around to overhear us. Let me come get you. We'll go somewhere to talk. Afterward, if you want to stay in Boston, rather than coming back to my place, I'll leave you there."

I start to say something else, but the voice mailbox cuts me off. It's fine. I've said enough.

I end the call and glance at the clock.

She's probably getting ready to take one of her finals. It'll be at least a couple of hours before I hear from her. Time to get on with my day. I've got my own schoolwork to wrap up.

So I do. All day.

Avery doesn't call me back until ten at night, which I know means we're not going out somewhere to talk face-to-face. Still, a live conversation is better than texts. I turn off the television and sit back on the couch.

"Hey," I say when I answer. "You listened to my message?"

"Yes."

"And?"

There are a couple beats of silence before she says, "And...that's all.

I listened to what you had to say." Her tone signals that none of her anger has worn off.

"I'll come in the morning. Tell me what time."

She exhales a scoff. "No. No way."

"Why not?"

"Look...it's more than just the video, which—I don't really believe you planned to keep to yourself. You made it portable for a reason, Shane. It could've stayed in storage with other files from that camera. That would've been plenty of insurance if you really thought I would lie and accuse you of something. Which I also doubt you believed. I think you had it on your phone so you could pull it out to show my mom if she pissed you off. Maybe you intended to show it to someone else, too. Declan or whoever. A lot of guys swap pictures and videos of girls they've hooked up with. There was a Beta House scandal last year, right? With a scoreboard or whatever? It's a common thing."

I'm not some douchebag frat boy, but I don't snap back because I don't want to add fuel to the fight. Instead, I keep my voice low. "I didn't show it to anyone, and I wasn't planning to."

"You made it portable for a reason. Why?"

"I don't know," I say honestly. "I didn't realize we'd been recorded until late on the first night you were here. I tapped the clip to watch it, and a copy downloaded. That's it. As soon as I realized what that camera caught on video, I went downstairs and unplugged it."

"I hope that's true."

I grind my teeth together. "Are you skeptical? Really? You know me. Do you honestly think I would let someone else watch you like that? Is that at all consistent with how I am when it comes to you? Like I'd be happy to share you? Give me a fucking break," I say with as mild a tone as I can muster. "I want you to myself. Always have. Which you know."

"I was shocked and felt sick when I saw that video on your phone. I still am," she says softly, which is like having a knife thrust into my heart.

"It was a mistake, and I'm sorry."

"Even if I could forgive you for the video, that's not the only issue." Her voice is so soft I almost can't hear it.

I press my phone's volume button to raise the sound all the way.

"What else, Avery? Tell me."

"You've got a lot of secrets—the locked room and whatever else. Things I don't even have a clue about. I can't be with someone who has so much to hide."

"Look, there are things—"

"I know! Shane, *I know*." She draws in a breath and exhales. When she speaks again, her voice is measured. "I'm sure you keep secrets for a really good reason. But I can't handle it. I was wrong to break into your phone, but I couldn't stop myself. It's better for you, and for me, if this thing between us ends now."

"I don't want it to end."

"We don't trust each other. It's already over."

My head tips back, so I'm staring at the ceiling. There are a lot of things I could say, but I doubt they'd be productive at the moment.

"It'll be a lot easier if we don't text or call each other—to give ourselves a chance to get over this."

I roll my eyes. We spent two years trying to avoid each other after a blowout, and it did zero fucking good to help us get over each other.

"Okay," she whispers. "Goodbye, Shane."

The call ends, and I toss my phone to the other end of the couch. Rubbing my forehead, I shake my head. There's no way our relationship's over. I don't know what, if anything, could break us apart, but it definitely hasn't happened yet. Whatever I need to do to bring her around is what I'll have to do.

30

AVERY

It's nine at night two days after my last conversation with Shane, and I'm sitting on my bed at Ethan's, quietly crying. I was a hundred percent right to end things with Shane, but that doesn't mean I can go more than five minutes without thinking about him. And nights are when I miss him the most.

There's a knock on the door, and my mom says, "Sweetheart, can I come in?"

"Just a sec." Shoving my laptop over, I get out of bed to grab a tissue. Quickly wiping my eyes doesn't fix them. They're really red, and I look tired.

Pitching the tissue in the trash, I walk over and open the door.

"I brought tea," Mom says, holding up a mug. "Ginger peach."

It's my favorite, and I take it. "Thanks."

"Can I come in?"

I shrug, glancing around for an excuse to remain alone. "Um..."

After Ethan caught me crying in the yard, he and Mom have been hovering constantly. I've told them repeatedly that everything's fine, but convincing them with words is apparently not possible.

"What's up?" I ask.

"Ethan said you got good news about your presentation?"

I nod, unable to muster much enthusiasm. "Smith-Hall gave me 'best in class' for it. Thanks again for your help. He agreed to write me a strong letter of recommendation for the internship. I submitted my application, so fingers crossed."

"That's great. And your last final is done?"

"Yeah, I took them both online. The teachers are good with that because of Casanova."

"Okay, good." She nods, then presses on, lingering in the doorway for as long as possible. "Ethan read in a Granthorpe bulletin that there was a boy in a bad car accident?"

"Yes, Todd Bardoratch. He died this morning. He had a really bad head injury, I guess, and they couldn't save him." My muscles tighten reflexively. I still wonder whether Shane had anything to do with what happened to Todd.

"Oh, honey, I'm sorry." She hugs me, and it feels really awkward. "Did you know him?"

"Yes, but we weren't friends. I'm sorry for his family, but I'm okay."

I pull away and take a sip of tea. "Anyway, I'm gonna go to bed and stream some movies, so..."

"Can we talk about what Shane did to upset you?"

"Who says Shane did anything?" I retreat with my mug in hand.

She levels a look at me. "Who else, other than him, ever makes you cry?"

Fair point, I think wryly. "I appreciate the concern, but if Shane and I have an issue, that's between us."

Mom purses her lips but manages to stay quiet.

"Thanks for the tea, Mom."

"It helps to talk..."

"Not always," I say firmly. "Sometimes it's better to just keep calm and carry on, as the Brits like to say. What *would* really help me is if you could just act normal, because I really am going to be fine."

"Hey," Ethan says from the doorway.

Oh, God. Now there are two of them. They are so sweet, but it's suffocating. Shane is lucky to have his own house right now.

"How is everything?" he asks.

I don't scream, but I'd like to.

"She's okay," Mom says brightly. "Gonna watch some movies."

"Good, good. Listen, Ave, I got your text about changing your flight to Colorado. In terms of holiday plans, what are we thinking?"

We're thinking I don't want to be in Shane's best friend's house for days. A place where Shane could show up any time.

"Not sure," I say, forcing a smile. "Some girls I know are talking about a girls' trip. I was thinking I might use the New Hampshire cabin and go cross-country skiing."

It's true that a girl at Granthorpe who went to my high school suggested I come on a group outing over winter break, but I think the only reason she reached out is that I've been seen with Shane and Erik Sorensen. Those guys are part of the GU crowd everyone wants to join. So, before I invest in new friendships, I want to see how people act next semester when they realize I'm not with Shane anymore.

"You think you want to do that instead of Aspen?" Ethan asks, the skin between his brows pinching together to form a vertical line above his nose.

"I don't know yet. I just finished finals. I'm gonna crash tonight and decide in the morning."

"A girls' trip is nice, but not over the holidays," Mom says. "The Heyworths—"

"You know Declan is Shane's best friend, right?" I blurt, cutting her off. "You remember that Shane lived with them when he was mad at us, right?" My voice is sharper than I mean for it to be. "Sorry. Just—can you guys do me a favor? Don't try to push me into going somewhere I don't want to go. And also, please don't tell anyone anything about my plans."

"Don't tell anyone?" Mom glances at Ethan, and they exchange a look.

"When you say anyone...?" Ethan says, tilting his head.

"I mean anyone. I want to be left alone right now to do my own thing."

My mom and Ethan share another look, and Mom nods. "Okay. If you want certain people to leave you alone, we understand. Maybe Ethan and I will change our plans by a few days, too."

Oh, God.

"You're crazy if you do, but I can't stop you," I say.

"Crazy?" my mom says, looking at me like I'm the crazy one.

"Why would you stay in Boston when I won't even be here? And miss out on skiing in Aspen? It's silly. Just go. Have fun. I'll join you guys there when I'm ready."

"We're going to leave you alone right now, so you can get some rest," Ethan says, tugging on my mom's arm.

They step back and close the door, but I can still hear them discussing me. I sigh and open my laptop. When I start my movie, I turn up the volume to drown out everything else.

This is what you get for hooking up with your stepbrother.

❦ 31 ❦

SHANE

I hold out for three days. No texts. No calls. No unannounced visits to my dad's house. I want to make contact with Avery the way I want water after a hard workout. But I don't let myself have it.

Props to her too for restraint. It's been radio silence.

Let's see how long she holds out when we're in the same house.

Declan confirms my family's flight, and that his stepmother is picking them up from the airport. I book the next flight out of Boston. This way there will be no scene at the airport. Dec will pick me up on the down-low, and then Avery and I will be in a house together for days.

Just because I haven't talked to her doesn't mean I'm not caught up. I had someone get me the class standings from her e-commerce class. She took the top spot, which is unheard of for a freshman. I'm proud of her.

The flight to Colorado is smooth, and Declan's waiting for me in baggage claim. We shake hands and exchange the usual greetings. On the walk to the car, the conversation's casual, but when we reach his jeep, he shifts gears.

"Let's stop and get a drink. I've got a problem I need to run by you."

"Happy to help, but let's just talk on the way," I say. "I want to get to the house."

He pauses, looking at me over the roof. "Did you come early to see *her?*"

I could lie, but there's no point. When I opted out of the triple-X celebration of my new membership in the Dark Knights, I told Declan the reason. There's only one woman I'm interested in, and of course, Avery is not now, nor will she ever be, on a Dark Knights' menu.

"Yeah, I want to see Avery sooner rather than later."

Declan taps the roof. "Did you tell her that?"

I cock my eyebrow. "No."

"Hate to tell you this, brother, but Avery didn't come with Ethan and Sheri."

"What? Why not?"

"I don't know. They said she's coming later." Dec starts to get in the car.

I do not. "When's she coming? Tomorrow?"

He stands again, looking across at me. "I don't know."

I take out my phone and call my dad. It takes a few rings for him to pick up.

"Where's Avery, Dad?"

"Hey, Shane. Ave decided to hang out and do her own thing for a few days. She's got an interview for the internship and wants to prepare."

I go still. "Is she on campus? She's not, right?"

"No, no."

In the background I hear Sheri's voice. "Don't tell him anything. Remember what she said."

Gritting my teeth, I scowl. Our parents' interference is more than unwelcome, it's a fucking blood pressure raiser. I try to focus on the more important issue.

"Dad, I don't want Avery on campus alone. Not even during the day. She's not planning to be in her dorm by herself, is she?"

"Easy," Ethan says. "No, she's not staying on campus. When she needs to go to Granthorpe, she'll take my car. Before the interview, she has plans with friends."

What fucking friends? "Who? Specifically."

"Look, I'm not at liberty to share her plans."

"Dad, listen, I know she might have told you not to tell me, but—"

"Shane, don't ask me to break her confidence. I won't do it."

For fuck's sake. "I'll talk to you later." I swipe a finger over the screen to end the call. "Fucking hell," I mutter.

Declan raises his brows.

"Sorry. I've gotta go back."

At this point, I won't reach Boston until three or four in the morning. It's a complete pain in the ass. But at least Avery and I will be alone for our reunion.

Declan falls in step with me as I start toward the terminal.

"What's going on, Shane? Seriously?" His tone is as grim as a fucking reaper. "She's coming eventually. Why wouldn't you wait for her here? Erik's at the house. I convinced him to come. The three of us can talk business. He and I have to go back for practice in a few days, so this is really our only chance."

"Yeah, the three of us will talk, but it's not urgent."

Declan scowls. "Now business isn't a priority? The thing that's urgent is that you see your little stepsister because she's in a snit about something? What's her problem? And why can't you just fly back tomorrow?"

"Snit. There's a word you don't hear every day. You have been hanging out with Sorensen. Has he been at the GRE test booklets between plays?"

Declan laughs, despite himself.

Sorensen once let slip he plans to go to grad school. And, between extended bouts of silence, he occasionally quotes obscure literature. The guy's an enigma.

"C'mon, man," Dec says. "Stay."

"Can't. I don't want her there alone."

"Where? Granthorpe?"

I nod, hustling across the street while traffic's light.

"Term's over. What the hell does she need to do on campus?"

When I don't answer, Declan blows out a frustrated breath. "You just got off the fucking plane."

"Yeah. Sorry for this bullshit pick-up. And listen, we'll still talk. I'll call you once I've booked a new flight."

Declan stops on the sidewalk just outside the terminal's sliding glass doors. "It's not a conversation for a public place. We'll talk when I see you next."

"All right." I shake his hand briefly before I walk back inside.

Not great to blow Declan off for Avery. I need to be better about that once things are back on track with her.

Inside, I get a seat on an outbound red-eye flight to Boston that's departing within the hour. Good. I want to see Avery tonight, and I'm going to. By the time I get back through security and to the gate, the flight is boarding. Also, good. I'm not in the mood to sit around in Colorado when she's in Massachusetts.

Once I'm seated, I start texting, knowing I don't have much time before the phone will have to go into airplane mode.

> Shane: heard from my dad you got an interview for your internship. Congratulations. proud of you.

> Shane: don't go to campus alone, Ave. not for any reason. if you have to go, let me be there.

The doors close, and the flight attendant starts taking drink orders.

> Shane: i wanna see you. i'll be in boston in the morning.

I hold the phone in a tight grip. I really want her to text me back before we take off.

I open email to sync the device before I go dark. I know it's unlikely Avery will have sent me anything, but back in high school she sent me a few emails, usually when she had something to say that was longer than she wanted to text.

The sync's done by the time we start to pull away from the gate. I switch the phone to airplane mode as directed and glance at my Inbox. Nothing from her. Just a few from Granthorpe that'll have links for grades.

Sitting back, I try to rest. Sleep and I haven't been on friendly terms lately.

I miss everything about having Avery in my bed. Sex the most, of course. But also how hard I crash afterward. Sleep was better when she was sleeping next to me.

APPARENTLY LACK OF SLEEP CATCHES UP WITH ME BECAUSE I CRASH for a few hours.

When I wake, it's four am Boston time. I open the GU emails to check my grades. There are no surprises. I've passed everything with decent enough scores.

The last email I open isn't course-related. Looks like spam. It's got rows of purple lines and only one line of text.

> YOU SHOULDN'T TOUCH WHAT ISN'T YOURS,
> MORAN. OR YOU MIGHT DISAPPEAR. LIKE HER,
> MY VERY CHERRY, A VERY CHER.

What the hell? What kind of bullshit is this?

I zoom in and realize the dots making up the purple lines are tiny rose emojis.

It takes a second for the email's message to hit me. And then my heart fucking stops.

It's from Casanova.

And he's threatening Avery.

32

AVERY

Darkness in the forest is different. It's full black, like charcoal briquettes.

The exposed parts of the cabin's wood floor are cold, so I'm happy to be tucked in bed under a stack of handmade quilts. When the three of us are here, Ethan builds a big fire and I'm missing that. I made a small one, but it's burned itself out. Tomorrow night, I'll use more wood.

Cell service is spotty, and there's no cable in the cabin, so I came to bed with a paperback from the bookshelf. Old school, as Ethan calls it.

I hope Ethan and my mom had a good flight and are enjoying their first night in Aspen, but I'm really glad I stayed behind.

The quiet calm of being surrounded by nature is soothing.

SHANE

I take my phone into the first class bathroom, turn off airplane mode, and wait for it to connect and update.

Come on, baby. Please have sent me a text.

The phone buzzes, which gets my hopes up, but no. It's all texts from other people.

I call Avery, and it goes straight to voicemail.

"Hey, it's me. Call me back. I got an email from Casanova, and I want to know you're all right."

There's a chime overhead, and the fasten-seatbelt light goes on. I ignore it and the turbulence that follows.

I call Pops, and he picks up after half a dozen rings.

"What's the matter?" The gravel in his voice drowns out his brogue.

"Sorry about the time. I need a favor. I need someone to go to Ethan's. Avery's alone, and the guy who's been stalking her may go after her there."

"Where are you?"

"On a plane. I'll get to my dad's place in an hour, two at the latest. But I want someone to check on her now. And if your guy can stay to keep watch till I get there, even better. I'll cover whatever it costs."

"This girl is expensive," he mumbles. "I thought the trouble was already dealt with?"

"Apparently not."

A flight attendant raps on the door, telling me I need to take my seat.

"Gotta go. I'll talk to you when I land."

I haven't made it out of the airport before my grandfather calls to tell me Ethan's house looks empty.

I call my dad immediately, but the call goes to voicemail. Understandable given the time, but I want to smash something. I retrieve my car from long-term parking and peel out of the lot.

On the highway, I try Sheri's number, which I've never called directly in my life.

After a few rings, she answers, sounding half asleep. "Hello?"

"Sheri, it's Shane. I'm sorry to wake you. I think Avery's in trouble."

"What?" Her sleep-roughened voice grows sharper. "What makes you say that?"

"She's not at your house. She's not responding to texts or calls, not even to say she's all right. And I got an email from Casanova that makes me think he might try to take her—if he hasn't already. My dad said she wasn't going to stay on campus. Do you have any reason to think she changed her mind about that?"

"An email from Casanova? How?"

"Sheri, can you answer me? Could she have gone to Granthorpe? If she did, I'm going to send campus police to her dorm."

"No, she's not at Granthorpe."

"Is she supposed to be at your house in Boston? Because she's not. I sent someone there to be sure she's all right, and she's not home."

"Are you—is this a trick? To get me to tell you where she is?"

"Of course not!" I snap. I regret it immediately. Sheri's cooperation is necessary. "I'm sorry. I didn't mean to raise my voice. Just tell me where she is. I need to know."

For the length of what feels like a hundred hours, there's nothing but the sound of her breathing and my dad mumbling in the background. On my end, the loudest sound comes from my pounding heart. They know something. I can't let Sheri end the call without telling me.

"No, I know," Sheri murmurs, but she's talking to my dad not me.

"Listen, I need you to tell me." We don't have time for this shit, I think, grinding my teeth. "If she's in trouble, and I'm too late because I don't know where to go—that can't happen. Please. I'll do anything you want."

I hate the desperation in my voice, but at the moment, it can't be helped. I'll do whatever it takes to find Avery, and Sheri needs to believe me that time may be running out.

"Avery doesn't want you to know where she is, Shane. And she's fine. We talked to her. She's fine."

"When? When did you speak to her?"

"Um, yesterday. When we landed."

"Is she staying with someone? Who?"

"I can't talk to you about this," she hisses.

MARLEE WRAY

"All right, do this. Call her right now. If she's all right, tell her I got a threatening email from Casanova, and I'm worried about her. Tell her to call the police. Tell her to say whatever it takes to get them to come to wherever she's staying. And then tell her to call me. I'll go and get her. Wherever she is."

My sense of urgency convinces Sheri. Or maybe it's just that I've suggested involving the police, which I would never do except in a dire emergency.

"I'll call her. I will," she says.

"If she's okay, call me back. Or just text me. I need to know you heard her voice and that she's safe."

"I will." Then the call ends, and there's dead air.

The entire time I'm driving, I wait for Sheri's call or text, but none comes. I hope it's because she's talking to Avery.

I reach the house, and it's dark. There's a sedan at the end of the driveway. When my headlights shine on it, my grandfather himself emerges.

I shove my door open and get out, shaking my head. "I didn't mean for you to come yourself, Pops."

"I know." He comes over to shake my hand. "Do you think this asshole took her?"

"I don't know. I hope not."

The phone rings, and I jerk it up. It's my dad.

I swipe the screen. "I'm here. Did Sheri talk to her?"

"No, we can't reach her—"

"Fuck!" The world blurs around me. I put a hand on the Porsche to steady myself.

If Casanova already has her, how am I going to find them? The police have searched for him for months with no luck. I have to figure out a way—I need to get Avery back.

"Where was she? Here? Or—?"

"Shane, calm down. She's not answering because there's terrible cell service where she is. She went to your Grandpa Moran's cabin in New Hampshire to cross-country ski for the weekend. Did you actually get an email from Casanova?"

"Of course. You think I'd make that up?"

"No, no."

"I've gotta go. I can get to the cabin in two hours."

"Shane, Casanova couldn't know where she is. She's been in Boston and just drove to New Hampshire yesterday. There's no way he could've followed her from campus. She hasn't been there."

"Maybe he didn't. Maybe she's fine. I'll go and make sure." I raise a hand to wave to my grandfather as he heads back to his car.

I drop into the driver's seat of the Porsche and close the door.

"Shane, why would Casanova email you? That doesn't make sense."

"I don't know," I say, though a part of me does.

Casanova and I share the same obsession. For a while, he wasn't able to take Avery because I was in the way. He was frustrated. Now I'm not in his way anymore, and he's gloating.

As I back out of the driveway, I grimace.

The thing that keeps hitting me over and over is I don't think he'd send an email unless he was sure I couldn't get to her in time.

33

AVERY

The trail is gorgeous. Nowhere is as beautiful as New Hampshire in the dawning light. I'm gliding along on fresh snow and work up a sweat by the time I reach the crumbling stone cabin from the 1800s. It's Shane's favorite destination on the trail. He showed me the spot on my first visit here.

The distant sound of skis swooshing through snow makes me smile. Someone else is up early and on the trails. There's a cabin about a mile from ours that belongs to a sweet young family of four. We sometimes bump into them on winter weekends.

I sit on the stones to rest. The approaching figure races through the trees. He's tall. Probably the dad then.

No, the man's dressed in head-to-toe black with goggles. It's not the kind of outfit I've ever seen the cheerful dad wear. It's not Shane, either. Too skinny. A scarf covers the man's lower face up to where his goggles hit, so I can't tell how old he is. From the way he moves, he's probably twenties or thirties. He's fit.

When he spots me, he slows down.

I smile, but only for a moment. The way he stares at me is intense,

252

and he doesn't wave or say hello like someone would who's casually passing.

The hairs on the back of my neck stand. Shane's words come back to me. "If something feels wrong, assume it is."

I keep my eyes on him, but I slide my hand into my coat's zipper pocket. Without looking down, I locate the knife with my fingers. I disengage the safety by feel and slip the knife out, keeping it concealed by my coat.

The skier stops a few feet away. He raises his goggles, and his eyes are familiar.

Who is he?

When he pulls his scarf down, I finally recognize him. It's Daniel.

"Hi, Avery."

My heart beats a thudding rhythm in my chest. What's he doing in our woods? He shouldn't be.

"Hey, Daniel. What are you doing here?"

"It was time." He looks around. "I can't believe we're out here alone. I thought it was going to be so difficult to arrange. I had this elaborate plan...but then you made it easy."

My boots are free of the skis. His aren't. Can I knock him down and get past him? Outrun him back to the cabin and the car? No, not unless he's injured.

He bites the end of a glove and pulls it off. Then repeats the move with other. When he unzips his jacket, my heart slams against my ribs. Why is he undressing?

"I was going to make it special. But you've been playing cum-dumpster for your psycho stepbrother," he sneers. "So, you'll be right at home here in the dirt."

So vile, the words suck the air from my lungs. My heart hammers in my chest, and the world starts to blur around the edges.

Don't. Don't you dare pass out!

Other than taking sucking breaths, my body remains still as my mind races. No matter what disgusting things he says, I can't let it distract me.

Daniel speaks again, but I don't hear him. For a second, my own thoughts drown everything else out.

What would Shane tell me to do in this moment? Give Daniel time to completely undress? Or strike before that? He'll be able to maneuver better out of his ski clothes, but he'll also have less protection.

Shane's voice comes rushing back, calm, consistent, firm.

Wait for your moment, Avery.

Wait for your moment.

"Why do this, Daniel?" My voice doesn't crack. A small victory.

He looks at me like I'm ridiculous. "Did you think you could just ignore me?" Scoffing, with a sharp shake of his head, he says, "I'd have broken you already if not for him. Todd was right; Moran's a thug. Like a dog with a bone, he didn't leave you alone for a second. Not at the party, not on campus, not even in his own house. Fucking frustrating. Until you left." His sinister smile makes him look like a maniac. "Thank you for doing that."

I stare at him silently. Daniel is crazy. He is.

Wait for your moment.

"It did make for a better game, I guess." Daniel stretches his arms out magnanimously. "You saved his life by leaving."

"Did I? What did you plan to do?"

Wait for your moment.

He grins and looks wolfish as he does. He jerks the goggles and scarf off and drops them on his discarded jacket. Only a knit shirt, ski pants, and boots left.

Wait for your moment.

Neck and chest are okay targets now. Upper thighs are still not good because of the thick ski pants.

Wait for your moment.

Imagining Shane's voice, so smooth and steady, makes me feel less panicked. I've been here before, on the mat. At least Daniel didn't grab me from behind and incapacitate me before I knew what was happening. That was the biggest danger. At least now, I have a chance.

Wait for your moment.

"Get undressed, Avery. I want you naked."

I want my bulky coat off, too. It'll be more difficult to move fast and strike hard with it on. Surreptitiously, I set the knife on the stone next to my thigh, making sure it's balanced and won't slip away. My coat's already unzipped, so it's easy to take off. I set it on the opposite side of me on the crumbled rock wall.

"Shirt next," he says, nodding encouragingly, happily. Crazily. "Shirt *next*," he repeats when I don't continue to undress. "Shirt off!"

No.

Fuck you, Daniel.

"It's cold out." My voice is still steady. Another minor victory.

Wait for your moment.

"Let's go back to the cabin," I say. "It's warm and dry there."

"I don't want you dry," he says with a leer.

God, I hate you.

"Besides, blood looks so good against the snow. Dramatic. Cinematic." He glances around. "I like it here. It's a spot I'll always remember."

Oh, God.

"Where have the other spots been, Daniel?"

If I stall long enough, someone else might come along. That could be a good distraction. It could also bring reinforcements, so it's more than just me against him.

Wait for your moment.

"Get out of your clothes," he says impatiently, his voice growing almost nasal.

"Where did you take the others?"

He smiles slowly until it becomes a sneer. Then he darts forward and grabs me.

It happens too fast. He's got my arms and I panic, trying to tear myself away.

You never know how you'll react in the moment, until the moment comes.

I fall over the rocks into the cabin's frame and land on the rotting floorboards. It's jarring, but I'm okay. The impact isn't as hard as when I was slammed into the mat while training with Shane.

Daniel hops the short rock wall and stands over me.

"I told you to undress. Stop stalling!" He punches me in the face.

More adrenaline pours into my veins as I gasp in pain.

His groin is protected. And if we're both standing, I won't be tall

enough to reach his throat. He'll spot the knife coming for sure. This
is not the moment.

If he pins your arms, you're finished. The knife will be useless.

Or he'll find it and use it on you.

My heart hammers so hard it feels as if it'll beat its way out of my
chest.

If you raise the blade, you can not hesitate! Shane's voice barks.

I plan my moves in an instant.

This is your moment. Take it!

I grab Daniel's sweater and jerk him down with my left hand. He
falls, landing on top of me. With my right hand, I press the knife's
button, activating its spring action.

Now, now, now!

The blade is silent as it emerges. My arm swings, and the knife cuts
through the air.

I slam the blade under Daniel's jaw until it can't go deeper, and
then drag my arm forward toward his chin. The practiced motion is
automatic.

At first, there's nothing but my ragged breath, and his confused
expression.

The blade hits something hard, maybe his Adam's apple. At the
same time, a gash opens in the knife's wake. Blood sprays out and
bursts upward as a beating, red geyser.

He jerks back, shocked.

The blade's caught, and I'm wrenched upward and forward, but
then the knife pulls free. I fall back onto the ground, knife in hand,
staring up at him.

He opens his mouth to scream, but there's only a broken, splut-
tering sound. Blood splashes outward in pulsing beats, and he grabs at
his neck to try to stop it.

Daniel staggers upright to escape, but instead of backing away, he
lifts his foot to stomp on my face.

I roll sharply to the side. His leg barely misses me when it pounds
down, cracking a board. Daniel teeters, trying to regain his balance.

Almost got me. Could've knocked me out. And killed me.

Shane's voice in my head says, *You don't stop 'til he's dead.*

I lurch up and shove Daniel with all my might. He topples and lands hard. Dropping down on top of him, I kneel on his arms.

His attempt to knock me off fails. He's weakening.

When I bring the knife down, he sees it coming and turns his head just in time. The blade skids off his cheekbone instead of entering his eye socket.

You don't stop.

I grab his hair, holding his head, and try again.

❧ 34 ☙

SHANE

"Avery!" My voice is ragged from yelling.

All I see as I run down the trail is the booted foot. The person's down and unmoving.

"Avery!"

I reach the broken stone cabin. There are scattered clothes.

The body is too big to be her. It's a man. Blood is everywhere, and half his face is cut up and unrecognizable.

My head jerks from side-to-side. There are two sets of skis. She was here. Is she wounded? Dying nearby?

"Avery!" I yell again, listening for her.

Please let her be alive. I'll do anything. Just let me find her alive.

I spot boot prints and a blood trail in the snow. I sprint through the woods, following the tracks.

When I reach the stream, I see her.

Avery stands at the edge with sleeves that are soaked and dripping. My black knife dangles from her fingers, pink droplets falling from the tip of the blade.

"Avery?"

She turns slowly, her expression vacant. Her pretty face bears a red scuff on one cheek, but it's not lacerated. Just wet and pale. Her shirt is soaked and so blood-stained I can't tell if she's wounded. It's also not clear whether she's been crying, but there's a shattered look to her.

I walk closer, but slowly. "Ave?"

Her throat convulses as she swallows. "I heard you, and did what you said," she murmurs. "I heard you. I waited for my moment." A long breath escapes through her pale, parted lips. "I didn't stop. Not until I was sure."

Jesus. As panic eases, realization dawns. *His mangled face, that was all her, and now she's in the aftermath.*

Her voice is like a haunted house, empty and creaking, whispering with tragedy.

"Good," I say gently. "You did what you had to do." My own lips are bone dry. I lick them, studying her.

I can't tell if she's physically injured or just in shock. I need to move close enough to check, but I'm afraid she'll bolt. There's a look to her that worries me. She reminds me of a deer that's caught a hunter's scent. Wary, watchful, spooked.

Her right hand shakes, the knife vibrating back and forth like a tuning fork. She tilts her head. "I don't know what to do now. We didn't talk about that."

"Come here." My hand reaches out, beckoning her. "Come to me, baby."

After a beat, Avery walks closer to stand a couple feet away. The knife twitches in her grasp, causing drops of bloody water to sway on the tip before they fall.

"Yours. I stole it." She lifts the knife higher and, when I don't reach for it, adds, "Want to hear something crazy? I don't know how to close it."

I take it and fold the blade away, then engage the safety.

She shivers, and her teeth start to chatter. Her eyes track the knife's path into my pocket, like she needs to see it reach a secure location.

"Are you hurt?"

"No. Nnn-ott me." Her voice is like chains rattling.

"I need to get you inside, someplace warm. Come here, Ave." I hold my arms out, beckoning her, and she finally walks into them. I press her against my chest, and for the first time in hours, I can breathe. "I thought I might lose you. Never been that scared in my life." My confession is barely louder than the wind.

"You knew I was in trouble." It's half question, half statement.

My lips press against her hair. "Casanova sent me a message. I didn't think I'd get to you in time." After the thud of a dozen heartbeats, I add, "Actually, I didn't." I draw in a shaky breath. He almost won. Almost took her away from me for good. "Thank God you had a knife and used it."

"You were here all along. You were."

I don't know what she means. It doesn't matter. At the moment, nothing matters except that she's not lost.

There's something that's been on my mind all day and night. The one undeniable truth.

It's not the right moment, but I can't keep myself from making one more confession into the wind.

"I love you."

🐿 35 🐿

AVERY

I n my mind, Shane becomes the wall I stand behind when I can't
face things.

The police arrive and take control of the property and the
crime scene. My words sound distant, like they're running away
through the trees. Their faces scrunch in confusion as they look
around and stomp through the snow. When Shane helps explain
things, it's much more clear, even to me.

They transport us to the station in the back of a sheriff's cruiser. I
sit so my body touches Shane, and he puts his arm around me, pressing
me against his side. It's shelter, like finding an awning to stand under in
a sudden downpour.

Shane's voice is low and calm, the same way it's been all along, as he
advises me of my rights and explains police interrogation tactics. He
speaks as if they are an enemy army that has laid siege to our home and
our persons. I listen carefully to everything he tells me, as though my
life depends on it. I owe him that, since without his advice, I wouldn't
be alive.

At the station, the police inform us of our rights and tell us we'll be questioned separately.

My gaze flicks to Shane's face.

"It's okay. I'm right here. I won't leave you," he promises as they lead me toward a door.

Taking a deep breath, I enter the cold room and settle into a hard chair. Across the rectangular table, there's a gray-haired detective with a stern expression who starts in with a million questions.

I tell the story and re-tell it.

A female deputy joins us. She acts kind but seems less genuine. To me, they look very bulky in their puffy brown coats and utility belts.

When my body starts to ache from sitting, I stand. "Is that enough?" I lick my lips. "I've told you everything. I want to go."

They take pictures and collect my clothes as evidence. I'm given prisoner scrubs, but they assure me it's not a reflection of their plans. They're not going to arrest me.

My words spill out slowly. "Never thought that. I only defended myself."

It's the truth, but their expressions appear skeptical. They don't speak again.

When they release me from the room, I overhear the sheriff say that, from the state of the body, it looks like a hell of a lot more than self defense.

His words cause no emotional reaction from me. None. I feel too numb.

My head turns, and I stare at the sheriff.

It feels as though I should say or do something, like be more emotional or smile gratefully for their help. But what if I make the wrong choice? It might be misinterpreted. Since I don't know how to proceed, I do nothing.

Watching me, the sheriff mumbles, "Jesus."

"Come this way, Avery," the female deputy says. "I'll drive you back."

Drop me off alone? "Where's Shane?"

"We're still talking to him."

My eyes scan the area, pausing on a closed door. He's on the other side.

"I'll wait." I sit on a bench near the front door. I'm freezing. It would be warmer in my car or the cabin, but the thought of going to wait farther away doesn't appeal to me.

Eventually the door to the second interrogation room opens, and Shane emerges.

As soon I stand, my muscles start to shiver. "I'm cold."

He crosses the distance to me and drags me up against him, wrapping his arms around me. "Where's her coat?"

"Everything she was wearing is evidence. We can give you a blanket."

"Yeah, give me one."

Moments later, he wraps me up and guides me outside to the cruiser. Time moves in fits and starts, as if I'm sleepwalking through patches of it.

Back at the cabin, my gaze travels over the cars. I drove here in Ethan's Lexus. Shane's Porsche is parked beside it. "Do we drive home separately?"

"Not right now. Come inside."

Relief washes over me. It wouldn't be safe for me to drive. I also don't want to be separated from him yet. The world is chaos. He restores order.

As soon as the cabin door is closed, I exhale. It's just the two of us now. Safe to talk.

Shane opens the front of the wood-burning stove and tosses some logs inside.

"They think I'm a psycho. They asked if I invited Daniel here. They wanted to know what kind of movies I like. The questions were crazy. They think I lured him here to kill him. *Me*."

"They're running down blind alleys because they've never seen anything like this. It's a small department. They're just covering their bases to be thorough." Shane lights kindling and tosses it in.

"Are we staying here long?"

"We don't have to." He closes the stove's grate. "We can stay long enough for you to take a hot shower and put on some warm clothes.

Or we can stay the night and leave in the morning. We'll do whatever you want."

"Did I go too far?"

"When?"

"When I defended myself. They called it overkill. Saying I had a grudge or something. They kept asking about my relationship with him. I told the truth, but I don't know...they exchanged looks as though I'd said the wrong thing. Just because he was an arrogant jerk at times doesn't mean I would plot to kill him."

When I look up, Shane is watching me. The quiet is unnerving.

"I didn't do very well," I say softly. "I should've cried, I think. Am I too calm?"

"No, you're in shock. Survival mode." His tone is reasonable. It makes sense. "Your mind is doing its job. To protect you."

"The police—"

"Fuck the police," he says coolly.

I blink and then glance at the door. They're still out there somewhere, collecting evidence. Better if they don't hear us cursing at them.

"I'm scared," I admit.

"You don't need to be." His big hand squeezes my upper arm so firmly it's almost painful, which helps. "You did everything right. There's nothing to worry about. I promise."

"I didn't tell them it was your knife, or that you taught me how to defend myself. I thought they might blame you."

"I told them."

My gaze snaps up, so our eyes meet. My concern for him is the sharpest thing I've felt since I walked away from Daniel's body.

"You—you told that part?"

He nods, the corners of his mouth twitching like they want to smile at my incredulity. "You were being stalked and assaulted on campus. You made a police report the night a rose was left in your bed, and campus police never even followed up. You had to protect yourself, Avery. No one from law enforcement was."

"Is that how you said it?"

"When they pushed me, yes."

Oh, my God. He's so reckless. And fearless.

"Adversarial, Shane. Best tactic?"

Now he does smile. "Probably not."

"I should've cried," I repeat in a whisper. "We want law enforcement to see me as vulnerable. We want them on my side when they write their report." Clearing my throat with a cough, I glance up at the exposed ceiling beams. "But I don't feel like crying. I don't—feel much. Just maybe relief. He wanted to rape me in the snow. He acted like there was no way to stop him. Like he could do whatever he wanted, and I could do nothing. I proved him wrong. And I'm not sorry."

"You shouldn't be." Shane's hard, resolute tone matches mine exactly. "Ever."

I nod, shuddering.

Shane's part monster. Thank God. He's the only thing keeping me anchored to the world.

"I'm glad you're here."

"Where else would I be?" When he's flippant and warm, that works, too. "Go take a shower." He turns and shoves some more wood into the fireplace.

In the rustic bathroom, light from the exposed bulb reflects off glossy knotty pine walls. A moment later, I'm standing under hot water, watching soap suds cover my feet and the slate tiles. I don't remember pouring shower gel into my hands or lathering myself up.

On and off, gaps of time continue to go missing.

It doesn't matter. You'll be all right.

When I emerge from the bathroom in a towel, I go straight to the bed. Crawling under the covers, I throw the towel out onto the floor.

"Shane?"

"Yeah?" He picks up the discarded towel and places it over the back of a chair near the fireplace.

"Do you have condom?"

He looks over his shoulder at me. "What's on your mind, Ave?"

"I want to."

Shane turns to face the bed. "I want to, too. Eventually. When the timing's right."

My thoughts are tangled vines that I don't want to unwind. "I need to feel something. Your body against mine feels better than anything, so that's what I want."

His voice is soft, like he's talking to a small child. "You're not your-self right now."

I can't argue that, but I still want what I want. From him. "I know what I need. It's you."

"I'll lie down with you." He hauls his shirt off, then sits on the edge of the bed to take off his shoes and socks. He pauses, his brows crin-kled, like he might waver. But then he stands and strips down to his skin.

When he joins me in the bed, I stroke his shoulders and press up against him.

"You don't need to rush this."

My hand moves to the back of his neck and pulls him closer.

We kiss as though the world's ending.

His hand slides between my legs and rubs my clit. I ease my legs apart, welcoming his touch. I place my hand over his, pressing it down harder, wanting something I can't name.

My other hand finds his hard cock and teases it. "I want all of you."

He raises his head to look down at me, his own fingers still stroking me. "I doubt you know what you want right now."

"I do."

"Let's start with an orgasm, and then see—"

"No," I snap. "Stop hesitating. Do you want me or not?"

His fingers grind to a halt, and his eyes narrow.

"Sorry." I lick my lips and tilt my head. "I just know...and I don't want you to be too nice. Be the way you normally are. What I need—" The words break off as I try to figure out how to explain myself. "I need—"

Shane lowers his head, so his mouth is near my ear. "Your beast?"

"Yes."

He understands. As usual.

"There will be no turning back from this." His voice is rough-edged and hard. "If we do this, don't expect me to let you go afterward because I won't."

I shiver and squeeze his forearm, my body sizzling with anticipation.

"Answer me, Avery." The dark command in his voice makes me squirm.

"What?" I whisper.

"You. Me. Inseparable. Say you understand."

Warnings drip off the edge of my mind like raindrops in the distance. I hear them, but don't care about them. Not now. There's blood on my hands, and the fear of what will happen next hovers all around me like fog. But here, with him, I can erase everything. Just for a while.

"I understand."

He rises from the bed and gets a condom from his wallet. Before his cock disappears under the latex, I see it's hard and dark with blood. Yeah, this is what we both want.

"Spread your legs," Shane orders when he returns to the bed.

My legs inch farther apart, and he moves above me and guides his cock to the soft aching entrance to my body. He kisses me, slow and sweet.

Then his hips rock forward ruthlessly.

Oh, my God.

My flesh reluctantly relents, tearing and spreading around him. It hurts, and every bit of my mind focuses sharply on the place inside me that he's stretching to accommodate himself.

"Fuck," he groans. "You're so tight and wet for me." He buries his head in my neck and starts to move.

My hands grab his shoulders.

There's another forceful thrust, and he's deeper.

My nails dig into his flesh. "Oh, my God. Wait," I say breathlessly. My hips twist, trying to ease him out.

"Look at me." His voice is rough, which I still love.

My gaze rises, and our eyes lock.

After a moment, I shift under him, the uncomfortable stretch intensifying. "You're too big, I think. For me."

"No, I'm not. Slide your hand down to rub your clit, baby."

His arm muscles strain under my hands. I can feel how hard his body is working to keep itself still. He wants to move. He wants to claim me.

"Do it. Move your hand there, kitten."

His voice is irresistible. My hand snakes down, feeling his abs and then lower. I find my clit and circle it.

After a few moments, the tingling arousal from my fingers connects to something deeper, where I'm so full. My hips move again, but this time it's not to escape. It's a small pulse that feels good.

His head drops low. "That's it," he says in a husky voice. "My cock is where it's meant to be, and I'm gonna fuck you with it."

I shudder and rub myself harder. The ache intensifies, but it's more anticipation than pain.

His pelvis draws back, and I feel my pussy losing him. Then he rocks forward, thrusting into me and hitting a spot deep inside me that is meant for him to touch. My walls contract, hugging him.

I groan, my fingertips pausing. "There," I whisper. "Exactly that."

For him, instinct takes over. The rhythm is steady and relentless.

My hips rise to meet his, and my fingers rub their own steady rhythm over my clit. He's so strong that the whole bed rocks every time he thrusts.

My free hand slides down his arm, so I can feel the groove of his triceps. His muscles are hard and rippling beneath his skin. There's so much power concentrated in his body, and he's forcing it all into mine.

Something primal and secret passes between us. We're as we're meant to be. Man. Woman. Interlocking bodies. Skin against skin. Flesh inside flesh.

I build toward an orgasm, and it breaks through me, waves overtaking the shore. It rips a moan from my throat.

He pumps faster, the bed banging the wall so loudly I worry he'll punch a hole through it.

Then he stiffens, tips his head back, and groans. "Fuck. Fuck. Fuck."

Shane exhales, pumping more slowly, now in sharp little pulses. His breath is ragged, and he lowers his head and kisses me, licking the inside of my mouth and my lips, and then sucking on me.

If he could, he would eat me alive. And I would let him.

"You can't know," he whispers. "You can't understand how right we are together, but I'm telling you..." He shudders and lowers his mouth to suck on my breast as his cock withdraws.

My body melts into the mattress, still humming from the aftershocks.

He licks my nipple and slowly kisses my breast. "You're everything. From the second I first set eyes on you." His mouth moves up to suck on my collarbone and then my neck. A soft groan tickles my ear. "You don't know."

"I do know," I whisper, my fingers stroking his back. "I love you, too."

36

SHANE

For twenty-four hours, we're caught in a rhythm that's all our own. The mood is *Moonrise Kingdom* meets *Hunger Games: Catching Fire*. She killed to survive and because of that, she's highly sought after. But what she needs is an escape, which is where the lovestruck guy with survival skills comes in. We'll call that guy Shane.

We return to my house first, and Avery pauses just inside the door. "Show me the locked room, okay?" Clear blue eyes trap mine, assessing me. Testing me.

"Being the keeper of my secrets is just more to carry. You sure you want that right now?"

She tilts her head, causing wild waves to fall askew over one shoulder. "Yes."

"My life will be in your hands, Ave," I say with mock gravity. "You'll have to protect me." My attempt to lighten the mood doesn't land.

With continued seriousness, she licks her pale lips and nods. "I can do it."

My smirk fades. "I know you can."

So for us, trust must cut both ways, dangerous or not. My hand catches hers, and I guide her upstairs and into the middle room.

Inside, I show her blank labels for bootleg liquor and start to explain how I lead people to pay me a thousand times what a bottle's worth.

Without warning, her attention wanders to an old scarred laptop on a stand in the corner. It doesn't turn on anymore, but the hard drive has spreadsheets from my first business on it, so I've kept it until I have time to destroy it.

Her fingertips drift over the cracked logo. "It's like an eye. That's broken." Her lids drift down, and she winces. I can guess which memory is projecting onto the backs of her closed lids.

"Come here, baby. Let me show you how I decide on the blend. I just bought a distillery to take this to the next level."

Nothing will persuade me to add to the blood she sees when she closes her eyes, so there will be no mention of the fight club or the pit right now. But I can talk about whiskey and my white collar crimes all day.

My mention of the distillery doesn't entice her back to me. Instead, her teeth sink into her lower lip as she turns. Eyelids at half mast, she murmurs, "I'll take some air." And she slips from the room as though she's made of whispers not flesh.

Stepping out and locking the door, I draw a deep breath. Back in apocalypse territory without a doubt. My gaze shifts to watch her descend the stairs.

She stops halfway down and looks over her shoulder. "You're coming with me, right?"

Yeah, anywhere and everywhere. Until I'm certain it's safe to take my eyes off you.

"Yeah. We can catch some fresh air on the walk to the car. We've gotta go to Boston, remember?"

"Oh right. Boston."

On and off, my baby is still walking through the New Hampshire snow, trying to find the stream where she washes off blood from her battle. I can't keep her from going, but nothing will stop me from meeting her there to take the knife from her hand. One more time or a thousand, it doesn't matter.

Avery exhales with an exaggerated grimace. "Could we skip Boston for a few days?"

"Not really."

My dad and Sheri flew home in a panic. I've held them off as long as I can. If I don't produce Avery in Boston in the next hour, they will be on my doorstep in two.

"All right." Her gaze rakes over me as I come down the stairs to stand next to her. "How will you make it up to me?"

My brow cocks, and the corner of my mouth tips up. "What did you have in mind?"

Her fingertips touch my lips. "Things."

"Yeah, sure." Leaning down, I kiss her. "I'll do *all* the things."

"Not now though?"

My king-sized bed calls to me like a trumpeting bugle.

"No, baby. Later," I force myself to say.

She nods and resumes her trek down the stairs, peach of an ass within reach. My cock curses me as a fucking idiot. I ignore it. Tonight when we're alone, I'll nail Avery to my mattress, fucking her so long and hard she'll lose her memory.

Like I said. Later.

As I drive her to the city, Avery stares out her window to watch the trees. "He's not taking the woods from me. If we were at the cabin, I would ski those trails today."

When she falls silent, I reach across and pull her hand to me, as though my physical hold on her will prevent her mind from drifting too far away.

When we reach Boston, Ethan and Sheri greet our arrival at their house with agitation. Avery immediately pulls out of their frantic hugs and circles behind me, saying she needs air. Without further discourse, she opens the front door and steps outside, coatless, with her breath fogging. I retrieve her from the step and usher her back inside, signaling for our parents to stay back a bit at first.

Once the four of us are sitting at the dining room table, Avery starts to relate what happened, but then she trails off in the middle before she reaches the killing. She glances at me, and I read the look. Without missing a beat, I pick up where she left off, glossing over the more graphic parts.

Sheri and Ethan ask a lot of questions. Under the table, Avery's hand squeezes my thigh, imploring me to answer, so I do. After a few minutes, they begin talking to me directly, with occasional concerned glances at her face.

Avery's expression is distant, as if we're talking about something we read in the newspaper, not something that happened to her, the girl they love beyond measure.

"Granthorpe emailed us, Ave," Ethan says, glancing between us. "They'd like you to be at the press conference if you feel up to it."

She grimaces.

"That's all right, honey. You don't *have* to do anything," Sheri says.

Avery's phone rings and buzzes, which it does constantly now. Everyone wants to talk to her. The FBI, the local police in Boston, GU campus police, administrators, people from school who've heard rumors that she's the girl who survived a Casanova attack.

Avery drags the phone to her and turns it off. She looks at me. "They're going to say it's him. They shouldn't until they're sure."

We've had two conversations where she's wondered out loud whether Daniel was really Casanova.

"What do you mean, Avery? It *is* him," Ethan says.

Avery's eyes bounce from my dad to the table before landing on me. "Shane?"

I shrug at Sheri and Ethan. "Avery and I wonder if Daniel might've been doing some half-assed Casanova copycat thing, so that Casanova would be blamed for what Daniel planned to do to Avery. Daniel *was* the one stalking her. We're sure of that. The police and the FBI found rosewater in a squirt gun. That tracks with something that happened to Avery. Daniel had lavender roses in his car when he came to the New Hampshire cabin, but the flowers looked days old. Wilted. Not freshly cut like Casanova usually leaves. And law enforcement found a GPS tracker on Avery's laptop, which she got from downloading software from him when they worked on their class project. None of the other missing girls had that software on their devices."

My thumb taps the table top. "Daniel asked people about Avery and kept tabs. A girl thought it was creepy and reported it to campus police. The investigation seems to show he didn't do that with any other women."

Avery glances out the window. "During the search of Daniel's place, they didn't find any trophies from the women who were taken."

With furrowed brows, Dad glances between us. "The FBI told you all this?"

"No, I've got a buddy from high school with an inside track," I lie.

The truth is I paid for the intel. Having cops on the take is essential to my operation. Turns out they come in handy in other ways as well.

"Well, it doesn't matter whether he was Casanova or not," my dad says, looking at Avery. "From the standpoint of the case, you thought he was Casanova. He threatened you and tried to sexually assault you. You acted in self-defense, period. I don't want you to worry about anything, Ave."

"I'm not worried. Not about myself." She tilts her head, her shiny dark hair falling over her shoulder. "I just thought that by killing him I saved other women, and that maybe we could even find out where the missing ones are." Avery rubs her forehead.

"It's enough that you saved yourself," Sheri says. "We're proud of you."

"Proud," Avery echoes. Then her big blue eyes turn to focus on her mom. "You should thank Shane. He's the one who taught me how to defend myself. It was his knife."

"We are thankful to Shane," Sheri blurts. She nods gravely at me. "*We are.*"

"Good, because without him, I wouldn't be here. Daniel let me see his face. He wasn't planning to leave me alive after he raped me."

Ethan and Sheri both wince and then look wrecked by the mental image those words conjure.

"Okay," I say, putting a hand on Avery's back. "Time for a change of topic. We need to eat something."

"Not hungry."

"I don't care," I say just as quickly. "You're gonna eat, Ave."

Her sapphire eyes rise to meet mine, halfway defiant.

"Pick something, or I will." She's eaten nothing since it happened.

"Maybe butter noodles."

I roll my eyes, and she rewards me with a small smirk.

"Yes," Sheri says, lurching to her feet. "Ethan and Avery like buttered egg noodles. But that's a little minimalist for Shane and me, so maybe eggplant parm for us?"

Sheri's eggplant parmesan is one of the best things about her. Also, I'm up for an olive branch, since she's offering.

I nod. "That would be great."

Sheri heads to the kitchen, and I wait to see if Avery will join her to help the way she used to. Avery doesn't move though, or even look in the kitchen's direction. Her gaze is on her hands. A crease reappears between her brows, and she picks at her cuticles. "Daniel doesn't fit the FBI profile. Do you think if the FBI advised against it, the dean would hold off on saying Daniel was Casanova?"

My hands close over hers to protect them. "Maybe, but you said you didn't want to talk to the FBI again."

"I don't." Her gaze flicks to my face, and she tilts her head forward, beckoning me to volunteer.

After a beat, I nod. "All right."

"Thank you." She leans closer and kisses my cheek. "I think I'll help make dinner." Avery slides from her chair and leaves the room.

Ethan stares after her for a long moment before he looks back at me. "How long have you guys been a couple?"

"Not long."

"At the risk of opening a can of worms..."

I wait, but incline my head for him to keep going.

"She's pretty fragile right now, Shane. It's not the best time to start a new relationship, is it?"

"Avery will be fine. She's not as fragile as she looks."

"Why? Because she managed to survive a violent attack?"

"Yeah, actually." I run a hand over the table's smooth surface. "And because she's always been able to handle herself where I'm concerned."

"What does that mean?" Ethan asks.

"It means...she's the one, and she knows it." I stand and stretch with a wry smile. "Sullivans don't talk to feds, Dad. We avoid them. Now excuse me while I find the card an FBI agent gave to Avery, so I can call him for her."

AVERY

On the grass of GU's main quad, Shane and I stand among a group of mostly female students. We're waiting about twenty feet from a wooden platform that's a makeshift stage for the upcoming announcement. News teams point their huge cameras at the podium.

Cold wind blisters my face as I pull my coat's hood tighter. The dean, the chief of the campus police and a woman who is probably from GU Media Relations walk up the steps to the platform.

There doesn't seem to be anyone from the FBI present. Or anyone from the city's police department.

The dean's gray hair ruffles in the wind. He wears a dark suit with a sprig of holly pinned on his lapel.

"Ladies and gentleman, thank you for coming. I will only make a brief statement today, out of respect for the families who even in the midst of this holiday season are uncertain about the fate of their missing daughters. Our thoughts and prayers are with them, as ever."

His cold-reddened fingers grasp the podium as his eyes scan the assembled faces. "It is with both sadness and relief that I'm here to identify twenty-one-year-old Daniel Taake as the criminal known as Casanova. A few days ago, he attempted to attack a female student who courageously defended herself. Thankfully, she is uninjured. He, however, is dead."

The murmurs begin immediately.

"Everyone involved is cooperating fully with law enforcement to try to quickly determine the location of the other young women he victimized. As soon as we have any updates, we'll communicate them without delay. Thank you for being here today and for continuing to help us search for our missing students."

Questions are shouted at the dean immediately.

I turn, shaking my head at Shane as my heart sinks. Deep down, I'm more and more convinced Daniel isn't Casanova.

"Dean! Dean! Can you tell us the circumstances of Casanova's death? Was he shot by law enforcement?"

"He was not shot. I'm not at liberty today to share the details of his failed abduction, but I'm sure the facts will emerge in due course."

It wasn't a failed abduction. He wasn't there to kidnap me.

"Dean! Who is the student? Is her name Avery Kershaw?"

I freeze. Someone leaked my name.

Shane's arm comes around my waist and guides me to a walking path. For a moment the dean's eyes lock with mine, causing at least ten heads to swivel in my direction. Shane moves around me in an instant, blocking their view of me.

We cut down a side path to the parking lot where the Porsche waits. Reporters and their cameramen pursue us.

A part of me doesn't want to run. A part of me is tempted to stop and share my concerns, so women don't return to campus unaware they may still be targets.

I don't speak though. My body hurtles along the path, feet crunching into snow and leaving dark footprints.

We reach the car, and Shane puts me in the passenger seat, ignoring the shouting reporters rushing toward the lot.

As ever, he is calm.

Once inside, he maneuvers the car around the throngs like a Formula One driver. "You all right?" he asks, glancing over.

"Yeah, I'm fine. I wish the dean had waited, but I trust the FBI will keep working on the case until they're satisfied it's really over."

Shane raises his hand to block the media from taking pictures of me through the windshield. My bodyguard until the bitter end.

Once we're out of the lot, he shifts gears and leaves everyone far behind. By the time we get on the expressway, we're lost in a sea of holiday travelers.

"Hey," he says.

I turn my head toward him. "Yes?"

"That settled it. We're going out of town for New Year's Eve. Pick a place, or I will."

"Edinburgh?"

"Yeah, sure."

His hand rests on the gearshift, and mine snakes over to cover it, stroking his knuckles.

"What made you choose Edinburgh? If we're over there, why not London? Or Dublin?"

"In his article, Erik made it sound like Edinburgh's Hogmanay is the best New Year's celebration in Europe."

"Sorensen? What article?"

"The one in the school newspaper around this time last year."

Shane's brows rise. "Last year? How did you see it?"

"I read Ethan's."

"I didn't catch it. Did they slide Sorensen's piece in on the break?"

"I don't think so. You know Erik writes under a twisted version of his name, right?" I'm teasing now. It's obvious that Shane didn't know until this minute about Erik's pen name.

Shane's eyes narrow, and he's silent as he thinks. "Is it Riksen? Something Riksen?"

"S. Riksen."

"How'd you find out it was him?"

"That's a secret."

His gaze cuts to my face immediately. "Not from me it isn't. Spill."

I smirk, despite how serious he sounds. "Are you jealous?"

"Maybe. Now spill."

My fingers move to the side of his face and trace a path through his stubble. "Maybe we can trade secrets." My concentration is getting better, and my interest in his secret room has returned.

Shane captures my hand and moves it to his mouth where he bites the flesh on the back of it.

"Hey," I protest, trying to tug it away.

His grip tightens, holding the hand captive. "You'd better tell me, kitten, before you get yourself in trouble."

A shiver of anticipation tightens my nipples. "You can't punish me. I'm still recovering."

He gives my hand a sucking kiss, then lowers it to rest on his thigh. "Right, because a beast is never what you need in bed."

My heart thumps harder, but my smile remains as I look out the passenger window.

Shane and I may not know all of each other's secrets yet, but the secret of what we are to each other is something we've always understood.

Deep down in the dark and hidden places is where we own each other.

THANK YOU FOR READING *INDECENT DEMANDS*!

Would you like to see where Shane and Avery spend Xmas? There is an exclusive bonus epilogue available for free.

Visit the "Connect" page of my website, www.marleewray.com, and use the "Contact" form to let me know you'd like to read *Xmas Eve Among Killers*. I'll send you the link to download it!

EPILOGUE

Dark Knights Bonus 1: Xmas Eve Among Killers is an exclusive bonus epilogue that includes the Xmas Eve party at Shane's grandfather's house and more. A newsletter sign-up is required to gain access to this and all MW bonus materials.

Visit the "Connect" page of my website, www.marleewray.com, and use the "Contact" form to let me know you'd like to read *Xmas Eve Among Killers*. I'll send you the link to download it!

WICKED DEMANDS

DARK KNIGHTS #2

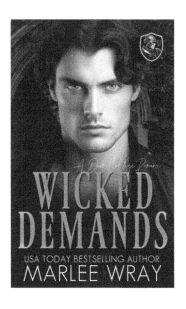

He has everything. Now he wants to own me, too.

Declan Heyworth is a star quarterback and the heir to a famous billion-dollar fortune. That gives him more power than one man should have.

When my family does something they shouldn't, he demands I make amends. Unfortunately, the only thing I have that's of value to him is my body.

Someone is targeting me. At first, I think I'll be safer in Declan's world. Then I realize the more time I spend with him, the more danger I'm in.

Will I survive two weeks with the arrogant superstar? Or will this end as badly as it begins?

<u>Wicked Demands Excerpt:</u>

CHAPTER 1

CAMRYNN

Every time the words "purity exam" cross my mind, my stomach knots. And now the driver who was sent to deliver me to the wretched exam tells me I need to be blindfolded for the ride.

"Blindfolded? Really?" I ask as my heart kicks into a galloping rhythm. My soft words are a stall tactic. I'm trapped between wanting to bolt from the car and trying to talk myself out of an impending panic attack so I can stay the course.

"Yeah, blindfolded," the driver says, his craggy face in shadow as he stands next to the black sedan's open passenger door. "You're going to lie on the back seat wearing a blindfold until we arrive."

Jesus. Am I really doing this? A creepy late night gyn exam, in preparation for a night that will change me forever?

I can't believe my family got us into a position where *this* is my only option.

As I grip the sides of the black leather seat, the surrounding darkness closes in. "No one warned me about this."

The driver clears his throat and shifts his bulky body. When he speaks, his tone is laced with skepticism. "No one said precautions would be taken to maintain privacy and security?"

I tilt my head before slowly shaking it. "All Mr. Stowe said was that discretion is critical."

Saying Brock Stowe's name sends a chill through me. The man's a ruthless snake who's facilitating his nephew's revenge upon my family.

His nephew. I'd like to stab Declan Heyworth in his filthy heart.

There's never been better proof that you can't judge a book by its cover, because Declan's exterior is gorgeous. He's tall and athletic with jet black hair and eyes as blue as sapphires. Beneath the stunning good looks and aloof charm however, lurks something wicked.

I suspected his taste for twisted sex, but not his capacity for unconscionable vengeance.

It's the twenty-first century, for God's sake. The taking of a virgin daughter as revenge went out with the dark ages, didn't it?

"The blindfold is nonnegotiable," the driver says. "You either go along with it, or you get dropped back off at home."

I wish.

It infuriates me that Declan involved these other people. His sending his uncle added insult to injury. Having a middle-aged man instruct me to have myself waxed... *Jesus.*

I've had bikini waxes for summer, but going completely bare on command has me feeling vulnerable. And humiliated.

And as Brock issued the mandates about grooming, birth control pills and the purity exam, he leered at me like I was a slice of glazed ham. I wanted to tell him to fuck off. I probably should have. At least then Declan would've been forced to talk to me directly. Something he hasn't done since the night we met.

"Well?" The driver is growing impatient.

My heart pounds as if I've been sprinting. I'd like to back out, but if I do, my family will be destroyed.

Licking my lips, I finally nod at the driver.

He steps back, affording me a view of the dark residential street that's a few blocks from the Granthorpe University campus. When I got my acceptance and scholarship to GU, it was a dream come true. I didn't realize my new life was being funded by extorted money.

The driver stares at me, waiting for me to step out of the car.

Declan and his goddamned minions.

Although maybe Declan involved more people when my family became a problem. The difference, though, is that I didn't involve my family. They involved themselves and never told me.

My mom's actions are definitely unacceptable, but her intentions weren't horrible. I can't let her lose the house, and more, when it's in my power to prevent it. Brock Stowe made it clear I'm our only way out.

This will be over soon, Cami. Stay the course.

All I have to get through is one clinic visit and then one night. Roughly ten hours of my life.

Emerging from the front passenger seat, I say, "Sure, fine." I'm doing my best to appear calm.

Ironically, when I think of remaining cool under pressure, the person who comes to mind is Declan. He's the heir to the legendary Heyworth fortune and our school's star quarterback. When he's on the field, he's grace under pressure. And afterward, when he's interviewed, he faces the news cameras like he's had a lifetime of media training, which he probably has. Because even with dark hair that's damp with sweat and tousled from being trapped under a helmet, he fixes his stunning eyes on the camera and speaks directly to anyone watching.

The driver clears his throat to reclaim my attention. "Sit with your body facing the driver's side."

I obey and, within seconds, a black sleep mask is placed over my eyes.

"I'll help you lie down."

The driver positions me on my side, and lying on the soft leather bench seat, I smell faint traces of bourbon and cigar smoke. Whose car is this? Brock Stowe's? It could be Declan's I suppose, but it doesn't feel like him. Not that I know him well. I've only met him once...on a night that's burned into my memory. And his, too, I'm sure, considering all the fall-out.

"How long is the drive?" I ask, trying not to sound nervous.

The driver has been nothing but professional, but it's nerve-wracking to be driven to a private clinic in the dead of night. Especially when the visit is to confirm my suitability as a virgin sacrifice.

"Not long." His disembodied voice hangs over me like a specter, adding to my uneasiness. "Just relax."

As if I could.

There are endless murky secrets surrounding this ride, and now I'm wearing a blindfold. I feel about as relaxed as a woodpecker on meth.

CAST | DK COMPANION

GU DARK KNIGHTS

- **SHANE MORAN** - GRANDSON OF JOE SULLIVAN
- **DECLAN HEYWORTH** - HEYWORTH HEIR, GU QUARTERBACK
- **ERIK SORENSEN** - GU DEFENSIVE CAPTAIN, SHANE'S COUSIN, ALSO KNOWN AS: S RIKSEN - STUDENT JOURNALIST ON THE *GRANTHORPE DAILY DISPATCH*

SELECT CAST

- BARDORATCH, TODD - GU STUDENT, BUSINESS MAJOR
- BRIGGS - HEYWORTH HOUSE CHEF
- BUCHANAN, EDEN - DANCE TEAM CAPTAIN, FAMILY LEGACY STUDENT AT GU , DECLAN'S EX-GIRLFRIEND
- CALLAHAN, AIDEN - BOSTON ORGANIZED CRIME, (APPEARS IN BONUS EPILOGUE #1)
- HALVERSON, EMILY - MISSING GIRL
- HEINRICH, MIKA - PULITZER-PRIZE-WINNING JOURNALIST, FACULTY EDITOR OF THE GDD

- HEYWORTH, HARRISON - HEYWORTH CEO, HEYWORTH FAMILY PATRIARCH, DECLAN'S GRANDFATHER
- HEYWORTH, ODETTE - CEO OF LABADIE COSMETICS, DECLAN'S GRANDMOTHER
- HEYWORTH, EMMANUELLE - DECLAN'S MOTHER
- HEYWORTH-STOWE, ELIZABETH - DECLAN'S AUNT
- HEYWORTH STADIUM - HOME OF THE MUSTANGS
- KELLER, ROXIE - ENTREPRENEUR, DIRECTOR OF FINANCE AND MANAGEMENT SYSTEMS AT RALSTON ENTERPRISES, AVERY'S IDOL
- **KERSHAW, AVERY** - SHANE'S STEPSISTER, GU FRESHMAN
- LONG, ISOBEL - MISSING GIRL
- MILLER, LEIGHTON - LAMBDA DELTA KAPPA MEMBER
- MORAN, ETHAN - DEFENSE ATTORNEY; SHANE'S DAD
- MORAN, SHERI - AVERY'S MOTHER
- MORAN, RIONA (SULLIVAN) - SHANE'S MOTHER
- MUÑIZ, OCTAVIA - GU BAND CAPTAIN
- NYBALL, ALLEN - GU DEAN
- PATRICK, ASHLING - TEEN SISTER OF C CRUE CRIME SYNDICATE FOUNDER SCOTT "TRICK" PATRICK (APPEARS IN BONUS EPILOGUE #1)
- PERALTA, ARYA - LADY KNIGHTS DANCE TEAM CAPTAIN
- RALSTON, DREW - BILLIONAIRE FOUNDER OF RALSTON ENTERPRISES, GU ALUMNUS
- REYNOLDS, CAMRYNN - GU TRANSFER STUDENT, *GRANTHORPE DAILY DISPATCH* STUDENT JOURNALIST
- ROCHE, GRETA - LADY KNIGHTS DANCER
- ROGAN, ROY - IRISH SOCCER PLAYER
- SMITH-HALL, WILLIAM - GU TENURED PROFESSOR, DEPARTMENT CHAIR COLLEGE OF BUSINESS
- STOWE, BROCK - GU ALUMNUS, DECLAN'S UNCLE, EX FATO MEMBER, SCHOLARSHIP SUGAR DADDY
- SULLIVAN, JOE - HEAD OF THE SULLIVAN CRIME FAMILY BASED IN BOSTON, GRANDFATHER OF SHANE MORAN
- SULLIVAN, SIOBHAN - SHANE'S GRANDMOTHER
- TAAKE, DANIEL - GU STUDENT, BUSINESS MAJOR

- TREMBLAY, JEFF - CEO TREMBLAY TELECOMMUNICATIONS, GU ALUMNUS, EX FATO MEMBER, SCHOLARSHIP SUGAR DADDY
- WILSON, JOSH - LAMBDA DELTA KAPPA VP
- WINTERS, CALVIN - GU KNIGHTS WIDE RECEIVER

PLACES & THINGS

- BEACON WEST - GU BUSINESS ADMINISTRATION BUILDING
- CAFÉ RAMEN - GU ON-CAMPUS EATERY
- COHEN'S DELI - SANDWICH SHOP IN COLUMBUS TOWER
- COLUMBUS TOWER - BUILDING ON GU CAMPUS, HOME OF THE GDD OFFICES
- COYNSTON - HOME CITY OF C CRUE CRIME SYNDICATE; ~ 90 MILES FROM FOXGROVE
- DARK KNIGHTS - SECRET SOCIETY FORMED FOUR GENERATIONS EARLIER AT GRANTHORPE. PURVEYOR OF VIGILANTE JUSTICE
- ESPRESSO YOURSELF - GU COFFEE SHOP
- EX FATO CLUB (BOSTON) - DARK KNIGHTS ALUMNI CLUB
- FOXGROVE - HOME CITY OF GRANTHORPE UNIVERSITY; AN HOUR DRIVE FROM BOSTON
- FOXGROVE MEMORIAL HOSPITAL
- GEL TRAIN - ALTERNATIVE ROCK BAND
- GRANTHORPE UNIVERSITY - ESTABLISHED IN 1898
- GRANTHORPE ALUMNI CLUB (FOXGROVE) - LOCATED ON THE GU CAMPUS
- *GRANTHORPE DAILY DISPATCH* - AWARD-WINNING NEWSPAPER, CONTINUOUSLY PUBLISHED SINCE THE EARLY 1900S; ALSO KNOWN AS *THE DISPATCH* OR GDD
- HEYWORTH HOUSE - HISTORIC HOME ON GU TOUR, OWNED BY THE HEYWORTH FAMILY
- THE HIDEAWAY - GU BAR & GRILL
- LABADIE COSMETICS - FAMILY OWNED COSMETICS COMPANY BASED OUT OF FRANCE

- LADY KNIGHTS - GU DANCE TEAM
- MUSTANGS - NFL TEAM, OWNED BY THE HEYWORTH FAMILY
- NOTABLE EVENTS - SPECIAL EVENTS COMPANY
- PALMETTO BOWL - COLLEGE NATIONAL CHAMPIONSHIP GAME
- REBEL'S CREED - MEN'S FRAGRANCE; DECLAN IS THE BRAND AMBASSADOR
- *REIBILIÚNACH* - IRISH WHISKEY THAT SHANE IS DEALING IN ILLEGALLY
- SCRIBE JAM - NEW YORK LITERARY FESTIVAL
- SEA STEED - HEYWORTH YACHT
- SHAMROCK CAFÉ (COYNSTON)
- STRYKER SECURITY - DECLAN'S PRIVATE SECURITY DETAIL
- TYNE RIVER - RUNS ALONG THE EAST EDGE OF FOXGROVE AND THE GU CAMPUS
- THE WOLFRAM HOTEL - BOUTIQUE HOTEL (BOSTON, NEW YORK)

TWISTED DEMANDS

DARK KNIGHTS #3

The Viking hates me. It's mutual. And now we have to live together.

ERIK SORENSON, THE TOWERING GU FOOTBALL SUPERSTAR, GOT HIS Viking nickname because he's blond, brutal, and ice cold. After a sordid promise is broken, we spend two years silently ignoring each other. Even in the same room, there's no conversation. No eye contact. *Nada.*

A serial killer is on a rampage. One day I see too much. *And the killer sees me.*

I'm forced to live with the Viking, and everyone expects me to follow his orders. Especially him. But considering what he wants from me... there's no way.

The gorgeous Viking doesn't let people defy him. *Too bad.* I won't be controlled.

Even while under threat, our chemistry is white hot, and it may burn until there's nothing left but ash.

AFTERWORD

The *Dark Knights* collection is set in the same universe as the *Rough Retribution* series of dark Mafia romances. (Joe Sullivan was first mentioned in *Used (Rough Retribution #3)*. The widow that Mr. Sullivan is dating in *Indecent Demands* is Scott "Trick" Patrick's mother.)

If you'd like to read all of Marlee's stories with dangerous, dominant heroes and the smart, engaging heroines they fall hard for, follow the link below.

HTTPS://WWW.MARLEEWRAY.COM/BOOKS

BOOKS

For Links to all of Marlee's books, Visit: https://www.marleewray.com/books

Dark Knights
(New Adult Dark Romance)

Indecent Demands
Wicked Demands
Twisted Demands

Knights of Wrath
(New Adult Dark Romance)

Pretty Threats

Rough Retribution Series
(Dark Mafia Romance)

Held
Pursued
Used
C Crue Afters (A Newsletter Exclusive)
His Prize
Ruthless Heart

Standalone Books
(Contemporary Romance)

Rulebreaker
Taking Her in Hand
Calling the Plays

Owned & Shared Series
(Sci Fi Romance)

Owning Their Pet
Taken by the Warriors
His Caged Princess
Taken Captive
His Caged Virgin

ABOUT THE AUTHOR

Marlee Wray is a USA Today and Amazon best-selling author. She writes books about dangerous, dominant heroes and the intriguing women they can't resist.

When she's not writing, Marlee enjoys traveling and taking photographs. She's also a voracious reader who is addicted to audiobooks.

Marlee loves connecting with readers and has a lot of FREE bonus content available through her newsletter. To subscribe and connect with her, visit her website at

HTTPS://WWW.MARLEEWRAY.COM/CONNECT

Made in the USA
Monee, IL
14 March 2025

13779430R00164